The Consulting Detective Trilogy
Part II: On Stage

Darlene A. Cypser

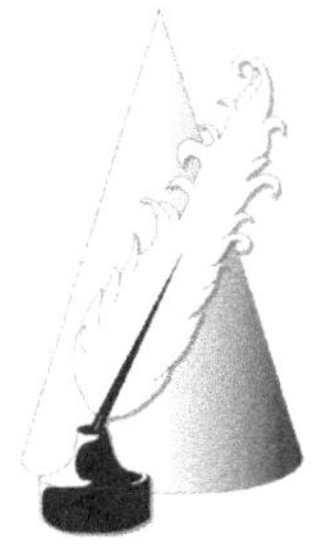

Foolscap & Quill

Set in Baskerville Classico & Times New Roman

www.theconsultingdetective.com

ISBN 978-1-938143-46-5

Foolscap & Quill, LLC
151 Summer Street #1018
Morrison, CO 80465-1018
www.foolscap-quill.com

Contents

Chapter 1

London

"I had not yet appreciated the part which they were to play in my life."
Sherlock Holmes, "The Gloria Scott"

Mycroft Holmes paid the driver and descended to the curb. The cab rattled off. Another hansom had stopped a few houses down the street. He was aware of it, but did not look towards it or make any outward sign that he had observed it.

The luncheon had been long and uninteresting with the exception of an occasional amusing observation and deduction, which he had kept to himself. The entertainments had been trivial and banal. He had been able to maintain a general air of amusement while analysing the latest developments concerning the Eastern Question. Mycroft disliked varying his routine, but when one worked for the government there were certain social invitations one could not refuse. The occasional sacrifice of personal comfort was likely to be rewarded in the long term. The schedule of the new housekeeper had already disrupted his Sunday routine as it was.

These thoughts flickered past in an instant as Mycroft mounted the front steps and stopped at the door to his lodgings. There was another set of footprints upon the mat. They had not been there when he had left. They looked very familiar.

There were new scratches around the keyhole. He turned the knob. The door was unlocked. He pushed the door open slowly, stepped in soundlessly, and closed the door quietly behind himself. He placed his hat and overcoat upon the rack and turned with his walking stick still in his hand. The intruder was lying upon his sofa reading his newspapers, some of which had cascaded onto the floor. Mycroft slid his walking stick into the umbrella stand as he spoke.

"Now you have added burglary to your hobbies?"

"I didn't think you would want me squatting on your doorstep with my baggage. Fortunately, my novice skills at lock-picking were sufficient to open the door," Sherlock replied without getting up. "I do need more practice. Oh, and based on my rudimentary studies of criminal law to date, I don't believe it would be considered 'burglary' unless I had stolen something or committed some other felony after breaking in. I don't think reading your newspapers on your sofa is a felony, though the way some of these writers butcher the facts should be."

"If you are going to make a habit of breaking and entering you might want to leave fewer scratches around the key hole in the future. It is quite obvious," Mycroft said seating himself in a chair across from his brother. "Unless, of course, you are breaking into the home of a drunkard in which case the key hole may be excessively scarred already, and the occupant too unobservant to notice. Perhaps I should invest in a more secure lock in any event, and provide you with a key. It wasn't necessary when Mrs Nugent was here."

The two brothers were alike in height when standing but they could not have been more unlike in build. Mycroft was massive and rotund though he moved with a grace that many large men lacked. Sherlock, who was stretched to his full length upon the sofa, was as thin as a beanstalk.

"Have you eaten?" Mycroft asked.

"Not since yesterday. It has been a rather eventful day and I used what funds I had to send Jonathan back to Yorkshire, and myself and my belongings here. I appear before you homeless and penniless," Sherlock explained.

"And in need of a bath," Mycroft observed. "Another accident at the lab?"

"Yes," Sherlock admitted, rubbing at the stains on his hands. "A somewhat unfortunate one. As a consequence, the college Master gave me until the end of the week to leave, but I saw no purpose in dallying."

Mycroft shook his head.

"Obviously I am being fed scraps of a much larger tale. However, it can wait until we have you cleaned up and we've seen to our suppers. Unfortunately, it is Mrs Denton's day off."

"Is Mrs Nugent not coming back?"

"She took the death of her husband quite hard. She's been with her sister since. It is probable that she is not returning. It is unfortunate. She was a most attentive landlady. The agent of the superior landlord has communicated with me about taking the lease of the whole house when the Nugent lease ends at Michaelmas. I am considering it, but that does not serve our immediate needs.

"Ah! I have just the thing!" Mycroft exclaimed, "Grab your hat and coat and come along, my treat."

The brothers donned their overcoats and hats and headed out, locking the door behind them. The air was crisp as they walked down Great Russell Street past the British Museum. They hailed a cab in Charing Cross Road. Traffic was light and they soon descended before Jermyn Street 76.

"The London Hammam," Mycroft announced. "The columned front is from the original St. James Hotel. The Turkish Bath was built primarily behind it where the stables had been."

Inside, Mycroft led Sherlock down the stairs. An attendant in the outer courts removed their boots and they padded along to the main chamber, or the "cold room," of the Turkish Bath. Here the whole atmosphere of the place changed from the London of January 1875 to some exotic land of another time.

The hall they entered was over fifty feet long. Ornate crossbeams held the sharply pitched roof more than forty feet above their heads. In the centre of the hall rose a fountain and beyond that stretched a long narrow pool of water with tropical plants growing along its edges and steps descending into it. Along the sides of the hall were small compartments each containing a few couches. These compartments were separated from each other by low walls and divided from the main hall by barriers of latticework. Thus, they provided some privacy while not inhibiting the view into the main hall. Some men lounged about on couches in the compartments; others walked the hall talking; while still others were entering or leaving the pool. At the far end of the room rose a large Moorish arch, nearly as high as the ceiling in this room, which marked the entrance to another hall.

The brothers were conducted to an unoccupied compartment to undress and hang their clothes next to the couches. An attendant assisted them in swathing one towel about their loins and wrapping another over their shoulders and upper body. The attendant massaged their feet and shoulders as they sat thus clothed upon the couches, then he led them past the fountain and the pool to the hot room beyond.

The room beyond the Moorish arch was dimly lit, illuminated only by scarce lamps about the room. The domed ceiling was pierced by windows through which light would have fallen from a noontime sun, but no light fell from them now. There were no furnishings in the room. A large square platform occupied the middle of the floor. It had a top level and an outer, lower level and steps leading to both levels. Steps also descended to the right and left of the platform to lower wings of the hall. Some men clothed only in the towelling about their loins sat upon cushions on the platform or lay upon towels upon it. Others walked about the room and spoke in hushed voices.

The heat in this hall was oppressive and sweat flowed freely. Their attendant had brought cushions and assisted them in laying their outer towels upon the platform. Mycroft seated himself upon the towelling on the lower level of the platform with the cushion behind his back. Sherlock chose to stretch out upon a towel next to Mycroft neglecting the cushion altogether. Both their bodies glisten from sweat in the heat. They said nothing. Mycroft sat with his eyes reduced to slits like some lost Buddha meditating. Sherlock, despite the heat, eventually nodded off.

It had been a very long day. Sherlock's mind wandered back to the experiment in the laboratory this morning. The flash between his hands, glass flying.... He snapped awake with a small cry. Mycroft said nothing but opened his eyes wider and looked at his younger brother. Sherlock responded to his look.

"I didn't sleep last night."

Mycroft suspected it was more than that. He saw the cuts on

his brother's hands and face, and the bandage on his arm.

"Come along, the next stages will wake you and then you can tell me about the accident in the laboratory."

From the hot room they went to the "shampooing" where they gave themselves into the custody of a pair of attendants who rather unmercifully rubbed and scrubbed skin and manipulated joints and stretched muscles and tendons. That was followed by the plunge into the pool in first hall and then back to the couches where they had started.

When Mycroft had arranged his bulk to his satisfaction under a mountain of towelling on a couch in the cooling room and Sherlock had stretched out on a second couch beside him, Mycroft urged his younger brother to tell him of the events of the day.

"I was attempting to make tri-nitro toluene this morning and it exploded prematurely during the nitrating process."

"Do you know why it exploded?"

"Impatience is the most likely cause."

Mycroft chuckled at his brother's self-indictment. He wondered if he would have admitted it to anyone else.

"Then you must learn patience. No one was seriously injured, I trust?"

"No. This is the worst of it," Sherlock said, touching the bandage on his arm. "But the explosion blew out a couple dozen windows in the college and destroyed most of the laboratory glassware."

"The college was not pleased."

"No. I was brought before the Master and he dismissed me from the college. He went as far as to say that my activities posed a danger to the college and brought it in to disrepute. He said they were going to strike my name from the rolls! That is far more galling than being sent down."

"I am sure it is."

"But there is nothing I can do to change that. I've had hours to think on the rest and I think it is for the best. I had reached the limits of what I could learn under academic constraints. They don't understand the value of my personal course of study. I must continue to study on my own."

"How do you propose to do that?" Mycroft asked.

"I can study crime and criminals anytime and anywhere. Here in London I have the resources of the British Museum, the courts, the hospitals. I need to develop additional connexions with the Metropolitan Police. I already have a better start here than with the Cambridge constabulary."

"And St. Bartholomew's?"

"I think I shall keep my distance from there for a little while. Word of what happened at Sidney might reach them through academic circles. I would not want to be barred from Bart's labs as well. Perhaps if I stay away until it is forgotten, I can return. However, I will need some method of supporting myself while I continue my studies. And no, I did not come to you for a loan. If you could just put me up for a while until I solve that problem."

"Certainly," Mycroft said.

"And there is also the question of my debt."

"To the college?"

"Yes. There will be a bill for the damage. I said I would pay it. I would not have them attempt to collect from Father. He has disowned me and it would only increase the disgrace to have him refuse to pay it. It was my fault and I will find a way to pay for it."

"I could inquire as to whether there are any government clerk positions available, but—"

"The dismissal from the college is not going to improve my references, especially when they learn of the circumstances. I think I will need to find a bit more tolerant employer than the government."

For a while the brothers lay there discussing positions that Sherlock might be suited for. Then they dressed and walked, hatted and booted once more, through the main hall and up the stairs through the colonnaded front of the old hotel. As they were leaving the Hammam they met a gentleman coming in. They tipped their hats.

"Good evening, your lordship," Mycroft said.

"Good evening, Mr Holmes," the man responded.

"May I introduce my younger brother, Mr Sherlock Holmes."

"Mr Holmes."

"Sherlock, Lord Stanley, Earl of Derby."

The earl nodded his head and Sherlock bowed slightly, "Your lordship."

"Good night, Mr Holmes," the earl said and proceeded in.

In the cab from the bath to the restaurant Sherlock said, "We are being followed. I saw the same man behind us when we came in."

"Yes, a clumsy fellow," Mycroft replied.

"You noticed?"

"Of course. He's been at it for a few days."

"We could intercept him and ask his business," Sherlock suggested.

"Well, of course, you would suggest an energetic solution. I merely determined based on my observations that he was a very junior member of her majesty's government."

"Why would such a person be following you?"

"Most likely because I refused to accept a body-guard earlier the same day."

"Your superiors thought you needed a body-guard?"

"Yes."

"Why?"

"A trivial matter I've been analysing. The precaution is entirely unnecessary. But I suppose if anyone was sufficiently idle to have designs upon my life then such an obvious tail might encourage them to seek other entertainment."

Sherlock laughed.

"Who would possibly wish to harm a junior clerk who audits some government accounts?"

"Precisely. Besides if my employers were so concerned about my well-being why did they allow someone to break into my lodgings earlier today unchallenged?"

Sherlock laughed again.

"That certainly was careless of them. I could have been an

assassin."

"Or a dynamiter."

Sherlock snorted.

"It is rather a wonder that you weren't detained by the police in Cambridge," Mycroft said, diverting the conversation away from the subject of his employment.

"The college accepted that it was an accident and the Chief Constable wanted nothing better than to have me out of his jurisdiction."

"Ah," Mycroft said.

"So, Mycroft," Sherlock began, returning to the subject of the man following them and the other man they had encountered on the steps of the Hammam. "The government has a man following you and the foreign minister knows you by name. These are deep waters," Sherlock said with a twinkle in his eye.

"And muddy enough without anyone else stirring them up," Mycroft warned.

Sherlock held up his hand as a sign of resignation.

"I shall leave it alone," Sherlock said, "for now."

"Yes, you shall."

Their "tail" hadn't far to go for their next stop was Simpson's in the Strand. After a light supper, they returned to their lodgings for the night. Mycroft's prescription worked well, for that night Sherlock Holmes slept more soundly than he had in many weeks.

Over the next few days Sherlock Holmes spent much of his time poring over newspapers in search of an appropriate position, with the expected detours to the crime news of the day and the agony columns with their usual mix of the mundane and the mysterious. Among the innumerable ads for cooks, housekeepers, and maids were a few for telegraphers, shipping agents, and junior clerks. He set out with the "Situations Vacant" columns in hand to apply to a few, but the positions had been filled. He should not have been surprised. The "wanted" ads for clerk situations outnumbered the "vacant" ads three to one. He returned to Montague Street each day disappointed.

On the third day after his arrival in London a telegram

came for Sherlock Holmes while his brother Mycroft was away at Whitehall.

"Evening attire. Be ready at 5. Mycroft," it read.

Obeying the command of his older brother meant diving into his trunk, which he had not unpacked since its delivery from Cambridge, and requesting assistance from the housekeeper to remove some unwanted creases from his evening clothes. But Sherlock was attired as requested when Mycroft appeared promptly at 5 p.m.

"What is the occasion?" he asked.

"You know what the occasion is," Mycroft replied from his bedroom.

"I was not expecting—"

"Exactly," Mycroft responded as he changed to his own evening dress.

Thirty minutes later the brothers were climbing into a cab.

"To the Lyceum, then?" Sherlock asked.

Mycroft smiled and held up the token for the box.

"To the Lyceum!" he told the driver.

"Irving's new *Hamlet* comes highly recommended," Mycroft said, "I believe this is their 57th performance tonight. A very long run is expected."

The portico of the Lyceum Theatre stood two stories over the public footway like a Grecian temple, with six ionic columns rising up from the ground surmounted by a massive cornice. It was a striking sight in Wellington Street, where most of the buildings were of a more ordinary type. Carriages were queued up along the curb, and people from all ranks of society flooded through the doors from the walkways and streets.

"Good heavens. It looks like half of London is here," Sherlock said.

"An exaggeration, of course, but they have been selling out every night. I was fortunate enough to know someone who had a box reserved."

The Holmes brothers managed to weave their way through the throng and up the stairs to their box well before the lights dimmed and the curtain rose. From almost the first moment Hamlet graced the stage, Sherlock Holmes watched like a man in a trance, leaning forward, studying every word, every movement. Even during scene changes, he remained silent and deep in thought. It was not at all like watching a play. It was like opening a window into a man's life and peering in. This new Hamlet was so simple, so quiet, so free from artifices. Other actors playing Hamlet shouted and raved and forced themselves upon the audience. Henry Irving made the audience come to him. He made them believe in his Hamlet and want to understand him. Rather than declaiming words on paper, Irving's Hamlet lived through the part. He breathed the line: "O, that this too, too solid flesh would melt," as one long yearning that brought tears to many. His eyes blazed with intelligence as he listened to Horatio's tale. He cross-examined the men with keenness and authority. His mental deductions as they answered were clearly shown upon his face. Melancholy, rage, sadness, anger, and weariness battled within throughout the play, and the audience felt it. After the final curtain fell, Sherlock stood with the rest of the audience and applauded this remarkable performance. Then Irving came out for the first of several curtain calls, first alone, then drawing out the rest of his cast. The rest had acted competently enough but were overshadowed by Irving's brilliance. Finally, the audience began to file out still dazed by the experience.

As they were leaving the box after the performance, a voice called out "Holmes!"

Both brothers turned around. Sherlock immediately recognized one of his fellow-students from Cambridge with a young woman on his arm.

"Lord Cecil!" Sherlock cried.

"Holmes!" the young man said, grabbing him by the sleeve. "I've heard rumours that you made a most spectacular exit from Sidney Sussex."

"I am surprised that you are not back in Cambridge yourself," Sherlock responded, trying to avoid the subject.

"Ah, thereby hangs another tale. However, I am being rude.

I should introduce you to the lady. This is Mr Sherlock Holmes. We were in the same college at Cambridge. Sherlock, Lady Elizabeth Bonstow.

Mycroft had seen his younger brother stiffen at the sight of the young lady, but he now bowed to her courteously.

"Please to meet you, m'lady. This is my brother, Mycroft."

"It is my pleasure to meet you both," she responded.

"Join me at my club for breakfast, Sherlock, and we shall exchange tales," Lord Cecil said making a note on his card and handing it to him.

Sherlock took the card, and he and Mycroft bid good evening to Lord Cecil and the lady. In the Strand the crush for cabs was ebbing and they secured one. Mycroft gave the driver the address of High Holborn 218 and they trotted off.

"Relations between you and the young lord seem to have changed substantially," Mycroft observed in the carriage.

"Perhaps. He came by my rooms before leaving Sidney for the holiday. He seemed to be experiencing some type of personal crisis."

"You don't trust him?"

"I don't know what to make of him. At times he seems profoundly shallow and at others profoundly deep."

"He seems interested in you."

"He's interested in a tale. The persons involved are often secondary considerations. In any case, I suppose I shall find out more on the morrow."

Soon the cabbie pulled up before a building with Holborn Restaurant over the door. They passed into the many-coloured marble hall where the maître'd greeted them.

"Good evening, Mr Holmes, we have your table ready."

They were led to a small room above the grand hall. The sounds of an orchestra drifted in from a distance. Mycroft had arranged for their courses in advance so no discussion of the menu was necessary. As they settled in a plate of oysters was set before them and champagne was poured.

Mycroft raised his glass and offered a toast: "To you, brother Sherlock, on the occasion of your 21st birthday, may your future be bright and prosperous!"

"Thank you, Mycroft. I have enjoyed this evening very much. I must admit that the year did not have the most auspicious beginnings."

"Then that must change as of today. This day shall mark a new chapter in your life. We celebrate new beginnings."

To which Sherlock Holmes also raised his glass.

Chapter 2

Tittle Tattle

"Dark rumours gathered round him in the university town"
Sherlock Holmes, "The Final Problem"

Unfortunately, the first post of the next morning brought bad tidings in the form of an envelope from the Bursar of Sidney Sussex College. The bill for damages was nearly double the Dean's original estimate and was far above the average annual wage of a junior clerk in London. It was more essential than ever that Sherlock find gainful employment at once. This thought filled his head as he dressed for his breakfast meeting with Lord Cecil.

"Perhaps I should send my regrets, forego this breakfast, and devote the time to seeking a position."

"Nonsense," Mycroft said, "Contacts with fellow students are often the best sources for referrals for gainful employment, especially when those fellow students rank among the nobility."

"I doubt we could be considered friends."

"That is of little consequence. The connexion was sufficient for him to invite you to join him for breakfast at his club. A personal reference is always valuable and there are many positions that are never advertised. Perhaps he has a relation in need of a personal secretary or a fencing tutor. Here is a loan for cab fare and miscellaneous expenses for the day. I insist that you take it. I have complete confidence that you will repay it shortly."

Sherlock Holmes had never been to a gentleman's club in London. He did not know what to expect. He took his brother's advice and hailed a cab in Great Russell Street and gave the driver the address. Soon he was stepping down in front of a refined, though unpretentious building. There was no sign in front identifying it as a club but the street address was the same as the one Lord Cecil had written on the back of his card. Sherlock Holmes mounted the steps and approached the double doors under the archway. As he passed through those doors, he realized that the simplicity of the exterior belied the luxuriousness of the interior. Even as he made a effort not to gawk like a simpleton from the provinces, he noticed the dense carpets under foot, the noble staircase of carved oak ahead leading up to the first floor, the elegant furnishings, and the exquisite paintings covering every foot of the walls.

He explained to the hall porter than he was a guest of Lord Cecil's for breakfast, holding up Lord Cecil's card with the address on it. He was led to a room with a long table in the centre and smaller tables along the walls. The walls above the tables were covered with paintings by Gainsborough, Reynolds, and Zoffany in a density more suggestive of an art gallery than a dining room. A few gentlemen were dining at the centre table. Lord Cecil sat by the window reading a newspaper with a cup of coffee before him, the soft sunlight lighting his strawberry blond hair and accentuating the sharp creases in his expensive suit. He folded the newspaper and stood as Sherlock approached.

"Holmes! So good of you to join me," he said, extending his hand. "I am not especially fond of mornings myself, but I have an appointment at ten o'clock and it might consume the rest of my day. I wanted to have a chance to talk with you first. What will you have?"

Despite the friendly greeting of the night before, Sherlock Holmes was uncertain how relations stood between them. They had not been friends at college. "Antagonists" was perhaps the closest term. Lord Cecil Hamley was the third son of the Duke of Whutsett. He had initially taunted Holmes, as he had all other commoners of their year at Sidney. He had spread malicious rumours about nearly everyone, including Holmes, sometimes with a factual basis and often without. The difference was that Holmes fought back both physically and vocally against Lord Cecil's abuse, earning both the praise of his fellow undergraduates, and the special hatred of Lord Cecil. However, two actions by Holmes had turned the tide and forced Lord Cecil to examine his own behaviour and re-assess the integrity of Sherlock Holmes. The first had been Holmes' saving the life of an undergraduate at another college when Lord Cecil's indiscriminate gossiping had put it at risk. The second had been saving Lord Cecil himself from a pair of blackmailers who preyed on students fond of gambling contrary to university rules. The latter action had resulted in complaint by the local constabulary and Holmes being gated by his college. Lord Cecil's new introspection had parted him from his former coterie. That was how things had stood three weeks before. But now as undergraduates at Cambridge were attending their lectures the two of them were sitting down to breakfast in London.

Holmes found that Lord Cecil had the same flamboyant manner and love of gossip as he had at college. The cloud that hung over him when they had spoken before the holiday had lifted and yet the inner strife he had been experiencing then had left its mark. He seemed more relaxed, and more self-confident than he had then, and yet less arrogant than he had been in the early days at college. Holmes was curious to know what had caused these changes.

Once the business of ordering was dispensed with, the young lord began to grill Holmes on his final days at Sidney. But Holmes put him off and repeated his surprise at finding him in London rather than Cambridge.

"Ah, I must give up my story first? I will if you promise to tell me of the explosion at Sidney afterwards."

Holmes agreed as their food was served, and over coffee, omelettes and rashers Lord Cecil explained why he had not returned to the university for the Lenten term.

"Well, I went home for the holidays, but I couldn't play the game anymore. I was finished with the lies and deceptions," Lord Cecil began. "I couldn't see that college was doing me any good either. I had no desire to be a scholar. I'm not cut out for politics or the army and would be bored out of my mind in the clergy. I needed something to do with my time other than idly sponging off the Duke. That would drive us both utterly mad. I haven't a head for business, nor the demeanour for charity work. The only thing I enjoyed any more—besides gossiping—and who knows how one could make a steady occupation of that. The only thing I am any good at is acting. I told you at college that I needed to decide who to be. Well, I decided to be an actor. I was done lying about it.

"You were correct two years ago when you suggested, during that little altercation, that my father wouldn't approve of my acting if he knew of it. I knew it was true then as well. When I told my father not only that I had been doing it, but that I intended to make a career of it, he nearly burst a blood vessel! I think the only thing that kept him from having me bodily ousted from the Hall was the presence of the holiday guests. A public scandal would be more abhorrent to him than anything else. He told me to leave the Hall and not darken the doorway again. He said he would continue to provide me a meagre allowance deposited periodically in a bank account in my name so no further contact would be necessary between us. He made it clear that any direct communication would be unwelcome. I think he was afraid that if he cut me off entirely the police would find me living in a gutter. The money is nothing to him, but he could not live with the disgrace. He insisted — for my mother's sake, he said, though I am certain it is for his own — that I practice my 'abomination,' as he called it, under an assumed name, which I had intended anyway.

"For her part, my mother asked me to keep in touch with her sister, my aunt, so that she would know I was well, but otherwise seemed little aggrieved by the whole incident. I moved to my club for the time being. I already had spoken to Sassanof and I started rehearsing with his company almost immediately. I'm enjoying it immensely.

"But enough about me, you promised to tell me the truth about dynamiting the college."

Sherlock Holmes looked around the nearly empty room.

"I did not dynamite the college and you had best not be telling such tales," he said in a low voice.

"Upon my word, I have said nothing about it to anyone! I have merely listened, as I am doing now," Lord Cecil said resting his delicate chin on one finely manicured hand and staring at Holmes with wide blue eyes.

The look alone was enough to make someone either tell all their secrets or burst out laughing. Holmes merely shook his head in wonder at this strange creature before him, but he did as he had promised and told what had happened Sunday morning at Sidney Sussex College in Cambridge.

"The facts are bare enough. The rumours are probably far more exciting. I was performing an experiment at the college laboratory between terms. It did not come off exactly as planned. The mixture exploded, starting a minor fire, and breaking a number of windows and most of the laboratory glassware. The Master was displeased and I was sent down."

Lord Cecil sighed and rearranged his napkin.

"Yes, you are correct. The rumours were far more interesting. They spoke of flying glass, billows of smoke, 40 foot tall flames, a student's gown on fire, and earthquakes that rocked buildings for miles around."

"There was undoubtedly flying glass and some amount of smoke," Holmes responded. "The flames were less than a foot tall and my gown briefly caught fire when I used it to smother them. The explosion did shake the laboratory. There may have been some buildings that shook as well. I was in the middle of it. I don't know how it felt elsewhere."

Lord Cecil looked Holmes up and down. The Turkish bath had removed the stains from his hands. The cuts on his face and hands had mostly healed, leaving few signs of the incident. Lord Cecil merely saw a tall, thin, dark-haired young man in a crisp morning coat, sedate tie, clean collars and cuffs, well-pressed trousers, and shined shoes.

"You do look remarkably hale for having been in the midst of a devastating explosion four days ago."

"Therein lays the proof that the rumours are false."

Lord Cecil sighed again and tossed his napkin upon his empty plate.

"The truth is so dry. It is hardly worth telling at all."

"Then please do not," Holmes requested earnestly. "I would rather the whole affair be forgotten. I have a debt to the college to repay and I need to find employment to do so. Such rumours do not help. Even the truth is hardly a good recommendation."

In the past, Lord Cecil would have scoffed at such an appeal and embellished the story to suit his whim. However, he had learned the dangers of spreading rumours loosely without due consideration of the consequences. Besides, he owed a debt of honour to Sherlock Holmes that had not yet been discharged. Lord Cecil looked thoughtful for a moment then quickly made up his mind.

"Well, come along with me then, if you are done with your breakfast. I'm heading over to the theatre. It is a new venture. Perhaps they have an unfilled position that would suit you."

While Sherlock had attended theatrical productions a number of times in his life at a number of different theatres, he had no idea what life was like backstage or what kind of positions they might offer. But Mycroft was right, he should take advantage of what connexions he had. He fell in with Lord Cecil's suggestion.

"So you are acting full time now?" Holmes asked in the hansom on the way the theatre.

"Yes. It is a small company that Sassanof just started building a couple months ago. Back before then I hear nothing of him; no connexions with English theatre at all, unless it was under another name or so far out in the provinces to go unnoticed. His antecedents are also unknown. Rumour is that Sassanof is the bastard child of gypsy king and a wayward duchess."

"You believe this?" Sherlock interrupted.

"Not wholeheartedly, but it does make a good story. Knowing what I do about duchesses that part is believable, but you would think a gypsy king would have better taste. Sassanof is not forthcoming about the truth. Nor does he deny the rumour. He merely snorts at the suggestion. I think perhaps he likes the idea.

"Sassanof is not a bad sort, a bit grumbly at times, but I think he really cares about his actors underneath that tough exterior and I think he believes in good theatre. Wherever he came from, he seems to have rounded up an investor in November, a Baron Von Marienburg—a baron from where I don't know. He's not in Debrett's. He has a slightly Teutonic accent. There are so many barons and such in that part of the world that it is difficult to keep track of them all. Regardless, he seems to have money to invest in the venture. It may not all be his. I believe he may have a syndicate of moneyed persons behind him. I have certainly seen some dowager duchesses upon his arm at the Café Royal.

"What did you think of Irving's *Hamlet* last night?" Lord Cecil asked, seemingly changing the subject.

"I was quite impressed," Holmes said. "The rest of the cast were somewhat stiff by comparison, but Irving seemed very much to be living the part. It was not like any play I had ever seen before. It seemed more like a bit of voyeurism rather than simple entertainment."

"Indeed. Sassanof and Von Marienburg seem to be of the opinion that Irving's *Hamlet* has begun a sea change, not just for the Lyceum, but for English theatre in general. They talk of a new naturalism that will bridge the mental gap between the proscenium and the seats. They leased this old theatre, the Corycian, brought builders in to fix it up and started hiring cast and crew. They have been putting things together fairly rapidly. Sassanof said, 'We may not be at the head of the fleet but we can at least keep ahead of the tide.'"

"They have expectations of making a profitable venture of this?"

"That is the plan. Von Marienburg seems to have little concern about the artistic merits. That is Sassanof's area. They have their own theories about how to outfit their dramatic ship. They've been hiring mostly young people, both on stage and backstage, with a few grey beards, perhaps to share their experience. Unlike most established theatrical companies, no one has been hired on the basis of established lines of business, at least by contract. We are all starting on equal footing. Sassanof assigns roles as he pleases. This produces various economies, though whether it will result in good theatre is to be seen. It is definitely a grand experiment. Sassanof wants to open in mid-March and he wants us to open with four plays ready so we can switch rapidly from one to another. As a result it is a bit chaotic in the theatre as everything is being prepared at once."

"Come along. We will see if you can find a place in this venture. Oh, and in the world of the theatre, I am known as 'Langdale Pike.'"

"After the mountains that overlook your father's estates?"

"Yes. I doubt the Duke would see the humour in it, but it amuses me."

They entered the Corycian Theatre by the stage door.

"Good morning, Frank," Lord Cecil said to the watchman at the door.

"Good morning, Mr Pike. Ian was looking for you."

"Then we shall press on to the stage to prevent them from making the error of proceeding without us."

Pike pushed Holmes quickly through the dimly lit backstage area. As they wove through a maze of passages Holmes observed numerous ropes and pulleys and tackle along with other equipment and bits of scenery. The air reeked of a multitude of smells layered upon each other. Holmes identified several types of paint mixed with sawdust, human sweat, and a general mustiness.

"Ian is the call boy," Pike pointed out as they went along.

As they approached the stage, they could hear voices followed by the sound of vomiting.

"That would be John Travis, if I'm not mistaken. He has two phases: in a fuddle or in the trembles, and he isn't a very good actor in either of them," Lord Cecil aka Langdale Pike whispered to Holmes.

"Get him off the stage. When he's fully sober tell him he's fired. Get that mess cleaned up," another voice cried.

"That's Sassanof," Pike said in a whisper just before they came on stage.

"Mr Pike, you are late," Sassanof growled as he spotted him.

Sassanof was a short, pudgy man with a crescent of greying hair around the back of his head and wire-rimmed glasses perched upon his nose. He reminded Holmes more of a schoolmaster than the scion of a gypsy king.

"I did my best. I even sprang for a cab to hurry back to your divine presence," Pike said.

"Enough of your nonsense. Who is this?" Sassanof asked.

"A friend from college, uh, William, yes, William S. Scott," Pike said.

"Can he act?" Sassanof asked.

"Of course, he can act!" Pike said.

"All right, Mr Escott, we are rehearsing Act 1 Scene 1 of *Romeo and Juliet* and we are now short a Tybalt. Mr Foster, give Mr Escott Tybalt's part," Sassanof said to Sherlock Holmes. Holmes took the papers. "You can have five minutes to review. Mr Foster will remind you if you miss something during the rehearsal."

Sassanof clapped his hands.

"Ladies and gentlemen, we shall start from the beginning of Act 1 in five minutes with our new Tybalt."

"What was that?" Sherlock asked pulling Lord Cecil aka Langdale Pike off to one side. "I've never acted before."

"First rule of acting: Never say you can't do anything. You said you needed a job. Here's your opportunity," Pike said. "Try it. What do you have to lose? If it is any comfort, I shall be with you on stage personifying Benvolio and thus you will begin by picking a fight with me."

"Turn-about—" Holmes said.

"Yes, yes, and I shall respond with utmost horror at your death."

"I'll do it."

Holmes was familiar with the play and he had few enough lines in this act. His character had more swordplay than words, but a sword fight was something Sherlock was familiar with. Sherlock was introduced to Sebastian Devigne and Anthony Dewitt who were impersonating Romeo and Mercutio. Joseph Reece, George Manson, Tom Leydon, and James Wyatt were the servants Sampson, Gregory, Abram, and Balthasar.

"Places," Foster called.

Reece and Manson entered as the Capulet servants looking for a fight and were soon followed by Leydon and Wyatt as the Montague servants they started the fight with. Then Pike entered the stage as Benvolio and drew his sword (in reality his walking stick) to part them.

"Part fools, put up your Swords, you know not what you do."

Then Holmes entered as the tempestuous Tybalt.

"What? Art thou drawn among these heartless hinds? Turn thee, Benvolio, look upon thy death," he said.

"I do but keep the peace. Put up thy sword or manage it to part these men with me."

"What? Draw and talk of peace? I hate the word as I hate hell, all Montagues, and thee! Have at thee, coward!"

"Then the supers will enter and part you. Enter Capulet!" Sassanof said moving the rehearsal forward.

"What noise is this? Give me my long sword!"

"A crutch, a crutch. Why call you for a sword?"

"'My sword' I say! Old Montague is come, and flourishes his blade in spite of me.

"Thou villain, Capulet. Hold me not, let me go."

"Thou shalt not stir a foot to seek a foe."

This exchange was followed by a long speech by the Prince then all exited but Benvolio and the Montagues who spoke of the fight and then of Romeo. Lord and Lady Montague asked Benvolio to find out what ailed their son. Then Romeo entered, and he and Benvolio exchanged words until the end of the scene.

"Not bad. Not bad," Sassanof said when they had completed the scene. "You looked like you know what to do with a sword, Escott,"

"I fence, sir," Sherlock replied.

"Ah, good, and respectful, too. You could learn something from your friend here, Mr Pike. And you did fair enough for a first run with your lines, Mr Escott. Come by my office after rehearsals and we shall talk terms."

Sassanof clapped his hands.

"Ladies and gentlemen, let's run through it again."

Sherlock joined the other actors in rehearsing the scene. Then he watched from the wings as the cast moved on through Scenes 2, 3, and 4 of Act 1. An older actor who was cast as Father Lawrence drew him further back stage as they waited and offered his hand.

"I'm Milton Hallows. You are new to this business, aren't you, Escott?"

"Yes, sir."

"Take the advice of a man who has been around it for a while. Take whatever Sassanof offers for a weekly rate. He's a fair man and he will offer a fair weekly wage, but make sure you get an annual benefit at 50 percent. It makes the world of a difference."

"What's that mean?"

"At your 'benefit' you get to choose the play and put the show together and you receive 50 percent of the ticket proceeds. Sassanof has agreed to allow me have mine in May. Help me with my benefit and I'll show you the ropes."

"Done!" Holmes said as he shook the man's hand before returning to the stage for the rehearsal of Scene 5.

"Did my heart love till now, forswear it sight, for I never saw true beauty till this night," said Romeo.

"This by his voice should be a Montague," Sherlock said as Tybalt. "Fetch me my rapier, boy. What dares the slave come hither covered with an antique face, to fleer and scorn at our solemnity? Now by the stock and honour of my kin, to strike him dead I hold it not a sin."

"Why how now, kinsman. Wherefore storm you so?"

"Uncle, this is a Montague, our foe. A villain that is hither come in spite to scorn at our solemnity this night."

"Young Romeo, is it?"

"Tis he, that villain, Romeo."

"Content thee, gentle Cuz. Let him alone."

"It fits when such a villain is a guest. I'll not endure him," Escott argued.

"He shall be endured," the other insisted.

"Patience perforce, with wilful choler meeting, makes my flesh tremble in their different greeting: I will withdraw, but this intrusion shall now seeming sweet, convert to bitter gall," Holmes aka Escott concluded.

Over lunch, Escott was introduced to more of the cast.

Rose Morris was Juliet and Maude Clement, Juliet's nurse. Bartholomew Renfield, and Annette Davenport were Old Montague and his wife. Weston Beaumont and Margaret Smithson were the Capulets. Clayton Ellsworth was impersonating Petruchio. Caleb Belmore was playing the Prince. Claude Dewarr was Paris. There were others in the company who played lesser roles, often several of them. They also understudied the other actors in case one took ill.

After lunch, they proceeded to rehearse Act 2. Sherlock stayed and watched from the wings. It was nearly 4 o'clock when they reached the end of Act 2.

Sassanof clapped his hands.

"Ladies and gentlemen, we shall reconvene at the usual time tomorrow. I hope everyone will know all his or her lines in *Romeo and Juliet* by next week. Mr Escott, if you would come along with me. Good night to the rest of you."

Sassanof led the way through the maze of the backstage area to a small cluttered room where a desk and some chairs held some of the debris off the ground. Sassanof took piles of papers off the chairs, placed them on the desk, and invited Escott to sit.

"Here is what I can offer: We'll try you at 30 shillings a week. Rehearsals are six days a week from ten o'clock until 4 o'clock until we open. After that ten o'clock until two o'clock or later if we need to, earlier if we have matinees."

"And an annual benefit?"

Sassanof smiled.

"Yes, I can do that."

"At 50 percent?"

"Someone has been coaching you. I'll give you 25 percent up to a half full theatre. Fifty percent if you fill it more than half full."

"Done."

"Here is a list of the rules and the fines for missing rehearsals and so on."

Sassanof quickly wrote out the agreement on a sheet of paper and handed it to a young man who had sat silently in a corner of the office at a wedge of a desk writing papers in neat script. He proceeded to make a second copy.

Sassanof looked William Escott over as the copyist worked.

"You might want to grow a bit of a beard to make you look older, and let your hair grow out a little. We will be doing mostly Shakespeare at least for a while. So the costumes will be provided. I am sure Ida will run you down sometime when you are in the theatre and take your measurements. You are not so unlike Mr Travis in build that much modification will needed to anything she has already completed for him. I expect you will be more reliable than Mr Travis."

"Yes, sir."

"You will need to provide your own make-up and tights. We are still a couple weeks from our first dress rehearsal, but you will need them by then."

The copies were completed and the ink blotted. Sassanof and Escott signed them both.

"Well," said Sherlock as he and Langdale Pike left the theatre together a little later. "That was astounding."

"Come, return with me to my club for dinner and we shall celebrate," Pike said.

The club was much more full now. In the hall they passed two barristers who were talking out the points of that day's conflict in court and the dining room held many faces that had appeared in newspaper and magazine sketches.

As they were seated at a table, Lord Cecil said, "I think we have nearly all the arts represented tonight. I just hope fisticuffs do not break out between the different schools of painters. John Everett Millais is in back in the northeast corner, William Powell Frith at the south end of the centre table, Lord Leighton against windows, Alfred Elmore, and Val Prinsep at the 2nd and 6th tables along the wall. That's the actor Charles Mathews whispering to Lord Anglesey across the table from Anthony Trollope. Tom Taylor, the new editor at *Punch* is dining with Edmund Yates and Charles Read, who undoubtedly is waiting for Bunsby Merewether QC to arrive for their rubber. Taylor will probably head toward the billiard room after dinner where he often plays with E. S. Dallas, the journalist, and Palgrave Simpson, the playwright. There's the former Attorney-General Lord James with architect John Connellan Deane and coming in the door is Frederick Clay, a composer. I hear he is working on a new comic opera with Gilbert."

Before Sherlock Holmes could respond to this synopsis of the more well-known diners, a man came up to their table and greeted Lord Cecil warmly and shook his hand.

"Pike! So good to see you. You must come around for supper on Sunday."

"So you can pick my brain?"

"Of course! Why else would I waste a perfectly good pork roast on you? I'm kidding! Lizzie will be delighted to have you. She says you always make her laugh."

"Allow me to introduce my colleague in the theatre, Mr William Escott. Escott, this is Mr Bromley, a prominent man on Fleet Street."

"Quite glad to meet you, Mr Escott. You are wise to cultivate this young man's acquaintance. He is the Tom Hill of his generation. It was said of old Tom that he happened to know everything that was going forward in all circles—everything came alike to him. We are always glad to hear Pike's stories at our table. But I should leave you to your suppers."

"He's terrified of me," Pike said after Bromley was out of earshot. "He's been trying to convince me to write for his rag. I don't know if he is more afraid that the *Daily Gazette* will recruit me first, or that I know of his affair. It doesn't matter because I am not interested in either at the moment. Nevertheless, I will eat his pork roast and tell his wife some harmless but amusing stories. Someone ought to make the poor woman smile."

"You are known by both names here," Holmes stated.

"Yes. That's what I love about this club. Here they don't care whether I am Lord Cecil or Langdale Pike as long as I am good company. You may be surprised to know that I was put up for this club over a year ago. Someone I knew at Sidney suggested it but there was a long line of seconds and no risk of a black ball."

"You knew something about the members?"

"Possibly. Or they might have only feared I did. There was no intimidation on my part. Most people didn't want to cross me because they have some guilty secret that I might know—except, of course, for you."

"I didn't like your attitude," Holmes admitted.

"You made that quite clear. I've changed, I think. I hope that I am better company now than I was and more worthy of membership here. This club was founded on the ideal of gentlemen and artistic persons being able to dine and engage in conversation on equal footing. Speaking of actors, you were surprisingly good for a first attempt. Are you sure you've never acted before?"

"Not unless acting respectful counts," Sherlock said cynically.

Langdale Pike laughed.

"Oh, yes, it should. I know very much what you mean. Oh, the performances I put on for my father before I tired of it and threw caution to the wind!"

"I did the same," Sherlock agreed. "It wasn't really the sanctions from the college after the incident with the blackmailers that caused my father to disown me. We had a row last autumn when I told him my career choice."

"Which is?"

"I plan to be the world's first consulting detective," Sherlock Holmes said.

"Now see, a bit of time trodding the boards will be perfect training for that. We shall make you a master of disguise!" Langdale Pike announced. Then he held up his glass. "To Sherlock Holmes, master detective!"

Sherlock Holmes smiled and heartily joined in the toast. It was not the last toast the two young men indulged in that night.

When he entered the sitting room at Montague Street later that night, Mycroft looked up from his newspaper.

"You have been drinking," Mycroft stated.

"A little bit," Sherlock agreed with a smirk and a twinkle in his eye. "We were celebrating."

"Celebrating what?" Mycroft asked.

"I have found myself a situation. I'm going to be an actor," Sherlock said with a wave of his hand. Then he tossed himself in the chair opposite. "It is a good thing I've already been disowned or this would assuredly do the trick. Of course, Father will probably never know unless you tell him because I'll be performing under a stage name: William Escott. Langdale Pike made it up spontaneously, but I think it will serve."

"Langdale Pike?"

"Lord Cecil's stage name. Don't you see, Mycroft? This is one thing we missed in our analysis! A knowledge of acting and disguises would be invaluable to my career as a detective, both for my own use and to understand the deceptions others might use," Sherlock said.

"That's true," Mycroft agreed.

"And I will be paid while I'm learning. It is not much, at least not at first. But I suspect my wages will increase as I improve, and I intend to improve. There is also the opportunity to make additional funds at a benefit performance. If you will allow me to share your lodgings for a while longer I will be able to send every shilling back to the college, after I repay your generous loan of this morning."

"You are welcome to stay, and do not feel obliged to repay my loan with any urgency."

"Thank you, Mycroft. Would you mind if I played my violin this evening?" Sherlock said.

"Not in the least," his brother responded.

Sherlock disappeared into his bedroom and a short time later Mycroft heard him tuning the violin. The sound of it reminded him that he had not heard his brother play since their mother's funeral over a year ago. Sherlock had stayed with him in London during the intervening Long Vacation but had spent all his time studying at St. Bartholomew's Hospital, reading at the British Museum, or watching trials at Old Bailey. He was rarely at the rooms and if he had brought the violin with him during that visit, Mycroft never heard it. But now he did, and it filled the air with rapid, lively airs, so different than what Sherlock produced in his darker moods. It was a good sign. With that thought, Mycroft retired to his own bedroom.

Chapter 3

The Corycian Company

"Watson insists that I am the dramatist in real life"
Sherlock Holmes, *The Valley of Fear*

Sherlock Holmes woke early the following morning and began copying the part of Tybalt in *Romeo and Juliet.* He wanted his own prompt-book with room for notes. Picturing the stage and the other players in his mind, he imagined the scenes to come and used those images to help commit his part to memory. Then he dug his epees from the depths of his trunk. He took them with him to the theatre. They would make rehearsing his fights with Dewitt and Devigne easier.

He walked from Montague Street to the theatre. The Corycian Theatre was off Tottenham Court Road. It was not a long walk. There was a light fog that morning. An occasional ray of sunlight pierced through with the promise of a warmer day. It was refreshing to walk amidst the bustle of London after months of being gated in Cambridge.

He arrived well ahead of time. He stood for a moment looking up at the theatre. Scaffolding covered the façade. Labourers were busy on the scaffolding and others were carrying lumber and fixtures in the front doors. Sounds of work could be heard coming from the interior as well. He walked around to the stage door where he had entered the previous day. Frank nodded to him as he entered. Once again he was assaulted by the sounds and smells of backstage. Paint, sawdust, and varnish battled with sweat, dust, and mildew in the old theatre. At the moment grinding, sawing, sanding, and hammering overwhelmed all other sounds. Then he heard footsteps directly above. He was looking up in the flies when Milton Hallows came in behind him.

"They are probably attaching back-cloths to the flies," he said. "Has anyone given you a backstage tour yet, Mr Escott?"

"No."

"Come along then. I'll take you to the haunt of the mistress of the wardrobe, the heavenly domain of the scene painter, the purgatory of the property master, and then back down to the green room and the dressing rooms where we lowly actors reside when not before the footlights."

As he followed Hallows' lead up the steep metal staircase, Holmes wondered if actors spoke like that all the time. The staircase creaked and groaned as they mounted through the ropes and blocks of the flies which supported and controlled the curtains and back-cloths of the stage, to a landing near the top of the building. The sounds of the workers at the front and the labourers backstage faded and were supplanted by other sounds and sensations. They heard machines chugging and whirring from a room to their left. Inside they saw racks filled with costumes and tables heaped with waiting sleeves, collars, and skirts. Two young women were feeding fabric through machines that they drove with their feet. A third woman was basting a hem by hand. She looked up at them and spoke.

"What can we do for you, Milton?" she asked.

"Giving a new player a tour. Ida, this is William Escott. Mr Escott, our mistress of the wardrobe, Ida Newton."

Ida Newton was not a young woman, but rather a matron with several decades behind her. Her greying hair was pulled up in a bun atop her head and glasses perched on the tip of her nose. She wore a simple smock dress with an apron adorned with pins and other accessories of her craft. She might be mistaken for a peasant if it were not for her air of authority. This was her domain.

"Mr Escott, is it? While I have you, I'll take a few measurements," she said setting aside her work and taking up a tape measure that hung around her neck.

William Escott stood still as Ida fussed around measuring here and there, much as a tailor would.

"Wirier than Mr Travis, and a little taller, but not so unalike that we can't make the adjustments," Ida commented as she noted his measurements. "You know you must provide your own tights?"

"Yes, ma'am."

"Ah, a gentleman, good. Now be gone, both of you. We don't need actors underfoot."

Having been dismissed, they returned to the landing where they were drawn by the reek of paint and turpentine to the scene painter's room. It was a room of vivid colours. Even the floor was splattered with a kaleidoscope of paint. Morning sunlight dimmed by the dispersing fog streamed in windows and skylights to light every corner of the room. It fell upon large canvases stretched on wooden frames that hung on the walls. On the far wall, a painter sat on scaffolding that was suspended by ropes before such a back-cloth. Next to him were buckets and tins of paints and brushes. He was painting a detail of a street in Verona that was sketched in charcoal on the primed white canvas. The completed portion sizzled with the heat of the Mediterranean summer sun even in January in London. Escott could imagine the scene backing their fights.

"That's Gus Webster on the scaffolding and his assistant Bob mixing the paint at the table," Milton Hallows whispered before they withdrew.

The next room was a shop filled with set pieces and properties in various stages of construction and the carpenters, welders, and other artisans working on them. Some looked up as they entered the room and went back to their work. Others never seemed to notice them amidst the cacophony of the room. Hallows and Escott turned and headed back down the stairs.

"You must excuse the crew. A theatrical company builds up a stock of back-cloths, costumes, properties, and set pieces that it recycles from production to production. A new company may purchase them from a defunct company or inherit them from the prior lessee of the theatre. The Corycian had been closed so long that everything found in it had gone to mould or fallen to dust. Sassanof wanted the crew to make everything from scratch. In truth, Ida and Lionel – the chief carpenter – arranged a few judicious purchases from other theatres to save time, but they are hard at work on the rest. To create everything for four productions in four months is extremely ambitious. The crew is feeling the strain to meet that deadline. I suspect they shall do it, and if not, we shall improvise. A good actor needs nothing to tell his tale and charm his audience."

"And the actors? They seem very relaxed."

"Oh, yes, now they are. Four months to rehearse four plays is a luxury for us. A veritable holiday! Why I've had to learn a new role in a day when a play closed early and we had to get a new one up straight away or lose the lease and our jobs. The workers behind the scenes feel they must please Sassanof. The actors will not meet their judge and jury until opening night when they stand before the audience. It is then they will feel the strain to do their best."

"The green room is the actors' sitting room, where most wait in makeup and costume to be called to the stage. Down here are the dressing rooms. Currently, we all share two dressing rooms. Others are still being renovated. The room for the gentlemen is on the right and the ladies on the left."

"You may have noticed these cards posted about saying smoking is not allowed backstage. Given the amount of combustible matter stowed in theatres the precaution is a necessary one, and anyone who disregards it is a danger to us all. I've lost friends to theatre fires. If you are a smoker, Mr Escott, it is best to do it in the alley outside the stage door."

"I shall remember that."

They entered a long room with rods and hooks down one wall with a long table attached to the wall on the other side. Above the table were mirrors and rows of gas lights. A few boxes and tins, brushes and combs lay on the dressing table and coats hung on the hooks.

"It will be chaotic in here once dress rehearsals begin. Bring in a box for your make-up kit. Put your name on it and place it here on the dressing table. I will give you a list of the items you will need. When you have your kit assembled, I can give you some basic lessons. Now, however, we should attend the stage."

Several of the actors were already on the stage when they arrived. Dewitt was there. Escott unwrapped his epees and handed one to him. Dewitt was delighted and soon the two were sparring downstage. Sebastian Devigne joined them when he arrived. Dewitt and Devigne took turns crossing swords with Escott. Since Mercutio never actually fought in the scene they were about to rehearse, they agreed that for the rehearsals Devigne would bring one epee on stage and Escott would retain the other. Sassanof and Foster joined them promptly at ten o'clock and called the actors to assume their places to rehearse Act 3.

Pike and Dewitt were first upon the scene as Benvolio and Mercutio. Escott entered as Tybalt with Clayton Ellsworth as Petruchio.

"Follow me close, for I will speak to them," Tybalt told Petruchio aside. "Gentlemen, Good den, a word with one of you."

"And but one word with one of us? Couple it with something; make it a word and a blow," Mercutio mocked.

"You shall find me apt enough to that sir, and you will give me occasion," Tybalt returned.

"Could you not take some occasion without giving?" Mercutio countered.

"Mercutio, thou consort'st with Romeo," Tybalt accused.

"Consort? What? Dost thou make us minstrels?" Mercutio retorted. "And thou make minstrels of us, look to hear nothing but discords. Here's my fiddlestick. Here's that shall make you dance. Come consort."

He gestured with his hand inviting Tybalt to fight.

"We talk here in the public haunt of men," Benvolio warned, "Either withdraw unto some private place or reason coldly of your grievances. Or else depart, here all eyes gaze on us."

"Men's eyes were made to look, and let them gaze. I will not budge for no man's pleasure!"

Then Sebastian Devigne entered as Romeo. Devigne was young and classically handsome with a good chin and thick, wavy blond hair. He had a good voice and played the dazed lover well.

"Well, peace be with you, sir. Here comes my man," Tybalt said, turning away to Romeo.

"But I'll be hang'd, sir, if he wear your livery," Mercutio spat. "Merry, go before to field, he'll be your follower. Your worship, in that sense, may call him man."

Anthony Dewitt was also in his twenties, of average height and looks. He hadn't Devigne's looks, but was nearly a matched for him in talent. He was well suited to Mercutio's word play. Coming from others the puns sometimes fell flat. Dewitt's delivery seemed quite natural. Sherlock Holmes found it easy to play the role of Tybalt when Dewitt and Devigne were on the stage with him. The encounters and the rivalries seemed real. It was a matter of act and react rather than declamation of lines. Clayton Ellsworth's Petruchio was stiffer. Ellsworth was middle-aged, red-head, and flamboyant, but he had a tendency to overact and Holmes had to avoid following his lead. The younger actors were following Irving's example of naturalness which some of the older actors were not accustomed to.

Tybalt insulted Romeo but he only responded meekly.

"Boy, this shall not excuse the injuries that thou hast done me. Therefore turn and draw!" Tybalt demanded in anger.

"I do protest I never injured thee, but loved thee better than thou canst devise till thou shalt know the reason of my love, and so good Capulet, which name I tender as dearly as my own, be satisfied," Romeo pleaded.

Shocked by Romeo's failure to respond to the insult, Mercutio challenged Tybalt on his behalf.

"Tybalt, you rat-catcher, will you walk?"

"What wouldst thou have with me?" Tybalt asked.

"Good King of Cats, nothing but one of your nine lives, that I mean to make bold withal, and as you shall use me hereafter dry beat the rest of the eight. Will you pluck your sword out of his pilcher by the ears? Make haste, lest mine be about your ears ere it be out," Mercutio responded.

"I am for you," Escott retorted.

"Hold Tybalt, good Mercutio," Romeo said as he stepped between them.

Tybalt stabbed Mercutio below Romeo's arm and ran off stage. Mercutio grabbed his side.

"I am hurt. A plague on both the houses. I am sped! Is he gone and hath nothing?" Mercutio cried in disbelief.

"What! Art thou hurt?" Benvolio exclaimed.

"I, I, a scratch, a scratch, merry, 'tis enough. Where is my page? Go villain, fetch a surgeon," Mercutio cried sinking to his knees.

"Courage man. The hurt cannot be much," Romeo said grasping Mercutio by the shoulder.

"No, 'tis not so deep as a well, nor so wide as a church door, but 'tis enough, 'twill serve. Ask for me tomorrow, and you shall find me a grave man. I am pepper'd, I warrant, for this world. What, a dog, a rat, a mouse, a cat to scratch a man to death. A braggart, a rogue, a villain that fights by the book of arithmetic," Mercutio cried, and grabbed Romeo's arm. "Why the devil came you between us? I was hurt under your arm."

"I thought all for the best," Romeo replied taken aback.

"Help me into some house, Benvolio, or I shall faint. A plague on both your houses. They have made worm's meat of me."

Benvolio helped Mercutio off stage while Romeo was filling with rage.

"This gentleman the Prince's near ally, my very friend hath got his mortal hurt in my behalf, my reputation stained with Tybalt's slander. Tybalt, that an hour hath been my cousin. O, Sweet Juliet, thy beauty hath made me effeminate, and in my temper softened valour's steel!"

Benvolio returned to the stage.

"O Romeo, Romeo," he cried "Brave Mercutio is dead, that gallant spirit hath aspired the clouds, which too untimely here did scorn the earth!"

"This day's black fate on more days depend. This but begins the woe others must end."

Tybalt re-entered the stage.

"Here comes the furious Tybalt back again."

"He gone in triumph, and Mercutio slain?" Romeo cried in anguish.

He exchanged more heated words with Tybalt before drawing his sword against him.

"This shall determine that."

The epees clanged as the actors fought and Tybalt fell to the stage.

"Romeo, away. Be gone," Benvolio cried. "The citizens are up, and Tybalt slain! Stand not amazed! The Prince will doom thee to death if thou art taken. Hence, be gone, away."

"O! I am Fortune's fool," Romeo declaimed.

"Why dost thou stay?" Benvolio said pushing Romeo off stage.

Sassanof clapped his hands and all the actors stood and assembled around him again. After a bit of discussion about the rehearsal, the caterers began bringing in lunch.

"Mr Escott, I presume these are your epees?"

"Yes, sir."

"I appreciate the initiative. We should have the property rapiers available for rehearsals in a couple weeks. Could I have a word with you, Mr Escott, Mr Devigne, and Mr Dewitt? And you, Mr Dewarr. The rest of you may see to your lunch."

"I like the realism that your knowledge of fencing is adding to these scenes. I think this is something unique that our company can add to this play and others. I would like to propose that you work with Mr Devigne to help him make his swordplay more exciting. We also need a shorter sword-fight between Romeo and Paris."

Escott agreed to work with the actors on their swordplay for *Romeo and Juliet*. It was decided that they should include not only Devigne, and Anthony Dewitt, who was Devigne's understudy for Romeo, and Claude Dewarr who played Paris, but also Joseph Reece, who was understudy to both Dewitt in his role as Mercutio and Escott himself as Tybalt as well as playing one of the servants. Once this was decided they quickly joined the other actors and conversed over the meal.

"Your death there was quite believable—until you got up and walked off. None of this malingering to spout puns like Dewitt here," Joseph Reece said to William Escott.

"It's in the script," Tony Dewitt protested. "Mercutio is a comic role. Tybalt is merely a firebrand. 'Dying is easy; Comedy is hard,'" he quoted.

"I've heard that. Who said it?" another actor asked.

"A comedian, no doubt," Devigne snorted.

After lunch, the company moved on to the next act. Once his character was deceased, Sherlock observed the rehearsals from the wings to study the other actors and their methods. He spent his Sunday studying his part. He was fortunate that Tybalt's death came early in the play for he was catching up with actors who had been rehearsing for weeks.

On Monday morning, the actors arrived to find the stage covered with sawdust and wood chips. The carpenters and other crew had begun assembling the set pieces for *Romeo and Juliet* on the stage that morning. Juliet's balcony was the most elaborate, but there were other pieces for other scenes to supplement the canvas back-cloths. The rehearsals continued despite the mess. All the actors knew their parts by the following week and as the scenes and properties were completed they began rehearsing their stage business.

From his observations and conversations, Sherlock Holmes learned much about his fellow actors. What he did not learn directly, Langdale Pike was all too eager to tell him, whether he wished to know it or not. The Corycian Company consisted of a couple dozen actors and actresses, plus the chorus, dancers, and supernumeraries. Many of the actors had not yet seen their 30th year, but a few such as Milton Hallows, Bartholomew Renfield, Annette Davenport, and Maude Clement were much older and more experienced.

Some of the actors, like Langdale Pike, were skilled at taking male or female roles. Some were better at comedic roles than drama. Some could sing or dance as well as act. Some, like Pike and Escott, were well-educated scions of the middle or upper classes. Others had received their education from the streets or the dance halls. Here class or education did not matter, for the theatre was a world apart, reviled by some and glorified by others. An actor's skill upon the stage was all that mattered here. That is not to say that all actors treated all others as equals. There were always some who took on airs and treated others with disdain regardless of whether there was any merit in it. Such behaviour often had little to do with age, experience, or talent.

Sebastian Devigne had spent two years acting in the provinces. In his mind, he had earned a leading position in London yet no one else had offered him one before Sassanof offered him the role of Romeo.

Holmes had never seen Lord Cecil act while they were in college. He was indeed surprised by how the young lord easily turned his nearly innate arrogance to self-depreciating comedy upon the stage. This explained his performance at their breakfast at the club. He could do serious impersonations, as he did in *Romeo*, but he was most effective in those with a comic twist.

Anthony Dewitt was a clown in real life and leaned towards comedy on the stage though he did drama well enough to fill Devigne's shoes if necessary. Dewitt came from a large family. His father was a London merchant who did well enough, but was hard-pressed to provide future prospects for all his children. He did not resist when his son announced he was going into theatre.

Milton Hallows and Bartholomew Renfield both claimed to have been leading men in the provinces in their day and lesser lights in London thereafter. Hallows had lost his hair and gained a paunch with age and Renfield's voice had nearly gone. He could only handle a few lines on any night in more than a whisper, though he could deliver those few lines with grace and majesty. Hallows had a wife who had retired from acting to teach elocution to young actors and others who needed to improve their speech. Between their incomes they managed a comfortable house. Renfield lived with a daughter and a son-in-law who both worked at a music hall. Renfield spoke as if he was helping them out by sharing his income with their household. He pitied their careers. Holmes suspected the young people saw it the other way round.

Annette Davenport had been a great beauty of the stage decades ago, but her blond hair had faded and more effort was required to cover the lines about her face. No one would mistake her for an ingénue, but she carried herself with regal grace that was ageless. Langdale Pike said that it was not commonly known she was a widow who had inherited a small house and some meagre investments from her husband when she was young. She had taken to the stage rather than drain those resources.

Maude Clement was short and round with wiry grey hair that evaded control by hairpins or nets. Some stray hairs were always escaping. She had a subtle skill with drama and comedy that seemed nearly unconscious. Maude was friendly and talkative, but very superstitious; she once flew into a wild panic when she mislaid her "lucky scarf." Her husband drove a hack. He picked her up at the theatre at the end of rehearsals each day.

Many of the younger actors and actresses lived together in lodging houses nearby, sometimes several to a room. They spent little time there except to sleep. The rest of the time, they were at either the theatre or a local café or pub.

Sherlock Holmes still had much to learn about the theatre. He found a box in his trunk that he could use for make-up and brought it with him to the theatre. As promised, Hallows provided him a list of other items to purchase and where to do so. He used his first week's wages to start his make-up kit. One morning he added his purchases of a few Leichner grease-paints, some lining sticks, Armenian bole in a tin box, a hare's-foot, powder-puff, violet powder, pink face powder, fuller's earth, a brush and a comb, a large tin of cold cream, and a couple of soft towels to his box in the dressing room. Then he collared Milton Hallows as the actors assembled on the stage. He asked if the offer of make-up lessons was still open.

"Of course, my boy. We can commence them directly after rehearsals have concluded for the day if that suits you?"

"It does indeed."

After a day of rehearsals, Escott and Hallows retired to the dressing room.

"Have a seat."

Hallows brought over his kit and sat next to Escott.

"To 'make up the face' is one of the most subtle arts of the actor. Yet each actor must develop his own tools and skills. It is a very personal thing. You can be taught the basics, but the rest is practice and experimentation. The advent of greasepaint to handle the harsher lighting changed that whole process. The gas lighting washes out the skin and makes even a swarthy man look ghostly."

The veteran actor guided Escott through the process by making up his own face as he spoke. William Escott observed and duplicated his actions.

"To make up with grease paint, first you must prepare the skin. Cold cream is the best preparation. I've heard some use cocoa-butter or lard, but there is a greater risk of rashes or blemishes than with cold cream. Spread it evenly and gently blot off any excess. Then take your stick of Leichner's 2 ½, smear a little on cheeks, forehead, and chin, and work it well over the face with your fingers. Use as little as possible to completely cover with a thin coat taking care to work it off the edges of the face under the jaw, chin, ears, and blend it into the colour of your neck. If it is cold backstage, it may be necessary to warm the grease paint by holding it over the gas for a few seconds, but not long. If your character has a darker complexion then you would want to use 3 or 4, but Leichner's 2 ½ works for average skin tones. Touch the lips lightly with carmine lip-salve; do not make the outline too sharp and be careful that they balance. Now your canvas is ready for work.

"If any modifications need to be made to your face for the part, now is the time to make them. Generally speaking, the effect of a highlight is to give prominence. A shadow reduces prominence. Do you wish to give prominence to the nose? Add a light colour on it. Cheek-bones may be reduced by painting high-lights above and below them, putting slight shadows on the cheek-bones themselves. Do you desire hollow cheeks? Rub some dark grey colour into their centres. You can make the chin and forehead broader or narrower by shading the edges with light colours or dark. If you need to appear sickly, then use a lighter shade with some hectic fever spots."

"What is termed 'lining' the face is the marking of it so as to represent wrinkles of age," Hallows continued. "When you are my age it is not necessary. In point of fact, you spend more time attempting to hide the lines you have earned the usual way. A wrinkle is simply an intensified shadow, which is deepened if a high-light is placed above and below it. Any colour darker than that for shading. Never use black for shading; Armenian bole is best, next to this are crimson lake, vermilion, and grey."

"The colour of the eyes may be altered by painting a line of the colour above the upper and below the lower lashes, care being taken not to touch the lashes themselves; I have known hazel eyes to appear blue, and blue eyes to suggest brown when treated in this manner.

"Yes, my boy," Hallows said with approval reviewing Escott's efforts, "You have the general idea. Perhaps a bit more colour to fill out the cheeks."

"You are now ready for the finishing touches. With a large puff, powder the face all over. Powder well down over the neck and throat, dabbing the whole 'make-up' thoroughly. The effect might look garish to someone on the street, but to the audience beyond the footlights it looks more usual than an unmade face."

"So if you were to be performing in a more intimate setting, such as a dinner party, you would want to tone it down?" Escott asked.

"Precisely so. You need to gauge the effect of the lighting and the distance of your audience and adapt accordingly," Hallows replied.

"One of the advantages of a beard is that there is less facial real estate to make-up. Some actors prefer artificial facial hair but I believe a natural beard can look more natural if the beard is sculpted and maintained. Would you allow me to offer some suggestions regarding your beard?"

"By all means. I am in your hands," Escott said.

Hallows stood behind Escott as they both faced the mirror. With his hands, he illustrated his instructions.

"Shave it off the cheek bones to just above the jaw line like this. Allow it to meet here. Give it another week or so to grow and then you will need to trim it to keep it the correct length."

"To remove the make-up, apply a liberal coat of cold cream to soften the grease paint then wipe it away with a soft towel. Then wash the cold cream away with a mild soap. Since our faces and voices are our stock in trade, it is essential to take good care of them."

After rehearsals, Escott put in extra time with Sebastian Devigne, Claude Dewarr, Tony Dewitt, and Joe Reece working on the swordplay. While Devigne considered himself the most experienced actor of the group, if he could learn something to improve his stagecraft from this novice, then he would. He took Escott's instruction on how things were done in fencing, a sport based on sword combat, and in turn he taught Escott how the moves must be modified to keep the action before the audience and make it seem real to them at a distance. This work was even more effective once they had received the rapiers that they would be using on stage. Sassanof was impressed with their efforts, but to Devigne's chagrin, he attributed the results more to Escott's contributions than his own.

"We could use your talents in more of our stage fights," Sassanof said to Escott, "You don't know anything about boxing, do you?"

"I do indeed."

Devigne's eyes blazed, but he kept his tongue. Romeo was his chance to show London what he could do and he was going to do nothing to jeopardize it, and do everything necessary to make it noteworthy.

By the end of February, they were cycling through rehearsals of all four plays that Sassanof had chosen for the initial repertoire: *Romeo and Juliet, Antony and Cleopatra, Twelfth Night,* and *Much Ado About Nothing.* The scenes, the properties, and the wardrobe were nearing completion, as were the renovations of the theatre itself. One day in late February when Holmes arrived at the theatre, the scaffolding was gone. He was looking up at the façade when Pike arrived in a hansom.

"Come, let's see how the old lady looks," Pike said, prancing up the front steps between the columns and opening the double doors.

The lobby was a large expanse of marble floor that would be

lit from above by chandeliers and from the sides by torch-like gas-lights. There were elegant staircases mounting to the boxes on the right and left. Directly before them was a larger than life fresco of the Greek Muses with Thalia and Melpomene, the muses of trage-dy and comedy, flanking the doors to the auditorium. They pushed open the doors and looked into the auditorium. The seats were all in place covered by cloths. The chandelier above was dark. The stage alone was lit by gaslight, the curtains drawn back. A back-cloth of a street in Verona graced the back of the stage, but all the set pieces were off in the wings.

As their eyes adjusted to the dark room, they could see the star-studded sky painted on the ceiling above and the elaborately carved woodwork surrounding the boxes. Rose Morris walked on to the stage, which immediately drew their attention. It was easy to see that despite the beauty of the theatre itself, when the lights were dimmed all eyes were drawn to the stage.

"It is hard to believe that dimming the auditorium lights is a recent innovation that some still oppose."

"That's what I was thinking. It seems so obvious when you see it."

"The theatre looks to hold around 800."

"And we shall have to fill it with regularity to earn our keep."

Other actors began to arrive on the stage. Pike and Escott mounted from the auditorium to join them for the rehearsal.

The first dress rehearsal for *Romeo and Juliet* was held on March 1st. The stage looked like a medieval marketplace, even though there were few set pieces on the stage. The actors were milling about the stage in full costume and makeup. Maude Clem-ent, dressed as Juliet's nurse approached the edge of the stage and began throwing things into the auditorium.

"What is she doing?" Escott asked Pike.

"I believe she is throwing coal off the stage."

"Why?"

"Some type of superstition about throwing coal off the stage to christen a new theatre before the first performance."

"What precisely is that supposed to do?

"Ward off evil, I suppose."

Escott snorted.

"She is already quite upset that opening night is a Friday," Pike said. "I would not be surprised if she came down with something that night."

"I don't understand how she can allow this nonsense to rule her life."

Pike shrugged. He was looking forward to opening night. Opening at a London theatre would validate his decision to split with his father and join this world.

Sassanof joined them on the stage and spoke a few words of encouragement before sending them to their places; some to the wings, and some to the green room. It was the first time they were working with their full complement of actors and supernumeraries in house at once. They needed the supers for the Verona crowd scenes, but it made backstage far more crowded.

Sassanof moved out to the gallery to watch the play through. He was pleased. He expected critics and audiences to be pleased. Rehearsals on the other three were not going as smoothly. He scheduled dress rehearsals for them as well but after them he was still convinced that *Romeo and Juliet* was their strongest piece. Opening day was drawing near. He scheduled a press night and invited all the London critics to see the theatre and view *Romeo and Juliet* before the opening.

Due to the promotional efforts of manager, Michael Sassanof, and his partner, Baron von Marienburg, the opening of *Romeo and Juliet* at the Corycian Theatre was a much-heralded event. It was covered by nearly every paper in the metropolis in some fashion. Much was written that had little to do with the performance. Critics discussed the reincarnation of the Corycian Theatre. Some wondered how many theatres London could support. Some praised the decor. Others discussed the revival of Shakespeare occasioned by Irving's *Hamlet*. The youth of the Corycian cast was mentioned. Some critics did write about the preview performance and some waited until after opening night. In general, the focus was on the star-crossed lovers and the actors who played them. Favourable comments were written about the portrayals by Sebastian Devigne and Rose Morris. They even managed to spell their names correctly, although one wit could not restrain himself from asking if a Rose by any other name could act as well. Some praised the energy and excitement of the sword fights and attributed their quality to a newcomer to the stage, William Escott, who appeared as Tybalt.

The box office receipts followed the notices and funds flowed into the Corycian coffers. So well received was *Romeo* that Sassanof allowed it to run alone for three weeks while rehearsals continued on the other plays. The actors settled in a routine of rehearsals and performances six days a week.

Chapter 4

Tangled Threads

"I have now in my hands...all the threads which have formed such a tangle."
Sherlock Holmes, *A Study in Scarlet*

It was past midnight. The streets were nearly deserted. The audience was long gone when the actors poured forth from the stage door of the Corycian Theatre. It was a week after the opening of *Romeo and Juliet* and the players had been celebrating with a special dinner. Everyone was in high spirits. They spread out into the surrounding streets, some seeking cabs and others walking to nearby lodging-houses. William Escott was among those walking. Langdale Pike was following him for no other reason than that no cab was yet available to take him back to his club.

"I think you have dying down to a science," Langdale Pike said.

"I suppose knowing how to die convincingly could be useful," William Escott responded. "However, I suspect audiences are more interested in how well Tybalt fights than in how well he dies."

However, Pike did not respond because his attention was drawn to something over Escott's shoulder.

"Look," said Pike, "Isn't that your boy?"

Escott turned around and looked the direction Pike was indicating. He saw a tall boy with light hair talking to a constable. He immediately recognized the boy as Jonathan Beckwith, who had acted as his servant for a number of years. Holmes had sent him back to Yorkshire to work for his brother when he left Cambridge.

"Jonathan!" he shouted.

The boy looked over at him, said a few words to the constable, and then ran toward them with the constable watching as he did so.

"Sir, I—" Jonathan began.

"What are you doing here in London?" Sherlock Holmes inquired.

"I came with your brother, Sherrinford, sir. He and his wife are having some fittings done this week."

"Yes, Mycroft mentioned that they were going to do such a thing. I did not know that they were bringing you. Be that as it may, what are you doing wandering about the streets at this hour?"

"He's learned your disreputable habits," the other teased.

"Hush, Pike," Holmes said.

Jonathan looked puzzled.

"Come, Escott," Pike replied, adding to Jonathan's confusion, "You can't complain about children doing what you've taught them! However, we should find another spot for this conversation before that constable decides we are not so harmless after all."

Holmes looked over at the constable and waved at him. He waved back and moved on down the street.

"Constable Thompkins won't concern himself with us. He and I've had a number of conversations as I have walked home from the theatre. Let's go to my rooms. They are just around the corner here," Sherlock said. "My brother Mycroft won't be back in town for a few days. So we don't risk disturbing him."

"I was thinking of getting a drop—"

"I'll take care of you," Sherlock said, "Come on."

Mrs Denton poked her mop-capped head out as he unlocked the door.

"Ah, I see you found him."

"Yes, ma'am," Jonathan said. "Thank you, ma'am. Sorry to have awakened you,"

"Good night, Mrs Denton," Holmes said.

Sherlock poured brandy for himself and Lord Cecil.

"Mmm. Your brother has excellent taste in brandy," the young lord said stretching out on the sofa and making himself quite at home.

Sherlock pointed to one of the chairs across from the sofa.

"Sit," he commanded Jonathan.

Jonathan obeyed.

"Now explain why you are wandering the streets of London in the middle of the night."

"I was looking for you, sir," Jonathan confessed. "I met a boy named Timothy. His brother, Samuel, is missing. Samuel had been working for your brother's tailor, but had given notice saying he had a better position lined up. Then he disappeared. Timothy thought a journeyman named Schnayder who worked for the tailor knew where Samuel had gone. Timothy kept trying to get him to tell him, but Schnayder sent Timothy away. This morning—"

"How long has Samuel been missing?"

"He set out for his new position two weeks ago and has not been heard from since."

"Tell me about this morning."

"While your brother and I were at the tailor's shop, Timothy came around again demanding to know about his brother and Schnayder began beating him. I stopped Schnayder from beating Timothy. Then your brother stepped in to save me from a thrashing. Your brother was rather upset with me. Timothy came around to the back door tonight and brought me to his house to talk to his mother. She's distraught. Samuel is younger than I am and has always been a good son. I thought perhaps you could help."

Holmes frowned.

"Timothy thinks this Schnayder is involved in his brother's disappearance?"

"Yes, and his mother said he had no enemies or any other reason to leave home. But Schnayder no longer works for the tailor. The tailor dismissed him today after your brother questioned the fact that he employed men who beat children."

"He is not likely to think fondly of you as a result," Holmes said.

"No, sir," Jonathan admitted.

"Sweaters," Lord Cecil said in the background, frowning into his glass.

"What?" Sherlock Holmes asked.

"While you have studied much about lawbreakers, Holmes, you are still a novice when it comes to the full spectrum of the evils of London. There are a great many crimes in this city which are perfectly legal and others that are questionable, but winked at. Ever read Kingsley's *Alton Locke*? No? It was written 20 years ago, but it is still true today. As you know, I collect gossip and my sources extend from low to high, from dustmen to dukes. Tailors are an especially interesting subject because I like fine clothes. An actor's salary is not high, as you know, but there are limits I will go to press a bargain. I think every man needs to know the integrity of his tailor. Not only to be sure that the man will keep his confidences, but to be sure that people are not dying to provide him with a waistcoat."

"Elaborate," Holmes said.

"There is the 'honourable' tailoring trade and the 'dishonourable.' The honourable trade have garments made on their own premises by journeymen tailors. The dishonourable trade includes the show-shops, that do a cheap bespoke business, and slop-sellers, who sell cheap ready-made garments. They contract with 'sweaters' who provide garments at a lower rate. The distance between the honourable trade and dishonourable is shorter than it might seem. The West End 'honourable' shops pay their journeymen tailors by the piece. There are those who are in constant employment at a particular shop as captains, and those who have the preference for work as leading men in particular shops, who are tolerably well employed during the year, but there are far more who are only casually employed by the honourable trade, either in the brisk season, or when there is an extra amount of work to be done. Many master tailors keep more hands than they have employment for, especially in the slack. But no work means no pay. Some of those journeymen can't pay their bills and take home 'sank work' of custom-house and post clothing. It's one step away from sweating. They contract more than they can do and recruit wives, mothers, or children to help. Soon they have slid from journeymen to middle men. They spend their time hunting other contracts for piecework and bring in other journeymen to do it. They may start out just to survive, but some go down a very dark road and set up sweatshops where workmen eat, drink, and sleep in one room; as many as the room will contain. The sweaters charge them for room and board, and deduct other charges and fines from their pay as well. Soon they owe more than the pay due them. The sweaters insist that they pledge their clothing to cover the charges and won't let them leave until the costs have been recouped. They are kept working fourteen or fifteen hours a day for days or weeks without receiving a penny.

"Some sweaters use a system of 'street kidnapping.' Young tailors, fresh from the country, are decoyed into their miserable dens with extravagant promises of employment, only to find themselves deceived. In less than a week, their clothes are all pledged and they are obliged to continue working under the sweaters. They are imprisoned and starved, unable to make their escape for months, perhaps years, while the sweaters collect income from their work."

"So one of these 'sweaters' could be holding Samuel prisoner?"

"Yes."

"And the law won't do anything about it?" Holmes said in disgust.

"If you point their nose at a particular case, then they might, but they aren't going to go looking for it."

"Like those blackmailers in Cambridge," Holmes said with a pointed look at Cecil Hamley.

All three of them knew that Sherlock Holmes was referring to the men who had the young lord in their grip while they were both students. Holmes had broken into the establishment and destroyed all the notes they were using to extort money from undergraduates. When the gamblers caught him and tried to kill him Jonathan had come to his rescue. It was that episode and the discipline by the college that resulted from their "interference with police business" that had led to Sherlock's father to discovering Sherlock's studies of crime and disowning him as a result.

"Yes," Lord Cecil responded, "but the police have a stake in turning a blind eye to this. Where do you think their uniforms come from?"

"Sir, there is something your brother said to me this morning," Jonathan began.

"Go on," Sherlock said.

Jonathan hesitated.

"It bears on your relationship with your father," Jonathan said.

"Go ahead, he knows I had a disagreement with my father and he disowned me," Sherlock said.

"It is our common lot," the young lord said languidly from the sofa. "Perhaps we should form a club."

Sherlock waved his nonsense off for he saw Jonathan was in earnest.

"Your brother was concerned that if the Squire were to associate me with your study of crime, or any involvement with police or crime, then he would dismiss me and the squire's ill will could extend to the rest of my family as well. I do want to help Timothy find his brother and if it was merely my position that might be at stake, I would not hesitate, but if it could threaten my mother—"

"No, we don't want that."

Sherlock readily believed that his father would act in such a fashion.

"I can make some inquiries. However, I have a heavy schedule of practices and performances right now. It would be rather difficult to canvas all of London looking for this boy. We need to narrow the search."

"Let me tap into my resources," Lord Cecil said, "I might be able to learn something."

"In the meantime, Jonathan, you need to go back to the house in Kensington."

They found a cab that Lord Cecil and Jonathan shared as far as St. James Street then Jonathan continued alone to Kensington.

On Saturday morning, Holmes wandered about the public houses near the tailor's establishment in his most threadbare jacket with a few coloured threads clinging to it and a measuring tape in his pocket. He did not shave that morning or comb his hair, which was enough to convince most that he was a down-on-his-luck tailor. Many people he spoke to steered him towards the legitimate societies for journeymen. He referred to Schnayder by name. One man had heard of his firing.

"Most likely trying to find a situation for hisself."

Holmes hurried to the theatre to keep his own position. In the dressing room as they made up for the matinee, he compared notes with Langdale Pike.

"I was able to make some enquiries this morning. Spitalfields seems to be the most likely place for the lowest sort of shop."

"Any more precise location?"

"Not yet."

Escott's beard did not grow fast and the grease paint was enough to cover a day's growth. By Sunday morning, the stubble on his cheeks was longer and a bit of fuller's earth made him look even more disreputable. He grabbed a ride on the back of carriage that took him east by way of the Holborn Viaduct. He walked through Cheapside and along Threadneedle Street to Bishopsgate to Houndsditch Lane.

The journey east from Bloomsbury was like a trip through purgatory. The streets became narrower and dirtier. The street hawkers seemed more desperate and the shopkeepers had to be more diligent at keeping the ragamuffins of the streets from pinching their produce. Holmes looked sufficiently down-on-his-luck that the beggars did not bother him. A few ladies of questionable repute looked his way but decided he wasn't worth an effort so early in the day.

He wandered the streets visiting public houses and asking after Schnayder. He found that the dingier the pub the more close the patrons were. Unless you bought them a drink, but even then they might know less than was useful, and he hadn't many pennies to spare.

By Sunday evening, Holmes still had not located Schnayder. He knew he was close. He caught another ride west and wandered the alleys and mews of Kensington until he came up behind his own family's townhouse. He was considering strategies to speak to Jonathan without revealing his identity in his current condition of dress. He was saved from employing any of them by the presence of a young boy by the kitchen door.

"Timothy?"

"Yes. Who are you?"

"I am a friend of Jonathan's. I have been looking for your brother."

"Have you found him?"

Just then Jonathan joined them carrying some waste for the dust bin. His eyes opened wide at the sight of his erstwhile master.

"Mr Sherlock!"

"Sshh!" Holmes said looking up towards the windows.

The last thing he wanted was his own brother to see him in such a disguise. He would surely think he had fallen on hard times.

"Sorry, sir. I can only spare a few minutes or they will miss me."

"To answer your question, Timothy: No, I have not found your brother yet. I have narrowed it down to the area near Houndsditch Lane. I need to try a different tack to find the right house. I am hopeful that we will find him in the next few days."

"We are returning to Yorkshire on Tuesday," Jonathan said.

"Then you will go on. If we have not found him by the time you leave, rest assured that it won't be long. We will find him."

"Thank you."

Holmes returned to Montague Street. Mycroft raised his eyebrows when he entered.

"Not a rehearsal, I presume."

"No, a different type of performance. A case took me to the East End. I'll tell you about it when it is concluded, but for now I need a bath, and given it is the help's day off I will need to heat the water myself."

Such were the hardships of a pair of bachelors rooming near the British Museum. Sherlock Holmes then had a bite to eat and tumbled into bed.

He believed that he was close to finding Samuel as he had told the boys. He mulled over his next steps as he dressed the next morning and walked to the theatre. The ragamuffins of the street might know something the adults did not. He would try to gain their confidence. That was his plan as he prepared for his next performance as Tybalt. But he had underestimated Timothy's determination and Jonathan's intrepidness.

That night as he was leaving the theatre, Timothy accosted him frantically outside the stage door.

"They have him! They have him!"

"Who has whom? Samuel? Have you seen him?"

"They have Jonathan!"

"What!" Holmes exclaimed.

He pulled the boy down the alley.

"Tell me exactly what happened."

Langdale Pike heard them and followed. Breathlessly Timothy told them.

"I saw Samuel. I went to the house in Kensington and told Jonathan. He said he couldn't come and you were busy at the theatre. I waited. He came out after sunset and I took him to the house. It was near Houndsditch Lane like you said. Each of the houses along the street is back-to-back with another one. It was in a window in the garret of the back one that I saw Samuel. I showed Jonathan the narrow path to get to the door of the back house. The yard is fenced all around where it is not blocked by any other buildings. There is no other way in or out. Jonathan said he would go down the path to see if he could find a way to get in the house without being noticed. He said if he was not back in a quarter hour to come after you here. I waited the quarter hour like he said and he didn't come. I crept down the path myself and he was gone! There is no other way out. They must have him in the house."

"And you are certain they are holding your brother prisoner in that house?"

"Yes! I saw him through the window! Oh, we must save them both. They will kill them!"

"Pike, you need to go for the police. Take Timothy with you."

"Aren't you coming?" Langdale Pike asked.

"No, I am going directly to the house to free the boys."

"We should help you," Timothy said.

"No, you are more useful going for the police, especially if I am unsuccessful. Tell them what you saw. Lord Cecil here has certain advantages that make it more likely they will respond quickly. At the very least, I may be able to prevent them from carrying out murder before the police arrive. Go."

However, before Sherlock hailed a cab and set out for the address that Timothy had given him he returned to his rooms for a couple items he needed. When he arrived he had the cab driver wait in the street. It was a rather sordid neighbourhood and if it had not been for his demeanour and the police helmet he had obtained in Cambridge, the driver probably would not have been willing to go there at all much less wait.

As Timothy had said, each of these houses along here was back-to-back with another one. Timothy said he had seen his brother in the window in the garret of the back one. The windows of the back house were all dark now and it was quite dark in the yard. The light from the street lamps did not reach this far. Most the windows of the house were boarded from the inside and all the windows were encrusted with grime. But there was a window in the garret that was not boarded up. The faintest of lights, as if from a single candle, came from that window. The yard was boxed in. He now understood why Timothy had been certain that Jonathan could not have come out without passing him. Holmes marched down the dirty path, up to the door, and banged his fist upon it.

"Open up in there!" he cried.

There was rustling inside but the door remained closed.

"It's the police. Open up or we'll break in the door," he cried.

"It's the peelers," someone said.

A man opened the door.

"No need for that, officer. How can we assist you?" he said.

"There's been a kidnapping reported," he said in an official-sounding voice.

"We know nothing about that, officer," said Mr Schnayder.

"The detectives are coming with a warrant," he responded.

"Not really necessary, constable—"

Holmes pushed past him and began opening doors, closets, and trunks then slamming them shut again.

"I assure you—"

He pressed on up the stairs.

"There is nothing to see."

"Unlock the doors then and let me see for myself or I'll bust them down" Holmes said.

"You can't do that, officer."

"You can argue that with the judge later. It's the son of a peer that's missin'. The peer's in the Home Secretary's parlour at this minute. If we don't come back with his son within the hour it'll cost us all our jobs, and I'll see it cost you your neck."

Reluctantly the man unlocked the door. The room beyond was dark and smelled of old sweat and human waste. Gaunt, strained faces of more than a dozen men and boys sitting cross-legged on a dirty wood floor stared at him. They squinted and covered their eyes against the light that streamed in the door and blinded them. All but one were pale like they had not seen daylight in many months. Most wore only tattered pants. Only one was wearing a shirt or shoes and that was the one he was looking for. As he felt a sense of relief, he also noted the dark stream down the side of Jonathan's face and it angered him. At that moment, Schnayder tried to turn and run, but Sherlock Holmes seized him with an iron grip and slapped derbies on one wrist and attached the other side to a gas pipe inside the room.

"Come, Jonathan, we need to get you out of here," Sherlock Holmes said entering the room.

Jonathan stood up, but swayed as he did and nearly lost his balance. A thin boy next to him grabbed him to keep him from falling and Jonathan returned the hold.

"This is Timothy's brother," Jonathan said.

"Then bring him along, but we must hurry."

Sherlock Holmes caught hold of both boys and half pushed, half supported them as the three of them passed through the house and out into the street. Schnayder howled, threatened, and pulled at the pipe. The other prisoners fled the room as fast as their curved, emaciated legs could carry them. Sherlock pushed both boys into the cab that waited on the curb. He examined the contents of his pocket and found it wanting. He did not have enough to take both of the boys home. Sherlock called out the address on Montague Street. He removed the bobby's helmet and coat and then took out his handkerchief and dabbed at the blood running down Jonathan's face.

"Are you all right?" he asked.

"I think so, sir," Jonathan said but he winced and drew away as Sherlock hit a sore spot.

"It looks like you took a few knocks," Sherlock Holmes said.

"Yes, sir," Jonathan said.

"You should have waited for us."

"I was going to, but he saw me before I could withdraw. Where is Timothy?"

"He's with Pike. They went for the real police."

When the cab stopped at Montague Street, Sherlock Holmes told the driver to wait and he ran inside.

Mycroft looked up from some papers as he entered and set down the helmet and coat.

"How much do you need?" Mycroft asked.

"A few shillings for cab fare to take the boys home."

Mycroft handed it over and watched the door close behind his brother. He expected he would hear more of the tale later.

Sherlock descended to the kitchen and raided the pantry. Sherlock came out of the building bearing a carafe of water and a bundle wrapped in a napkin. He climbed in and handed the bundle to Samuel.

"This is what food I could find on short notice," he said then knocked at the trap and gave the driver the address of his family's house in Kensington.

Samuel took the bundle with trembling hands and untied it. Inside were some rolls, a lump of cheese, and some apples.

"Thank you," he said before attacking the food.

"Why aren't we taking Samuel home first?" Jonathan asked.

"What if Timothy brought the police there looking to see if Samuel had returned home?" Sherlock said as he wet the handkerchief in the water from the carafe.

Then he handed the carafe to Samuel who gulped down the

water, slopping some down his bare chest.

"The only way we can keep you out of it is prevent any contact between you and the police. That's why I marched you out of there before they showed up. I only took Samuel because I knew you would not leave without him."

"That's true," Jonathan conceded.

"Lean back," Sherlock said and wiped the rest of the blood off Jonathan's face and then folded the wet cloth and held it against the growing lump on Jonathan's head. Jonathan had to smile at the role reversal. He had tended Sherlock many times when he had been ill or injured.

"I promised—" Jonathan said.

"You fulfilled your promise and found Samuel. I promise that I will take him home directly. I suspect we barely escaped before the real police arrived to clean up the rest. I am sure Pike's performance was grand. He's good at melodrama. By now Schnayder has been arrested and the men freed. There isn't really much for any of us do. Besides, you aren't too steady on your feet. You took a bad knock there."

"He was out for some time after Mr Schnayder dumped him in our room," Samuel said.

"We need to get you to bed."

Jonathan scowled, which caused a particularly hideous effect on his battered face lit by the flicker of passing street lamps. Samuel reached over and took his hand.

"You are injured," Samuel said. "Listen to this man."

"You are right," Jonathan conceded. He looked back at Sherlock who still held the cloth against his head. "Thank you for coming for me."

Sherlock was silent for a moment in the dark carriage.

"I would be a most ungrateful brute if I had not," he said looking out the window. "Driver, pull around in the mews. Out you go."

Sherlock helped Jonathan down.

"I will be back in a minute," he told the driver.

As they entered through the backdoor and passed quietly

through the back hall, Sherlock was struck by memories of creeping down this same hall as a small child. He had lived in this house many years ago. Jonathan staggered and Sherlock caught his arm. He realized that he probably knew this route better than Jonathan did in the dark. Jonathan found the door to his room. They entered and closed it behind them.

"The house is fairly empty," Sherlock whispered.

"Yes, just your brother, his wife, her maid, and the housekeeper," Jonathan said. "Cook is coming in days."

"Ah, and housekeeper's room is on the other side."

"Yes," Jonathan said suddenly feeling exhausted.

"Those clothes are filthy. Take them off and tumble into bed. I'll see Samuel home."

Jonathan did as he was told.

Sherlock quietly left the room and tip-toed to the housekeeper's room. He tore a sheet from his notebook, wrote on it, pushed it under the edge of the door, tapped on the door, and then made his way rapidly out of the house. He returned to the cab, directed the driver towards Samuel's house where he left the boy in the arms of his grateful mother.

The sun was rising as the cab returned him once again to Montague Street and he paid the driver. He tumbled into his own bed to get a few hours' sleep before he had to be back at the theatre. But on his way to the theatre he sent a telegram to his brother Sherrinford in Mycroft's name asking if everyone had arrived back safely at the Hall. The response the following morning reassured him that all was well.

Chapter 5

The Play's the Thing

*It was not merely that Holmes changed his costume. His expression, his manner,
his very soul seemed to vary with every fresh part that he assumed.*
Dr Watson, "A Scandal in Bohemia"

Romeo and Juliet was doing well. Sassanof was less pleased with how the comedies were progressing in rehearsals and hoped to push them further before opening them. He tried swapping actors in different parts. At the urging of the Baron, he opened *Much Ado About Nothing* on April 5th. If the play had been left to Dewitt, Pike, and a few others it might have come off. Some of the cast lacked timing and proper inflection for the comedy. Some lines felt flat and some were "so overacted that they became dizzy from the rarefied air and wandered off without purpose" as one critic wrote. It ran for two weeks to plummeting ticket sales. Sassanof wanted to hold off opening *Twelfth Night* but his partner pressed him so he opened it directly after *Much Ado* closed. *Twelfth Night* closed a week later. The box office receipts could not justify holding it longer. Only the banter between Dewitt and Pike was keeping the audience awake. The other performers were unconvincing. "Comedy is not this company's forte," one critic wrote.

That comment stuck in Sassanof's mind. Perhaps he was right. Perhaps they should steer clear of comedies. They re-opened *Romeo and Juliet* while still rehearsing *Antony and Cleopatra*. He had greater hopes for *Antony and Cleopatra*. It had some characteristics in common with *Romeo and Juliet*—romance and fights. Hallows' benefit was also coming up.

"There are several important ingredients to a successful benefit," Matthew Hallows had told Escott a few weeks earlier. "First is choosing the correct play to highlight your own talents and draw a large audience. The second is choosing a good cast. The third is shameless promotion, for without an audience a play is nothing. A benefit can only be successful if you fill the theatre. You must ask everyone you know, high and low, to buy a ticket.

"For your cast you can draw upon any actors from any company who are willing. I have offered my services to a great many others for their benefits over the years. Therefore, I am not limited to Corycian's rather young and inexperienced members, but can call upon actors with greater experience and notoriety from other companies. By aiding me you will have a chance to work with these other actors and come to know them and perchance recruit them for your own benefit."

"I have chosen *King Lear* because the age of the title role fits me and I enjoy the variety of the role. The king alternates from regal to comic to dramatic to tragic all in one play. Thus, I can demonstrate my versatility. *Lear* also has a number of roles for older men allowing me to make good use of some of my close and very talented friends. However, there are also good roles for younger men and women. There is romance, betrayal, intrigue, and a few sword fights – all good elements to draw an audience. I have hopes that if we do well with *Lear* at my benefit that Sassanof will add it to the repertoire.

"There are costs associated with putting on a benefit. You must bear the costs of printing the circulars and the tickets. I have known actors performing in the provinces to overspend on these and yet fail to draw sufficient audience to cover those expenses. It is possible to lose money on a benefit. Yet here in London where there are so many theatres calling for attention, good circulars are essential. I will introduce you to the printers who do mine and teach you how to get the best dispersal."

"What assistance do you ask of me?" Escott asked.

"I ask you to personify Edgar, the son of the Earl of Gloucester, who is betrayed by his half-brother. He must flee for his life and goes into hiding as Mad Tom. I also ask that you plan the sword fights by the other actors as well. I hope that good stage combat will draw younger audiences who are less familiar with the plays of Shakespeare, but always willing to see some good sword fighting.

"I have asked Devigne to impersonate Edward, your duplicitous half-brother, who not only betrays you to gain favour in your father's sight, but uses his handsome looks to entice the married daughters of the king, and betrays his own father.

"Miss Anderson, Miss Parker, and Miss Clinton have agreed to take the parts of the king's daughters. Pike has agreed to be the fool. My friends Runnison, White, and Bannock shall play Gloucester, Kent, and Albany.

"For scenery and costume, we shall borrow those from *Romeo and Juliet,* and thus incur no new costs there."

So began the rehearsal for *King Lear*. It was a very different play from the others. Less romance and more intrigue. Hallows knew what he wanted from the players and how to get it. Rehearsals proceeded smoothly.

The Sunday after they began rehearsing *Lear*, Jonathan Beckwith answered the door at the Holmes' residence in Kensington. He had known that Mycroft Holmes would be joining them for dinner and was bringing a guest. As he entered, Mycroft asked Jonathan to forgo announcing them and allow him to introduce his guest. Jonathan took their hats and coats and allowed them to proceed to the sitting room unannounced.

Mycroft entered the sitting room silently as Mycroft always entered a room.

"Mycroft!" Sherrinford said rising and coming forward.

"Greetings, brother!" Mycroft said.

"So good of you to come," Amanda said offering her hand.

Mycroft took it, squeezed it warmly, and continued on, waving his other hand towards the young man who followed him into the room.

"I would like to introduce you to the actor, William Escott, currently performing at the Corycian Theatre."

The newcomer was tall and thin with black hair worn artistically long and a slight goatee and moustache. He was smartly, though not expensively, dressed.

"Pleased to meet you, Mr Escott," Amanda said offering her hand to him as well.

"My pleasure, madam," said Mr Escott as he bowed towards

her.

"Mr Holmes," he said bowing towards Sherrinford.

"I am glad to make your acquaintance, Mr Escott. Come in, have a seat. Would you like a drink before dinner? No? Well, if there is anything that we can do to make you more comfortable, do not hesitate to ask," Sherrinford said, and then turned back to Mycroft. "I thought perhaps you would convince Sherlock to come along."

Mycroft raised his eyebrows and did not respond to this remark, but Mr Escott walked up behind Sherrinford and threw his arm over his shoulder.

"Would you know him if you saw him?" asked Sherlock in his normal voice.

Sherrinford spun around and grabbed him by the arms with his eyes popping.

Mycroft chuckled.

"Oh, you, and you, too," Sherrinford said, nodding his head briefly at Mycroft.

"It is indeed like old times, isn't it?" Mycroft said.

"Amanda, my brothers were always playing tricks on me when we were growing up. Sherlock was often the perpetrator, though I think Mycroft did the planning."

"Oh, not this time," Mycroft said claiming a comfortable chair, "I merely provided the introduction."

"But Sherlock, you have gone to quite an extreme this time to fool me, growing your hair and beard out."

"Ah, but that was not really a trick. This is how I am wearing them these days. Mycroft's introduction was accurate. I am currently performing at the Corycian Theatre under the stage name of William Escott."

"Good heavens, if father knew—"

"He'd what? Disown me? He's done that already," Sherlock waved his hand dismissing the subject. "I needed a job and I found one that will suffice until I've paid my debt to the college. I'm actually rather enjoying it. I had to come here looking like Escott because I have a performance tomorrow and I can't possibly grow back my beard that fast. So I thought we'd just see if you recognized me."

"You did it well. I was totally taken in."

"With all due respect, Sherrinford, you are not much of a test of anyone's acting skills," Sherlock said.

As Sherrinford swatted his youngest brother, a bell rang. Amanda laughed.

"Despite Sherlock's comment, Sherrinford," Mycroft said. "You will note that he did not dare come as close to you as he did to Amanda, who seems to have divined the truth the moment he looked her in the eye."

"Yes, I recognized him then," Amanda said.

"I admit that I avoided eye contact with Sherrinford because I was afraid it would give me away," Sherlock said. "He is my brother after all."

"Well, that was the dinner bell. We should go in," Amanda said. "Do try to behave yourselves over dinner, gentlemen."

"Yes," said Sherrinford, "no turning the rolls into frogs or the roast into a turtle," as they filed into the dining room. Jonathan followed silently behind to assist with serving.

"It was Mycroft who taught me my skills at legerdemain at an early age," Sherlock said.

"Yes, but you were bolder at using them," Mycroft said.

"In occasionally inappropriate circumstances," Sherrinford said

"I seemed to remember some encouragement, even occasional dares, from my older brothers," Sherlock countered.

"I confess," Sherrinford said as he held Amanda's chair for her.

"Guilty as charged," Mycroft agreed.

"Now that we have convicted all three you for something," Amanda Holmes said. "I would like to hear how Sherlock has been doing."

"What would you like to know?" Sherlock asked.

"Did you really blow up the college laboratory?"

"Amanda," Sherrinford chastised her.

"No, it's all right," Sherlock said. "I was doing an experiment at the laboratory and it exploded. It was an accident. I was sent down as a result and I agreed to pay for the damage, which is why I must sweat before the footlights."

"So now you are acting on the stage?"

"Yes."

"How long have you been doing that?"

"I started rehearsing with the company three months ago. We opened *Romeo and Juliet* in late mid-March. We had short runs of two other works but will be performing *Romeo and Juliet* this coming week while rehearsing for the opening of *Anthony and Cleopatra* in ten days. We are also rehearsing *King Lear* for Milton Hallows' benefit."

"You are living in London?" Amanda asked.

"Mycroft is putting up with me, or rather putting me up."

"Both equally accurate, I imagine," Sherrinford said.

"Since the evening performances began, Sherlock is rarely there when I am," Mycroft said. "We occasionally see each other on Sundays."

"Most of the performances are in the evening," Sherlock agreed. "We have rehearsals in the mornings and afternoons when we do not have matinees. The rehearsals for Hallows' benefit are in addition to those."

"What of your plans to become a detective?" Sherrinford asked.

"I am still intent upon that," Sherlock said. "This is not merely a hiatus to pay my debt to the college, I am also learning many things that will be very useful to me in my future career."

There was a brief silence at the table for they all knew that it had been Sherlock's announcement that he intended to become a consulting detective that had caused his father to his disown him. He was not welcome at the family estate where his father still ruled, but Squire Holmes could not control what Sherlock and his brothers did here in London.

"Could we attend one of your performances?" Amanda asked, trying to break the mood.

"Most certainly," Sherlock said.

"We should do that, Ford."

"Yes, dear, we should."

"I must ask that you preserve my identity and promise to refer to me by my stage name at the theatre."

"We promise," Amanda said. "It will be fun! Like a play within a play."

"Are you going to be spending the whole Season here?" Sherlock asked.

"Yes. We have a busy schedule of teas, brunches, and balls lined up already. It will be so different from the quiet life of Yorkshire."

"Indeed," Sherrinford agreed.

"The nurse will be bringing the boys up in a few weeks," Amanda said.

"We are still not decided on how long they will stay," Sherrinford said.

"London is rather a dirty place for children of that age and they aren't old enough to appreciate its merits," Amanda said.

"While we love our boys," Sherrinford said, "we need a bit of time for ourselves to have a little fun."

"Before we are old and decrepit," Amanda teased.

"You will never be decrepit my dear," Sherrinford said, picking up Amanda's hand and giving it a kiss. "You shall be exquisite when they lay you in your coffin—"

"If you will excuse me," Sherlock interrupted laying down his napkin and quickly leaving the room.

"Oh, my God," Sherrinford said in his wake. "I just didn't think. He seemed so much like his old self—"

Jonathan stepped forward.

"Sir, if I may?"

"Yes, go ahead," Sherrinford said.

"He is still sensitive to some things, especially when he lets his guard down," Mycroft was saying as Jonathan left the room.

Jonathan followed the direction Sherlock had taken. He found him in the sitting room. Sherlock looked up at him as he entered.

"You seem to have recovered from that beating at the sweaters."

"Yes, sir."

"You had quite a knock on the head."

"Yes, sir. I was a bit sore for a few days. Your brother threatened not to let me come back to London unless I told him the whole story."

"So you did?"

"Yes, well, mostly. The essential parts."

"He was satisfied."

"Yes, sir. He said I should be careful."

"You are here for the whole Season?"

"Yes, sir, unless your brother should change his mind."

"How have they been treating you back in Yorkshire?" Sherlock asked him.

"Very well, your brother is an easy person to work for," Jonathan said.

"No problems with the Squire?"

"I rarely interact with him. When I do, it seems to be with the same indifference that he treats all the servants. Your brother is almost affectionate in his handling of the staff."

"I can imagine," Sherlock replied.

At that moment Mycroft appeared.

"Come, Sherlock, join us for brandy in the library. I've promised Sherrinford you would run through a few scenes of *Romeo and Juliet*."

"Good heavens, are you going to be Mercutio, Mycroft? Sherrinford obviously has taken Romeo. I don't suppose you know any of the lines from *Romeo and Juliet*, Jonathan?"

"I'm afraid not, sir," Jonathan said.

"At least you would do justice to the swordplay. Well, I suppose I am stuck—"

"That is the idea, is it not?" Mycroft responded.

"Ha! Lead on, Mycroft. It will take quite a bit of brandy to survive this."

Hallows' benefit performance of *King Lear* was held on May 5th before a packed house. Sassanof used the opportunity to promote *Antony and Cleopatra*, which was opening the following evening. Hallows' *Lear* was evocative and thought provoking. It was about age and illness, but it was also about ignorance and selfishness. The critics were kind. Those less interested in the battles between an arrogant father and his self-centred daughters found the intrigue between Edgar and Edward more engaging.

The next night *Antony and Cleopatra* opened. The critics were not as kind. They found Devigne believable as a lover, but not as a soldier. In a desperate attempt to save the play, Sassanof swapped Dewitt into the lead, but then it became a farce. He tried a couple of the other male actors before changing back to *Romeo and Juliet*. They could fill the theatre with *Romeo and Juliet* and pay the rent, but how long could they survive on one play? Shakespeare was still in vogue and Sassanof intended to stick with it. He studied his stack of play scripts. Perhaps he should try Devigne in a more villainous role. Then his eyes fell on Cibber's staging of *Richard III*. The Monday after *Antony and Cleopatra* closed the Corycian Company began rehearsing the Cibber version of *Richard III* with Sebastian Devigne as Richard, Duke of Gloucester.

William Escott was beginning to be annoyed at this long string of failures.

"Upon what basis does Sebastian Devigne merit first pick of the lead?" Escott asked Pike as they reached the street.

"A handsome face and a couple years performing in the provinces?"

"Not by talent then."

Pike laughed.

"He's no worse than the rest of us and only slightly better than some. Despite how he behaves, he does not have the lead by right of contract. He is contracted like the rest of us without a designated line of business. I suspect that Sassanof holds out hope of signing a star and did not want to limit his options too soon. It is a little unusual, but there are many changes occurring on the London stage and this is not the strangest experiment I have heard of.

You can learn a great deal by treating some of the greybeards to a few pints."

"But the point is that Devigne could be overthrown?"

"If better came along, undoubtedly. Are you planning a *coup d'état*?"

"No, I just find his arrogance out of alignment with his talent."

"You don't suffer arrogant fools well, do you?"

"No."

"Then how do you now put up with me?'

"I keep asking myself that question."

Pike burst out laughing.

"My dear Holmes, pardon me, Escott, if I had known you were so witty I'd have cultivated your friendship earlier."

"I doubt that."

"Are you coming?" Pike asked as a hansom pulled up.

"No. I have work to do," Escott said waving the script.

Pike made an elaborate bow.

"As you wish," he said and climbed into the cab that dashed off.

Hours later as Lord Cecil was engaged in a delightful discussion of someone's tawdry affair in one of the parlours of his club, a note was brought to him by one of the footmen. He glanced at it and told the footman to show in his guest. He excused himself with an explanation that a friend wanted a word with him. When Escott appeared before him, he did not immediately sit down, but walked back and forth fuming.

"Have you read this, Pike?"

"Not yet," he responded. "I read the play once in college. Why? What's the matter?"

"Cibber's arrangement of Shakespeare's *Richard III* bears hardly any resemblance to Shakespeare's."

"True, but it is the version that has been performed for 175 years!"

"A folly perpetuated for 175 years makes it no less a folly! The differences are so great that I think that merely applying Shakespeare's name to it would be an act of fraud."

"Oh, it is a crime now? You certainly take your art seriously, but aren't you exaggerating a little?"

"It is appalling. The writing does not approach Shakespeare's original. It contains poor, and sometimes quite execrable, verse. It guts Richard's opening soliloquy, which is a marvellous speech, and stuffs the remains in Act 5 Scene 6. While Shakespeare's version may be a little long for a modern audience without some trimming, it contains psychological complexity and well-crafted verse that are lacking in Cibber's. Cibber's rubbish is merely intended to shock audiences on a visceral level rather than make them think!" Escott declared and flung his copy upon the floor.

The script slid across the highly polished hardwood floor and stopped under the foot of one of a group of men seated at a table. The man bent over and picked it up with his long, thin fingers and held it out. In his rage against the play script, Sherlock Holmes had failed to observe the other people in the room. Now his eyes grew wide when he saw who was holding the script out to him.

"My apologies, Mr Irving," he said.

"It sounds like it had it coming. Pull up a chair and tell us your objections to Cibber's rendering of *Richard III*."

Escott and Pike quickly pulled two chairs to Mr Irving's table.

"I'm William Escott and this is Langdale Pike."

"On stage, at least," Mr Irving said with a twinkle in his eye.

"Yes, sir."

Sherlock Holmes explained his objections, thumbing through the script and pointing out examples to the great actor.

"Macready tried it in 1821 and Phelps in 1823, but both failed to win the audience over," one of the other actors at the table said.

"It is always a risk to break from what the audiences are accustomed to," Mr Irving said.

"But you yourself have done it with your Hamlet," Escott said.

"That's very true and we had no idea how well it would be received. The first night the auditorium was as silent as a tomb for the first two acts," Henry Irving said.

"No one backstage dared make a comment about it," said one of the other actors at the table with Irving, "but we were all holding our breath. Then the audience rose and applauded in the third act and we knew everything was fine."

"But you do not have Mr Irving's experience, Escott," Pike said. "You'll never get Sassanof to agree to it."

"Not in the regular repertoire," Holmes said with a twinkle in his eye, "but I have a benefit coming up."

"You wouldn't!" Langdale Pike exclaimed.

"I think it is worth a gamble, and that, my dear Pike, is a rumour you are free to spread."

"It could be a disaster," Pike said shaking his head.

"Or a triumph, Mr Escott!" Irving said.

Sherlock Holmes beamed, his eyes shining at the challenge before him.

"Please keep me apprised of the progress of your experiment," Henry Irving said, "I am curious how it turns out. For now, however, we must be going. We have another long day of rehearsals tomorrow."

"As do we. Thank you for kind words, Mr Irving. Good night."

"Good night."

After they were gone, Sherlock turned to Pike.

"Did you know he was a member of the club?"

"Yes. There was a big scandal when he was initially blackballed a few years ago, but many prominent members asked him to resubmit his name for consideration and he was accepted later that same year. You don't mean what you said, do you? About your benefit?"

"I most certainly do."

Pike shook his head again.

"You are certainly more energetic than I am. Even the thought of such a project exhausts me. I think I shall retire. Good night!"

"Good night."

While Sherlock Holmes memorized his lines as Richmond in Cibber's arrangement of *Richard III*, he also began reviewing Shakespeare's version and plotting his own staging of the play.

They rehearsed the Cibber version of *Richard III* with Sebastian Devigne in the title role for a week and opened it on May 24th.

"That did not come off well," Pike said, adding another newspaper to the array around him. "Vacuum in the centre," he read pointing to one. "Unbalanced performance," he said indicating the next. "Shallow" he read from a third. "A tragedy becomes a comedy," he read from a fourth. "But this one said good things about you: 'The young actor who came on in the fifth act as Richmond was far more noble and believable in his role. He handles a sword like a master in this and his other roles. I predict a great future for Mr Escott.'"

"Do you think it will close?" Escott asked.

"I thought it might last a few weeks, but after this, I'd be surprised if it lasts through tomorrow."

Langdale Pike's prediction was accurate. The auditorium was nearly empty that night and Sassanof told them that the rest of the run of *Richard III* was cancelled. As Escott was leaving the stage after this announcement, Sassanof called to him.

"Escott, hold up a minute," Sassanof said.

"Yes, sir," Sherlock said.

"Pike tells me you've been to France."

"Yes, sir. I lived there a number of years."

"So you know the language well?"

"Yes, sir."

"Then I'd like you to come over with me to Paris. There is an English actor living there. I have heard good things about him and I want to take a look at him."

"I would be glad to. When were you thinking of going?"

"Tomorrow. Meet me at Victoria for the first train to Dover. Pack for a couple of days. I'll cover the expenses."

"I will be there."

Chapter 6

The Tragedians

"This, then, is the stage upon which tragedy has been played."
Sherlock Holmes, *The Hound of the Baskervilles*

The morning fog was still masking the dilapidated buildings of the Chatham and Dover Railway at Victoria Station when they boarded the carriage for the journey to the coast. Their train would meet a packet ship at Dover that would take them over the Channel to Calais, where they would take another train to the *Gare du Nord* in Paris. The journey would last nearly eleven hours.

At the commencement, William Escott feared it would seem substantially longer. As they pulled away from Victoria Station, Sassanof began to talk at length, almost more to himself than to his travelling companion. It came out in a flood with eddies that cycled back to things he had already said. Mostly he talked about the Corycian Company and his hopes and concerns for the theatrical venture. Undoubtedly, the failure of *Richard III* was foremost on his mind, following as it did on the heels of the failure of the comedies and *Antony and Cleopatra*. Sassanof had left the Corycian Company to repeat *Romeo and Juliet*. Joseph Reece was filling Escott's role as Tybalt while they were gone. However, one of Sassanof's greatest fears was that they would become known as being capable of only one play. No theatrical venture could survive on a single piece. Baron Von Marienburg seemed patient enough, but how long would that last if they kept losing money? Hallows' *Lear* benefit had been well received. Sassanof hoped to mount *Lear* with a few changes but he doubted its endurance. His purpose in travelling to Paris was to recruit an actor with greater experience with tragedies than his current cast. No one could do *Hamlet* in London as long as Irving's lasted but there were other plays. He repeated those thoughts amidst complaints about the caprices of critics.

Escott feared Sassanof would ramble on in the same way the entire journey. He nudged the conversation in other directions, thinking to explore the mystery of Sassanof's background, yet instead he found himself talking about his own past. When he asked if Sassanof had ever been to France, the answer was a quick negative. Then Sassanof asked how he had come to know the country. Aware that he was constructing the back-story for the fictional William Escott, yet knowing that staying close to the truth would make it easier to be consistent, Sherlock Holmes told stories of his family's stays in France. In the midst of his tales, he inserted questions about Sassanof's own childhood. In each case, they were deftly deflected by a question about his past. Holmes found it to be an interesting mental exercise, an attempt at interrogation without interrogating. Yet the result was utter failure. He learned nothing about Sassanof beyond what he had learned when he first laid eyes on him.

What he knew about Sassanof was far more than Langdale Pike's fantasies. He had detected no hint of a foreign inflection in Sassanof's speech patterns, at least no more foreign than Liverpool. The fact that his regional accent was nearly nonexistent suggested that he had travelled frequently in his youth. It was also obvious to Holmes that Sassanof had evidently been in the theatre for many years. Holmes had not perceived any indication of any other career. It all suggested that Sassanof came from a theatrical family and had been raised travelling about Britain acting from a young age. It was not for him a career, but a way of life. He had given no indication to the Corycian actors that he ever intended to take to the stage himself, unlike the prominent actor-managers of the day. Perhaps he had some reason for choosing exclusively to manage. Yet the thought of leaving the theatre was like the thought of ceasing to breathe. It was not something he could even contemplate.

All this was reflected in his current concerns. The Corycian was important to him. It was not merely a business venture. The mystery of his background was merely a role, perhaps his final role, and the world was his audience. Holmes' attempt to force him out of that role was unsuccessful, but it made the trip less interminable than Sassanof verbally churning over the business concerns of the theatre. However, failing to provoke Sassanof to reveal his memories did not prevent Holmes' mind from wandering to his own. He had intentionally avoided talking about their final year in France and return to England in the spring of 1871. Nevertheless, the human mind links memories to other memories, and a few times he found himself clenching his fist as if to physically clamp down on the memories of that year as they attempted to come forward. He believed his efforts went undetected; at the very least Sassanof made no comment.

When they arrived in Dover, a vigorous wind was blowing off the channel that discouraged conversation. The wind also made for choppy seas. Sassanof was looking a bit green by the time they reached Calais. He spoke little as they found their carriage on the train to Paris. Grateful for the silence, Escott leaned back and closed his eyes. Soon enough they arrived at the *Gare du Nord* and engaged a cab to take them to the *Hotel du Louvre*. Once there a late supper and clean sheets satisfied their needs after a day of travelling.

Sherlock Holmes was up and dressed early the next morning. They had arrived after dark the night before and had seen little of the French capital. He wandered from the hotel down the *rue St. Honore*. Sherlock and his parents had been in France in early 1871. They had heard reports of the Commune de Paris, but had left the country before its peak. They had sailed directly from the south of France to Whitby in the north of England. He had not seen any of the conflict first hand. It had now been a half dozen years since he had last been in Paris. He was shocked to see the morning sun shining through the charred shell of the Palace de Tuileries. It had survived convulsions of revolution and empire only to be gutted during the Commune. Repairs were continuing on the Louvre, which had suffered far less damage. A guidebook for visitors back at the hotel had listed other buildings that had been destroyed. Some had been repaired or demolished, but no decision had yet been made about Tuileries. It sat like an open wound between the Louvre and the Palace Royal. Despite the scars in the French capital and the early hour, people strolled the boulevards and filled the cafes. Paris, like the proverbial phoenix, was rising from her ashes to proclaim once again her place in fashion and culture.

Sassanof had told him that the actor they had come to see was playing Laertes in *Hamlet* at the *Theatre Français*. Holmes found the theatre a short distance from their hotel. A banner was suspended from the pillars of the building. "Lablas" was written across it in large letters above "Hamlet." The other performers' names were below in smaller print. He was not familiar with this Lablas, but assumed he was an actor of some renown.

Escott returned to the hotel and joined Sassanof for *petit dejeuner*. Sassanof was impressed by his description of the ruins of the Palace de Tuileries. He wanted to see it for himself. They walked past the ruins and then spent some time at the galleries at the Louvre. The library and other portions of the Louvre had been fired by Communards and entirely destroyed. The museum itself had miraculously been saved. They purchased tickets at the theatre and returned to the Louvre Hotel for lunch.

They spent part of the afternoon sampling the wide selection of English, American, German, and French periodicals in the hotel lounge. Then they dressed for dinner, dined early at the hotel, and strolled over to the theatre in anticipation of crowds. The *gardiens de la paix* were already in place at the theatre to preserve order. They were arranging patrons in queues to await the opening of the doors, and keeping traffic in front of the theatre moving. Sassanof looked up at the banner as they waited.

"That's our man, Henri Latour," Sassanof said.

"The name sounds French," Escott replied.

"Oh, it is. His father - deceased now - was a Frenchman, but his mother is English. His brother is attending Edinburgh University. His mother would like to return to England but hasn't the funds to do so, and while Henry is acting in Paris...."

"I see. Are you a friend of the family?"

"More of a friend of a friend. I said I would look into it. With the failure of *Richard III*, I have another motivation. I need to bring in a tragedian. I'm forced to admit that Devigne is not convincing in that type of role."

Seven o'clock struck as Sassanof was speaking and the waiting throng filed into the theatre. From the vestibule, an elegant staircase led up to the foyer of the theatre, where a statue of Voltaire stood on a pedestal of blue-tinted marble. The interior form of the house was elliptical and substantially larger than the Corycian. Sassanof wanted to be close to the front so he could get a good look at the actors. A nervous-looking fellow was also heading towards the front row and bumped into Sassanof as he brushed past.

"Excuse me, sir," he said.

"Ah, you're an Englishman like ourselves!"

"Oh, glad to meet you. Sorry to be so boorish, but my friend is performing and he insisted that I get as close as possible."

"Well, it looks like there is still plenty of room in the first row," said Sassanof, waving his hand at the empty row. "So take your pick."

The nervous English young man chose the seat in the exact centre of the front row with only the orchestra intervening between him and the footlights. Sassanof sat next to him and introduced himself.

"I'm Michael Sassanof. I manage an English acting company and this is one of my actors, William Escott."

"Barker's the name. What are you doing over here?"

"I'm looking to see if there is any talent here worth importing. Yourself?"

"What? Oh, just visiting friends."

Mr Barker seemed very distracted, but that did not prevent Sassanof from babbling on about theatre.

"We can't approach the French on 'touch-and-go' comedy," Sassanof said. "It's their strong point. However, when it comes to Shakespeare, they are lost, sir, utterly lost. If you had seen the Hamlets I have seen — Macready, the older Kean, Irving—"

Sassanof's reminiscences were cut short by the raising of the curtain. The first few scenes were tame enough.

Sassanof leaned over to Escott and whispered, "It's better in English."

William Escott had to grin at that since Sassanof didn't speak a word of French. However, it wasn't the language that was attracting his attention. There seemed to be some special tension between the actor who was playing Hamlet, the Lablas mentioned on the banner, and this Latour fellow who was playing Laertes. While Lablas' performance was good --though not on par with Irving's--, Sherlock heard whispers in the audience that this seemed an off night for him. On the other hand, Latour's Laertes scintillated. The spirit and the fire of his performance seemed to captivate the audience and he was roundly applauded. There was something more than good acting going on here. As student of the darker side of human nature as well as a student of theatre, Sherlock Holmes saw drama behind the drama. There was a smouldering glint in Latour's eyes when he looked at Lablas that went beyond mere acting, and true indignation rang out in the words: *"Ma soeur a été jetée dans un état désespéré! Mais ma vengeance viendra!"* (My sister was thrown into a desperate state! But my revenge will come!) While Sassanof did not know the language, he knew the play like his own heart beat and knew the intent of the words.

"By Jove!" he exclaimed, "Those last words were nature itself."

Latour was called before the curtain for an extra bow at the end of the fourth act, but it was in the scene at Ophelia's grave that he surpassed himself. His howl of *"Que le démon prenne ton âme!"* (The devil take thy soul!) as he sprang at Hamlet's throat fairly brought down the house. Mr Barker next to Sassanof sprang to his feet, but sat down again as Laertes shook himself free of Hamlet. There was no doubt in Holmes' mind now that Latour was the friend Barker had come to see and his nervousness was related to the tension Holmes saw on the stage. The theatre was filled to the brimming. The vast audience hung on every word that passed between Hamlet and Laertes.

"You'll get an English actor to make more stage points," Sassanof commented enthusiastically, "but there's a confounded naturalness about all this which is wonderful!"

There was a great hush in the house as the curtain rose upon the final scene. The king and queen of the Danish Court were seated in the background under a canopy of purple velvet. There was a clear space centre stage with a swarm of men-at-arms, courtiers and members of the royal household on either side. Laertes was leaning carelessly against a scenic pillar while Hamlet was conversing with a courtier with a confident smile upon his face. Near Laertes was a man-at-arms with an ill-fitting suit of armour. Size wasn't the only thing wrong with his costume. By his side was a delicate rapier instead of the Danish broad sword that was fitting to the costume. Osric came tripping forward with the bundle of foils. Hamlet and Laertes chose their weapons and saluted each other.

"Gad!" whispered Sassanof as the combatants had saluted each other, "Look at the man's eyes! I tell you it's unique!"

Sherlock grabbed Sassanof's arm and whispered urgently, "There is something wrong here. Those aren't foils. They aren't properties. They're sabres, real sabres."

Before any more could be said there was a quick stamp and the ring of steel upon steel.

"Damn it, Sassanof! Property swords don't ring like that. You know that!" Sherlock said.

The combatants were evenly matched; first one then the other seemed to gain temporary advantage.

"The deception is admirable. You'd swear there was blood running down the leg of Laertes. Capital! Capital! The business is perfect!" Sassanof exclaimed.

"It is blood, real blood! We have to stop them!" Sherlock said rising.

But Sassanof grabbed his arm and pulled him back into his seat. Just then Laertes rushed at Hamlet furiously driving him into the crowd of courtiers. Hamlet gave a deadly lunge under the guard driving his sword through Laertes' left arm. Then Laertes sprang forward and ran his sword through Hamlet who fell upon his face at the footlights.

There was a hush in the audience and then a loud cheer went up. The whole house sprang to its feet with round after round of applause. Like the rest of the audience, Sassanof was on his feet, but he wasn't applauding. From the front row, he had seen something terrifying in that final lunge that most of the audience could not have. In his shock, he had let go of Sherlock's arm and Sherlock had vanished.

Sassanof convulsively grabbed the Englishman to his left by the wrist and whispered, "I saw it come out of his back!"

He stood there stunned. The audience continued to stand and applaud expecting Lablas to stand and take a bow. Lablas just lay there stiff and stark with a scowl upon his white face and his blood running down the stage towards the orchestra pit. Silence spread over the pit as a musician noted the blood running onto his music and alerted his fellows. Sassanof now saw that Sherlock had made his way on to the stage and was gesturing and calling for the curtain to be dropped. The curtain came down as a great stillness fell upon the theatre.

The audience slowly filed out of the theatre, bewildered, and then horrified as the rumour spread that the great Lablas had died on the stage before them. Bucking the tide towards the exits, Sassanof and Barker attempted to reach the stage, but were turned away by *gardiens de la paix* who had swarmed up onto the stage. Stunned and not familiar with the language, Sassanof clung to the Englishman Barker as they flowed with the human torrent out into the street. Barker seemed a tumult of emotions himself. Horror and relief seemed to fight for supremacy on his face.

"I can't believe he did it," Barker said over and over.

"Most extraordinary thing," Sassanof mumbled. "Don't abandon me yet, kind sir. I don't know the tongue here. Where has that boy gotten off to?"

The *gardiens de la paix* were directing people away from the building. They expanded their cordon towards the street, urging people away. The doors to the theatre opened to reveal another *gardien* with his hand on Escott's arm directing him out the door. Some words were exchanged between them. The *gardien* shook his head. Escott looked down the steps and saw Sassanof and Barker. He descended towards them.

"Is he really dead?" Sassanof asked.

"Yes," Escott said.

"And Henry? How badly is he injured?" Barker asked.

"Not badly. He should recover," Escott responded.

"You know Henry Latour?" Sassanof asked Barker.

"Yes. I said a friend was in the company. It was he," Barker said.

"Then tell us what was really going on there," Sherlock Holmes said grabbing Barker's arm. "This wasn't just a play."

"I don't know what you mean," Barker said.

"They were real sabres. I examined both of them before they removed me from the stage."

Barker blanched, but did not say anything.

"You were nervous from the start. You knew something of the sort was going to happen," Holmes accused him.

"Something of what sort?" Sassanof asked.

"That was not a stage fight that we saw. It was a duel," Sherlock Holmes said.

"My God, is duelling legal in this country?" Sassanof asked.

"No, it's not," Sherlock Holmes said. "But some people do it anyway. You knew about this, Barker."

"I can't tell you anything," Barker said.

"And from the ferocity of Latour's words I suspect his sister is involved," Sherlock said.

Barker blushed and turned away.

"I can't tell you anything. I really must be going," he said hurrying away.

Holmes started after him, but Sassanof stopped him.

"Let him go, Escott," Sassanof said. "What can we do about it anyway? There'll be some type of inquiry, won't there?"

"Probably not," Holmes said with disgust. "The *gardiens de law paix* merely came in to restore order. They distinctly told me that they considered it an accident, even when I pointed out that the actors were using real swords. They proposed that the two actors both accidentally chose real swords from the lot, which I find to be highly improbable. I think they understand what happened and they don't intend to do anything about it."

"Amazing," Sassanof said shaking his head. "I don't know how much of that was acting and how much was real, but the whole thing has left a bad taste in my mouth. I've a longing to just get back to a civilized country."

Despite Sassanof's desire to quit the country immediately, the next train to Calais did not leave until morning. They were up and packed betimes and off to the station with the dawn. The sun rose red that morning and tinted the ruins of the Palace Tuileries as they road past it, as if to remind them of the bloody passions of the Parisians. They needed no reminder. Sassanof was haunted by what he had witnessed. Escott had already turned his mind to other things.

Sassanof and Escott were quiet on the journey back to London. For Sassanof's part, it was a lingering horror of what they had seen in France combined with his concern for the Corycian Company. He believed a strong tragedian could turn their fortunes around. He had hoped to convince Henry Latour to join their company but having just seen him kill another actor on stage. Sassanof shivered. A black mood enveloped him.

Holmes was plotting. On the train from Dover to London, he finally broached the subject on his mind.

"I want to take my benefit in July," he said.

"Might as well," Sassanof replied.

"I want to do *Richard III*," Escott said. "Shakespeare's *Richard III*, not Cibber's, and I want to play the lead."

"You can do whatever you want for your benefit. Just give me the date," Sassanof said glumly.

Holmes wasn't even sure he was listening. He would have paid more attention if he had realized how important this announcement would be to the Corycian Company.

Chapter 7

To Prove a Villain

"I think, perhaps, it is almost time that I prepare for the new role I have to play."
Sherlock Holmes, "A Scandal in Bohemia"

Romeo and Juliet had gone as well as usual while they were in France. It remained their biggest draw. They continued the performances of *Romeo* for the next few days as they rehearsed *King Lear* and the scene painters created back-cloths specifically for *Lear*. On Friday, the Corycian Theatre opened *King Lear* with Hallows in the title role and most of the Corycian actors in the roles they had volunteered for his benefit performance. Where he had used actors from other companies, members of their company replaced them. On Saturday, they performed *Romeo* for the matinee and *King Lear* in the evening. The combination was well received. For the next two weeks, they offered *King Lear* six evenings a week with *Romeo and Juliet* for the Saturday matinee. Unfortunately, Milton Hallows could not keep up that pace of performances. Rather than attempt to switch the lead, Sassanof changed the schedule. They offered *Romeo* Monday through Wednesday evenings in addition to the Saturday matinee and *Lear* on Thursday through Saturday evenings. These changes boosted the box office receipts and Sassanof felt more confident. Yet disaster continued to stalk the Corycian Company.

On June 28th during the evening performance of *Romeo and Juliet*, the cast and supers were scattered between the wings and the green room during Act 2 Scene 2. Only Sebastian Devigne and Rose Morris were on the darkened stage lit by a shaft of limelight that fell between them. The audience was enthralled as the two lovers spoke.

"By a name I know not how to tell thee who I am," Devigne cried as he stepped from the shadows, "My name, dear saint, is hateful to myself, because it is an enemy to thee. Had I it written, I would tear the word."

"My ears have yet not drunk a hundred words of thy tongue's uttering, yet I know the sound," Rose responded. "Art thou not Romeo, and a Montague?"

The illusion of two lovers conversing in the moonlight was complete as the actors spoke—except Juliet's balcony seemed to be leaning a bit too much and continued to slowly tip forward.

"Neither, fair saint, if either thee dislike."

Rose screamed as the balcony fell. Devigne initially backed away, then stepped forward again and caught her as the balcony crashed with a cloud of sawdust at his feet. The curtain rang down. The other actors and backstage crew spilled out on to the stage. Sassanof was on the stage in seconds.

"Are you hurt?" he asked his actors.

Rose was clearly shaken from her fall, but she was unharmed because Devigne had caught her. She was still gripping his arm and thanking him profusely. Devigne shook his head. He was speechless, staring at the debris inches from his feet, and the twisted pile of lumber where he had been standing. The only words that came to mind were not ones he would say in the presence of a lady, even if she were an actress.

Lionel Palgrave, the chief carpenter, pushed through the throng and expressed great shock at the damage. He seemed less concerned about the presence of the ladies. Sassanof quickly surveyed the damage to the stage floor as well the twisted wreck of the balcony and made the painful decision to cancel the rest of the performance. He went before the curtain to speak to the audience. The audience began filing out. The actors retired to the dressing rooms to change.

Escott had been in the wings on the opposite side when the balcony fell. He crossed over the stage and examined the remains as the stage hands disassembled the balcony and carted it off stage. There was twisted and broken lumber and sawdust. Was it due to poor construction or weak materials? He could not find any obvious explanation in the cursory examination possible. He joined the other actors changing out of costume. News from the stage filtered back to them.

Sassanof insisted that the repairs to the stage floor be given priority over the balcony. They would have to bring in special lumber to make those repairs and it would take two days to tear out the damaged boards and replace them. The Tuesday and Wednesday performances of *Romeo and Juliet* would have to be cancelled, but they should be able to go on with the Thursday performance of *King Lear.*

Reconstruction of the balcony was not complete before the Saturday matinee, but it was ready by Monday evening and they resumed their previous schedule. William Escott had used the evenings off to work on his version of *Richard III.* He had already spent several weeks on the script and was still refining it. He had begun with Shakespeare's own plot line and dialogue from the 1597 quarto and trimmed characters, scenes, and dialogue. The arguments between Richard and Lady Anne had seemed far longer than necessary to convey their antipathy and subsequent alliance. The speeches in the last scene seemed anti-climactic. He chose instead to end the play at Richard's death at the hands of Richmond.

Escott also acted as a promoter. He posted bills and handed out handbills. He tested new versions of speeches in Regent's Park, Hyde Park, and near the Tower of London. This was also a new role for him, but he had taken Milton Hallows' instruction on how to run a benefit performance to heart. He dispatched circulars to numerous potentially interested parties, including to Mr Irving.

They began rehearsals on the new *Richard* in early July. Escott had recruited a number of the company to take on roles, including Devigne, Dewitt, Pike, and Reece. Hallows was to play Edward IV with Annette Davenport as Elizabeth his queen. Dewitt would be Lord Stanley, Pike, Buckingham, and Reece, the Duke of Clarence. Elspeth Anderson, a steady and versatile red-haired actress agreed to be Lady Anne.

Sebastian Devigne had agreed to impersonate Henry, Earl of Richmond. Devigne was still stinging from his failed attempt at the Cibber version of *Richard III.* While Henry was not the title role, it was the chief protagonist. In this version, he would literally be the last man standing on the stage when the curtain came down. Devigne understood the cooperative nature of benefit performances, and realized that he might want Escott's aid with one of his own. He also had more experience at self-promotion than Escott had, and had gladly agreed to recreate one of their stage fights in Regents Park to promote Escott's benefit, the theatre in general, and, of course, himself.

These efforts were having some success at driving ticket sales for the benefit but Escott had also taken Hallows' advice to engage family members in the promotion of his benefit. While he had been inspired to demonstrate his ability to play the villain as Shakespeare had written him, the potential financial rewards in terms of an early retirement of his debt to the college forced him to swallow his pride and ask for his brother's assistance. Mycroft did not hesitate. He took the tickets for the boxes and the dress circle and passed around circulars among his acquaintances. He made no mention of any familial relationship, only that these tickets were for a benefit performance for a young actor who had the temerity to revive Shakespeare's *Richard III*. The tickets sold rapidly in his hands. Mycroft filled the dress circle with junior government clerks and the boxes with senior clerks, saving one for himself and one for Mr Irving. It was from William Escott that Irving received the invitation to *Richard III* with the token for the box left for him at the box office.

They used the scene-cloths and costumes from the Cibber arrangement in the new version of *Richard* and the stage business and stage combat were adapted to the scenes. As the day of his benefit grew closer, Escott continued to refine the production.

Chapter 8

The Lost Boys

"His complete suppression of every reference to his own people"
Dr Watson, "The Greek Interpreter"

Late one Sunday morning, Sherlock was at the table in the sitting room in Montague Street with a cup of coffee at his elbow scribbling away at his plans for *Richard III* when there was a violent knock at the door. It was the housekeeper's day off so he answered the door himself. Jonathan Beckwith stood there with a troubled look on his face, and grass and mould on his shoes.

"What's the matter? Did something happen at the Gardens?" Sherlock asked before Jonathan could speak.

"Your nephews are missing," Jonathan said, but he had not completed the last syllable before Sherlock had thrown aside his dressing gown.

"You have a cab waiting?" Sherlock asked as he pulled on his coat.

"Yes, sir," Jonathan said, "Is your brother Mycroft here?"

"He is at a meeting at the Russian embassy. We will drop a note there on our way," Sherlock said grabbing his comb.

He combed his hair up and back on his head. Once he donned his top hat, the length was less noticeable. He still had the beard he wore as the actor William Escott. Sassanof had been right. It did make him look older than his twenty-one years. That might be useful. Soon Sherlock and Jonathan were heading across London.

"Tell me what you know," Sherlock said.

"The nurse, Agnes, took them for a walk in Kensington Gardens—How did you know it happened there, sir?"

"The mould on your shoes. I know Kensington Gardens well. Go on."

"Agnes took Arthur and Edward out to the park like she does every day it is fair. Her feet were sore and she sat down to rest along the Flower Walk. She tried to get them to quietly play catch with a ball. She began talking to another nurse and when she looked up the boys were gone."

"How long ago did this happen?"

"About an hour and a half ago now."

"The police have been called in?"

"Yes. Constables were searching the Gardens when I left. There was a Scotland Yard inspector there who spoke to your brother."

"The inspector's name?"

"Gregson," he said. "He said other children have disappeared in parks recently."

"What? There has been no mention of such a thing in the newspapers. I read all the crime news."

"He said they have been keeping the investigation quiet."

"Obviously. To the sorrow of more parents."

"There is something else I think you should know. Your brother's wife is with child, or at least the maids think so. We believe your brother was attempting to talk her into returning to Yorkshire before this happened."

"I will keep that in mind," Sherlock said and banged on the trap. "Driver, stop here. If you could pay the man, Jonathan, I shall take a look around."

Sherlock began by standing at the Palace Gate and looking over Kensington Gardens from where he stood. Most of the 275 acres were hidden by the trees that were in full leaf. The Broad Walk stretched out in front of him and the Flower Walk curved off to his right but they were both unusually quiet. On a normal day there would be couples strolling, nurses pushing prams, and children running about. Now all he heard were the birds and the vehicles behind him on Kensington High Street. The only people he could see were two constables approaching him.

"Sorry, sir, the Gardens are closed today," one said.

"Yes, because a pair of young boys have disappeared," Holmes said.

One constable squinted at Sherlock Holmes.

"And what you be knowin' about that, sir?" the other constable asked with a touch of suspicion.

"They are my nephews," Sherlock said as Jonathan ran up beside him.

One of the constables recognized Jonathan as the servant who had been with the father of the boys earlier.

"He's all right."

"Excuse me, sir. I was not aware."

"Can you show me where the nurse was sitting?"

"Yes, sir. This way, sir," the first constable said. "Not quite as far as the Albert Memorial."

As they walked down the Flower Walk, they saw more constables searching the gardens.

"Was the ball found?" Sherlock asked.

"Um, no, sir, we've been concentrating on finding the children, not their toys."

"The toys might lead you to the children."

When they reached the bench, to the surprise of the constable, Sherlock Holmes took out a magnifying glass, handed his top hat to Jonathan, bent down on his hands and knees and began studying the area under and around the bench. Jonathan watched him, wondering what he was looking for.

"Here, what is this?" asked another voice.

Sherlock Holmes stood up, brushed the grass off his hands and knees, put his top hat back on and greeted the Scotland Yard inspector like a colleague.

"Ah, Inspector Gregson. Sherlock Holmes. I was searching for clues regarding my missing nephews."

The Scotland Yard inspector gave the young man an amused look.

"Surely anything small enough to require a magnifying glass couldn't be of much significance?" he said.

"On the contrary," Sherlock said, "I have found that the smallest details are often the most significant."

"You have, have you?" said Inspector Gregson with a smile.

"Yes," Sherlock said as he began to walk off away from the path, staring at the grass.

Jonathan, Inspector Gregson, and the constable followed.

"I would have been able to discover more if the scene had not already been trampled by an army of constables."

"Such as what, young man?" Inspector Gregson asked, clearly amused by the lecture.

"Oh, such as more details about the captors — height, weight – though the shoe size gives a general range – state of health, occupation, perhaps even their current location."

"From the earth?"

"Yes. But I have mostly seen partial prints and not often consecutive ones. It makes it much more difficult to extract information, though it does provide the general direction that they travelled."

"They came this way?"

"Yes," Sherlock Holmes said as he examined some broken branches and picked up a dirty rag from the ground beneath them and stuffed it in his pocket.

"What were their shoe sizes?" Inspector Gregson asked he followed the young man down a slight decline.

"The woman – the nurse was an accomplice – a size 8 ½ and the men a size 12 and a 10 ½. Well-worn and straight last, suggesting people of limited means."

Inspector Gregson could not control himself any longer and burst out laughing.

"Mr Holmes, perhaps this incident has you a bit rattled—"

Sherlock Holmes seemed to be more intent on something mostly hidden in the ground ivy. He pulled it out and held it up.

"Jonathan?"

"Yes, sir, that's it," Jonathan responded.

"My nephews' ball," Sherlock Holmes said handing the ball to the inspector.

Then he dug the rag out of his pocket and laid it on top of the ball.

"And the rag dipped in ether that was used to silence them, which caused Edward to finally lose his grip on the ball."

Then he walked briskly on, still looking at the ground. Jonathan tried to keep up with him. Inspector Gregson stood staring at the ball and the rag in his hand. He handed them off to the constable and began to run forward.

"Now hold up there, Mr Holmes," Inspector Gregson said.

Sherlock Holmes stopped and turned back to him.

"Yes?"

"How did you find those things? We've had people searching everywhere."

"As I noticed. But they were merely walking around looking for two boys. I found the ball where I knew it would be."

"And how did you know that?"

"From the evidence that your men had not managed to trample yet."

"How did the ball get this far away?"

"Have you ever tried to remove something from the grasp of an eighteen-month-old child? Infants are born with a phenomenal grip, a throwback perhaps to our brachiating ancestors, but their natural instinct is to grasp on to things and not let go. They lose that tendency over time. If Arthur had had the ball, he probably would have tossed it away, but Edward's instinct would be to hold on to it. Since it was not found near where the boys were last seen I concluded that Edward had it. The branches back there were broken when they pulled the children behind these trees. Near them I found the rag that still has some of the ether clinging to it. There, entirely surrounded by a thick screen of bushes and trees, is where they used the ether on the two boys and the ball was finally dislodged from Edward's hand. But there is a small basin here so the ball naturally rolled down hill and lodged in the ground ivy heaped at the lowest point where I found it. It is a clear indication that their captors brought them this direction. I suspect here they put them in a pram or wrapped them in rugs to hide them before they went out onto the public streets. As you can see once we pass through the trees on the other side of this triangle, we are but a short distance to the Palace Gate and Kensington High Street. The carriage drive also converges here but they don't impress me as the kind of people to own a carriage. You could question people in this area about whether they saw someone carrying something, though I don't know how you would distinguish them from all the normal traffic through this gate. I don't believe I can do any further here."

Sherlock Holmes turned back the way he had come and left the inspector gaping. He walked out the gate and down the few blocks to his family's house. He knew the route well. As they approached the house, Jonathan ran forward and opened the front door. Sherlock entered, removing his hat as he did so.

"I was beginning to worry about you two," Sherrinford said as Sherlock handed his hat and coat to Jonathan. "Mycroft said that you had probably stopped at the park to investigate."

"And he was correct. Shall we convene in the library?"

"Yes, Mycroft is there already. Do you want to speak to Agnes?"

"No, I don't think she can tell me anything I don't know already. Do you have any large scale maps of the Gardens?"

"No. I don't think so."

"Some large sheets of paper, then, so I may draw a map?"

"Jonathan, go to the nursery and get some of the drawing paper and bring it to the library."

After Jonathan left the room, Sherrinford asked, "Is there anything else you need?"

"I will let you know if I think of anything."

"Amanda is very upset about this."

"In the circumstances—" Mycroft began.

"I understand that she is with child," Sherlock interrupted.

"Yes, but how—" Sherrinford said.

"She should go back to Yorkshire," Sherlock said.

"She won't do it," Sherrinford responded. "I suggested it before this happened. I know that there is no use arguing with her. She refused to leave off tending you when you were ill and she was further along with Arthur than this. I know she won't leave when her own sons are missing."

"Ah, the paper," Sherlock said as Jonathan returned. "Bring it over here."

As Sherlock took the paper and began to spread it out on

the table, the door opened again and Amanda entered. Her eyes were red and her blond locks tumbled chaotically about her shoulders. Sherrinford stepped forward and put his arm around his wife.

"Is there any news?" she asked Sherlock, holding his eyes for a second.

Her face was composed, but the tremor in her voice revealed the fear within. Sherlock looked away and reached into his pocket for his pipe and his tobacco.

"The police had no news to report when I spoke to them," he said as he packed his pipe. "But I found the boys' ball and followed the track of their captors for some distance."

Leaning over his pipe to light it, Sherlock did not see Sherrinford's scowl.

"Their captors?" Amanda asked. "What do you mean their captors? I thought they had wandered off and become lost."

"Two men and a woman snatched Arthur and Edward from the Gardens," Sherlock said.

"My God. How do you know this? Did you know this, Sherrinford?"

"The police said it was possible that they had been taken. They weren't certain."

"But now they are?"

Sherlock answered between draws on his pipe.

"Well, no, the police aren't certain. But I am," he said, "I followed their footprints as far as I could. I was about to draw a map of what I had seen so we could analyse the data further."

"Why would they do that? For ransom? We'll pay anything. Won't we, Ford?"

"Yes, dear."

"We don't know yet why they took the boys," Mycroft said, "but I have some theories."

"I don't want theories. I want my boys," Amanda said breaking free of her husband and moving forward to grasp Sherlock's arm. "Sherlock, I know you are clever. I remember the thimblerigging at the fair."

"That was an insignificant trick," he replied, not looking at her.

She referred to a time of which he dared not think.

"But it was more than that. You understood the whole game and spotted the shills. A small thing to you, perhaps, but it makes me believe you when you say you know more than the police. I have but one question for you: Will you bring my boys back to me?"

For an instant, all of them were silent, not even breathing. Sherlock fought back the waves of emotions and memories that her words evoked. He knew that maintaining control right now could be a matter of life or death for the boys. His whole soul cried out that this was the very reason that he had chosen to become a detective. There was only one answer and he gave voice to it.

"I will," Sherlock responded.

Sherrinford wrapped his arms about Amanda and urged her towards the door.

"Come dear, my brothers need to concentrate."

"Yes. I'll go now," she said, but she turned back to Sherlock as she reached the door. "I believe you," she said to him.

When the door had closed behind her, Mycroft said, "I would warn you about making promises that you may not be able to keep—"

"I will keep it," Sherlock snapped.

There was steel in his grey eyes when he said it. Then he closed his eyes and drew upon his pipe trying to concentrate.

"I hope to God you can," Sherrinford said sitting down, suddenly overwhelmed.

"Here, Jonathan, hold the paper," Sherlock said, getting back to the task at hand. He leaned over the table and began to sketch out the landmarks of Kensington Gardens and the surrounding streets. Mycroft got up from his chair and loomed over the table as Sherlock worked.

"So you believe they are still alive?" Sherrinford asked.

"Yes," his brothers answered simultaneously.

Then Sherlock added the location of the footprints he had observed to the map and marked the places where he had found the rag and the ball.

"What are those theories, Mycroft?" Sherlock asked as he set the pencil aside and relit his pipe.

"Well, ransom is an obvious one, but it seems less likely when there are multiple incidents near in time and space."

"Why?" Sherlock asked.

"Because in order to collect the ransom you must name a location for the ransom to be paid and run the risk of capture when you collect it. Usually kidnappers ask for sufficient ransom to leave the locality and live well elsewhere. They don't run the risk over and over in the same city."

"The police said none of the other children have been recovered."

"Another indication that ransom was probably not the motive."

"I agree."

"Then our other possibilities are some form of deviant sex trade," Mycroft said.

"Oh, my God!" Sherrinford cried. "You are not to mention that to my wife!"

"No, we won't, and they are too young," Sherlock said.

"Yes," Mycroft agreed. "Slavery?"

"Also too young. They would be a liability until they were old enough to work."

"Baby trafficking?"

"A possibility."

"You think someone would try to buy my sons?" Sherrinford asked. "But the boys would know they weren't their parents."

"They would at first and they might cry and even try to run away," Sherlock said, "but in time they would forget."

"But how can someone forget their parents?"

"Do you remember anything from when you were three years old, Sherrinford?"

"Well, no."

"You see? That's why their ages are perfect for it."

"There are still other—"

"I don't want to hear any others!" Sherrinford said raising

his voice and approaching the table.

Jonathan backed away from the table to the corner of the room.

"How can the two of you go on like this is a philosophical discussion of the evils of society? We are talking about my children!"

Sherlock turned two steel grey eyes on Sherrinford as smoke curled about his head. He looked much older than his twenty-one years at that moment and his voice was cold and firm as he spoke to his brother.

"If we are to defeat evil in the world, then we must acknowledge that it exists and try to understand its habits and motivations. If we allow emotions to cloud our minds then we will not be able to find your children."

Sherlock understood Sherrinford's emotions far too well. Nevertheless, he knew that if he allowed them to overwhelm him, the result would be devastating to himself and his nephews. The ice in Sherlock's tone reminded Sherrinford of what Sherlock had been through and he struggled to control his fears.

"I'm sorry," Sherrinford said. "You are right."

Mycroft stared at the crude map on the table.

"We need to put this incident in context," he said as if the interruption had not occurred.

"Yes. I need more information from the police," Sherlock said.

"They may not want to give it to you."

"That is true," Sherlock said thoughtfully, "but I will get it."

"I must go," Sherlock said quickly and began rolling up the map, "May I take Jonathan with me?"

"You won't get the boy in trouble?" Sherrinford asked.

"No. I need someone I can trust to assist me and to run errands."

"Then yes," Sherrinford said.

"And there is the matter of expenses, I don't—" Sherlock began.

He had recently sent a draft to the college and was without

funds until he received his next wages from the theatre.

"Yes, yes—" Sherrinford said distractedly.

He went to his desk and took out his chequebook.

"Will that be enough?" he asked when he handed the draft over.

"Certainly," Sherlock replied.

"Well, unless I can be of further—," Mycroft said.

"No, I don't see that you can do anything further here."

"I will make myself available if I am needed. Please send word to me of any developments," Mycroft said as he donned his hat and coat.

"Thank you. I will," Sherrinford said. "Sherlock, you must keep me abreast of your investigation."

"I will."

"I want my boys back, but I don't want to lose anyone else."

"Tell me immediately of any news you hear from the police," Sherlock responded.

Jonathan followed Mycroft and Sherlock Holmes out to the street. He hailed a cab as the two brothers spoke.

"The moon is full tonight," Sherlock said.

"A pagan ritual?" Mycroft said.

"Possibly. I will look for any pattern like that."

"When is your next performance?" Mycroft asked.

"Tomorrow night. I will deal with that when the time comes."

A four-wheeler pulled up.

When they were all seated, the cab started off across the cobblestones. Mycroft took out his pocketbook and extracted a few bank-notes. He handed them to Sherlock.

"Until you can negotiate that draft on Monday."

Sherlock took them without a word.

"Will you be coming back to the rooms afterwards?" Mycroft asked.

"I expect so, unless some other line of investigation presents itself. I don't know how long it will take."

"Then I will expect you sometime this evening."

"Yes. If something comes up I will send a message to you."

"Have you ever investigated something like this?"

"No. But I have read of many similar cases."

"Be careful."

"I will find them," Sherlock said and turned his head to look out the window.

The brothers rode the rest of the way in silence.

Sherlock Holmes descended from the cab in front of Scotland Yard. He walked briskly up the steps as if he owned the building with Jonathan trailing slightly behind.

"They have a fascinating collection of weapons and other artefacts of crimes here. P. C. Randall manages the collection. Last summer I met him at the Old Bailey and he let me see it one evening. I haven't had a chance to visit since I came back to London. Do you have your notebook?"

"Yes, sir," Jonathan said.

"Well, get it out and take notes of anything and everything. You never know what might be useful."

"Yes, sir."

"And take this," Holmes said handing him the rolled up map.

"May I help you, sir?" a police constable asked as they entered.

"Yes," said Sherlock Holmes offhandedly, pitching his voice a bit deeper than usual, as he had learned to do for some roles. "Remind me which direction it is to Inspector Gregson's office."

"That way, sir."

"Thank you. Come, Jonathan."

They found Inspector Gregson at his desk.

"Hello again, Inspector. Any news about my nephews?"

"Oh, it's you, Mr Holmes. Nothing so far. We have expanded the search to houses near where we found the ball."

Holmes noticed the "we."

"There has been a rash of child disappearances recently."

Inspector Gregson frowned.

"I wouldn't call it a rash. There have been a few. Enough to get the Yard's attention."

"I need to know the details of those other cases."

"Now Mr Holmes—"

"This is not just morbid curiosity. I need the information to find my nephews."

"We don't even know if the cases are related."

"That's what I need to determine," Sherlock Holmes insisted.

"I'm willing to humour you to a certain extent, young man, you being the boys' uncle and all, but this isn't a game for amateurs."

"And the police don't need any help with it?" Sherlock said sarcastically. "Tell me you've found the boys and I'll go home."

"Well, no, we haven't."

"Tell me that your police constables didn't walk past the ball and trample the cloth soaked with ether into the ground and nearly obliterate all the footprints on the scene."

"I still don't completely understand how you found that ball when no one else saw it. But you are asking for information that has nothing to do with this case."

"It has everything to do with this case," Sherlock Holmes said. "It will allow me to determine if this is a random act or part of some pattern or plan. If there is a pattern then clues from the different crimes can be used to find all the boys."

"How did you know they were all boys?"

"I didn't until you just told me. That's the type of information I need: genders, ages, class, locations, dates, and so on."

"This is official police business, young man. We have our best men working on it."

Sherlock Holmes fixed an icy stare on the Scotland Yarder.

"Inspector, if you do not tell me what I want to know, I shall walk down Fleet Street and in a few hours every street corner is going to be shouting that children are being snatched right and left in London parks and the police are covering it up. You can calculate your chances of retaining your position after that," he threatened.

"Why should they believe you?" Inspector Gregson countered.

"The police have been all over Kensington Gardens today. I'm sure the press would like to know why."

"And I'll have you in gaol for interfering with a police matter."

"You'll still be looking for new employment."

"All right. I'll tell you about the other cases, but I want your word of honour that this information is only for the purpose of finding your nephews and catching the crooks. I don't want to see it on any rags in the morning."

"On that you have my word," Sherlock said.

"Stay here," the inspector said and left the room.

He returned in a few minutes with a box of files.

"Here are the files."

"That seems to be more than a few, Inspector."

"They are probably coincidences. Children wander off sometimes. Kensington Gardens is notorious for tykes fallin' out of their prams. Sometimes their nurses spot 'em and sometimes they just vanish into thin air."

Sherlock began leafing through the files.

"Some are runaway apprentices. I think we can eliminate those."

Sherlock began sorting the files into a series of stacks on the desk under the Inspector's watchful eye.

"These are apprentices," Sherlock Holmes said indicating one pile. "These are all over the age of ten and seem more likely to be runaways as well," he said pointing to another. "But the remainder, with two exceptions, are all under the age of four. Those two exceptions are the oldest cases in this group from nearly two years ago. Adam Hamilton and George Wilson, two boys of seven and eight."

"Those really shouldn't be in there at all," the inspector said.

"Why not?" Sherlock asked.

"Because they were found."

"Where?"

"Just wandering around the streets. Seemed no worse for

the wear. Might have been runaways.”

“Were any of these others found?”

“No.”

“Any bodies of children found?”

“Always plenty of street urchins dying of somethin’ or other. No matches to these cases.”

“Jonathan, take notes.”

“Yes, sir.”

Sherlock began reading off the names, ages, dates, and locations of the lost children from the files as well as their parent’s names and addresses. Jonathan took it all down.

“Now don’t you start disturbing those grieving parents,” the inspector insisted, “or we will find a gaol cell for you.”

“I think I have all I need, Inspector.”

“So what have you learned?”

“I don’t know yet. I will let you know if I find any new information. Come Jonathan.”

They left Inspector Gregson shaking his head at these youngsters and their notions.

In the rooms that he shared with his brother, Sherlock shed his top hat and coat and donned his dressing gown. He relit his pipe and began examining his brother’s stock of reference books.

“Ah, here we go,” he said, pulling Whitaker’s Almanac from the shelf.

He thumbed through the pages.

“Read off the dates.”

Jonathan pulled out his notebook and did so.

“No correlation with the phases of the moon,” Sherlock said snapping the book shut and laying it aside. Sherlock spread several atlases on the table.

“We need to map where the other children were last seen.”

Jonathan read out the locations and Sherlock marked them on the map. They were scattered about London. Sherlock had begun comparing them with the locations of other characteristics of the city when Mycroft arrived.

“Any news?” Mycroft asked as he hung up his hat and coat.

"No, but I did extract the data from Scotland Yard."

"Are these the locations where the other children were taken?" Mycroft said leaning over the table.

"Yes."

"None are far from an underground station."

"True, but is it significant?" Sherlock asked.

"Perhaps. Note that the nearest stations are all on the southern part of the Circle Line. If you look at the stations as points on that line, you notice how they cluster out in either direction from there, leaving a centre station, Charing Cross, that doesn't have any children missing near it."

"Not wanting to soil their own backyard?"

"Or more likely, given that neighbourhood, it isn't an area where children usually go. Even if your theory is correct and these child-snatchers have their headquarters somewhere in this area, we don't have the time and the men to search every building."

"A search like that would also alert them."

Sherlock stood up and paced the floor. He stopped before the fireplace. He picked up his pipe and began cleaning out the bowl.

"We are going about this the wrong way. We are not looking for a place," he said. "We are looking for people."

"Correct," Mycroft agreed.

"People are itinerant," Sherlock continued as he packed his pipe, "and they have reasons for where and why they go places. They may be frivolous or irrational reasons, but they are reasons. If these people have gone into hiding then they will be very difficult to find in their hole. We aren't looking for a foxhole. We are looking for the fox. So like a good foxhound we must find the scent – the traces that these people left behind going to and from their headquarters. What we need to do is figure out what motivations distinguish these people from the other four million people in the city."

Sherlock picked a hot coal from the fireplace and used it to light the tobacco in his pipe. When it was drawing he looked up at Jonathan.

"You take my bed, Jonathan. I have some thinking to do," Sherlock said.

"I will be retiring as well unless you feel you need my assistance," Mycroft said.

"No, I can think this out best if I am alone."

Chapter 9

Fire and Water

"If the law can do nothing we must take the risk ourselves."
Sherlock Holmes, "Wisteria Lodge"

Left alone in the sitting room Sherlock sat thinking and smoking. Sometimes he consulted the books and maps on the table or pulled others from the shelves. Mostly he sat and thought. He looked at a list of adoption agencies in a directory. He estimated how long it would take to talk to each one. It would take days. Perhaps one would give him a clue or perhaps the traffickers used other channels. In such case, that time would be wasted. They did not have time to waste. There must be a more direct path of investigation. He looked over Jonathan's notes again. There were the two boys who had reappeared. They also had vanished from Kensington but they had reappeared at other locations. The files had not included any statement from the boys. If the police had interviewed them, there was no indication of what they said. No arrests were made. Could the boys describe their captors? Did they remember anything about where they were held? Was anyone else there when they disappeared who may have seen something?

Regardless of how long his investigations would take, it was impossible for him to make the performance at the theatre that night or even be able to concentrate on it. Just the fact that he had the commitment was a distraction. He drafted a note to Jonathan instructing him to take the accompanying note to Frank at the stage door of the Corycian Theatre to give to Sassanof. His note to Sassanof begged off from his performances for a few days citing a family crisis and asking that an understudy take his place. He wrote that he willingly would accept any fine the manager chose to charge against his pay. He completed those notes shortly after dawn. With the notes on the table and off his mind, Sherlock Holmes dressed to interview the very people that Scotland Yard had warned him not to. If he had planned to leave without the boy, he had clearly underestimated Jonathan's own intentions to help with this case. When he turned to the door to leave, Jonathan stood there with the notes in hand.

"Then come along," he said.

Jonathan hailed a cab for him on Great Ormond Street. The cab turned into Tottenham Court where the boy hopped out and delivered the note to the theatre. Then they continued on to the Hamilton residence in Kensington.

Sherlock Holmes apologised for interrupting her morning and explained the purpose of this visit very thoroughly, but Mrs Hamilton was hesitant. Since Adam had returned she had been very protective of him.

"I understand your reluctance but my nephews are missing and your son might know something that can help us find them."

"I-I."

"Imagine the sorrow of another mother? You know how frightened you were. What if someone had known something?"

She relented.

"Mary, please ask Adam and Mr Rogers to join us. Mr Rogers is his tutor. He goes everywhere with Adam now. That's the only thing that keeps me calm."

"Was Mr Rogers his tutor at the time Adam disappeared?"

"No, he had a governess, Mrs Blightly. She left us right after Adam vanished. She was so distraught. She blamed herself."

"I know someone of that name. Is she a young, plump lady?"

"Not at all, middle aged, thin, quite aesthetic and scholarly."

The boy and his tutor entered the room and introductions were made. Holmes explained to the boy why they wanted to talk to him.

"Anything you can remember, no matter how small, can help us."

"I am sorry, sir. I don't really remember anything."

"Well, let's just think back to that day. What was the weather like?"

"Warm and sunny, sir."

"Did you go out?"

"Mrs Blightly took me out to the shops. I stopped to look in a window. I don't remember anything else."

"Mrs Blightly said she turned around and he was gone," Mrs Hamilton said. "The police kept suggesting that Adam had run away."

"I assure you, mum, I did not!"

"I know, Adam."

"What was the next thing you remember?"

"The birds. I heard the birds and woke up in the park."

"What park was this?"

"A constable found him early in the morning in St. James Park," his mother said.

"You don't remember anything else?"

"Not a thing."

"Oh, but he has nightmares," Mrs Hamilton said.

"What do you see in your nightmares, Adam?" Holmes asked.

The boy hesitated.

"It is not a sign of weakness, my boy. Sometimes we remember things in our dreams that we do not remember when we are awake."

"Yes, sir. I have this one dream of waking somewhere dark. I can hear water. People are arguing. Something about 'too old' 'get rid of them' 'not murder," and "drop them somewhere.'"

"You said you hear water in these dreams? Is it water dripping?"

"No, like a stream or a river."

"Mrs Hamilton, do you have a forwarding address for Mrs Blightly? I have some questions for her."

"Unfortunately, no. The last Christmas card I sent to her was returned."

"Thank you, we won't disturb you any longer."

They took a cab to the second address. Holmes once again explained their quest to a protective mother and convinced her to allow them to interview her son.

"He went out to the bakery with his governess, Mrs Walton," Mrs Wilson said. She said that he just vanished while she was paying for her purchases."

"Tell me what happened, George," Holmes said.

"It started raining. The bakery was very warm and smelled delicious. I was looking at a display of biscuits near the door. There was a funny man waving to me outside the window. I think I stepped outside. I don't remember anything else until I woke up on the bench." George said.

"Where was that?" Holmes asked.

"Vincent Square in Lambeth," Mrs Wilson said.

"Had Mrs Walton been with you long at that time?"

"Just a few weeks. Then she left. She blamed herself," George's mother said.

"Can you describe her?" Holmes asked her.

"Do you think she was responsible?" Mrs Wilson said.

"I want to eliminate that possibility."

"I can do better than describe her. Here's a picture of her with George."

"May I borrow this? Thank you," Holmes said tucking the photograph away in his coat pocket.

"We must speak to Agnes," Holmes said to Jonathan back in the cab.

When they arrived at the Holmes' house, Sherlock Holmes stayed in the cab and sent Jonathan in to speak to Agnes. He did not want to deal with a hysterical nurse or risk another encounter with his sister-in-law. He lit his pipe. His tactic of sending the boy in, however, did not prevent his brother from coming out to him.

"Any progress?" Sherrinford asked.

"I am hopeful."

Jonathan came out. From the excited look on his face, Sherlock knew they had the answer they needed.

"She said it was the same woman. She said her name was Nancy."

"Probably another alias. Did she see anyone else with her?"

"When I asked, she remembered seeing Nancy in the distance with two men when they first arrived at the park. One was pointing towards the street. She thought perhaps they were asking directions."

"No doubt they were setting up their rendezvous."

"What does this mean?" Sherrinford asked.

"I have determined that at least two of the previous abductions were associated with a woman in the employ of the family, the same woman Agnes spoke to. I believe she is working with two men."

"What are you going to do now?"

"I need to narrow the search further. We must be off."

The evidence seemed to indicate that the boys were kept in a building near the Thames, not on the Embankment, yet not far from Charing Cross Station. There was a pedestrian bridge that crossed the Thames there next to the railroad bridge. He had the cabby drop them off on Waterloo Road in the South Bank. Holmes knew they had to stay near the Thames. He stopped in at a pub on Waterloo Road and showed the proprietor the picture.

"Sure I saw her. She left here a little while ago. Took some sandwiches with her. She asked for something I don't get much call for 'round here."

"What was that?"

"Milk. Guess she had some young ones."

They walked to Commercial Road and then along Belvedere Road. It was an industrial area featuring iron works, white lead works, distilleries, and breweries. They spotted a woman with a packet entering an old abandoned brewery. She matched the woman in the picture.

"The two of us just can't crash in there in broad daylight," Holmes told Jonathan. "They might take off with the boys and we would be back where we started, or worse."

They walked quickly back to Waterloo Road and returned to Scotland Yard where they attempted to enlist the aid of the Metropolitan Police.

"It is an abandoned building," Sherlock said.

"It may be run down, but it belongs to someone," Inspector Gregson said.

"Anyone else can wander into it, but the police can't?"

"We can't do anything until we have a warrant."

"They might be gone by then!" Holmes cried in frustration.

"I'm not sure that the magistrate will even grant one. What do I have? Just your theories."

"My theories, as you call them, found the ball and the ether rag."

"Well, yes, I've seen a few positive results."

"And they have uncovered a baby trafficking scheme that has been operating under your noses for two years!"

"That's what you say. That's a lot different from finding a ball. I need something concrete before I act upon your theory."

"If you act now you can find my nephews and catch the men who took them and possibly discover where the other children went. I'm offering you a chance to be a hero."

"Or a dupe. If we go in there without a warrant, we'd probably have to turn them loose anyway and the press will be all over us for that. It'll cost me my job."

"Bah!"

"Look. We will have some constables patrol the area and look for suspicious behaviour."

"And they'll find nothing," Sherlock Holmes said and turned and left the room.

Jonathan followed.

They found a hansom on the street and Sherlock gave the driver an address a few blocks from the abandoned building.

"You should stay behind with the cab," Sherlock told Jonathan as they rode along.

"You need me, sir," Jonathan replied. "When was the last time you saw your nephews?"

"Over a year ago."

"They were both infants. They won't remember you and you may not recognize them. I know Arthur and Edward by sight and they know me."

"Yes, that could be useful. An extra pair of hands and eyes could be useful as well. But we are heading into trouble here and I don't want you in the midst of it."

"This is not the same as the other business. My duty to your family, whether to you personally, or to your brother, or the squire, demands that I give you what assistance I can. I will come with you."

"Good heavens, you are growing up," Sherlock exclaimed. "No longer afraid to speak your mind, are you?"

"Not when it is necessary."

"What of your family?"

"My father lost his life in the service of your family. My mother would understand that I can do no less."

"Well, I hope it doesn't come to that. I suppose that the squire couldn't object to the quest. It is the presumptive heir to the family estate that we are trying to rescue. Driver, we will get out here."

The building was dark and dirty. There was an open yard in front of it next to the street. Perhaps it had been meant as space for delivery vans. They skirted along the edge of the lot rather than walking through the open space. Sherlock concentrated on watching and listening and Jonathan followed him silently. They found an unlatched door and Sherlock opened it slowly and carefully. He slipped inside and closed it behind Jonathan.

It was dark inside the building. Small patches of light filtered in from dirty windows and leaky roofs. From somewhere inside, they could hear banging. It was the kicking and drumming of small fists. Sherlock headed towards the sound and it grew louder. Now they could hear it was accompanied by a small voice.

"That's Arthur," Jonathan whispered to Sherlock.

Just then they heard other sounds in the building, footsteps, rustling. Someone else was in the building. Sherlock signalled Jonathan to silence. They crept along until they came to the door where the banging was occurring. Sherlock tried the latch, but it was locked. The door and the lock seemed newer than the rest of the building. Someone had made an extra effort to secure this room. Sherlock pulled burglar's tools out of his pocket and set to work on the lock while Jonathan watched down the hall. It was dark and he saw no one but the sounds of someone else in the building continued and there was a new sound, a kind of crackling, and they could smell a faint whiff of smoke. Then the lock sprung. Sherlock grabbed Jonathan, pushed him through the door before him, and shut it firmly behind them.

"Yonatin!" Arthur exclaimed in his childish rendition of Jonathan's name.

Jonathan squatted down to the boy as Edward toddled up.

"Shh. We have to be quiet," Jonathan whispered as the boys wrapped their arms around him.

"Who dat?" Arthur whispered.

"A friend," Sherlock whispered quickly before Jonathan could answer.

The smell of smoke had increased.

"You must take the boys out of here," Sherlock said.

"I have them," Jonathan said, standing up with one on each arm. "Let's go."

"Go. I will release her," Sherlock Holmes said looking beyond Jonathan and the boys.

Jonathan was puzzled and turned to face the direction Sherlock was looking. There was a woman gagged and tied to a chair. It was the woman in the photograph. She, too, smelled the smoke and her eyes were wide with fear.

Before Jonathan could speak, Sherlock said, "Your duty is to save the boys. Run, now!" and pushed him out the door into the smoke-filled hallway and slammed the door behind him.

Sherlock pulled out his knife and began cutting the woman's bonds. The old building was burning rapidly and flames were now reaching through the walls of the room. As soon as he had cut her free, Sherlock pulled the woman up from the chair. He grabbed the chair she had been tied to and threw it through the window behind her. The window shattered as the chair hit it. Air rushed into the room through the broken window and fanned the flames higher. The flames surged in around them. The woman screamed.

Sherlock grabbed her and threw her on his shoulder, climbed on the crate under the window, stepped onto the windowsill, and then jumped out into the space beyond. In an instant, they went from the searing heat of the fire raging behind them to the chill of the murky Thames. Sherlock had been expecting the plunge, but the hysterical woman he was holding had not. She flailed as they submerged. She beat at him and tried to grab for his throat as they sank in the river. He flipped her around, caught hold of the pieces of rope still trailing from her wrists in one hand to tow her, and swam up for the surface. His lungs near bursting, Sherlock brought his head above the river. He pulled on the ropes and she surfaced behind him gasping and choking. As he looked for a safe landing point, a constable spotted them.

"What are you doing there? Fellows, there are some folks in the river!" the constable called to his fellows.

"Let's fish them out!"

Sherlock released the woman as the constables' hands grabbed both of them and pulled them from the river.

"Who are you, and what are you doing with this woman all tied up?"

"My name is Sherlock Holmes," he gasped still catching his breath. "She was tied up in the burning building. I cut her loose," Sherlock said. "The only way out of the building was into the river."

"And a clever one it was indeed, Mr Holmes, but what was she doing in there?"

"She's an accomplice to the kidnapping of my nephews."

"Then we'll just take care of her."

"Here, take this blanket. Wrap it around you. You are sopping wet."

"There was a boy with me, a servant. He was carrying the boys. Did he get out of the building?"

"Aye, he did. He looked near to faintin' but he wouldn't let us take the boys from him. Right terrified they were and clinging to him. He said you were still in there. We were thinking you'd been toasted. We sent them home."

"Can you find me a cab? I need to get to my brother's

house."

"Come along. We'll get you there."

The four-wheeler pulled up before the house and Sherlock descended to the drive. He was hatless, his hair and clothes were wet, and he had the blanket pulled around his shoulders.

"No, constable, I will be fine. I'm sure that my brother can find me some dry clothes."

"I'm thinking I'll make sure everything is all right."

"Well, come along then if you wish."

The front door was thrown open before Sherlock Holmes made it to the steps.

"Oh, thank God!" Amanda cried from the doorway.

Sherlock could see his brother, the Scotland Yard inspector, and most of the household behind her in the hall.

"This fish insisted on coming here directly to confirm that your boys had made it back safely," the constable said.

"You must excuse the condition of my attire," Sherlock said, "but given the choice between a stroll through the burning building and a plunge in the Thames, I chose the latter. Unfortunately, my companion was less keen on the idea and I had to struggle with her a bit."

"We are so glad to see you alive that you could have come stark naked," Sherrinford said, putting his hands on his youngest brother's shoulders and guiding him to a chair in the sitting room. "But come in here by the fire before you catch a chill. We've been through that too many times."

"I'll have Annie draw you a hot bath," Amanda said and hurried off.

"Are the boys all right?" Sherlock asked sitting by the fire and accepting the brandy his brother offered.

Jonathan threw more coals upon the fire, and then drew back from it with a series of coughs and lost his balance.

"Yes, they are fine," Sherrinford said directing Jonathan back to the sofa and pouring more in his glass.

"You did well to trust them to this lad," the first constable said. "He brought them through the smoke and fire right to us."

Sherlock held up his glass to Jonathan.

"As I wrote to you, Sherrinford, there is no one more faithful and trustworthy. Thank you, Jonathan."

"Just doing my duty, sir," Jonathan said and then coughed some more.

"Are you all right?" Sherlock asked.

"Just the smoke," Jonathan said, but he was feeling a bit light-headed.

"He inhaled a quite a bit of it getting through the building with the boys," the first constable said. "The cough should pass in a few days."

"I think you've gotten him a bit tipsy, Sherrinford. He's not used to strong drink. In fact, I don't think he's ever had spirits before."

"No, sir," Jonathan said.

"Well, he fainted in the driveway," Sherrinford explained. "At first we were just trying to get him alert enough to find out what had happened to you, and then the cough. Well, it'll help him sleep tonight. Tell us how you got out of the building alive."

"I presume that Jonathan told you how we found them. Someone else was in the building while we were there, though we never saw them. We were guided to the correct door by Arthur's banging, kicking, and yelling."

"Yes, that sounds very much like Arthur. He can be a little hellion," Sherrinford said.

"I suspect that they had been keeping the boys under with the ether, but stopped dosing them when they figured the game was up. So the boys woke up in a strange place and wanted out. As I was picking the lock to the room where the boys were, it became obvious that the other person in the building was setting fire to it. I knew that the old building wouldn't last long. I initially planned that we would grab the boys and run. When we got inside the room, I saw the 'Nancy' we had been looking for tied up inside there. She must have disagreed with their plan and been left to be burned alive as well. I couldn't leave her there. I sent Jonathan out with the boys. By the time I had cut her bonds the flames had reached the door to the room. I knew that the building backed onto the Thames so I picked her up and jumped through the back window.

"Unfortunately, the woman was unfamiliar with the art of swimming and fought me. The Thames is not the most pleasant river for swimming at the best of times, but swimming in the dark with an uncooperative companion is worse. As you know, I did that once before long ago. I learned from that experience. I flipped her around and used the ropes still trailing from one of her wrists to tow her on her back. That way I was able to find a safe landing point without drowning us both. The constable here heard the ruckus and drew some of his fellows from watching the fire. They helped us out. When I explained the situation, they took her into custody and helped me to a cab back here."

Amanda had returned to the room while Sherlock was telling his story. She now knelt down beside his chair and took his hand. Sherlock stared off into the fire.

"Thank you, Sherlock. I believed you would find the boys. I am very glad that we did not lose you in the process."

Sherrinford squeezed his wife's shoulder, and she stood and hugged him.

"I'm afraid we are wearing Sherlock out, dear. You should stay here tonight," Sherrinford said to Sherlock. "Don't argue with me. I want to be certain you aren't going to be ill before I send you back to Montague Street. There is a hot bath waiting for you and they are lighting the fire and warming the bed in your room."

"I am feeling rather done in," Sherlock confessed.

"Then it is settled."

"I don't want anyone fussing over me."

"Most certainly not. I'll call upon you myself in the morning and bring the papers to you so you can read them and solve seven impossible crimes before breakfast."

"It looks like your brandy has put Jonathan to sleep."

"We'll take care of him. Off you go."

Sherlock stood up and allowed himself to be led towards the hall. Inspector Gregson followed.

"I will come back and talk to all of you in the morning, most especially you, Mr Sherlock Holmes," Inspector Gregson said. "Good evening."

"Good evening," the two constables echoed in his wake.

Then the three policemen left and Sherrinford saw to it that the two heroes were tucked away in their beds before dismissing the servants for the night and finding his way to his own bed.

The following morning Sherlock was sitting cross-legged on the bed smoking his pipe and reading the *Times* when Jonathan knocked at the door.

"Good morning, sir," Jonathan said. "Your brother Mycroft brought some of your clothes."

"Ah, that was considerate of him. Obviously Sherrinford's are a bit too big," Sherlock said indicating the dressing gown he was wearing, which was much more roomy than necessary.

"Yes, sir."

"Have you seen the papers yet?" Sherlock asked.

"I saw the *Telegraph*."

"My brother brought me several. The *Times* seems to have the most details. 'One young man escaped from the burning building carrying two small children. A man and a woman jumped into the river to avoid the fire and constables pulled them out. While it is unknown why these persons were in the abandoned building, the police do not believe the men are responsible for the blaze. The woman was taken into custody as having some connection with the arsonists.'"

Sherlock shook his head.

"People will remember the melodrama of the fire at the end and forget all the observations and deductions that got us there."

"I won't, sir. Without your deductions, we'd have never known where to look for the boys."

"Ah, thank you, Jonathan. It is good to know someone will remember my contributions. Your cough sounds a little better this morning."

"Yes, sir."

"Well, I suppose I should dress for breakfast this morning before I return to my Bohemian ways. Since I work at night, I am less accustomed to these early mornings. Is Mycroft staying for breakfast?"

"I believe so. Oh, and the cook is brewing your coffee. Is there anything else I can do for you?"

"No. Thank you."

Inspector Gregson stopped in as the family was finishing breakfast and they invited him in for a cup of tea.

"Good morning, Mr Holmes, Mrs Holmes, Mr Sherlock Holmes."

"This is my other brother, Mycroft."

"Good morning, sir."

"How are your young'uns?"

"They are fine."

"No ill-effects?"

"No, sir."

"Very good."

"I think my wife and I are more shaken than they are. We are planning to return to Yorkshire in a few days."

Then Inspector Gregson turned to Sherlock Holmes.

"My superiors are wondering why I was requesting a search warrant for a building a few hours before it goes up in flames. An odd coincidence, is it not?"

"Not a coincidence at all. I told you that they were desperate."

"So you took matters into your own hands."

"I went to save my nephews."

"And then risked your life to extract that woman."

"I couldn't leave her there to burn. Besides, she is the key to finding the others. Men like that don't stop when things like this happen. They start over again somewhere else."

"She has been very helpful already. She is not only helping us find her accomplices but is providing us with information to help locate the other missing children. We must be very discrete. Some of them have been placed with very well connected families. We would appreciate it if this matter could be kept quiet."

"I don't see any reason for us to do otherwise," Sherrinford agreed.

"But I want you to explain to me how you located them," the inspector said, "for my report, you understand. So if you could come by the Yard...."

"I could come by tomorrow morning and explain it all to you," Sherlock Holmes said.

"That would be most appreciated."

Inspector Gregson bid them good day.

"I should be getting to the theatre," Sherlock said as he rose from the table.

"We can share a cab," Mycroft said, rising after him.

Sherrinford followed them both out to the hall.

"Sherlock, I don't know how to thank you. It is clear to me that Scotland Yard would not have found the boys. You seem to have convinced the inspector that you have something to contribute."

"That may be very valuable to me in the future."

"I think that Father will see your career choice in a new light now," Sherrinford said.

"No," Sherlock said, stopping in the hall. "I do not want you to mention my role in this."

"Surely, if he understood how you saved his grandsons—"

"I will not purchase my father's respect," Sherlock snapped.

"As you wish," Sherrinford responded. "Thank you. Thank you both. Good day."

124

Chapter 10

Son of York

*"A flush of colour sprang to Holmes's pale cheeks, and he bowed to us
like the master dramatist who receives the homage of his audience."*
Dr Watson, "The Six Napoleons"

"How did you do it?" Tony Dewitt asked after a look into the audience before Escott's benefit. "Isn't that the foreign secretary? I think you have half of Whitehall and most of the Foreign Service here."

"I have some connexions."

"Good heavens, Irving's here," Langdale Pike said after taking a peek at the audience himself.

"Wonderful!"

"Aren't you nervous?"

"Only of the pit. If they don't follow me all is lost," Escott said with a twinkle in his eye.

His staging of the first scene was simple. He stood on the dark stage with a single limelight on him with a scene painting of London faintly visible behind him. The costume was the same that Devigne had used for the Cibber version but William Escott had managed to transform himself into a far more malignant figure than Sebastian Devigne had ever achieved. There was no artificial hump on his back, but a twist to his neck and shoulders that followed the twisted nature of his soul. While his dialogue said otherwise, one began to wonder if nature had changed to follow spirit rather than spirit having responded to physical nature. Long before Richard showed his true villainy, Escott's voice sent chills down the spine of the audience as they heard his first speech.

It began pleasantly enough...

"Now is the winter of our discontent made glorious summer by this sun of York and all the clouds that lowered upon our house in the deep bosom of the ocean buried. Now are our brows bound with victorious wreaths...."

...until he revealed his plans with a quiet malignancy that no end of shouting could produce. Escott seemed to understand the vile, manipulative nature of the man and it showed in his voice, his stance, his every move.

"Plots have I laid, inductions dangerous, by drunken prophecies, libels, and dreams, to set my brother Clarence and the King in deadly hate the one against the other."

William Escott controlled the stage in each scene and controlled the audience as well. The actors who had volunteered for his benefit performance joined him in creating a world that held them until he fell to the stage as the dying Richard and the curtain fell breaking the thrall. He was master of it all. There was hardly a moment of silence before the applause roared and the audience demanded a curtain call and another....

The critics shared in the enthusiasm and the papers were filled with praise the following morning:

"In a daring departure the little Corycian Theatre revived Shakespeare's original *Richard III* play for the benefit performance of one of its young actors. This was especially daring after the poor reviews of the earlier production by the Corycian Company of the standard theatrical version arranged by Cibber. Actor William Escott arranged and produced the play as well as taking on the title role. Prior to his benefit, Mr Escott read scenes from the play in the parks about town to draw people into the theatre. The audience also had a heavy representation among government officials, suggesting that Mr Escott may have friends or family there. The performance drew the audience into the story, breaking down the barrier between the actors and the audience with a naturalism that nearly rivalled Henry Irving's *Hamlet*. Mr Irving himself was present in a box at the Corycian for this performance and joined the audience in a standing ovation for Escott and his supporting cast. It is to be hoped that the Corycian will be scheduling repeat performances of this version of *Richard III* so that more members of the public may experience this remarkable event."

"Incredible!" another critic wrote, "It is difficult to find words strong enough to recommend Escott's performance as Richard III. This tiny theatre has pulled off a triumph."

"'Now is the winter of our discontent made glorious summer by this sun of York....' So begins Shakespeare's *Richard III*. Nevertheless, for 175 years those words were not heard by audiences on an English stage. Why? Because theatres were using an 'adaptation' written by Colley Cibber in 1699 that had an entirely different first act. Twice in the early part of this century actors Macready and Phelps tried to return to the original but audiences did not approve of their rendition. Where they failed, William Escott has succeeded with the Corycian Company."

Escott's benefit was wildly successful. It was rewarding for him financially and in other ways. Sassanof wanted to make a few small changes and add it to repertoire. Sebastian Devigne fumed when Langdale Pike told him of Sassanof's plans.

"How long have you known this rogue?" Devigne asked.

"We met in college. We weren't exactly on good terms."

"Was he in theatrics there?"

"No, not at all."

"I believe that. He so obviously came amongst us with no knowledge of stagecraft and here he is stealing a leading role after a few months."

"You don't think he has earned it?"

"I think this is a flash in the pan and will not last. It is part luck and part on the backs of the more experienced cast members that his benefit worked out as well as it did. I doubt he will have the stamina to maintain his performance night after night."

"I suppose we shall see," Pike responded.

Devigne's thoughts turned from Escott's performance to his own.

"I was stuck with the Cibber script. If Sassanof would let me do *Richard* from this script—"

"From Escott's?"

"From Shakespeare's!"

"You think you could do better?"

"Undoubtedly!"

With that thought in mind, Devigne extracted Sassanof's

agreement that he could understudy Escott for *Richard III*. He would still play Henry with Dewitt as his understudy, but if Escott became indisposed, he would take the role of Richard. That at least gave him a chance of being able to show what he could do with this arrangement of *Richard III*, and perhaps absolve himself of responsibility for the failure of the Cibber version.

"I have no interest in rivalries," Escott said when Pike told him of the exchange.

"Don't tell me that. You set out to take the lead in *Richard*. You plotted it for months."

"Because I detested Cibber's script and because felt I could play the role better. I think I have a better idea of the evil in men's hearts than Devigne. I have dealt with men like Richard."

"Perhaps that is the reason. But it is obvious you enjoy the audience's applause."

Escott smiled. That was something he could not deny.

They continued their performances of *Romeo and Juliet* and *King Lear* for the next five days while they rehearsed the new version of *Richard III* to Sassanof's satisfaction. Then on August 2nd, they opened *Richard III* for an indefinite run with *Romeo* continuing to be offered as a Saturday matinee. This allowed Devigne the satisfaction of killing Escott on the stage seven times each week. It was cathartic for him. It was also very lucrative for the theatre. Reviews and word of mouth drove the curious to see this new *Richard III*. Weeks passed with no decline in ticket sales. William Escott's name spread across London. Fortunately, he looked different enough without his make-up and costume that he was not recognized and molested on the streets by strangers.

Chapter 11

A Mad Man

"Holmes...here is a madman coming along.
Dr Watson, *"The Beryl Coronet"*

On September 1st, William Escott exited the stage door after another successful night playing Richard III. Most of the actors had left long before. Langdale Pike was directly behind him, but stopped at the threshold.

"Wait. I forgot my stick. I'll fetch it and join you directly," he said.

The stage door swung shut behind Pike. The light from inside had illuminated Escott in the alley. As the light vanished with the closing of the door, he heard a sound behind him. He threw himself to the side and flattened himself against the dark wall next to the door. As he did, he felt a sharp burning sensation on his left hand and heard a voice curse. Then the door swung open again bumping whoever was there. Running footsteps faded away as Pike looked out at Escott who was binding his left hand with a bloodied handkerchief.

"Hello! What happened to you? I leave you for a moment and you seem to get into some adventure!"

"Someone attacked me with a knife."

"What!"

"I'll hold the door open," Escott said, holding out his right hand for the door and then turning and leaning his back against it. "Go ask Frank to bring his lamp out here so I can look around."

Pike ducked back inside.

In a moment Pike was back with Frank and his lamp.

"You aren't hurt too badly, Mr Escott?" Frank asked.

"No."

"We should call a constable," Pike suggested.

"What good would that do?" Escott said. "The man got away. I didn't see him at all."

"He could investigate," Pike suggested.

Holmes snorted.

"I will investigate."

"He'd make me feel safer," Pike admitted.

Langdale Pike was not a physically brave person and not one thrilled by the idea of exploring dark spaces peopled by robbers with knives.

"You stay here and keep the door open," Escott said. "We need all the light we can get."

Frank and Holmes began exploring the alley as Pike stayed at the doorway. He kept the door open so the light continued to spill into the alley as far as it could. He also took up singing multiple parts of music hall songs in different voices to entertain himself, and perhaps to convince the imagined gangs of assassins that there were multiple people guarding the stage door. This produced the rather surreal effect of strains of Gilbert & Sullivan's *Trial by Jury* filling the air as Sherlock Holmes examined footprints in the dust and dirt of the alley. Holmes found signs that someone had stood and smoked cigarettes about twenty feet from the door. There were matches, cigarettes, and liquor bottles of varying ages in the vicinity.

"Thank you, Frank," Holmes said as they returned to the stage door.

"I'll be sure to lock up, Mr Escott," Frank said.

"You do that, Frank. Let's just keep this between us for now."

"Yes, Mr Escott."

Pike began walking quickly towards the lighted street as the stage door slammed behind them and they heard the bolt slide in place. Escott followed him. Pike inhaled deeply and waved desperately as he saw a hansom on the street.

"I definitely need that drink now. I'm sure you do, too."

Escott hesitated.

"Surely you don't want to walk home after that."

Holmes shrugged. He didn't expect the man to be back that night and he was less concerned about walking the streets alone than he was about enduring the young lord's frenzied babble. He was in the habit of conversing with the constable on the beat on his way home from the theatre, which may be why the man had never tried to attack him before. Lord Cecil seemed much more distressed than he about the whole incident. But Holmes thought talking out his observations and deductions with someone might be useful and Mycroft would be abed at this hour. In the end, he decided to join Lord Cecil at least as far as a drink at his club.

"You don't seem very disconcerted by the attack," Lord Cecil said on the way to the club.

"On the contrary, I am most grateful for the timing of your exit," Holmes said. "My eyes had not yet adjusted to the dark and I could not see him at all. I merely heard him and managed to dodge far enough to keep him from stabbing me in the back."

"Stabbing you in the back!"

"The cut on my hand is testimony to the sharpness of his blade since it barely nicked me. His eyes were obviously accustomed to the dark and thus he had the advantage of me. I am not certain that he would not have attacked me again before I could have opened the door. You actually hit him with the door when you opened it. I heard the impact then heard him take to his heels. He had been less than two feet from me at the time."

"So he had been waiting out there for the next person to come out the door? Are we in danger of being robbed and murdered each time we leave the theatre?"

"Oh, no, he was waiting for me," Holmes said as they arrived at their destination.

"What? You horrify me even more! But come along. The porter may be able to find a more satisfactory bandage for your hand."

Gauze, soap, and water were found and soon Holmes' hand had a fresher, cleaner bandage.

"Now tell me why you believe the man was after you. Was it a result of your investigations in the alley?"

"Yes. The footprints, the bottles, and the cigarette butts in the alley indicated that not only had he stood there for hours but that he had made a regular habit of it for weeks, if not months."

"Why does that indicate that you were the target?"

"Because many people have gone in and out that door in that length of time. He never revealed himself to them nor attacked them. If robbery had been his motivation, then why not attack Clayton Ellsworth or Caleb Belmore who dress much more expensively than I do? They often leave the theatre first. This is the first time I've left the theatre alone after dark. He was close enough to see who I was in the light from the door. He attacked immediately after the door shut. He would have heard your words and known you would follow shortly. He obviously intended to make a murderous attack on me and take off before you returned. There wasn't time or light for rifling pockets. This was no robbery. He intended murder and he knew who he was attacking."

"And yet you do not want the police called in?"

"Not yet, they would have swarmed all over the evidence before I could examine it and then they would have done nothing because I could not identify him."

"But you think he will try again?"

"Oh, yes, this is a man with patience and a man filled with rage."

"The 'patience' I comprehend from his waiting in the alley, but how do you know about the rage?"

"The speed and virulence of the attack. If he had come up behind me with more stealth I might not have heard him until it as too late, but in his rage he ran forward and that was the sound that warned me."

"But you aren't afraid to go home alone."

"No, he will not come again tonight. He will wait until he thinks I am no longer on my guard, until I have dismissed it as a random robbery attempt."

"But surely you must go to the police and have them increase patrols?"

"I don't want to scare him off. I want to catch him."

"By letting him try again?"

"Yes."

"This is insanity. You could be killed!"

"It is the only way to stop him. It must be properly arranged."

"Who would want you dead? That fellow with the sweaters outfit?"

"No, he's still in jail."

"Those men who kidnapped your nephews?"

"No, they were both arrested."

"The blackmailers from Cambridge were surely a murderous lot. They nearly killed you then."

"It is not them unless they've taken to following you and happened to recognize me. They never knew who I was and they never knew of any connexion between us. If they had been following you for some reason, why not take care of you first before attacking me and showing their hand? No, I don't believe it was one of them."

"You are not thinking it is Devigne?"

"No, he may give me murderous looks sometimes, but he would not risk his theatrical career by doing such a thing. Besides, he does not use tobacco."

"Who else have you been making enemies of?"

"No one that I know of. It could have been some insignificant slight that enraged an unstable mind."

"You are telling me this was the work of a mad man?"

"Quite likely."

"With such patience?"

"Oh, yes. Some of the insane have great patience when they are obsessed with something. You forget I studied with Dr Mackenzie for a few months. He told me many interesting tales."

"If I knew I was being stalked by a murderous madman, I'd hardly be so calm about it," Lord Cecil said.

"It is surprising that you are not stalked, given your hobbies."

"My enemies make pretence of being civilized. They don't stalk in dark alleys. Their back-stabbing is unlikely to be quite so literal. How do you know your mad man won't attack you in broad daylight? You don't even know what he looks like."

"I know he is about my height and build. He smokes. He's a drunkard who is down on his luck and is familiar with the theatre."

"And he believes he has a grudge against you?" Cecil Hamley asked thoughtfully.

"Yes."

"Travis. John Travis," Lord Cecil said.

"The actor I replaced as Tybalt?" Holmes asked.

Lord Cecil nodded.

"And all his other roles in the opening repertoire."

"I never even saw him."

"He fits your description to a T."

"I remember that Sassanof said we were alike in build and Ida Newton said something similar."

"Travis was dismissed that morning for being worse for drink. It was not the first time. You immediately stepped into his roles and have gone on to greater successes."

"Which he undoubtedly feels should have been his. What has become of him since he left the Corycian Company?"

"I have not heard a word. I will inquire."

"We don't want him to get the wind of us," Holmes said. "Even if he is no longer acting he may have friends in theatrical circles who might tell him if anyone is asking after him. We have no proof. The only way we can stop him is to catch him in the act."

"That is a dangerous game."

"I will be prepared for it, but I don't want him to know that I am. We must tell everyone that it was merely a footpad who accosted me outside the theatre and that he is probably long gone."

"That you can leave to me," said Lord Cecil.

On his way home, Sherlock Holmes located Constable Thompkins on his beat near the Corycian Theatre. In a quiet corner a few hours before dawn, he explained the situation and the difficulty in catching the man. Constable Thompkins was diligent and ambitious. He agreed to keep a look-out for Travis during his rounds, but not do anything to scare him off. Holmes and Constable Thompkins spoke several times over the next three weeks as they planned the trap. Holmes examined the alley each morning until fresh signs of his adversary appeared. Thompkins gave Holmes a police whistle. Holmes explained the plan to the doorman at the theatre.

The night came for the implementation of the plan. *Richard III* was presented as usual. Escott and Pike stayed later than the rest of the cast and stage crew. The fewer theatre people involved the better. Constable Thompkins was nearby awaiting the signal. He had alerted other constables that there might be some trouble. The theatre was unnaturally quiet. As Escott approached the stage door from the interior hall, he heard the snap and hiss of a match. Then the gaslights went out in the hall. He heard a pop and flutter and saw the pulsing flame of an oil lamp.

"Why the oil lamp, Frank?" he asked, despite having asked Frank to light it.

"Gas fixture is not working right. I'll have the gas man look at it tomorrow," Frank responded as they had agreed.

Escott waited a few minutes impatiently staring at the wall. He looked at his watch in the faint light. He waited a few more minutes. Then he opened the door. The dim light from the oil lamp spilled out the door.

"Pike is taking forever to change tonight," Escott said from the threshold. "I'll just step out for a smoke."

"Be careful, Mr Escott," Frank responded.

Holmes stepped out the door and let it close behind him. He saw the outline of a figure in the dark. He struck a match and held it close to his chin as if to light his pipe. The figure lunged at him. However, the item in Holmes' left hand was the police whistle, not his pipe. He blew the whistle as he ducked away towards the back of the alley, avoiding the blow, and blocking his assailant's retreat. The figure lunged at Holmes again as Constable Thompkins ran down the alley. Holmes knocked the knife from his attacker's hand and grabbed his assailant about the waist. He and Constable Thompkins wrestled him out into the street. There they were joined by more constables drawn by the whistle.

"What is this?

"Here hold him. He attacked this man with a knife," Thompkins said.

"Where's the knife?"

"Back in the alley. I heard it fall," Holmes said.

Holmes and some constables went back into the alley with a bull's-eye lamp. By then Frank and Langdale Pike stood in the stage door, the gas full on now.

"Is it safe?" Pike asked.

"Yes," Escott replied. "They have him cuffed out on the street. They could probably use your help identifying him."

Holmes saw the knife not far from the door and pointed it out to the constables who took it up. In the light, they could see it still had dried blood on it from the first attack. Pike walked with them out to the street. He had no trouble identifying John Travis. His hair was wild and greasy, his face dirty, and his hands stained by cigarettes, but he was unmistakably the former actor. Travis said nothing but scowled at them. The constables had delivered the standard police warning and Travis had chosen to hold his tongue. Soon the Black Maria arrived to haul the prisoner off.

"You will need to come to the station tomorrow and make a statement," Constable Thompkins told Holmes.

"Gladly."

Chapter 12

Return to Cambridge

*To admit such intrusions into his own delicate and finely
adjusted temperament was to introduce a distracting factor.*
Dr Watson, "A Scandal in Bohemia"

Richard III continued its remarkable run to packed houses through late October. Then one night as Escott fell to the stage as the dying Richard III he heard an odd sequence of sounds from above just off in the wings. There was a creak, a screech, a slither and – Escott threw himself back at Devigne, pitching both of them to the opposite side of the stage – a whoosh and a crash as a jet of flame shot out from a broken gas pipe, and the fixture on the wing light fell to the stage where they had been. A gasp went up from the audience. Elspeth Anderson screamed as the wing curtain next to her ignited. The gasman from his position on the prompter side of the stage shut the valve to the line, darkening the OP side of the stage. Scene-changers dropped and smothered the curtain before the audience could rise. Escott and Devigne stood and assured the audience that all was well, before they recommenced their final combat, Devigne re-killed Escott, and the curtain fell.

As they left the stage, Sassanof thanked them. Fire was the greatest danger in a theatre. Second to that was a panic in the audience that could lead to a stampede for the exits, which could cause many injuries and deaths. The stage crew had done their part in averting the first and the actors had done theirs in averting the second. They had all acted knowing that if the stage had caught fire none of them would have exited alive. Even as a movement was afoot to improve fire safety in theatres, the stage itself remained a death trap.

Miss Anderson had been taken to a hospital. Some of the other actors were so shaken they could not wait to be gone from the theatre, leaving before changing their costumes or removing their make-up. Others were more curious. After the curtain fell, a ladder was brought into the wings and the gasman scrambled up to inspect. When he came down the ladder, an actor was waiting for him.

"What happened?" Escott asked.

"Can't tell. It's all melted up there. We'll be working on removing the damaged parts overnight. We won't know until then how bad it is. The whole line to the junction may need to be replaced."

"May I have a look?"

The gasman shrugged.

"Don't touch anything. The whole theatre could go up."

Holmes looked, but the gasman was right. The jet of burning gas released when the fixture fell had melted the metal. He had already examined the twisted fragments of the fixture that the stagehands had carried off the stage and drenched in a bucket as a precaution. An accident? Perhaps. There seemed to be too many accidents. Thoughtfully, Holmes wandered back toward the dressing room. As he was going in Sebastian Devigne stopped him.

"There you are. I've been looking for you. You saved my life. That thing would have fallen right on me if you had not thrown me out of the way."

"It would have hit both of us."

"Yes, but you could have saved your own skin without worrying about mine. How did you know it was going fall?"

"I heard it."

"I heard something but I wasn't sure what it was. I'm glad you figured it out. Thanks again."

Devigne offered his hand and he – more Holmes than Escott at the moment – shook it, while wondering if it was just a coincidence that the fixture fell at the moment that the two leading actors of the company could be predicted to both be under it night after night. Other than that fact, he had no data. Why would anyone want them maimed or killed? How could anyone have done it? Why would anyone take the risk of setting the whole theatre on fire? Any member of the cast or stage crew would also be at risk of death, as well as the audience. Perhaps he was trying to see villainy where there was none. Perhaps it was just an accident. Nevertheless, his brain continued to churn. What of the collapse of the balcony? It had nearly fallen on Devigne. Seconds later, he would have been climbing it, which would have made it impossible for him to escape injury. Was Devigne a target, or were they just two unrelated accidents months apart? Holmes would not accept Miss Clement's superstitions. The range of plausible explanations traversed coincidence, incompetence, and villainy. It annoyed Holmes that he did not know to which class they belonged.

The following day was a Sunday. Holmes spent two restless nights and a restless day. Without rehearsals or performances to hold his attention, he kept returning to the misfortunes at the theatre. He hated unsolved mysteries. On Monday, when the company assembled at the theatre they saw banners across the broadsheets at the front announcing that the performances had been cancelled for the week. All the gas lines to the stage were shut off, so they assembled in the foyer of the theatre. Sassanof addressed them.

"I have a few announcements to make. First, Miss Anderson is doing fine. Her burns are healing well. However, she has informed me that she will be leaving us. As a result, I'm going to be auditioning for a new girl to join the company. Miss Louise Harris will step into Miss Anderson's roles and the new girl will take her role. Second, due to the repairs needed to the gas lines, we won't be performing at the theatre for the next two weeks. During that time, I have booked us to perform three nights in Cambridge. We will leave from Bishopsgate station for Cambridge on Wednesday the 10th. We will be performing *Richard III* all three nights. Take the rest of today to make any arrangements necessary. Be ready to continue rehearsals tomorrow."

"I suppose you didn't anticipate returning to Cambridge so soon?" Pike asked Escott as they were leaving the theatre.

"No," was his only reply.

Escott did not anticipate being recognized in the town as the former student named Sherlock Holmes. His make-up in *Richard III* remarkably altered his appearance and even without it, his hair, beard, and dress as Escott were different. He did not intend to wander about town in any case. No, it was not the imminent return to that university town that disturbed him over the next two weeks. It was a cascade that began with the fall of that gas fixture and the puzzle it held. Other events followed fast upon it and nearly pulled him under.

Rehearsing in the foyer of the Corycian theatre rather than on the stage was bothersome. The acoustics were very different in the foyer. Words meant to reach the farthest extremes of the audience echoed off the walls and tangled with the following lines. The marble floors were too slick to rehearse the fights. The actors adapted and attempted to concentrate on what they could do but they were on their own during the first day of rehearsals in these new circumstances.

The manager, Michael Sassanof, and the prompter, Randy Foster, were holding auditions for Elspeth Anderson's replacement. Young women flocked to the theatre seeking a chance to fill the position. Since the stage was out of bounds, the auditions were held in the back of the auditorium. The stream of young women entering the theatre was cordoned off from the actors, yet there they were, looking, and chattering. Too many and in too close a proximity. Escott felt as if they were looking for him, looking at him, and pointing him out to each other. On stage, he basked in the applause, but this celebrity was different from an audience's admiration of a performance. It felt as if they expected something from him personally.

Miss Harris had been understudy to Miss Anderson and easily stepped into the role of Lady Anne. She ran through her lines with Escott with ease but he seemed on edge. She asked him if she was doing something wrong. He said no. After a couple hours, the actors retired for the day. Escott breathed a sigh of relief as he left the building. He stopped in front of the theatre, lit his pipe, and smoked as he walked home. He had not realized how tense the circumstances of the rehearsal had made him. He tried to shake it off. When he arrived back at the rooms, he took up his violin to sooth his nerves. He could neither concentrate on the mysterious accidents at the theatre because he had no data, nor concentrate on his acting under the current conditions.

Escott had expected that rehearsal would be easier the following day. However, Sassanof wanted to try out the candidates with the cast. They were a mixed lot of young blondes, brunettes, and redheads. There was one with especially dark, long, waves of hair, so like— He cut the thought off and avoided looking at any of them. Initially they read with the other actors and actresses. Then Sassanof had them read some of Lady Anne's lines with him. He had been performing the scenes in which Richard wooed Lady Anne with Miss Anderson for months with ease. It was a role, nothing more, and the actresses of the Corycian Company were extremely professional and intent on upholding the integrity of the profession from unseemly accusations. His difficulty the previous day had been unrelated to Miss Harris, as he had told her. But this was different. The lines, the very lines he had been performing for months now, escaped him. Sassanof's look said he noticed Escott was off his form, but he said nothing before the outsiders. Sassanof slowly dismissed the candidates until one remained. It was she. That was not surprising. Her performances were good. Her name was Jenny Mayne. Escott had bowed courteously, if stiffly, when they were introduced. She was more enthusiastic in the meeting. She gave him a fetching smile and told him she loved his performance as Richard III and she had seen him as Tybalt as well. He was polite, but glad when it was over.

The following day they attempted to rehearse again. The acoustics were a problem; the floor was a problem; but worse than that was Miss Mayne's presence. She seemed to be constantly appearing in his range of vision. Perhaps it was his imagination. Perhaps it was just because there was nowhere else for the other actors or actresses to go, no wings to hide them.

Finally, Sassanof spoke up.

"Mr Escott, you are having an off day."

"Yes, I know. It's — well, everything. I can't rehearse under these conditions."

To his relief, there was a murmur of agreement among the other actors. After brief consideration, Sassanof decided that it was probably worse to continue than not to rehearse at all. He gave them the next few days off and told them meet him at the station on Wednesday next.

"Don't forget to pack your costumes!"

There was a murmur of approval and the actors streamed towards the dressing rooms to gather coats, costumes, and make-up boxes. In the dressing room, there was the familiar crush of men, but as he headed for the stage door, there she was again. She seemed to be making her way towards him through the backstage throng. He turned, saw Pike at the door, called out to him, and pushed ahead to join him.

"Ah, this is an unexpected holiday."

"Yes."

"Want to join me at my club?"

"Yes."

They exited to the alley and walked to the street. As they were hailing a cab Escott heard her come out behind them, but Sebastian Devigne seemed to be talking to her, momentarily occupying her attention.

On the way over in the hansom, Pike asked, "Nervous about returning to Cambridge?"

"No."

"I'm actually looking forward to it. I expect to meet with some of my former colleagues in the FootLights and I've made arrangements on the Saturday with a young lady of my acquaintance who lives there. She and I once— but you are not listening, are you?

"No."

"Something else has you off besides the intolerable conditions."

Escott did not reply as they arrived at the club. He relaxed as they were seated in the dining room. Like in most gentlemen's clubs, women were not permitted. However, the subject of them still seemed to follow him.

"Miss Mayne has potential as an actress," Pike began, "She is obviously quite beautiful. However, the competition for her attention seems to be quite thick."

"Surely, the fact that you are a member of the nobility would turn any girl's head."

"A card I will not play with the ladies who don't already know it. In any case, it seems she's more interested in you than me."

"What do you mean?"

"Did you see how she looked at you?"

"No, I was attempting to think of my lines," Escott said, not quite truthfully.

"Interesting. I've noticed that before. Women seem invisible to you. You look around them and through them, but not at them. For most of us men, when a beautiful woman enters the room that's the only thing we see, but you don't see her."

"She has pale skin with freckles and long dark hair. Today she was wearing a light blue dress with white ruffles at the wrists and neck, shoes to match, and a silhouette broach. Would you like to know her shoe size?" Sherlock Holmes replied.

"No, thank you. How clinical! But you don't really see her. Are you one of them?"

"One of whom?"

"With different tastes; certainly enough of them in the theatre."

"No."

"Don't you get the urge to wrap your arms around a pretty thing like that and—"

"Pike, this isn't a topic I have any interest in."

"It's not that simple, Escott. I may not be as observant as you, but I've noticed that you go out of your way not to even look her direction. I've seen you flub a line when she came into view unexpectedly. Maybe you two have some secret liaison—"

"Enough!"

Holmes rose to leave, but Lord Cecil laid one hand on his sleeve and lifted the other as a sign of surrender.

Lord Cecil changed the subject and prattled on. He was never one to be at a loss for conversation. Holmes indulged him for the sake of the sanctity of the club and the invitation that he believed had rescued him from an undesired encounter. After lunch, he walked home. While he lived not far from the Corycian Theatre, the actors were likely to have dispersed about the city by now. He informed the housekeeper that he would be home for supper and took up his violin when he arrived at the rooms. That evening he explained to Mycroft the situation with the gas lines at the theatre. For a week, Sherlock Holmes lived like a hermit, content with studying his books, playing his music, and never going out. His brother and their housekeeper let him be.

On the appointed day, William Escott arrived at Bishopsgate Station by hansom in good time. The actors began gathering in a knot waiting for the train. Escott leaned against a post studying his notes on *Richard III*. It was odd not to have performed the role in over a week after doing so for three months straight. Pike found him there and accosted him.

"You must hear this. I just heard Miss Mayne talking to Sebastian Devigne. He was going on about the roles he had played and generally attempting to impress her. Then she asked, 'Have you learned a lot from Billy?'"

"Billy?" Escott said.

"Don't interrupt," Pike said. "She went on 'I mean William, William Escott, our lead actor.' Devigne turned several shades of purple and sputtered that he had taught you everything you know and that normally he played the lead character, but he was trying to broaden his depth and try other roles. She just smiled."

"Billy? Neither she nor anyone else has ever called me 'Billy.' I've hardly even spoken to her."

"Regardless, I think she has set her cap for you."

"Nonsense."

"Well, it's just as well because Devigne has his eye on her and her interest in you has made him all the hotter to have her."

"As I told you the other day, I'm not interested in the subject."

"It's not like there is anything better to do waiting for the train."

"I need to practice my lines."

"Bloody hell you do. You know the play better than any man on Earth. I'd wager you could recite it backwards."

"I am sure I could. But it is not the words I am working on but the nuances in their elocution."

"I'll drop it for now, Escott," Langdale Pike said. "But my curiosity is piqued and you know how dangerous that is."

Escott stuffed his notes in his pocket and bought a couple of papers to read on the train. He chose a smoking carriage in hopes of avoiding the actresses and most of the company in general. If what Pike was saying was true, it was worse than he had imagined and he wished to avoid Miss Mayne at all costs.

There was the usual chaos of finding conveyances at the Cambridge railroad station and making their way to the hotel. While most of the company were sharing rooms, Escott had used his leverage as the lead in *Richard* to obtain separate quarters and once there settled in for the night. He had brought his violin. He played a few pieces before turning out the light. Nevertheless, he spent a restless night. Despite what he had said, the sights of familiar locations had brought memories of his time here. He and Cambridge had not parted on good terms. There were older memories that he had buried here as well. His mind was awhirl and would not rest. He rose and dressed. He stopped at a cafe and bought a cup of coffee. As he was purchasing a newspaper, a police officer passed him without notice. That brought a brief smile to his face. Chief Constable Blevins had not recognized him. No doubt he would have run him out of town if he had. The year before he had been gated by his college at the university at Blevin's insistence.

Escott returned to his room, gathered up his costume, and walked to the Corn Exchange. According to Sassanof, the Corn Exchange had only recently been converted to a theatre. Cambridge had no other theatre and the university discouraged theatrical performances. He had never been inside the Corn Exchange, but he knew how to climb to the top of its roof. It was not knowledge he planned to use this trip. Inside he found his way to the dressing rooms. The stagehands were setting up for the performance that night.

Rehearsals started well enough. He gave his opening speech and his exchange with Clarence but when he turned to the Lord Chamberlain, there she was in the wings. He stumbled over his words. The prompter corrected him. They started again. He changed his position slightly so he could not see her and they moved on. There she was again. Sassanof called a five-minute break.

"Mr Escott. What is the matter? I know it is a smaller stage in an unfamiliar theatre—"

"Too many distractions. Could you have the wings cleared?"

"Yes. Now just take a moment and clear your head."

"I am going to step outside for a smoke.'

"An excellent idea."

When Escott returned to the stage, the wings had been cleared of actors and supers and Sassanof had even asked the scene-changers to take a break from their work for an early lunch. The actors continued through the last act. The only interruptions were those necessary to adjust stage business to the smaller stage. Then lunch was brought on stage for the actors. The stagehands returned to their work.

Escott was not hungry. He went outside for another pipe. When he returned lunch was being packed away. They began rehearsals from the beginning again and ran straight through to the end. Then Sassanof sent them off to the dressing rooms to get in costume and makeup while preparations on the stage were completed. They completed a full dress rehearsal before curtain time.

The house was packed. Prior to the conversion of the Corn Exchange Cambridge had no theatres and the only theatrical performances were the somewhat clandestine ones offered by groups of university students. They were starved for good theatre and very excited that the Corycian Company had come down from London to perform their rendition of Shakespeare's *Richard III* that had caused such a buzz there.

The tangle of actors in the wings parted as Escott came forward dressed as Richard. As Escott drew next to Sassanof, the manager gave him a pat on the back.

"You look good. Just do what you've done for months. Break a leg."

As Escott took a step forward, someone bumped into him. He turned to see Miss Mayne. Suddenly she kissed him on the cheek, her dark curls cascading about his face as she did. He continued on to his mark on the stage. As it had been in London, the stage was empty except for him standing before a back-cloth of a London street scene, nothing to detract from Richard and his opening speech. The stage was dark. The curtain rose, the lime light fell upon Escott and his eyes rolled up into his head and he pitched forward to fall upon his face on the stage. The audience's gasps joined those of the actors and stagehands who ran forward on to the stage. The company found him insensible.

"Is there a doctor in the house?" Sassanof cried as he knelt beside his unmoving lead performer.

A man with a black bag stood up in the audience and the crowds parted.

"Let's carry him off the stage," Sassanof ordered.

The man with the black bag mounted the stage and followed the people carrying the actor backstage. They laid the actor down on a sofa in the green room and left him in the doctor's care. In minutes, the actors and scene changers were back at their places and the sound of Devigne giving *Richard III's* opening speech could be heard in the distance. Devigne had his chance to show Cambridge, if not London, how well he could perform in the lead of this version of *Richard*.

The doctor leaned over the actor and examined his breathing and pulse. No one saw the look of surprise on the doctor's face as he recognized his patient. The actor's hair was much longer and he'd grown a beard, but from close up the doctor had no doubt as to William Escott's true name. He rolled up Escott's shirtsleeves, took his pulse, which was rapid, and he searched the young man's arms and hands. He found nothing unusual. Escott's head rolled from side to side and his hand reached out as if to catch himself from falling. The doctor grasped the hand and called, "Sherlock!" His hand was trembling. Sherlock's eyes blinked opened.

In his mind, the actor known as William Escott was falling and the snowstorm was fading to darkness but someone grasped his hand and called his name. He looked around. In the darkness, he noticed a row of blurry lights. He blinked his eyes and tried to focus on the lights.

"Sherlock?" the voice said again.

It was odd, the actor thought. He recognized the voice. It was a voice from his past. Which past? Not the past of the snowstorm. Everything was jumbled up in his mind. He had to concentrate. Where was he? He was lying down somewhere. The lights. He must be backstage. Backstage where? Not the Corycian. Who was calling him by his real name in a theatre? He turned his head. Next to him he saw a familiar face. Who was it? It was face he had seen from this position before. A doctor. A doctor, yes, but more.

"Dr Mackenzie," Sherlock gasped with some surprise. "Where?"

"Backstage at the Corn Exchange in Cambridge," Dr Mackenzie said.

"Cambridge?" Sherlock said with some confusion. He had lived in Cambridge once, but not now.

"You collapsed on the stage," Dr Mackenzie said.

"On the stage...." Sherlock said. "Then I was performing?"

"Yes. How do you feel?" the doctor asked.

"Disoriented," Sherlock said.

"Yes. One of your attacks?"

"Yes," Sherlock said.

"I think it would be best if we speak in more detail later. Not here," the doctor said as Sassanof entered the green room.

"Yes," Sherlock agreed.

"Ah, I see Mr Escott has decided to re-join us," Sassanof said when he saw Sherlock's eyes were open.

"He's still somewhat shaken," Dr Mackenzie said.

"I'm sorry," Sherlock said to Sassanof.

"You're not drunk, are you?" Sassanof asked

"No," Sherlock said.

"Are y'sick?" Sassanof asked.

"No, I don't think so," Sherlock said looking to the doctor.

"It was an attack of some kind. It has passed," Dr Mackenzie said. "I would like him to come with me tonight so that I can observe him further," Dr Mackenzie said.

"Just have him back here by noon tomorrow," Sassanof said and headed back to the wings.

"Are you up to walking?" Dr Mackenzie asked.

"Yes," Sherlock said.

He was still feeling drained and disoriented and he allowed Dr Mackenzie to lead him to his carriage. In the doctor's carriage, Sherlock leaned back against the cushions.

"I was confused when I heard you calling my name."

"I had no idea until I saw you up close that William Escott and Sherlock Holmes were one and the same, but when I did, I understood what was happening," Dr Mackenzie said.

"You were in the audience?" Sherlock asked.

"Yes," Dr Mackenzie said.

"What did you see?" Sherlock asked.

"When the curtain rose you were standing alone on the darkened stage. When the light came on you pitched forward on the stage," Dr Mackenzie said. "What did you see?"

Sherlock waved his hand dismissively. He did not want to talk about the visions he had seen during his nervous attack, but he and Dr Mackenzie had an old pact between them. So he summarized them briefly, trying not to really think about them as he did.

"It was the same thing, as it happened. I was following her in the storm. I lost her and then was lost myself. It was growing dark and then I fell. That's when I heard you call my name—Confound it! This hasn't happened in years. Why now?" Sherlock asked.

"I am not sure I can answer that. However, here we are," Dr Mackenzie said as the carriage pulled through the gates and into the grounds of the Fulbourn Asylum. As the medical superintendent of the asylum, Dr Mackenzie had a house on the grounds, separate from the main building and surrounded by a small stand of trees.

Dr Mackenzie led Sherlock to a guest room. He sent a maid

to the kitchen for hot water and towels for Sherlock to remove his make-up. He loaned him a dressing gown so he could remove his costume. Afterwards Sherlock sat down before the fire and leaned his elbow on the arm of the chair and rested his head in his hand.

"Have you eaten?" Dr Mackenzie said.

"No, we usually eat after the performance," Sherlock said.

"Then I will have the cook prepare some supper," Dr Mackenzie said.

"Thank you, but I'm not really hungry," Sherlock said.

"Sherlock, you should eat," Dr Mackenzie said firmly.

Sherlock looked up at Dr Mackenzie. Dr Mackenzie was reasserting their respective roles as doctor and patient from Sherlock's early days at the university. Sherlock remembered how much Dr Mackenzie had helped him then. He knew he should trust him now.

"Yes. Yes, I should. Then go ahead. I would like to just sit here quietly until it is ready. I'm still rather foggy," Sherlock said.

Dr Mackenzie left Sherlock alone gazing into the fire until the cook had laid out a cold supper in the dining room. He then called on Sherlock who hadn't moved and led him to the dining room.

"If you don't mind, I would be interested in hearing how you ended up as an actor. Last time we spoke you were still intent on becoming a detective," Dr Mackenzie said over supper.

"I suppose you heard that I was sent down from the college," Sherlock said.

"I believe everyone in the town heard about that." Dr Mackenzie said. "Some rumours have set you up as a latter day Guy Fawkes who tried to destroy the whole university."

"That is quite an exaggeration," Sherlock said. "It was an accident. An experiment I was working on went bad. It didn't even damage the building much, mostly just broke windows and glassware. I was standing over it when it went off and I lived to talk about it."

"That's how rumours are," Dr Mackenzie said. "When I heard about the explosion at Sidney Sussex College, I enquired after you, but was told that you had already left town. I have heard nothing of you since."

"I left town rather hurriedly," Sherlock said. "When I left I insisted on paying for the damages myself. I needed funds. I was offered a position as an actor and I took it. That's what I've been doing since I left. My brother, Mycroft, whom you met briefly, has been putting me up while we are in London so nearly every shilling has gone to the college."

"And you receive no support from your father?"

"None. He disowned me when he learned of my plans to become a detective. From what I have heard, he does not even allow my name to be mentioned in his household. In my father's eyes, I am no longer his son. It stands to reason then that I no longer have a father. With my mother gone for two years now, I am an orphan," he said bitterly.

Dr Mackenzie absorbed both the facts and the sentiments behind their expression and decided to change the subject.

"Do you still plan to become a detective?" Dr Mackenzie said.

"Yes and my brothers are supportive of my study and training in that direction. I think this stint as an actor will be very useful to me in that career. I have learned a great deal about disguises and other tricks of the trade."

"I can see how that could be useful to a detective," Dr Mackenzie said. "Back to this evening. Do you know what precipitated the attack?"

"No," Sherlock said looking down at the table. He didn't really want to think about it.

Dr Mackenzie noticed the sharp change of mood as he brought the conversation back to the attack. Sherlock seemed alert and good-humoured when they were speaking of other subjects, with the exception of his father.

"It seemed to start when the light hit you. I remember bright lights or snow sometimes seemed to bring on the attacks," Dr Mackenzie said.

"I have been performing that scene under a similar light for months. I have had no difficulty with it."

"I believe your state of mind is a factor. Was there anything unusual that happened before you went on stage?"

"I don't know," Sherlock said shaking his head. "I don't remember anything."

"Think back," Dr Mackenzie said. "What occurred just before?"

"Everyone was getting ready backstage. I can't think of anything unusual," Sherlock said shaking his head again.

It seemed to Dr Mackenzie that Sherlock was not making an effort to remember. Slightly over a year ago, Sherlock was analysing minute details in someone's handwriting or clothing and describing their occupation and personality. Yet now he was answering with broad statements. Whether consciously or unconsciously, he was avoiding thinking about something. Dr Mackenzie went through his own memories of the evening.

"Let's try a different tack then. I noticed one actress with dark curly hair seemed especially concerned about you," Dr Mackenzie said.

"That would be the new actress, Jenny Mayne—"

Sherlock Holmes began then he stopped and placed his hand upon his cheek. He paled, his mouth opened, and his eyes grew wide.

"What is it?" Dr Mackenzie asked.

"She kissed me," Sherlock said. "She kissed me on the cheek right before I walked on-stage. I didn't have time to think about it. I went on stage, the curtain went up, I saw the light and then everything was gone."

"You may not have had time to think about it, but you may have felt something about it. It may have stirred up old memories," Dr Mackenzie suggested.

"Yes," Sherlock said leaning his forehead against the heel of his hand.

"You didn't intermingle with many women at the university," Dr Mackenzie said softly.

"No, I didn't," Sherlock agreed without looking up.

"I remember how you reacted to that one woman in the asylum. Have you interacted with very many women at all since—"

"Not on a personal basis. There was my mother before she died and occasionally with my brother's wife.... The actresses in the company are very professional."

"But not Miss Mayne."

"No. She's young and new to the business."

"What does she do that is different?"

"She seems to go out of her way to be where I am in the theatre, sometimes in my line of sight during rehearsals. Tonight there was no reason for her to be where she was. I was about to go on stage. She should have been keeping out of the way of the actors set to perform."

"Anything else?"

"I have been told by other actors that she watches me and talks about me."

"How do you react to her?"

"It is very awkward for me. I try to avoid her if I can. Otherwise, I try to be polite, but—"

"But you are afraid."

"Yes," Sherlock whispered.

"Afraid of stirring up old memories?"

"Or worse," Sherlock said and buried his face in his hand.

A moment later he shook his head and looked up at Dr Mackenzie with a pained look in his eye.

"I won't ever be free, will I?" he said. "I know that I cannot love again. Not now, maybe not ever. I'd be afraid that something I'd do would—."

He broke off and looked away.

"And if I'm going to be a detective it might not be a good idea to have such personal relationships. They would interfere with my work."

Sherlock looked back at Dr Mackenzie.

"But is some part of my brain going to explode every time some woman shows me any type of affection?" Sherlock asked. "Does that fear run so deep that I have no control over it whatsoever? Must I find some cloister away from the rest of humanity to keep my mind at peace?" Sherlock demanded fiercely and buried his face in his hands once more.

"Sherlock?" Dr Mackenzie said fearing that this was the start of another attack.

Sherlock looked up at Dr Mackenzie. He stared at Dr Mackenzie for a moment then he steepled his fingers together and leaned his forehead against them. His conversations with Dr Mackenzie had always been enlightening. What was it the doctor had said to him years ago? "You change what is going on inside your head, not me." Dr Mackenzie provided clues. Sherlock knew that he was the one who had to act upon them. He rose from the table and paced the floor.

"I have been lax. I have let my guard down. I should know by now the consequences of that," Sherlock said as his face becoming stony and his grey eyes as cold as steel. "I know what I must do."

Dr Mackenzie watched the transformation with fascination. Dr Mackenzie had last seen Sherlock on Christmas Eve nearly a year ago. He had seemed quite well and in control of himself. This attack was a serious setback. Sherlock seemed to be recovering from it faster than others, even though he had been quite shaken by it. But his mood and mental acuity had fluctuated widely during the short while they had been together this evening. Now he saw Sherlock rein in his emotions by force of will. If the change had merely been internal the doctor might not have noticed, but it was reflected in Sherlock's stature, gait, and facial expressions. Never before in all his studies of the sane and insane had Dr Mackenzie seen such an effort at control, or such success. He had no doubt that the storm was still raging somewhere deep inside Sherlock but it had been banished for the moment from the surface. Now he understood how Sherlock Holmes had weathered the shocks of the last few years. Yet this amazing physical and mental control had been torn asunder by a kiss.

But the hour was late and despite his control, Sherlock looked tired.

"Whatever it is, it must wait until morning," Dr Mackenzie said. "For now you should get some rest. You look done in."

"Yes. Thank you for your hospitality," Sherlock said.

Dr Mackenzie walked Sherlock back to the bedroom and then went thoughtfully to his study. He sat down at his desk and poured a brandy. He was fond of this young man, more than he dared show. He had been concerned when Sherlock had suddenly left town. It had required great restraint to keep from inquiring about him further than he had. Dr Mackenzie felt towards him like the son he had never had, would probably never have. Yet he knew it was necessary to keep his distance and let Sherlock step out of his life again as quickly as he had fallen back in. Perhaps there was something else he could do. Dr Mackenzie set the empty glass aside and headed off to his own bedroom.

In the morning, Sherlock appeared for breakfast looking haggard. Obviously his control was still imperfect.

"Nightmares?" Dr Mackenzie asked.

"Yes," Sherlock said.

He ate for some moments in silence. He wasn't hungry, but he knew Dr Mackenzie would insist.

"You are welcome to stay here as long as you need to, though I do have to attend to my rounds at the asylum," Dr Mackenzie said.

"No. I can't hide now," Sherlock said. "Dr Mackenzie, I need this job to pay my debt to the college. To keep this job I need to perform well tonight."

"And you are afraid you won't," Dr Mackenzie suggested.

"Correct," Sherlock responded.

They were both silent for a moment. Dr Mackenzie thought he knew where the conversation was going, but he wasn't going to help it on its way.

"Do you remember that drug we experimented with?" Sherlock asked.

"Yes," Dr Mackenzie responded as his suspicions were confirmed.

"Do you have any of it?" Sherlock asked.

"A little," Dr Mackenzie said. "I don't normally prescribe it for patients."

"Would you give me some now? Just enough to get me through the performances for the next two days. I'll pay you for it," Sherlock said.

Dr Mackenzie laughed.

"What would the world think of me for taking money from an impoverished, debt-ridden actor? I'm sure Dante had a special level of hell for such behaviour! Yes, I will give you some. No, you will not pay me for it. When you become a detective, I shall call upon your services gratis and obtain my compensation that way."

"Thank you, Dr Mackenzie," Sherlock said.

"Do you remember what the counter-reaction was like?" Dr Mackenzie asked.

"Yes. But we have Sunday off. I could sleep all day then. I have my violin at the hotel. I will manage," Sherlock assured him.

"You will send for me if there is a problem?" Dr Mackenzie said.

"Yes, I will," Sherlock said.

After breakfast, Dr Mackenzie gave Sherlock a ride to the hotel where the company was staying. Most of the actors had already gone to the Corn Exchange to rehearse. Escott washed, changed, and walked to the theatre. He encountered Sassanof as he arrived.

"If we lost money last night, then take it all out my wages. I won't have the rest of the company suffer for my weakness," Escott said to the manager.

"I appreciate that, Mr Escott, but I don't think they issued any refunds. I think most of the audience found your performance a bit shorter than expected — your character is not supposed to die until the end — but we started again with Devigne almost immediately. We'll see how it goes tonight. If the press about last night packs the house again, all's good. If it drives them away, then we will have problems," Sassanof said.

"I understand," Escott said. Then he asked, "Press, sir?"

"You haven't seen it?" Sassanof said, passing some newspapers over to Escott.

"Actor Makes Dramatic Entrance" and "William Escott Collapses on Stage" the headlines read.

"Good heavens," Escott said.

"That's one way to make headlines. You may keep them. I've got some matters to attend to before rehearsal," Sassanof mumbled as he walked off.

As Escott wound his way through the Corn Exchange, Miss Mayne spotted him.

"Billy!" she cried, "You seemed to have recovered."

"Yes," he said flatly. "Miss Mayne, I need to talk to you."

"Certainly, Billy! What would you like to talk about?"

"About last night—"

"Yes."

"You kissed me right before I went on stage," he said.

"It was for luck, Billy. I just wanted you to do well. I like you, Billy," she said wrapping her arms around him and smiling.

Escott steeled himself, peeled her arms away firmly, and stepped back from her.

"Please, Miss Mayne," he said, trying very hard to be both firm and polite. "Please, do not do that again. It was not lucky for me. It broke my concentration and—"

"You don't think I caused that?" Jenny Mayne cried, sounding offended. Her face was growing red.

"I don't know," he responded. "Now I need to get ready—"

Before he could turn away she reached out and slapped him and ran off. He stumbled back holding his hand to his cheek. He'd never been slapped by a woman before. But he remembered now looking through the window of his father's study and seeing Violet slap his tutor, and he remembered racing out after her and the snowstorm.... When Sherlock came out of the second attack, shaken and trembling, he found that he was sitting on the floor in a dark corner of the building. He heard voices in the distance.

"Have you seen Escott?" Sassanof's voice said.

"No, but I've been looking for him," Devigne's voice replied.

Sherlock sat quietly for another minute gathering his

wits. Two attacks within twenty-four hours! He remembered the contents of his bag. Where was it? He must have dropped it. He searched for the bag and found it on the floor not far from his feet. Sherlock stood up and continued towards the dressing rooms. Devigne approached him.

"There you are! What the bloody hell did you say to Jenny? No, don't bother lying, she told me. How dare you blame her! You come down with an attack of stage fright—"

"It was not stage fright," Escott said.

"I don't care what it was. After all your scoffing at Maude Clement's superstitions you parade out one of your own. Couldn't handle home-coming night? Trying to blame it on someone else? Now we are starting to see your true colours. You are a cold-blooded monster. I should—"

He took a swing at Escott who dodged it. Even on his worst days, Sherlock Holmes was a better boxer than Sebastian Devigne, but he did not swing back at Devigne. Devigne made several attempts before Sassanof stepped from the shadows and grabbed his arm.

"I will not have you mussing up the face of my lead actor tonight. Now get yourself ready for rehearsal and leave Mr Escott alone," Sassanof said.

"Devigne didn't land a blow?" Sassanof asked after Devigne stalked off.

"No."

"I need you to perform tonight with your face intact. Richard III may not be a handsome fellow, but I don't want him starting out with a black eye. But it looks like someone has already been messing with your face."

"It's nothing," Escott said.

Sassanof looked closely.

"Miss Mayne slapped you, didn't she?" Sassanof concluded.

"Yes," Escott admitted.

"Well, it will cover. I don't know exactly what is going on here, but backstage romances create too many complications."

"My thoughts exactly," Escott said.

"I will tell Miss Mayne to keep in her place, to stay in the green room when not needed, and stay out of the wings. If she is disruptive we will dismiss her, but you and Mr Devigne need to get along."

"Yes."

"You make good theatre together. Keep the drama on the stage."

Then Sassanof shivered.

"But not like what we saw in Paris."

"No. I assure you not."

"Good, then I will remind them of the rules before rehearsal. You are looking worse for wear. Are you sure you are going to be ready to perform tonight?"

"Yes, there should not be a problem," Escott said.

"Good."

Escott continued on to the dressing room. There he opened his bag and took out the wooden box. He saw no signs of leakage but he opened it carefully. The syringe was the same one that Dr Mackenzie had loaned to him to take on his trip back to Yorkshire several years ago. It was metal and unharmed. Inside the box with the syringe were four small bottles wrapped in wool to keep them from banging together. They were intact. Dr Mackenzie had mixed the cocaine himself. The concentration was the same as they had used before. Each bottle would only last a few hours. While Dr Mackenzie understood that the drug helped Sherlock after these attacks, he also had a distrust of it. With trembling fingers, Sherlock filled the syringe, rolled up his sleeve and plunged the needle into his arm.

That evening as the curtain was raised, William Escott once more stood alone as the twisted Richard. Behind him was a backcloth of London. Otherwise the stage was dark and empty. He was careful to look away from the limelight as it came on and he began his speech: "Now is the winter of our discontent made glorious summer by this sun of York...."

As he recited it, the rest of the cast let out their breath and fell into their parts. The play went well and he reached his final line without difficulty.

"A horse! a horse! my kingdom for a horse!" he cried before Devigne returned to the stage for their final battle.

The critic's comments on Devigne's performance on Thursday night had been "workmanlike" and "solid." Devigne had not been able to project the same intense malevolence that Escott demonstrated to Cambridge on Friday and Saturday. Yet Devigne had an evil look in his eye as they crossed swords in the last scene. It reminded Escott far too much of the duel he had seen in France. Yet he knew that even if these swords had been real, Sebastian Devigne was no match for him with a blade. The fight went as planned and the audience applauded as he fell to the stage on cue this time as the dying Richard III.

Chapter 13

After the Storm

*His aversion to women, and his disinclination to form new
friendships, were both typical of his unemotional character*
Dr. Watson, "The Greek Interpreter"

Around noon on Sunday, someone banged on the door of
Escott's room at the hotel, waking him up.

"Go away," Escott mumbled.

"It's me, Pike. I've brought you some food," Langdale Pike
said through the door.

"Go away," Escott repeated.

There was some scratching at the door and then it opened.
Pike pushed it closed with his foot as he spoke.

"Any idiot can open the doors in this place," Pike said, "and
that includes me. Didn't your university education teach you the
benefit of chapel Sunday mornings?"

Escott opened his eyes and scowled at him.

"No, it taught me that it was best to hide from marauding
dogs on Sunday mornings," Holmes grumbled.

"Ha ha! Yes. I remember! A nasty bite, wasn't that? Good-
ness, you look awful," Pike said. "And you didn't even indulge with
us last night. Or did you have your own private party?"

"No," Holmes replied, shutting his eyes again.

"Here, maybe some food would help," Pike said, dropping a
hamper on the bed next to him.

"What is the purpose of this intrusion?" Holmes growled.

"I wanted to speak to you," Pike said as he began digging
into the contents of the hamper.

Holmes had to admit that the contents of the hamper
smelled good. He turned over, sat up, and pulled it toward him.

"Concerning?" he asked as he explored its contents.

"Concerning what happened Thursday evening," Lord
Cecil said. "Does this town cause some type of reaction in you?

After you collapsed on the stage I remembered that you had been ill your first year at college and I remembered hearing that you had collapsed once in the courtyard at Sydney."

Holmes seemed to ignore Lord Cecil as he tore a large piece from the loaf of warm bread he had found in the hamper and bit into it.

"Is there something to drink in here?" he asked, looking into the hamper again.

"I recognized Dr Mackenzie when he came on stage. You know bloody well that I knew you and he had some prior relationship, a professional one, I assume," the young lord continued, ignoring Holmes' question.

Holmes wiped his lips after drinking milk from the bottle he had found in the basket. Sherlock Holmes did not know where he had found the food on a Sunday morning, but the milk was fresh.

"Then I heard that you went home with him that night. I know that Dr Mackenzie is the medical superintendent at the asylum. The audience here knows it. The company doesn't — not yet. But, Sherlock—"

Sherlock Holmes did not like the direction Pike's monologue was heading.

"Please stick to 'Escott,' unless you wish me to address you as Lord Cecil," Holmes said icily.

"Yes, yes. Quite correct, especially here in Cambridge," Langdale Pike continued. "What I was saying was that someone in this town might tell one of the other actors who Mackenzie is. They might think nothing of it. They might just think it was a coincidence that he was the only doctor in the audience that night."

"It was," Escott said.

"Or they might start wondering. I know that he used to go to your rooms. I know there is a connection. I'm not going to tell that to anyone in the company—"

"Thank you," Escott said with relief.

"Don't misunderstand me. Though I still have a reputation as a rumourmonger, I am much more careful about what I say than I used to be. You taught me several things at college. One was that you could easily thrash me if you wanted to. More importantly, you taught me there are still men of integrity in this world and you are one of them. I still owe you for getting me out of that gambling mess. I'm not going to do or say anything to harm your reputation—."

"Such as it is in this town," Escott said rolling his eyes, "The Sidney Dynamiter."

"But I would like to know what is going on. It won't go any further," Pike concluded.

Escott bit into an apple from the hamper looking thoughtful. Pike waited in silence.

"Dr Mackenzie was treating me for a nervous condition while I was in college," Escott said finally. "I had a recurrence on the stage Thursday night and I am still recovering from it."

"Ah, well, that's really all I wanted to know. I won't pry further. I hope the food helps. If there is anything further I can do—"

"No, I'm just going to try to sleep some more. Thank you for bringing the food."

"If you should have another of these attacks—"

"I hope not," Escott said.

"But if so, is there something special we should do?"

"No, just leave me alone. I'll come out of it eventually on my own."

"Well, then, Mr Escott, I'll let you get back to sleep. The rest of the hamper is yours."

With that, Langdale Pike bowed his way out of the room, locking the door behind him.

Monday morning the actors of the Corycian Company returned to London. The gas lines had been repaired and they put on *Richard III* that very evening and resumed their previous schedule. Though few would believe it who had already seen the play, Richard III grew colder. Yet he continued to draw audiences even as the actor who portrayed him became more distant from them and his fellow cast members. Escott rarely socialized with the other actors after the company returned from Cambridge, even Langdale Pike.

Some of the actors thought that somehow in playing Richard Escott had absorbed too much of the villain's cold-bloodedness. Many of them had heard legends of actors who so lost themselves in a role that they lost their grip on reality. Others thought it merely a case of swelled-headedness, and attributed whatever rumours they heard of his interactions with Jenny Mayne or Sebastian Devigne at the Corn Exchange to the same cause. They all observed that the long-standing rivalry between Devigne and Escott had devolved to antipathy on Devigne's part and a more active indifference on Escott's. On stage, Devigne and Escott were professional as always. Off stage, they did not acknowledge each other's presence.

It was during this time that some individual dressing rooms were finally completed at the Corycian Theatre, having been constantly delayed by repairs and other projects. Escott and Devigne were each assigned their own, which warmed some of the chill that had descended on the dressing room used by the rest of the actors. However, it also ended the egalitarian atmosphere in the company that had encouraged Escott to claim a leading role. Even if the move was primarily intended to separate them from each other, the assignment of the dressing rooms anointed them the male leads of the company. What the ranking was between them depended upon whom you asked.

As for Jenny Mayne, she remained in the cast for a few more weeks under the injunction from the stage manager that she not go anywhere near where Escott was likely to be, either on stage or off. This rather limited her participation in *Richard III*, but she began performing small roles in the *Romeo and Juliet* matinees after Act 3 Scene 1, as Escott often left the theatre after Tybalt's death, returning in time for the evening performance of *Richard III*. Sassanof had offered to cast another actor as Tybalt, but Escott remained fond of his first role and Sassanof was not going to take it away from him if he still wanted it. However, major upheavals were about to take place in the membership of the Corycian Company in any case and Jenny Mayne would be swept away with a number of others when the changes came. Perhaps on some level, Sherlock Holmes was relieved, but by then he was building stronger walls separating himself from William Escott. Escott was becoming no longer just a stage name, but a separate entity, a role he played, a layer of clothing for him to shed when he reached his brother's rooms.

The first Sunday afternoon after they returned to London, Mycroft spoke up. Sherlock was on the sofa in the sitting room with his shirt sleeves rolled up restringing his violin. He had felt the pressure of Mycroft's gaze for some time before Mycroft spoke.

"What happened in Cambridge?"

"What do you mean?" his younger brother responded.

"Since you moved to London you have been very vibrant and energetic. Not even mentioning the lives you have saved in your off hours, you have risen dramatically in the ranks at the theatre company with good notices of your performances. Suddenly you are quiet and lethargic. I might think that you had a poor reception at Cambridge except I have seen the notices. There is also this," Mycroft said rotating Sherlock's left arm to show the nearly healed puncture marks. "A week old, I surmise."

"And this," Mycroft continued as he tossed a newspaper at Sherlock that was folded to expose a circled article. It mentioned Escott's collapse on the first night.

"A relapse?"

"Not precisely. A nervous attack."

"Like the ones you used to have?"

"Yes. An isolated case, I believe."

I hope, Sherlock thought.

"Dr Mackenzie happened to be in the audience," he told Mycroft. "He provided me some of the drug to help me through a few performances."

"What precipitated this attack?"

Sherlock grimaced.

"Something unprecedented?" Mycroft asked.

"An actress kissed me."

Mycroft raised his eyebrows.

"That caused you to collapse?"

"Yes. It is difficult to explain."

"You are certain that was the cause?"

"Yes."

"I have seen the way you react to women, or rather try not to react to them."

"This incident," Sherlock said, pointing to the article, "demonstrates that I must be more vigilant to avoid such interactions."

"Why?"

For an instant anger, frustration, and pain flashed up within him and Sherlock wanted to scream "You know why!" but he inhaled deeply and suppressed the emotions.

"It is a part of life I am not meant for," he said calmly.

"And yet one you must endeavour to understand."

"Why?" Sherlock asked.

"Affairs of the heart are obviously at the core of many crimes. You cannot solve such crimes if you do not understand the underlying passions."

"I understand them too well, but I must view them dispassionately to follow the chain of logic. Emotions are fine things for driving a man to commit crimes or for pulling the wool over a detective's eyes."

"True, but many men would find such a path difficult."

"In my case it is the only possible path."

"If it is how you can find contentment...."

"L'homme c'est rien—l'oeuvre c'est tout."

It was not a sentiment with which Mycroft could or would argue. His own life was bound to the pleasure he found in resolving the complex problems of government and he had seen Sherlock's enthusiasm for solving crimes. It might be a lonely life before him but it could be fulfilling.

Sherlock Holmes did not like discussing the inner workings of his mind or his heart with others. It was difficult enough to express what he thought to others in ways they could understand. But what he felt? He was not always certain he could explain that to himself. Both were perhaps best kept tucked away for the most part.

He knew his brother Mycroft had his well-being in mind and would cease prying once satisfied. Sherlock had not forgotten the promise he had made to Mycroft in Yorkshire, nor the fact that he had broken it once before. For those reasons, he accepted Mycroft's interrogation. He had a pact with Dr Mackenzie as well and he owed the man much for the assistance he had given him in his early days at Cambridge.

Chapter 14

The Curse

Many startling successes and a few unavoidable failures
were the outcome of this long period of continuous work.
Dr Watson, "The Solitary Cyclist"

The talk of the "Curse of the Corycian" had begun some months before. It was likely that the phrase was first used by Maude Clement, but it was the newspapers that carried it and amplified it with each accident and each failed play. It was easy for a superstitious person to find evidence for the curse. The weeks and months of successful runs by the Corycian Company were often forgotten in the strain occasioned by the next accident. Such talk was another reason that Escott had endeavoured to keep Travis' attack and detention quiet. The story of a crazed, murderous former member of the company would only add to the noise.

However, Langdale Pike reported that Sassanof's business partner in the Corycian Company, Baron von Marienburg, frequently and adamantly denied that any curse hung over the theatre when he held court at the Café Royal. Often such denials only increased the attention paid to the subject. When productions were successful and box office receipts were good, the rumours faded. In the face of the near tragedy the night of the 4th of December 1875, they returned fourfold. The results undoubtedly could have been much worse, but as it was, it was impossible for the company to continue as they had been.

The curtain had descended on the matinee of *Romeo and Juliet* without incident on that Saturday and *Richard III* had commenced at the usual hour. The trouble came in Act 2 Scene 1 when Milton Hallows as King Edward, Miss Davenport as Queen Elizabeth, Tom Leydon as Dorset, James Wyatt as Hastings, and a number of others were assembled upon the stage. They had just received news of the death of the Duke of Clarence from Richard, Duke of Gloucester (Escott). Then Derby arrived on stage to ask a boon of the king. As Hallows responded to Derby, "You straight are on your knees for pardon," a shiver passed across the stage, similar to an earthquake. Hallows saw no sign that the audience felt it and did not miss a beat in his speech, but at his line "O God, I fear thy justice will take hold on me, and you, and mine, and yours, for this!" there was another, and some of the actors looked about nervously. As he finished with, "Come, Hastings, help me to my closet. Ah, poor Clarence!" there was a mighty crack and Hallows, Leydon, and Wyatt vanished, with only a cloud of sawdust to show where they had been!

Those familiar with the play knew this to be a deviation from the script even before the curtain rang down. A hole some four feet wide had opened in the stage and the actors had fallen through it. Escott and Pike (as Buckingham) had each been several feet from where the hole had opened. Sassanof directed his actors off the stage. He was concerned that additional weight near to the hole would cause more of the stage floor to collapse. Several of the stagehands went around to come up from below and aid the actors. The younger actors, Wyatt and Leydon, were unharmed by the fall except for some scrapes and bruises, but Milton Hallows was in much pain. He feared he had broken his hip. A doctor was summoned and a pallet was assembled to bring him up from the nether regions. Soon the actors and the audience were dismissed leaving the stage manager and crew to handle the aftermath. However, as the actors and actresses were leaving the building some began voicing their theories.

"This theatre is cursed," Maude whispered, "Did anyone look into why it had closed? Likely some disaster. Perhaps someone died. I know there is a curse on it. Don't know if I can stay here. It is too dangerous."

The next day was Sunday and Sherlock Holmes heard nothing more. He put no stock in the "curse." He had no more data than he had before that there was any connexion between these various accidents other than that they had all taken place in an old theatre. In this particular case, there were a number of actors on the stage, including himself, at the time it collapsed. Devigne was off in the green room. Unless, of course, the collapse had occurred prematurely.... He forced himself to stop theorizing without data and spent his time studying the recent crime news in the papers.

Monday morning he was reading the newspapers over a cup of coffee when Mrs Denton came in bearing an envelope.

"A boy just brought this by," she said.

His name and the address were written across the envelope in a neat and elaborate hand. He tore it open and read the contents:

Would you mind if I dropped in your rooms this morning? I went to the theatre hoping for news. Sassanof and the Baron were going at it. They nearly came to blows. Sassanof calmed down after the Baron left. He came up with a new plan, as he always does. He wants to speak to you. I told him that I would hunt you up, but I think it would be best if I brought you up-to-date first. Devigne and a few others are here. We could speak more freely there. I'll follow this note in about twenty minutes, if you will receive me.

Lord Cecil

He tossed the note aside and told Mrs Denton that Lord Cecil would be visiting shortly.

"A real lord? And this place a mess!" she cried gathering up the cups, saucers, and newspapers.

"We were at college together."

"Oh, in that case...."

"Yes. Just show him in."

Not long after the flustered housekeeper showed in the dapper young lord.

"Good morning, Holmes, though I suppose that is a matter of perspective."

"You have more information about the theatre?" Holmes asked.

"Yes. You might have heard some people in the theatre on Saturday batting around the theory that Hallows had fallen through an old trap that had been inadequately covered. However, the matter seems much more serious than that. Between the dismissals by Sassanof and the Baron there have been a few people let go this morning, including the chief carpenter Palgrave. The Baron is threatening to have the lawyers after the firm that restored the old girl. He says he had a new man in to inspect who claims the entire proscenium and its support beams must be torn out and replaced, which would close the theatre for nine to ten months. Sassanof was irate. He wanted to know why this not discovered before and blamed it on the Baron's hiring practices. Baron von Marienburg proclaimed his innocence in the matter, expounded on the construction firm's incompetence, and threatened legal action against them. Sassanof was ranting that we were just starting to make headway. The Baron suggested that perhaps the company could tour the provinces. Sassanof was not convinced. He enquired about the costs of repairs. The Baron insisted their investors had faith and would not abandon them. Sassanof was still fuming when the Baron left."

"Do you know what his new plan is?"

"He wants to talk to you before talking to the rest of the cast, but I believe that he is thinking of a tour of the States. He was dictating some telegrams to New York to his assistant."

"Fascinating."

"Yes, this could be a jolly romp. He's probably already discussed it with Devigne because he was at the theatre when I left. I believe he plans to talk to the rest of the cast this afternoon provided he can speak to you before then. I think he wants to know if his leads are on board before he decides who else he can take."

"So the entire company is not coming?"

"I don't believe so, but that is speculation on my part."

Langdale Pike and William Escott arrived at the theatre a little while after. Pike's surmise had been correct.

"I have connexions in New York, Mr Escott," Sassanof said, "who can book us in a theatre there and who will be able to provide me with introductions to others in Chicago, Philadelphia, and San Francisco. I am making arrangements for passage on a ship. We can make this work. We do a nine-month tour. The Baron has promised the work on the theatre will be completed by the time we return. He has also promised to arrange for a triumphant welcome for the internationally famous Corycian Company after the tour!"

It was another example of Sassanof's skill at quickly turning around disaster. At times like this, his mythical background as the son of a gypsy king almost seemed believable. Escott agreed to the plan, as had Devigne. Sassanof asked them both to stay for his announcement to the rest of the company as a show of unity. They agreed.

Only about half the cast could go. The dancers, the supers, and most of the minor players would be left behind. They would leave the orchestra behind and be dependent on local musicians in the cities where they performed. The wardrobe mistress and one of the dressers would be coming, and Walter Blanchard, the assistant carpenter. They would take their costumes and a few properties, but their back-cloths and sets would be left behind in storage.

Sassanof had the callboy intercept actors not on the list as they came in and he spoke to them individually and sent them off with their pay, until only those whom he was inviting on the tour remained.

"Ladies and gentlemen," Sassanof said to those assembled. "We have some good news and some bad news. One piece of news that I just received is that Milton Hallows has a broken leg, but the doctors expect him to be walking by next summer. The bad news is that the stage will require extensive repairs that will last months."

Groans rose from the company.

"Now, now. You must hear the good news. I have arranged for the Corycian Company to tour the States."

Excited murmurs passed through the company.

"We are making plans for a nine-month tour. We sail next month for New York. You have a few weeks to get your affairs in order. You can go through the stage door to collect your things from the dressing rooms. Wardrobe and carpenters are already crating up what we need to take with us. The rest will go into storage until we return. Then we will turn the theatre over to the workmen who will tear down and rebuild the proscenium."

That evening Sherlock Holmes spoke to his brother.

"Mycroft, you will be glad to know that you will have your

rooms to yourself for a while. We are going to tour the States."

"How long?"

"At least nine months."

"That should be interesting."

"Yes, I'm looking forward to it. However, I need to make arrangements with Sidney Sussex. I wouldn't have them believing I have run out on my debt. Perhaps I can arrange to wire my wages directly to them from America."

"Why don't you just wire them to me and I'll make the payments to Sidney on your behalf?"

"A generous offer, Mycroft, which I am inclined to accept. This will be a great opportunity to learn the criminal history of that country. We will be starting on the east coast and heading westward."

"You may meet some criminals who are not purely historic. I have heard tales of the lawlessness in the American West."

"Criminals see new frontiers as a place of opportunity just as much as anyone else."

"Well, in your pursuit of understanding lawbreakers, just be careful that you do not fall victim to them."

"I suspect that most of my researches will involve nothing more than long hours at courthouses reading old cases, when I'm not required at the theatre, of course."

Chapter 15

Journey to America

But there was no great difficulty in the first stage of my adventure.
Dr. Watson, "The Man with the Twisted Lip"

In mid-January 1876, Sherlock Holmes bid farewell to his brother Mycroft at the door to the rooms in Montague Street. He stepped out into the cold, damp air with a small bag and his violin case in hand. The sun had not yet risen and each breath hung in a cloud before dissipating. The cab driver was nearly finished tightening the straps around his trunk. Sherlock climbed into the cab and set down his bags. It was not much warmer inside. He tugged at his gloves and pulled his scarf tighter. He felt the driver climb up to his seat, and took up the violin case again before the cab lurched off.

The streets were all but deserted in Bloomsbury. The clop-clop of the horse's hooves seemed louder without the normal hubbub of the city. Wisps of fog hung about the streets and hoar-frost decorated the lampposts. The fog thickened as they drew near the docks. A forest of masts loomed out of it, towering over where the Thames must be. People, too, were thicker here, more densely packed like the fog. At the London docks, a new day had already begun for the servants of the tide.

Carters and porters materialized and vanished in the fog as they moved bales, baskets, and hogsheads to and from ships. Clerks and tidewaiters scurried about with pencils and ledgers. Sailors, firemen, lascars, and passengers rubbed elbows. The mists muffled the sounds of the docks to a deep murmur, punctuated now and then by shouts and steam whistles. The damp air was pungent with coal smoke, sweat, and creosote.

The driver stopped the horses at the pier before a steam packet ship called the *Athenian*. A stevedore helped the driver unload the trunk and took custody of it as Sherlock Holmes dismounted and looked up at the ship that would be his home for the

175

next week. The *Athenian* was a middling size for a steamship, but she loomed over the dock, her funnels and masts fading into the fog above them. She could carry fifty-two first and second class cabin passengers, and several hundred steerage passengers, in addition to her crew.

A crowd had gathered before the ship. The members of the Corycian Company had begun to cluster together. The sheer number of the steerage passengers, many of whom were poor, emigrant families, overwhelmed their small group. Children whined and parents shivered in the cold. Holmes set his violin case and bag between his feet and dug his pipe out of a pocket. In the damp air, it took several attempts to light the match and ignite the tobacco. The pipe was just beginning to draw as another cab pulled up. Lord Cecil Hamley flounced from the door as it stopped. He wore a fur-lined hat and pulled a matching cape around him.

"I would wish you 'good morning,' Escott, but I don't think it is morning yet and I don't find this weather very 'good.' Tis an hour I prefer to retire, not rise."

"Good morning, Pike."

They joined the others from the Corycian Company. There were six actors, six actresses, Sassanof and his secretary, the prompter Randy Foster, Ida, the mistress of the wardrobe, Sally, a dresser, and the assistant carpenter, Walter Blanchard. There were eighteen of them all told. They would be sharing seven second-class cabins, four with three berths each and three with two berths each. Escott was sharing a cabin with Pike and Dewitt. Devigne was bunking with Claude Dewarr and Joseph Reece. Sassanof had arranged a further reduction in the company's fare by agreeing to provide entertainment for the other passengers.

The rail-gates were opened. Corycian group tried to stick together as several hundred people surged up the gang-plank. The majority of the crowd streamed towards the steerage level. Dewitt joined Pike and Escott as they looked for their cabin. It was a small room with three berths, two lower and one above. Dewitt scrambled up and claimed the upper bunk, leaving the two lower ones to Pike and Escott. They arranged what luggage they had carried with them.

"I didn't know you played the violin, Escott," Dewitt said.

"I do. It helps me concentrate."

"Will you be playing for us?" Dewitt asked.

"Possibly. But right now I am going up on deck."

"I'll join you," Dewitt said.

"I think I shall turn in," Langdale Pike said.

The two young men headed up. The ship throbbed as the engines built up steam and the whistle blared. As they arrived on deck, the gang-plank was being pulled up and the rail-gate was closed. The whistle sounded again. Then the *Athenian* began to pull away from the pier. Soon her prow was cutting through the Thames as they left the docks behind. They passed other steam packets, cargo ships, sailing ships, and tugs pulling barges. They pushed through banks of fog that whirled in their wake as they slid past the Isle of Dogs. The sky was starting to lighten as they passed Woolwich, but it mainly made the fog brighter. Visibility was less than a tenth of a mile. It was still cold and damp, and most of the passengers had decided to remain below, perhaps to catch up on sleep lost due to the early rising. William Escott leaned against the rail, smoking his pipe, and staring off into the fog. Anthony Dewitt stood nearby. Neither said anything.

The ship took its time manoeuvring around Gallion's Reach, the whistle announcing their presence, the engines whirring and throbbing, and the water slapping against the ship. By Gravesend, the sun was cresting the horizon. It was but a bright blur through a swirl of white. They reached the sea cloaked, disguised, but not silent.

As the fog began to burn off in the Channel, Randy Foster came searching for them. The Corycian Company was meeting for breakfast in the second-class dining room. There was tea and coffee, toast with marmalade, oat porridge with milk, poached eggs, and kippers. After all eighteen of them had gathered, the first mate joined them. He expressed his appreciation.

"When the weather is fair," the first mate said, "the passage can be a tedious one for both passengers and crew. Any new form of entertainment is welcome. Unfortunately, beside the deck itself there is nowhere large numbers of people can gather at once. I recommend that instead you arrange small performances in the lounge of each class. There is a small stage in each lounge."

After some discussion, the company decided to tour the ship after breakfast to better understand how they could arrange performances. Each class of passengers had its own smoking-room, lounge, and dining-room. The steerage section was divided, with portion of the third-class passengers forward and another portion located aft. While their quarters below were more cramped than those of the other classes, steerage class had a whole deck to themselves for taking the sea air.

The Corycian Company's tour also allowed them to become better acquainted with their fellow passengers. Among the first class cabin passengers, there were six ladies, two children, and five men. Besides themselves, there were six second-class cabin passengers, all of whom were servants of the first class passengers. There were many more passengers in steerage. Due to the cold weather, most of the passengers were staying below decks amusing themselves by reading, writing, knitting, walking, and playing checkers or chess. Children were running up and down the halls of the steerage sections playing tag and other games. The passengers were excited by the news that there would be plays performed during the passage.

Sassanof had informed the cast before they left London that they would not present any of their previous repertoire on the ship, but instead use the captive audiences to test three new plays, *Henry VI Parts 1-3*. They had used the weeks between their last performance at the Corycian Theatre and their sailing date to learn their parts. They had no scenery and limited costumes available to them while they were at sea. Therefore, the results would entirely depend upon the skills of the actors. The size of the company meant more doubling of roles, and some characters had been dropped or combined with others. They would begin with two performances of *Henry VI Part 1* in steerage in one day and then separate performances for the first and second cabin class passengers the next day.

After that, they would move on to *Henry VI Parts 2* and *3*, repeating the sequence of performances to each class of passenger. This meant that after one day for rehearsals they would be performing twice a day throughout the whole voyage.

The ship arrived at Havre, France, in the early afternoon of their first day at sea and took on some additional passengers. The actors were taking a break from rehearsing and Holmes had come up on deck for a pipe. The sun was bright, but the wind was cold. He returned below deck shortly to work on their new plays.

While they were at sea, Sherlock Holmes began most days by rising from his berth near dawn, donning his hat and overcoat, and walking around the promenade. He would light his pipe and proceed like the ship itself, leaving a trail of smoke behind him. He observed the sea, the weather, and the sailors at work. The sea that early in the morning was grey-green, broken by foam where it collided with the ship or when the wind churned up caps. The sky stretched on and on. The weather held quite well with sun, few clouds, and a light wind most days. Sometimes the wind rose and they unfurled the sails to supplement the steam-powered screw. The first mate said they were making good time.

Very little changed from day to day, but the pipe and the brisk air cleared the fog from his mind, if not from his lungs, and spared him from Lord Cecil's complaints about rising. Anthony Dewitt, coming from a large family and being of a comic bent, was perfectly willing to bait and tease his fellow actor in response to his complaints. Holmes would eventually make his way from the deck to the second-class dining room where he would have some coffee and toast. He missed reviewing the London papers with his morning coffee. He strolled back to the cabin about the time the young lord was prepared to break his fast. Holmes took that opportunity to wash, shave, and change.

Often he had some time left to review the scripts they would be rehearsing that morning before joining the cast in the lounge. The rest of the day would be taken up with rehearsals, meals, and performances. Holmes would retire to his cabin directly after the last performance and play his violin a while before sleeping. Lord

Cecil and Dewitt shared a few drinks and levity with the other passengers. They would roll into their berths a few hours later and the cycle would begin again. Holmes liked his solitude, yet the press of presenting new plays on a short schedule kept his brain busy most of the day. Lord Cecil had in the past never travelled less than first class in any form of transportation, nor had he ever shared quarters, but he was a gregarious sort. Aside from the shipboard hours, he was enjoying himself, especially the companionship of his fellow actors and other passengers. Dewitt, on the other hand, was relishing being free of the throng of younger siblings at home.

Initially some rehearsals and performances were complicated by seasickness among the actors, but that abated after a few days. The seas were fairly calm during their passage. Acting on a moving deck required some adjustment, but none of the cast injured themselves before they got their sea legs. However, there were some comedic touches added inadvertently that Shakespeare had not anticipated working on an immobile stage.

It was not possible for the company to rehearse without observation, but some passengers and members of the ship's crew seemed fascinated by the process. They watched as the actors rehearsed their lines and arranged their stage business on the stage in the second-class lounge. The staging of the scenes was limited by the smaller stage, which was much closer to the audience. However, in the circumstances the actors were less concerned with creating a sensation to impress London theatre critics and more concerned with providing a bit of diversion for their fellow passengers. The ship had a small printing press on board which the crew used to create daily newsletters and other announcements. The first mate saw to it that the schedule of performances was published and signs were posted as reminders. No tickets were required and there was little to no competition for passengers' time. The result was that all performances were filled to capacity. Off-duty crew members filled in the performances in the second-class lounge since the Corycian Company itself made up two-thirds of the second-class passengers.

Otherwise, the passage was uneventful. No storms arose to toss them about. There were no plagues or fights among the passengers. Devigne and Escott stayed out of each other's way when they were not performing. The performances went well. The steerage passengers were not a particularly discerning audience. Few of them had ever seen a play and fewer had read Shakespeare. They were so incredibly bored at sea that the company probably could have done nearly anything and still won their applause. First and second-class audiences were polite, as could be expected. For all of them, actors and audiences alike, these performances helped pass the time.

For Sassanof, the eight days went quickly. He was always working, evaluating the performances and planning ahead. With the addition of the three parts of *Henry VI*, Sassanof hoped be able to put on the entire tetralogy with *Richard III* in New York. He was also tempted to try the Scottish Play, but not on the ship. Perhaps he would test it in some American city. If they could polish it before they returned, they could put it on in London after. If that were added to the War of the Roses tetralogy and *Romeo and Juliet* they could have six successful plays, and if Hallows returned to them in London, then Lear would make seven.

On their last day at sea, Sherlock Holmes rose before dawn as usual. He had not been long on deck when a cry came from the crow's nest. The sky had just begun to shift from inky black to mottled grey. It must have been a sharp eye with a telescope that spotted the winking light upon the horizon. It was another quarter hour before the first mate confirmed it himself and by then the distant light was fading into the growing dawn. It was the Montauk Point Light on Long Island, their first sight of North America.

Soon a sliver of land appeared along the starboard bow and slowly grew along the horizon. As it did, the twilight also revealed other ships in the distance around them drawing closer as they all bore down upon the port city somewhere beyond the horizon. Ahead there appeared an armada of swift schooners seemingly on a collision course. But the *Athenian* held her course without concern. As they drew closer, Holmes could see that each of these tiny sailing ships bore a number upon her sails. Then one out-distanced the others and began to draw towards the leeward side. *Athenian* cut her engines and furled her sails. A man on the schooner raised his arm, and the captain, who had joined the first mate, responded in kind. A deal was struck in that exchange and the other vessels drew away in pursuit of other ships. Sherlock Holmes now understood that these were harbour pilot ships vying for the custom of the ships approaching the harbour. To the swift went the prize.

The schooner drew up beside the *Athenian* and a rope ladder was dropped. The pilot scrambled up. No sooner was he on board than the pilot ship pulled away seeking other ships for the pilots still on board. The pilot was received with much ceremony by the captain and other officers, and the helm given over to his command. By now, word had begun to spread among the waking passengers about the slice of land on the starboard horizon. A scattering of them watched with Sherlock Holmes as the pilot from Sandy Hook took command of the ship and they got underway once more. The clouds began to break up as the sun rose aft. The pilot steered the steamer toward the starboard until the land spread out before the bow to both port and starboard.

The dark strip on the horizon had texture now, of a rough sort. Then a bight opened directly before them. To the port side, low hills appeared, topped by a pair of lighthouses. As the ship rushed on, a low rocky spit of land stretched out below those hills. It, too, hosted a lighthouse. The proliferation of lights spoke of unseen sandbars, shoals, and other dangers. To the starboard side the forbidding Fort Lafayette scowled from its island perch. Hardly more than ten years before a confederate rebel had been hanged at Fort Lafayette for plotting to burn the city it guarded. Additional forts bristled with guns on the east and west shores as they passed through the Narrows. They sat as warnings to potential intruders, and reminders of the troubles this nation had come through not too many years past. Then a cemetery came into view on a hill to the east as a final reminder of the costs.

Many other ships were leaving the harbour and all those coming and going came closer together as they passed through the Narrows. The skill of the pilots and the conventions they followed meant that ships passed quickly through this gateway without incident. Beyond the Narrows, the inner harbour opened into a series of bays both port and starboard. Ferries, barges, tugs, and small excursion and fishing boats darted among the ships approaching from the sea. Small islands were scattered before them and beyond those islands appeared the larger island of Manhattan. The shores of the bays were mostly wooded down to the water's edge, broken by villages, farms, and country mansions. From this distance, Manhattan Island was an unimpressive cluster of boxes with a few steeples piercing the sky above. At the southern end of Manhattan were the remains of an old battery once used in the island's defence. More prominent now in the area of the old battery was Castle Garden where the steerage class passengers would be inspected by immigration officials after first and second-class passengers had disembarked.

They were heading eastward and Castle Garden was sliding away to their port when the *Athenian's* engines stopped once more. A tugboat approached and the docking pilot scrambled aboard. While lines were being laid from the tug to the steamship, an immigration inspector came aboard and spoke to the captain. Soon they were underway again and the passengers who had been on deck scattered to their respective cabins to gather their possessions.

In their cabin, Sherlock Holmes found Dewitt fully dressed and packed, sitting on the upper berth threatening Pike below.

"You tell him, Escott, that it is time to be going."

"Is it true, or is this clown just playing with me?" Langdale Pike grumbled.

"They are towing us to the pier now. You are welcome to stay abed, but the immigration inspectors are on board. I can see the headlines in the *New York Herald* now about them interviewing you in your night shirt."

Langdale Pike could imagine the headlines, too. Undoubtedly, they would want to know his real name and social status. He jumped up and began changing as Dewitt and Escott headed up to the deck with their bags. The young lord made quick work of it and joined them less than ten minutes later. By that time the tugboats were manoeuvring the steamship alongside the pier. The first and second-class passengers had mostly gathered on deck by this time. Any steerage passengers who came up were directed below again.

"What is that?" Pike asked pointing to a large structure in the making a few blocks to the north.

It towered over the *Athenian*. An identical structure stood on the eastern shore. One of the other passengers responded.

"It's a new bridge over the East River. Some believe it is a boondoggle and will never be completed. They have been working on it for six years now. Too much sand and silt down there. Hard to find bedrock. The original designer was killed in a freak accident surveying the site for the east tower over there in Brooklyn. Been many men injured in the caissons, including the chief engineer. Hear his wife is trying to completed it now, if you can believe that."

"Indeed?"

"Crazy, isn't it?"

The immigration inspector began cursory interviews with the passengers as the ship was moored and the gangplank readied. Soon the first and second-class passengers were streaming down the gangplank to the Pine Street Pier.

The air was warmer in New York than it had been in London when they left, and the morning sun was shining. The members of the Corycian Company stood together as arrangements were made for their luggage and transportation to the hotel. The pier itself was very long, over three hundred feet. There were three and four story buildings along the streets at the end of the pier. Some looked to be warehouses and at least one seemed to be a tavern of some sort.

Chapter 16

Stages, *Times,* and Trains

The carpet round his chair was littered with cigarette-ends
and with the early editions of the morning papers.
Dr Watson, "The Norwood Builder"

The Corycian Company and their luggage were crammed into a number of carriages and wagons that set off from the East River Docks. The young actors and actresses craned their necks to see this mythical city of New York as the drivers turned their horses westward along Pine Street then north on Water Street. The buildings near the waterfront were mostly brick and stone stained with smoke and time. There were taverns, warehouses, and shops catering to seamen and their ships. They turned west again on Fulton Street. Then they turned north on Nassau Street to Centre Street which merged with Fourth Avenue after a mile. As they drove north, the buildings seemed to grow newer, larger, and more dramatic as if they represented the character of the town through time. Another mile up Fourth Avenue the carriages turned west on 23rd Street and north again on Fifth Avenue. Fifth Avenue was arrayed with a number of hotels and theatres. They stopped before an immense structure of white marble called the Fifth Avenue Hotel. It was six stories tall and covered the entire block between 23rd Street and 24th Street. Though undoubtedly of American design there was an Italian influence in the architecture of the hotel, most notably in the pillars with Corinthian capitals. The hotel faced Madison Square Park across Fifth Avenue. However, on that morning in January only leafless trees and brown grass stared back.

They descended from their carriages and passed under the portico to the main entrance. The floor of the entrance hall was laid with a pattern of white and dark red marble. The ground floor included a telegraph office, a bookshop, a barbershop, and a restaurant. The floor above had carpeted corridors lined with double rows of Corinthian columns and lit by eleven chandeliers. On that same floor was the main dining room and another for early dinners and breakfast as well as a ladies' tea room. The guest rooms were all richly furnished. With the exception of Langdale Pike, the actors and actresses were not accustomed to such luxury. They were awestruck.

"They haven't kept up with the latest fashions, but the hotel seems to have aged well," was Pike's critique.

What amazed the actors more than the decor and furnishings was the 'perpendicular railway' that intersected each floor. It was a steam-powered vertical screw lift that saved guests the effort of mounting the stairs between floors. The desk clerk insisted that this was the first hotel in the country to have one.

It took some time for all eighteen of members of the Corycian Company to be assigned rooms and their luggage distributed. They broke their fast in the smaller dining room while that was being attended to. The crates of costumes and properties were sent over to the theatre with a note that Sassanof would be around in the afternoon. That had the unexpected result of earning them a visit in the dining room of the hotel from Mr Palmer, the manager of the theatre.

He approached the table with hat in hand.

"Mr Sassanof?" he asked.

"Yes," Sassanof responded.

"I am Mr Henry Palmer," he said.

"Oh, Mr Palmer," Sassanof said rising from his chair and extending his hand. "Please join us."

Mr Palmer shook his hand, but declined to sit.

"No, thank you. I just wanted to come over and tell you in person once I knew you were in town."

"Tell me what?"

"There has been a bit of mix up," Mr Palmer said.

"What sort of a 'mix up'?" Sassanof responded looking somewhat annoyed.

"A scheduling mix up. We aren't ready for you. We have another performance booked. The theatre won't be available to you for another two weeks."

"Your wire said it was all arranged," Sassanof replied

"I know, and it is entirely our fault. By the time I discovered the error, you were already at sea. We will compensate you. I've made inquiries. The Globe Theatre in Boston has some openings and would love to have you for the interim. You can rest up today and take the train over tomorrow. It is only five hours. Your company could take the stage the day after. Waller is the manager's name at the Globe. Here's his telegram. You can respond directly. I'll pay for the train tickets and I'll hold your hotel rooms here for you. I can ship your crates there today."

Sassanof was still sceptical. Mr Palmer continued to try to persuade him that this arrangement was the best for everyone.

"Let's work out the schedule of performances for when you return. I will have the playbills printed and notices sent to all the papers while you are in Boston. We will lionize you and fill your first night if I have to buy all the tickets myself and hawk them on the street."

"Agreed, sir," Sassanof said at last. "I will hold you to that. If you can fill the first night, I know my actors can fill the rest."

They shook hands on it. Sassanof excused himself and went downstairs to the telegraph office where he began exchanging wires with Mr Waller in Boston. Arrangements were made in a few hours. They would arrive in Boston the following afternoon and go directly to the theatre to rehearse. Their luggage would be sent on to the hotel. The property and costume crates would precede them and Mr Waller agreed that they would unpack the costumes and air them upon arrival. Mr Palmer sent over the railway tickets that afternoon.

The members of the company explored the hotel and its services in the morning. After lunch, some of them wanted to see some portion of this American city before being whisked off to another. It was a very mild day for January. Several knots of actors and actresses spread out to stroll amongst the trees of Madison Square Park or down Fifth Avenue. At first, it was difficult to understand the speech of the people in this city. They were undoubtedly speaking some form of English, but they spoke very fast and their consonants had a way of wandering off and attaching themselves to other syllables. Sherlock Holmes wondered how many variations of English there might be in this country stretching from the Atlantic to the Pacific. He made a mental note to listen carefully and attempt to learn the various dialects he encountered. Such knowledge would be useful to both an actor and a detective. He also collected a number of New York newspapers from the shop in the hotel to study on the train to Boston.

The next day they were crowded into carriages again and taken to Grand Central Depot, a massive train station facing 42nd Street between Vanderbilt and Fourth Avenues. The walls were brick with iron trimmings and the wrought iron roof was supported by semi-circular trusses spanning hundreds of feet. Based on the signage, many trains of several railways left from this station daily for points east, west, and north. The railway maps were a cobweb of different routes. Some routes went through the southern part of the state of Connecticut along the coast of the Long Island Sound and then north to Boston. Their tickets took them north through the Hudson Valley to Albany, and then east the length of the state of Massachusetts to Boston.

The carriages, or "cars" as they seemed to call them, on these American trains were different. Rather than being divided into separate compartments with facing seats they each consisted of a single compartment with all the seats facing forward. Sherlock Holmes' first thought was that this arrangement would make it more difficult for passengers to murder one another without observation. It brought to mind the murder of Thomas Briggs in a first class carriage in England in 1864. He didn't think that American railroad carriages – cars – were designed that way for that purpose. It was more likely an attempt to fit as many seats as possible in each car. Profit was the more probable motive than crime prevention. This did not mean that railway travel was entirely egalitarian in the States. He had heard that the very wealthy travelled in sumptuous parlour cars and sleeper cars. Such isolation made an attack easier – unless they had servants, and anyone able to afford to travel in a parlour car most likely had servants.

The train itself broke his train of thought as it lurched forward and pulled away from the city, passing through fallowed fields, pastures, and forests. There was no snow on the ground. The days had been warm, unseasonably warm, some passengers said. The Hudson River was itself remarkable. In some places, it was as wide as some seas and it had carved its way through immense cliffs.

Holmes was sitting next to the aisle and saw these things over the shoulder of Anthony Dewitt who was seated beside him. Dewitt was looking out the window. He was raised in London and rarely had been out to the country, even in England. The New England countryside was a fresh sight for him.

Pike, Devigne, and the other two actors were attempting a game of whist despite the seating arrangements. Ida was sewing something. One of the actresses was knitting. Two others were reading, one a novel, and the other, a script. The other three actresses were chatting and laughing. The ladies' dresser was staring out the window. Their manager was dictating something to his secretary, and the prompter was talking to Blanchard the carpenter, who seemed very bored.

Sherlock Holmes arranged his pile of papers on his lap and immersed himself in them. There was a great deal of political news related to the city of New York, the state of the same name, and the national government. The New York papers also reported news that came to them from other states. It did seem that the governing system of the United States provided more employment opportunities for politicians. Some of the opportunities were not consistent with the law. Some reports in that vein included the continuing efforts to retrieve William M. "Boss" Tweed after his escape from custody of the New York police the previous year.

Police in Newark, New Jersey, were looking for a thief who used an elementary ruse to steal cash from bank customers. In the most recent occurrence, a man was counting his money and arranging it into piles prior to making a $1000 deposit. A gentleman tapped him on the shoulder and asked if he had dropped a one-dollar bill that was lying on the floor at his feet. The man looked down and responded in the negative and the other man left the bank.

However, when the teller counted the bills, $450 was missing. The same thing had happened at the same bank a few months before.

The newspapers contained lists of indictments for a number of petty thefts and assaults in New York without any details. They also reported that a man left his home in New York to attend a lecture and never returned. A New York patrolman had been accused of feigning illness in order to avoid testifying at a trial, and a captain was charged with neglecting to arrest liquor dealers for selling liquor on Sundays in violation of the excise law. Scarlet fever was on the rise in Baltimore, and a bucket of water had exploded in Nevada. There was an interesting article on the murder of Madame Mazel in Paris in 1698. The *New York Times* also had a long, depressing article about actors who were seized with paralysis or apoplexy while on stage, many of whom subsequently died.

As Holmes finished with each paper, he handed it over to Dewitt. In time, they had accumulated quite a pile of papers on the floor below. Another passenger asked after the papers and they passed them on to him. Dewitt returned to staring out the window and Holmes leaned back and took a nap. In a few hours, they arrived at the city that had begun the American revolt against the British Empire. Unfortunately, they did not have time to explore sights, but were immediately whisked off to the Globe Theatre while their luggage was sent ahead to their hotel.

Mr Waller greeted them at the front entrance of the theatre and gave them a tour. The Globe Theatre was much larger than the Corycian.

"How many patrons does the auditorium hold?" Sassanof asked.

"Twenty-two hundred," Mr Waller responded.

"I hope we can fill them. Though on short notice—" Sassanof began but Waller cut him off.

"We have a head start. One hundred and fifty of the seats are 'leased' — paid in advance. We papered the town with play-bills yesterday afternoon. Come along and I will show you the notices in this morning's paper. I think you will receive a good response. We have had a number of actors from England come to visit and they have been treated kindly by our audiences."

Sassanof and his secretary followed Mr Waller. The actors and actresses of the Corycian Company were left upon the stage. They were not entirely alone. Randy, their prompter, was with them. He was suggesting that they proceed to set up a rehearsal when a tall, thin young man rushed on stage from the wings.

"Sorry, I am late," he said. "Professor Monroe kept us late, then I ran into Thomas Watson who was babbling on about some machine of Bell's. I could not shake him—"

He stopped when he realized he was addressing strangers.

"Where is Mr Waller?" he asked looking around.

"He has wandered off with our manager," one of the actors responded.

"You must be the actors from England," he said.

"Indeed we are," said Dewitt.

"It is the most remarkable thing, Escott," Pike said. "You and this fellow could be twins."

"Are you an actor?" Escott asked.

"Yes, indeed. I've been filling in as a utility actor here at the Globe while attending lectures at the Boston University School of Oratory. I've previously performed in New York, Buffalo, and New Orleans."

"Glad to meet a fellow thespian," Devigne said extending his hand. "I am Sebastian Devigne."

The American actor shook his hand.

"Will Gillette. Good to meet you. And you, sir?" he said offering his hand to his doppelganger.

"William Escott," he responded.

When introductions were completed, Pike suggested that he join them in their performances.

"After all we have this very large stage to fill and there are only a dozen of us," Pike said. "There are certainly parts available and space for bodies in some scenes."

"I would be honoured!" Will Gillette responded.

"We can discuss it with Mr Sassanof when he returns," Randy said. "In the meantime—"

"We need somewhere to put our coats," Escott interrupted. "Mr Gillette, could you show us to the dressing rooms?"

"Will, please. Of course. Follow me," he said and led the way.

They found when they arrived at the dressing rooms that the costumes had indeed been unpacked and hung up. They doffed their hats and coats and claimed their spots on the tables in the dressing rooms. Separate rooms had been set aside for Escott and Devigne, but they found it necessary to claim their costumes from the main actors' dressing room. The properties were there, too, including their swords.

The stage was larger than the Corycian Theatre's and immensely larger than the space they had to work with on board the ship. When their manager returned to the stage, he informed them that Mr Waller had shown him what backdrops and set pieces they had available. The ones he selected were being brought to the stage from storage. As they rehearsed the stage crew made efforts to make the stage seem less vacant with appropriate placement of back drops and set pieces.

Sassanof's plan was still to run the three parts of *Henry VI* in order followed by *Richard III*. If that tetralogy succeeded the first time through then they would repeat it twice more in Boston, encouraging audiences to return several nights in a row. William Escott was portraying three generations of Richards in the tetralogy and Sebastian Devigne was impersonating Henry VI and Henry VII. Sassanof was now glad that they would have the opportunity to polish *Henry VI* before opening it in New York. It was a gruelling first day of rehearsals, especially for the parts of *Henry VI*. The cast had been through *Richard III* numerous times and settled for a cursory review to establish the new marks. Will and several other local utility actors filled in as soldiers and courtiers as needed.

Early the next morning they had their first dress rehearsal and completed *Henry VI Parts 1* and *2* before lunch and *Part 3* after lunch. The only hitch was a miscommunication. The English theatrical company discovered that in the States the "Prompter" and the "Opposite Prompter" sides of the stage were the reverse of the way they were accustomed. Since they were going to be performing on American stages for the next few months, they would have to adapt, at least as far as giving instructions to the lighting and stage crew. The cast was given a couple of hours rest before the curtain rose.

They learned in Boston that American audiences differed from English audiences. They seemed less sophisticated and more easily pleased. They were more respectful to the actors. They never hissed. If a play was particularly bad, they might leave before the last act, but in general, if they did not like the play, they merely left at the end of the night and did not return. A first night could be packed and the second night empty. The Corycian Company did not suffer such a fate. To Sassanof's pleasure and surprise, they ran through the tetralogy three times in Boston to packed houses. Some of the papers commented on the innovation (at least to them) of running the plays in historical order, and the difficulty of doing so with such a small cast. They were impressed with the naturalism that this company brought from the "old country" and speculated that Irving's style was spreading among young actors in England and might do so here as well.

It was a whirlwind of two weeks rehearsing and putting on four different plays three times each. Before the Corycian Company knew it, they were on a train heading back to New York. The return trip was much like the one to Boston had been. Once again Sherlock Holmes accumulated a stack of papers to read on the train.

He read that there had been a successful raid on a "panel house" led by Inspector McDermott of the 2nd precinct in New York. A severed head had been found in Brooklyn. The previous owner of the head was quickly identified and a co-worker arrested. A man who had been arrested for throwing red pepper in a man's eyes was being extradited to Michigan for another offense.

As the train rolled on, Holmes read a report about "sawdust frauds." It was not clear how the name was derived. The paper explained that the swindlers sent out circulars to people in the western territories offering them a stock of goods obtained through questionable means with the proposal to split the proceeds if the recipient agreed to help them sell the goods. A correspondence ensued in which the swindler eventually asked for a sum of money for shipping the goods. If the money was sent, the swindler was never heard from again. The circulars seemed to originate in New York and a police detective named Kealy had been assigned to investigate. Detective Kealy and some other police officers had arrested two men and seized a large number of envelopes and circulars that were ready to be mailed. The prisoners were presented before a magistrate at the Washington Place Police Court for arraignment. After all their work, the magistrate discharged the prisoners, claiming the complaints against them were invalid.

Sherlock Holmes shook his head at this disappointing outcome. It did no good to catch criminals it they were merely set free again. It seemed a straightforward case to him. He wondered what the magistrate found unsatisfactory about the work of the police and what more he required to prosecute the men.

Several articles told of a man named Ezra D. Winslow whom the Boston and New York papers referred to as the "Boston forger." The story was of the downfall of respected citizen, or perhaps, it was the revelation of the true nature of a man. Winslow had been a Methodist minister who contributed to the temperance and the prohibition movements. He was also active in politics and held a Senate seat for a term. He was chief proprietor of the *Daily News* and had purchased the *Daily Post* the previous May. The purchase of the *Post* seemed to be where the trouble started. Winslow paid $160,000 in cash for the *Post* but he seemed to have raised that money by giving his own notes for $70,000 or more. Shortly after buying the *Post*, he created a stock company for it nominally valued at $150,000. The newspaper reporters speculated that his intent had been to sell at least half the stock to raise funds to pay back the notes. Unfortunately, he had not sold enough of the stock and the notes had matured a few days before. He seemed to have resorted to forging signatures on renewal notes. When that succeeded, he flooded the local banks with forged instruments of different types. Some gentlemen bought up notes circulating under their forged signatures and forced Winslow to pay back the money under threat of exposure, but his house of cards was falling. The extent of his forgeries was thought to exceed $400,000 and touched numerous banks. Banks began refusing any notes from him and freezing his accounts. It was also suspected that he sold more *Post* stock certificates than the total capital stock allowed, but who held that diluted stock was unknown.

Detectives Dearborn of Boston and Kealy – Kealy again – of the New York Central Office were working on the case. A few days previously, they had discovered that Winslow had been making inquiries regarding sailing times of steamships from New York. Dearborn and Kealy visited the offices of the various steamship lines, but found no trace of Winslow until they reached the offices of agents for a Dutch line of steamers sailing between New York and Rotterdam. They discovered that a man answering Winslow's description had called at the office and inquired about passage for himself, his wife, and children. The agent said that the man bought the tickets under the name of John Clifton. The steamer agent positively identified Winslow from his picture but the ship had left port on Friday. It seems the man had escaped. Holmes realized there could be more to the story. Perhaps if he had time he would call upon this Detective Kealy who seemed to have his finger in every pot in New York.

When they arrived in New York, it was cooler than it had been when they left. They pulled their coats and wraps close as they bundled into carriages for the drive from the depot to the hotel. Leaving their luggage in the custody of hotel employees, they made their way to the dining room for supper and then retired for the night.

<h1 style="text-align:center">Chapter 17</h1>

<h1 style="text-align:center">Artful Dodging</h1>

He was still, as ever, deeply attracted by the study of crime.
Dr Watson, "A Scandal in Bohemia"

Sherlock Holmes rose early the next morning and proceeded downstairs to ask the desk clerk for the address of Western Union. When he arrived at their offices, Holmes entrusted the majority of his pay from the two weeks in Boston to Western Union with instructions that the funds be wired to his brother in London. Then he returned to the Fifth Avenue Hotel and joined the remainder of the Corycian Company for breakfast.

It was a warm day. After breakfast, Sassanof recommended they walk the block west to Booth's Theatre rather than order carriages. After a brief stroll, the acting troupe found themselves before a colossal granite building with a mansard roof and three towers. Booth's Theatre was not merely impressive in height and design. It stretched one hundred and fifty feet wide. An attached five-story wing took up another thirty-four feet of the block. The theatre had been built under the direction of the celebrated Edwin Booth himself. He had managed it for a few years before turning it over to others, confessing that his skills lay in acting, not in theatre management. These days he travelled across the United States and Europe performing. Even when he was back in New York, he often performed at theatres other than that which bore his name.

Several arched doors led to a grand vestibule paved with Italian marble featuring a large statue of Edwin Booth's father, the Shakespearean actor, Junius Brutus Booth. The ceiling above was covered with frescoes. As members of the Corycian Company stood looking about the vestibule, they were joined by Henry Palmer, whom they had met briefly two weeks before. He and Henry Jarrett were managing Booth's these days. Mr Palmer led them on a tour of the theatre starting with the auditorium, which was lavishly decorated. In the centre of the stage, above the proscenium arch, stood a statue of Shakespeare surrounded by busts of prominent actors, including the English actors Garrick and Kean.

"The house seats 1750 patrons with standing room for more," Mr Palmer told them. "We have a sprinkler system for fire prevention and the entire building is heated and cooled with forced air for the comfort of both players and audience. Come up on the stage and I will show you some of our other innovations.

"As you see," he continued when they were all on the stage. "We have done away with rectangular side-wings. Side scenes are solid walls of rooms or outdoor scene paintings. The stage uses hydraulic rams to raise and lower scenery, and has electric spark stage lights. We also have a very well stocked prop and scene room. Our carpentry shop is located under the sidewalk along 23rd Street. Backstage there is a green room, star dressing rooms, and thirty other dressing rooms."

"Over thirty dressing rooms?" Sassanof asked.

"Yes, indeed. Given the small size of your company, we can assign a separate dressing room to each of your actors and actresses."

That sent a murmur of approval through the company as they considered the idea of each having his or her own dressing room rather than sharing cramped quarters.

"In fact, we can go there now and each of you can stake your claims."

Mr Palmer led them through the backstage area to a hall of doors. They each chose one and removed their hats, gloves, and coats.

"Now what would you like to see next?" he asked.

"Lead us back to the stage so my actors can begin their rehearsals," Sassanof said. "Then you and I can inspect your prop and scene room."

Having spent two weeks in Boston rehearsing and performing the tetralogy, the cast knew their lines well. Little adaptation was required at this theatre. The stage was similar in dimensions to the one in Boston. The rehearsals concentrated on teaching the theatre's own crew when scene changes were required for each of the four plays. The stagehands at Booth's had never done a repeating tetralogy before, but they were accustomed to putting on new shows on short notice. They adapted quickly.

Mr Palmer was good to his word and filled the theatre the first night. Sassanof was also correct that it filled again on the second. The New York critics were initially uncertain as to how to review a series of related plays. Like those in Boston, they were mostly kind to this young cast from overseas. They were intrigued by the naturalism of the characterizations and enjoyed the energy of the sword battles. They sang high praises for Escott's *Richard III* when it came around on the fourth night. Inevitably, there is some critic who disagrees and finds some nit to pick, but enough of the notices were positive to make more people curious about the idea of serial plays and want to see all four in order.

The day after their return to New York, Holmes read in a newspaper that the house of Winslow, the "Boston Forger," which had been heavily insured, had burned a few weeks before. The article also revealed additional details about the total amounts he had defrauded. The police believed the man was bound for the Netherlands and diplomatic attempts were being made to intercept him there. Holmes still had many questions about the case.

Soon the Corycian Company settled into a regular schedule of evening performances six days a week and matinees on both Saturday and Wednesday, as was the custom in New York. Except on days when there were matinees the actors were on their own until the late afternoon. Sherlock Holmes took advantage of this schedule to take a hackney cab down to the police headquarters at 300 Mulberry Street. After some inquiry, someone showed him to a door marked "Kealy." A tired young man in shirtsleeves and a waistcoat looked up over a desk piled with files as he entered.

"Hello. My name is Sherlock Holmes. Are you Detective Kealy?"

"No."

"Is Detective Kealy in?"

"No, he's out detecting something," the man said.

"Do you know when he will be in?" Holmes asked.

"No. You're not from around here. England?"

"Yes."

"Immigrant?"

"No," Holmes replied.

"You want to report a crime?"

"No."

"Then how can I help you?"

"As I said, I am looking for Detective Kealy."

"Why?"

"I wanted to talk about some of his cases."

"Why?"

"Because I am a detective, or rather I am training to be a detective. I have been reading about some of his cases in the newspapers. I know those are incomplete. I thought I could gain some additional insight from him," Holmes said.

"This ain't a school."

"I know—"

"Done any detective work before?"

"Yes."

"Anything that would have been in the papers?"

"Some of it was in the London papers, but my name was not mentioned—"

"Why not?"

"Because I allowed the regular police to take the credit," Holmes said.

"That's a good deal. I wish the Pinkertons worked that way. What are you doing in this country? On a case?"

"No. I am here as an actor."

"An actor? Is this some kind of joke?" the man said starting up.

"No. I have been acting to learn skills that might be useful to me as a detective."

"Say, that could be handy. Are you any good at it?"

"You can come to the Booth Theatre and find out. My stage name is William Escott," Sherlock Holmes said, somewhat exasperated by this man.

"I might do that. Not acting under your real name?" the man said.

"No."

"I guess that's pretty common."

"Yes. May I ask what your name is?"

"Hargreave. Wilson Hargreave."

"Are you a detective?" Holmes asked.

"As far as it matters to you," Hargreave responded.

"What does that mean?" Holmes asked.

"It means, like you, I am training to be a detective, but I am doing it from inside the police not on some stage."

"No offense was intended," Holmes said.

"None taken," Hargreave said. "None intended to you either. We have our ways."

Holmes took out a visiting card and wrote "at Fifth Avenue Hotel" on it and handed it to Hargreave.

"Please give this to Detective Kealy when he comes in."

"Okay."

"Good day."

"You, too."

Holmes left the building uncertain whether Hargreave would give his card to Detective Kealy or whether he would ever hear from either one of them again. He returned to the hotel, picking up some newspapers on his way up to his room. In a few hours, it was time to walk over to Booth's Theatre and prepare for the night's performance. He liked this theatre. It was both aesthetically pleasing and a pleasure to work in. It was easy to tell that an actor had designed it. As usual, that evening Holmes left the theatre after the other actors and walked the short distance along 23rd Street. As he approached the door to the hotel, a man stepped out from a corner of the portico. He placed his hand on Holmes' elbow and urged him through the doors, saying, "Let's talk." They entered the hotel and found their way to one of the parlours on the ground floor.

"You have a peculiar way of making appointments, Mr Hargreave," Holmes said as he removed his hat and overcoat and sat down.

THE CONSULTING DETECTIVE PART II: ON STAGE

"It was effective," the New York policeman said. "I knew you would be coming back from the theatre soon. So I just waited."

"You came to the theatre tonight?" Holmes asked as he lit his pipe.

"I took a look, like you suggested. You're good. Can you do other voices? Accents? Can you play a New Yorker?"

"I have had very limited time to study the New York accents—"

"Well—"

"I knew you would be coming back from the theatre soon," Holmes said repeating the words in Hargreave's own accent and inflection. "I took a look, like you suggested."

"Oh, you are good. I could use someone like you."

"I cannot guarantee that I wouldn't make an error. I need to hear more of it. Perhaps if I could shadow you for a while I could—"

"Okay, here's the deal. You can follow me for a few days if you think it will help you impersonate a New Yorker. Then I want you to do a bit of detective work for me. There is no pay in it."

"That would be an effective way to improve the dialect and vocabulary as well as allow me to observe your methods. However, I can only do it when I am not required at the theatre. We will also be moving on eventually."

"It's a deal," Wilson Hargreave said offering his hand.

"Then I will see you tomorrow morning at 300 Mulberry Street," Holmes said shaking his hand.

Hargreave was not much for formal greetings. The following morning he handed Sherlock Holmes a map in a sleeve as soon as he entered the office marked "Kealy."

"Since you are an actor, you can memorize things, right?" Hargreave asked.

"Yes."

"Good. Memorize this map. It has the streets and the precincts. You will need to know your way around. I'll be telling you the rest. Come along."

Sherlock Holmes went with Hargreave as he travelled about

the city interviewing witnesses and suspects, and following up on clues to different cases. Most of the interviews were for Detective Healy's cases, but Holmes never met Healy himself. According to Hargreave, Healy assigned much of the routine work to subordinates, particularly those like Hargreave who wanted to move up to detective. When Hargreave and Holmes were alone on the streets, or in cabs between interviews, Hargreave talked about their "deal."

"I – well, Healy, really, but he set me on it – I need someone who is not connected with the New York police and who has no affiliation with any of the other factions in the city. That's where you come in. Oh, and I asked Scotland Yard about you. Got a wire back from an Inspector Gregson. He said you were okay."

"Did he say anything else?"

"It was an international wire. He wasn't wordy. Why?" Hargreave responded.

"Curious."

"This could be dangerous. Does that bother you?"

"No. Are you going to tell me what 'this' is – beyond delving into police corruption?" Holmes asked.

"How'd you find that out?" Hargreave asked suspiciously.

"Why else would you need someone from outside?" Holmes said.

"You are quick. Soon enough. Let's work on your character."

"Would it be more appropriate if I had just come over?"

"No, some folks don't like immigrants. You are more likely to blend in if they think you are from New York. If they wonder why they've never met you, say you've been living up in White Plains in recent years with a sick relative who died leaving you nothing but debts. However, I want you to seem familiar with the city, like you lived here as a kid. Oh, and find some American clothes. Those would give you away."

"I might be able to borrow something from the theatre," Holmes responded.

They chose the name "Will Taylor" for Holmes' alias. Holmes was used to responding to William or Will, and Taylor was a common name. Hargreave filled Holmes in on the intricacies of uptown versus downtown, and east side versus west side. He told him the history of the gangs of the Bowery and the Points, police riots and draft riots, and the various political factions, including Tammany Hall. At the mention of Boss Tweed, Holmes interrupted.

"I understand he was convicted, but escaped."

"Escaped! It wasn't much of a detention. Who lets a man convicted of over 200 crimes sit in his own home and sleep in his own bed? Someone arranged the 'escape.'"

"I see."

"I don't know what the point was. I think they will bring him back to finish his sentence. I'm not sure his replacement at the Hall is much better. All crooks, if you ask me. You are better off not having an opinion about any of this, however. It's not your problem."

"Not something I need for your plan?"

"You need to know the history, but not take sides. When it comes down to it, you will be working for your own side — your character's, I mean. That should be your only alliance. Just follow that."

After a few hours of shadowing Hargreave, Holmes took a cab to the Booth Theatre to reassume the identity of William Escott. It was a Saturday and they had a matinee. Sassanof had them running a separate sequence of the tetralogy in the matinees. Thus, a patron could see the entire tetralogy either by attending only matinees or only evening performances. Holmes understood that the company was drawing substantially more income because these theatres could hold larger audiences than could be seated in their theatre in London. In addition, there had been no accidents to break their run. However, no one alluded that point, as if even the mention of it would bring bad luck.

On his Sunday off, Holmes walked the streets of Manhattan matching what he saw with the map that he had committed to memory. Diagonally across Fifth Avenue stood the Hotel Brunswick, a favourite of New York society. The Coaching Club met at the Brunswick. The broughams and victorias of Fifth Avenue's wealthy residents passed up and down the street. On Sundays, the sidewalks were crowded with men in grey toppers and girls in bonnets and billowing skirts. Not far was the St. James Hotel, a gathering place of the theatre, while further up Broadway was another theatrical rendezvous, Gilsey House. On the west side of Broadway, between 24th Street and 25th Street, was the Albermarle Hotel, small, select, and discreet. Next to it was the Hoffman Hotel boasting the longest bar in America, which attracted sporting men and wealthy playboys, as well as connoisseurs of Bouguereau's paintings of naked nymphs frolicking with satyrs.

Heading downtown along Broadway, Holmes found a mix of buildings devoted to commerce and amusement. Wallack's Theatre, one of the leading theatres in the city, occupied the corner with 14th Street. Nearby was a sewing machine company building, Union Square Theatre, a German savings bank, four hotels, and Tiffany & Company, a jeweller. He continued into the part of lower Manhattan called the Bowery. Here the tenement houses loomed above him. The population was very dense and far less fashionable. To the east was the part of the city called Little Germany then on to Five Points and uptown again.

For a few days the following week, Holmes alternated between being under the tutelage of the New York policeman in the mornings and performing Shakespeare in the evenings. After the first two meetings at Mulberry Street, he met Hargreave at different spots in the city to limit the time they were seen together at the Central Office. Holmes remained in his own person when they met so "Will Taylor" was not seen with the policeman.

Beyond Hargreave's history and geography lessons, Holmes learned that the methods of the police in New York were not that different from those of Scotland Yard. They primarily consisted of tedious legwork and countless interviews. They depended more on luck than skill to catch criminals. Unless there was an eyewitness, or someone who confessed, there was little chance that anyone would be charged, much less convicted. There were exceptions, but they were rare. The London police seemed more polite than their New York counterparts. However, neither took kindly to a lack of cooperation. Holmes asked Hargreave about the magistrate who released the men in the "sawdust fraud" case he had read about in the newspapers.

"That was a bad deal," Hargreave said, "I think someone paid off the magistrate. We had them dead to rights. They left town after they got out. They probably are continuing their game somewhere else."

"Is bribery of magistrates all that common here?" Holmes asked.

"Far too common. But you can just forget I said that."

"What about the Boston forger case?"

"The same, someone was not doing their job, but there is hope that we'll get him back. He made the mistake of stopping off in London. Scotland Yard seems willing to cooperate. I expect we will hear news of an arrest in a day or two."

"Perhaps you can keep hold of him this time."

"We would have to fight Boston for him since there are charges pending in both cities."

When he walked the streets, Holmes wore some American clothes that he borrowed from the stock costumes at Booth's Theatre. He matched his stance, his gait, and his demeanour to the neighbourhood, being especially alert in the poorer ones. He offered no challenges to anyone, though he would not back away from a fight. He tested his rendition of the local dialects at taverns and coffee shops. He repeated his walks about the city any time he was not needed at the theatre. He became a familiar figure around town and being familiar, began to disappear.

Finally, Hargreave explained what he wanted.

"Look, Talbot Smith has this saloon up on 29th street, just a few blocks north of your hotel, called the *Silk Glove*. We think he's running a panel joint and that's just the beginning."

"A panel joint?"

"A swindle house. Pretty gal gets a fellow to go to a room with him and when his pants are down her partner sneaks in through a false panel and robs him. Some hotels and saloons specialize in them, often in combination with Murphy jobs and badger games. We're pretty sure it's going on in the *Silk Glove*, but the local precinct says there is no proof, no complaints."

"You think someone is protecting Smith?"

"Yes. Others, too. They've had token raids on other places up that neighbourhood. Rarely the more fashionable places. Never there. They are open 24 hours, plying their trade."

"Doesn't that violate the liquor law?"

"Yes, but that's not being enforced either."

"I read articles about police officers being disciplined for not showing up to court or only enforcing the excise laws on some saloons and not others."

"That's part of it. We don't know how the pressure is being applied. Are the police being blackmailed into providing protection, or they being paid? Is something else at work here? What we need you to do is to find out who is involved. Patrolmen? Roundsmen? Warders? The District Attorney? The Magistrates? We don't know how far it goes. We want you to observe and report back to us. That's it. Just observe."

The next day presented Holmes with an opportunity. A fierce snowstorm struck the city on February 17th. In the late afternoon, he stumbled into a saloon as Will Taylor in his American clothes with a notebook and pencil in his pocket, clearly seeking shelter from the storm. He unfolded a newspaper and began reading. Sometimes he would circle articles or take notes. After a while, he moved on to another location. He repeated this performance at a number of places over the next few days. Once again, his goal was to become familiar, and thus invisible.

On Sunday, February 20th, it was warmer and slush was everywhere. Holmes sloshed his way about the streets to the saloons in the guise of Will Taylor. The following day it rained then turned to snow. The snow fell even heavier on Tuesday, and Thursday the temperature dropped to five degrees Fahrenheit and everything turned to ice. The ice and snow was not good for attendance at the theatre and several performances were cancelled. Holmes used this opportunity to spend more time at the *Silk Glove* and other saloons north of 23rd Street.

He had noticed that the neighbourhood was in decline. What may have been stylish venues at one time had run to seed and squalor. At first, he chose the saloons at random as if trying to find a new 'local,' but at last he settled on the *Silk Glove*. The *Silk Glove* was located on the ground floor of a four-story building made of red brick. It was probably originally built two or three decades before as a personal residence and converted later to public use. The custom of the saloon included a steady flow of regulars. It was likely that there were more who came in during the evening hours while he away at the theatre. Nevertheless, the place was quite lively in the hours after he returned. The regulars were mostly clerks and day labourers.

He'd show up in the early afternoon many days, but leave by 4 p. m. on days he had to be on stage. Then he would come back late at night after the theatre let out. When performances were cancelled due to weather, he'd spend longer drinking, reading, and scribbling in his notebook. Eventually the bartender, Nelson, made some comment about his hours. Holmes told him he was a playwright and he had to go to theatres to talk to the managers and seek wealthy patrons to finance his next production.

"Any luck with that?" Nelson asked.

"Not yet. I need to come up with a new play. No one wants to pay you while you are sweating over the next one."

"So that's what you've been writing in your notebook?"

"Yeah. It's a good atmosphere here to write."

"What kind of play you writing?"

"Don't know yet. Something modern, I think. Like what goes on around here. Anything exciting go on around here?"

"If there was any excitement would I be talking to you?"

Being a playwright not only explained the hours he kept, but it also allowed him to randomly take notes or ask questions. He also read a lot of newspapers. He mostly read the crime news as he usually did. There were some interesting reports. The Boston Forger had been arrested in London and arraigned. There were reports of a numerous local thefts and assaults. There were a number of articles about the arrest of members of gang called "Molly Maguires" in Pennsylvania for the murder of a coal mine boss. Another forger named Williamson was arraigned, and diamonds were seized at the Custom House. There was an inquest related to a fire on Broadway and a sailor met with foul play.

He was somewhat disturbed by an article in the *New York Times* on February 18th, that discussed a select committee that had been appointed by the State Assembly the previous year to investigate the increase in crime in the city. The *Times* alleged that the committee's report accused several police captains of habitually protecting gamblers and panel thieves who gave them large payments. The newspaper also said that the detective force was implicated. The detectives had aided the captains in setting up systems of blackmail, and stood between criminals and enforcement of the law. Additional blame was thrown on political interference in the department and insufficient numbers of policemen. To Holmes it sounded like everyone was pointing fingers at someone else. He was not surprised that the committee made no recommendation on how to fight such corruption. The committee seemed more like a political manoeuvre to achieve re-election than a serious effort to stop crime. Perhaps the detectives planned to use the information he gathered to attempt to vindicate themselves.

There were a number of newspaper articles related to "Indians," as they called the natives of these lands. It seemed the U. S. president had ordered all Indians to move to parcels of land called "reservations" by the end of January and some of them had not complied. The articles concerning Indians seemed to be of two minds. Some articles were shocking reports of Indian "depravities." Others complained of the federal government's failure to make payments required by a treaty with a tribe called Utes and blamed the actions of the Indians on the government's lack of fair dealing with them. They proposed that Indians were starving as a result of the failure of the payments and were stealing cattle and other livestock to feed their families. The western settlers shot Indians caught stealing and the tribes retaliated in kind, resulting in a murderous cycle.

Over and around his newspapers and notebook, Holmes watched tradesmen, coachmen, and clerks come through to have a drink and some conversation. He soon determined that, with the exception of some cards in a back room and the violation of the excise laws about serving liquor on Sundays, most of regulars were not connected to any illegal activity. That latter vice was useful to Holmes since he had Sundays off from the theatre.

"Making progress on that play?" Nelson, the bartender, asked one evening.

"Got some ideas. Needs romance, intrigue, betrayal."

"Huh."

A police officer came in.

"Maybe I should include a cop as a character."

"He'd make a good choice — a real ladies' man."

Such Holmes had already surmised. Policemen were regular visitors to the *Silk Glove* both in and out of uniform. Perhaps some were merely there for the drinks and the camaraderie but Holmes doubted that any trained policeman would miss the illegal activities. At best, they were turning a blind eye, and at worst, they were benefiting. He listened for names and made a mental note of them.

There were others who were intimately connected with the illegal activities. He had no doubt that the bartenders were involved. He saw them slyly accepting envelopes or actual cash when no drinks were poured. There were also the "panel girls," who lured men into the place. Some were young, but others were not as young as they tried to seem. Some were flamboyant and some played sweet and innocent. They didn't start their nights at the *Silk Glove* but they ended them there, again and again. They were bait tossed in the stream of commerce and reeled in. While the girls might talk to the regulars, they never tried to hook them. The regulars knew the game even if they did not play. The marks were mostly buyers or salesmen from out of town. The girls would find them at another saloon nearer to buildings devoted to dry goods or manufactures, or a hall where a convention was being held and, after a few drinks, they would entice these men to make a night of it. Eventually they ended back at the *Silk Glove*, asked the bartender for the key to the upstairs room at the end of the hall, and went up with their companions. Holmes saw coffee and tea dealers, fish factors, dry goods buyers, and when the American Book Trade Association's fair was at Clinton Hall, a whole string of book buyers and sellers, go up those stairs and come swiftly down. Little note was made of their arrival by the regulars and even less when the men stumbled down the stairs a short time later red in the face with their clothes in disarray. The victims tended to startle if anyone addressed him. The bartender would ask if he could get him a drink, if he was not otherwise engaged and invariably the man would respond by grabbing at the wallet that was no longer there. Holmes witnessed this performance when uniformed patrolmen were present. The sight of them tended to make the victim exit more rapidly. The patrolmen made no motion to help them.

Holmes believed some of the officers were participating in the badger games, appearing at the appropriate time to confront the victim and frighten him into paying money. The marks of the badger games and other forms of blackmail were more likely to be local men, especially the younger sons of prominent families. Sometimes they were used when the profit was potentially higher, or if for some reason the panel swindle could not be run. Sometimes it was part of a longer swindle. One landsman in New York to recruited investors in farmland in the San Luis Valley of the Territory of Colorado had the misfortune of landing in the *Silk Glove* one night. He had made a big sale and was celebrating while trying to sell anyone else within earshot. After much pitching and more drinks he mounted the stairs with a blonde he thought was to be his reward. A policeman in uniform followed up the stairs not long afterwards and escorted the man out the door. Newspapers later reported that he had embezzled funds from the land company. They were unable to determine where the money had gone.

Holmes could not interview these men without exposing his position. He did endeavour to bump into a panel victim on his way down and ask him if he was all right. The man took flight without a word. That was the benefit of this type of swindle. The victims of panel heists, who were often married men, feared exposing themselves more than anything else. The girls liked it because they made good money without giving up what they would have had to in a bordello.

Beginning on the 25th, a number of articles appeared in the papers that raised much commentary and cursing in the *Silk Glove*. Police captains were now being required to complete daily report books listing all the places they had been during the day, the names of the people they spoke to, and the number of hours they spent in their homes. A new system of espionage was to be started using patrolmen in plain clothes to determine if the captains were filing true reports. One police captain resigned over the new policies. Holmes wondered if any of this was related to his own work. He doubted it. There seemed to be much confusion over what the problems were, and how to resolve them. The solution was a job for administrators, not detectives. He had agreed to observe. Nothing else.

It was an interesting exercise. Developing characters for the stage was initially challenging and the applause of the audience was rewarding, but repeating the same plays became almost automatic after a while. The repeating tetralogy did keep the actors on their toes, but even that became a habit. Playing Will Taylor, the playwright, was more stimulating because there was no script; each day the interactions were different. Yet it was even more important to stay in character, and to keep this character separate from both William Escott and Sherlock Holmes. That included coordinating his surveillance with his complex performance schedule in which he was playing four different characters on different nights. He had to remind himself who he was supposed to be at the moment. It was a unique challenge that he savoured.

Sherlock Holmes kept his American clothes in his dressing room at the theatre and went from there to the *Silk Glove*, which was only a few blocks from the theatre. He usually waited until all the actors had gone. However, one night Sassanof called a meeting after the evening performance to announce to the cast that Philadelphia is out of the tour schedule.

"I've received a wire from the theatre in Philadelphia cancelling the engagement. They said that due to the Centennial Exhibition there will be no rooms available in town and they are afraid no one will be going to the theatre. I am attempting to rearrange the schedules here and in Chicago to fill the gap."

"You aren't going add another city?" Devigne asked.

"No. The southern states are entirely out of the question. There are riots and outbreaks of yellow fever. Some of the smaller cities are unlikely to provide the box office receipts that we have been receiving. I hopeful that Chicago and San Francisco will be as kind to us as New York and Boston have been."

Holmes was thus late returning to the *Silk Glove*. He thought all the actors had left as he headed out in his Will Taylor attire but he had misjudged and bumped into Langdale Pike on the way out.

"Excuse me – Good heavens! What are you doing in that costume?" Pike asked.

"Rehearsing another role."

"Gutter rat?

"No."

"Drunken sot?"

"Not quite."

"You aren't going to tell me, are you?"

"No."

Pike let it pass, but Holmes should have known that was not the end of it.

There was one policeman, a Captain Bernard, who was on especially good terms with Smith, the owner of the *Silk Glove*. Holmes had no doubt that money was passed to him, but there was more to the relationship than paid protection or blackmail. It was almost like a joint venture or a brotherhood. Holmes decided that he needed to know more. He tried to concentrate on those two as he drank their beer, read newspapers, and jotted scene notes. He gradually pieced together hints that there was some type of secret society behind it. He began hearing mentions of an upcoming meeting of that society as the Corycian Company's time in New York was growing short. Sassanof had extended their run in New

York a few weeks but the Booth Theatre had another booking coming up and their manager had arranged for them to move on to Chicago soon. As Holmes was seeking the details about the meeting of the secret society, his investigation was nearly waylaid.

It was a busy Friday night in early March. The days were lengthening and there had been a hint of spring in the air. The theatre had been full and there were more people out on the street that night coming and going to and from restaurants, saloons, and theatres. Sherlock Holmes was on his way to the *Silk Glove* when he realized something was not right. He stopped and listened. One set of footsteps stopped. He walked on. One set of footsteps started. He stopped to look up at a building as if looking for an address. The footsteps stopped and sidled away as he looked back. He walked again. He recognized the cadence of the steps. His pursuer was light on his feet, but an amateur at this game. Holmes walked on. He passed a group of people and ducked behind the front steps of a building when the group was between him and his follower. Holmes heard the familiar steps pass and then pause. He reached out and pulled his follower into the shadowed corner next to him.

"What do you think you are doing?" he asked.

"Satisfying my curiosity," Lord Cecil said.

"I didn't know that was possible."

"For short periods of time it is."

"You are not very good at following people," Holmes said.

"At least not very good at following you," he conceded.

"You don't want to get involved in this. It could be dangerous. Your presence would likely increase the danger to both of us."

"What is it you are doing that is so dangerous?"

Holmes sighed.

"I am investigating a matter for the New York police," he whispered. "It is a situation where my acting skills are also called upon. As long as I remain in character, I should be safe, but a slip could be very perilous."

It was not clear that Lord Cecil accepted the reality of the danger. He enjoyed drama and did not always recognize the line between drama and real danger.

"Ah, pursuing the detective business?" he asked.

"To some degree. It is an elementary investigation, but it has allowed me to learn more about the methods of both the police and the criminals in this city without interfering with my schedule at the theatre. It is good practice for other surveillance."

"You aren't going to tell me anything more?"

"Revealing more could place your life in danger," Holmes said.

"Perhaps after we have left New York?"

"Perhaps, but in the meantime, I must ask that you refrain from following me or take any note of my leaving the theatre. It is just as well that the other members of the company believe I am merely being antisocial," Holmes insisted.

"As you like," Lord Cecil said with a wave of his hand.

"Then go back the way you came. I will continue after you are out of sight."

The young lord strolled back the way he had come without the clandestine moves he had attempted the first time. Then Holmes continued on his way to become Will Taylor once again.

Holmes was frustrated by the difficulty in finding out when and where this meeting was. It was Saturday, March 18th, the day of their last performances in New York, between the matinee and evening performance of *Richard III* that he finally heard that the meeting was that very night. He still did not know what time the meeting was or where. Short of feigning illness, he could not get out of the evening performance, or the inevitable curtain calls. If he seemed to the other actors to be a bit preoccupied, then they were correct. Several of them set it down to conceit and were not shocked when he vanished almost immediately afterwards.

He rushed to the saloon in time to see Captain Bernard mounting a carriage. Holmes climbed on behind. The wheels of the carriage threw up dust and debris from the street and thus the ride did not improve the look of his attire. When they arrived at the destination, Holmes quietly hopped off the back of the carriage. He stayed behind it for a moment as Bernard stepped out and entered the building. Holmes had not been able to see most of the street signs during the ride, but he believed he was in lower Manhattan, not far from Water Street. There was an old red brick tavern before him much older than the *Silk Glove*. Quite a number of people were walking towards the entrance and carriages were driving up and discharging passengers at a rapid rate. It was an unusual hour for such a congregation.

He found his way around to the trade entrance and let himself in. With food and drink orders flying fast, it was easy enough grab a measure and follow another man up to the first floor – the second floor – in the American way of thinking. Everyone was heading to a long room full of men. Holmes recognized some of them. He ducked away from the man he had been following and found a corner behind a wood beam to tuck into. He concentrated on separating voices and hearing names and forms of address. He saw a number of policemen of different ranks. However, he also saw businessmen, including Smith, and some government officials. There was some mingling before the meeting got under way. It was during this time that he saw an envelope pass from Captain Bernard to a man Holmes believed was a police magistrate.

Finally, the meeting was called to order with much ceremony. It seemed it was called the Polar Star Lodge. They went through old business and then started new business, which included vigorous discussion of the new police notebooks, recent prosecutions of officers, and the captain's resignation. There was disagreement among the members about what actions, if any, should be taken.

Holmes had to memorize everything. He could not take notes. After a while he felt he had heard and seen enough. He was considering how best to make his exit when he was collared by the employee of the tavern he had followed up the stairs.

"There you are. What are you doing skulking back there? Help me bring the food up before you are given notice."

The man continued to mumble about the inability to find good help as Holmes followed him downstairs. Then Holmes slipped away from him again and out another door, which was a mistake. The lodge had posted guards at that door to keep out newspapermen. One of them was a great bull of a man. He grabbed

Holmes by the right arm and held him in an iron grip. Sherlock Holmes could have felled a smaller man but he could not even reach this man's face, and the body blows he delivered with his free fist had no effect. His captor half-led, half-dragged the struggling young Holmes into a stone building behind the old tavern. The second guard reappeared shortly with a couple of men from the meeting. One was Captain Bernard.

"Here, what are you doing prowling around?" Captain Bernard asked.

"I was just looking for inspiration," Holmes said in character.

Bernard looked more puzzled than convinced.

"Search him. See if he is armed."

The second guard patted Holmes down. He pulled Will Taylor's notebook out and handed it to Captain Bernard.

"Just this," he said.

Captain Bernard flipped through it.

"I've seen you around before. You are that guy who writes plays?"

"Yes. Sorry to interrupt your meeting. I was curious. Always looking for fresh ideas for a play."

Bernard scowled and pulled out a pair of handcuffs.

"Cuff him to that post. We will deal with him later."

The giant dragged Holmes over to a post and thumped his back against it. The other guard pulled his arms back behind the post and handcuffed them together.

"Now get back to your positions," Captain Bernard said.

The two guards left. Captain Bernard stuck Will Taylor's notebook full of play notes and ideas in his pocket.

The second man had said nothing but as they left the room, he whispered to Captain Bernard, "Do you think he works for the *Times*?"

"We'll figure that out later."

Holmes concluded that he did not want to be there later. Left alone he sat down on the dirt floor and leaned back on the post to think. He was confident he could unlock the handcuffs if he could find something to use as a pick. He felt up the post but found no nails he could reach. There was straw on the ground beneath him. Just straw, and he could not pick a lock with straw. Looking around he realized this was the saddle room of a small stone stable. It looked older than the main building. It might date back to the days of the Dutch East India Company. The stable might have once been a larger carriage house. Now it was only big enough to weather a wagon or small carriage and a pair, and the saddle room was hardly more than a closet. There were no horses or carriages in it now. Yet it must be used because there were two fresh bales of hay stacked against the wall of the saddle room. Where there were bales there was baling wire. He knew it was not uncommon for a careless stable boy to cut the baling wire and let it fall were it may and get on with the feeding. The very fact that there was loose straw on the floor of this room pointed to the existence of a careless stable boy.

Holmes stretched out one foot as far as he could and caught the corner of the lower hay bale with his boot. He rotated the stacked bales towards himself, then grasped the lower one between his feet and dragged them both towards him. Next he used his legs to knock the top one off and to push the lower one up beside himself. He twisted around and struggled until one hand could reach under the bale. There he found a loose piece of baling wire that had been under the bale and dragged along with it. It was much longer than he needed. He grasped it in his hands and bent it back and forth until it grew hot and snapped. Then he began working with the small piece of wire until the handcuff latch released and he had one hand free. He quickly left the stable and made his way uptown to the Fifth Avenue Hotel.

Their agreement had been that Holmes would not contact Hargreave until he finished his observations in order to avoid compromising his identity. So Wilson Hargreave had not been surprised when he had not heard from Holmes for the first two or three weeks. He checked the theatre notices regularly. As long as Escott was continuing to appear on stage, he assumed all was going well. Then he saw that the Corycian Company were ending their run soon. On the afternoon of March 18th, he received a telegram to meet him at the hotel late that night. It was unsigned and did not say where. He knew. He arrived at the hotel about ten and sat down to read a newspaper. Eleven passed, and midnight came, but there was still no sign of the actor. Hargreave had stepped out for a smoke after one o'clock in the morning when he saw him coming down the street.

"I was beginning to worry," Hargreave said.

"Let's get off the street. Come up to my room," Holmes said and led him up the stairs.

"You look a bit of a mess," Hargreave said noticing the dirt and straw on Holmes' hands and clothes.

Holmes did not answer as he unlocked the door.

"What did you discover?" Hargreave asked as they entered Holmes' room at the hotel.

"More than you may want to know. Are you familiar with the Polar Star Lodge?"

"Polar Star Lodge? Is it involved? That could mean connections to Tammany, even the Freemasons. This could reach into the highest levels of government. It may be a lot bigger than Kealy thought."

"Unfortunately, when I followed one of them to the Polar Star Lodge meeting at a tavern downtown, I was caught," Holmes said as he closed the door.

"You were caught!"

"Yes, but they left me alone for a few minutes and I escaped. Would you mind?" he said holding up his right wrist still bound in the handcuffs.

"Where did that come from?" Hargreave asked as he took out his keys and unlocked the cuffs.

"They handcuffed me to a post in the saddle room of a stable which is the reason for all the muck."

"This is one of ours," Hargreave said as he examined the handcuffs.

"They belonged to Captain Bernard," Holmes said tossing off the hat, overcoat, and coat. He poured water to wash with and began unbuttoning his shirt.

"How did you open the other one?" Hargreave asked.

"I picked it with baling wire. It took a few minutes. I did not waste time removing the second. I wanted to be gone before they noticed," Holmes said washing his hands and face. He towelled off and donned his dressing gown and then discarded the mucked up trousers.

"Supposed to be unpickable," Hargreave said.

"Hardly. I did it entirely by touch."

"Glad you are not a criminal," Hargreave said putting the handcuffs in his pocket.

"It seems you have quite enough local ones without importing more," Holmes responded.

"That's for sure. Could they have followed you here?"

"I am certain they did not," Holmes said as he filled his pipe and held a match to it.

"Do they know who you are?"

"I stayed in character. Captain Bernard recognized me as Will Taylor, but has no reason to trace me back here."

"You might just want to stay out of that character."

"Yes. I have no intention of returning to the *Silk Glove*."

"They know someone was snooping."

"They seemed to think I was a reporter for the *New York Times*."

"That would make sense. Maybe that will put them off the scent. I don't know what they would do if they were to find you again."

"We are scheduled to leave tomorrow."

"Good. Now tell me everything you learned," Hargreave said taking out a pencil and notebook.

"That will take some time."

"I have all night if we need it."

"I can confirm that Talbot Smith is running badger games, panel games, murphy games, and probably many more swindles in his saloon at Fifth Avenue and 29th Street. Police officers are receiving money from Smith and passing it up the ranks. Captain

Bernard is heavily involved, but it seems to be much more widespread than that. There are many other public officials involved as well. I saw an envelope passed to a magistrate. Most of the people seem to be connected with the Polar Star Lodge."

"They have your notebook. So they will know what you were observing."

Holmes smiled.

"No, it was part of my disguise. I knew that taking notes of my observations would be dangerous. The notebook contains snatches of dialogue and bits of scenes for a play as well as some notes about stories I read in the newspapers."

"So you made what could have been a liability into proof of your background story."

"Precisely. I memorized names and important observations and wrote them down afterwards."

Sherlock Holmes opened a bureau drawer and took out a few pieces of paper. The top one contained a list of names and nothing more. He picked up a pencil and added a few more.

"Here are names of people I know are involved."

Hargreave took the paper and read it. He shook his head.

"Deeper than we thought. Might require a state investigation to uproot this, but go on. Give me everything you have."

Sherlock Holmes started back on his first day of clandestine surveillance and recounted the relevant activities from memory, giving Hargreave dates and times. He provided in-depth descriptions of people when he did not have names. It took a couple hours and filled up Hargreave's notebook, but the New Yorker was quite satisfied with the results.

"What do you plan to do?" Holmes asked.

"I'll give this information to Kealy, but I think he is going to lay off it for a while. They are going to be on their guard. This may take years, maybe even decades to crack if the roots are that deep. This information will help us convince the right people that an investigation needs to start higher up. Thanks for your help," Hargreave said extending his hand.

"It has been an interesting experience," Holmes replied and

shook his hand.

"Stay in touch once you return to England," Hargreave said. "Maybe there will be other opportunities for us to help each other out."

"I will do that," Holmes said.

Hargreave left. Holmes finished his pipe and caught a few hours' sleep. Later there was a knock at the door. Holmes snapped awake.

"Who is it?" he asked.

A child's voice said, "Excuse me sir, but I have a note for you."

Holmes rose from the bed, picking up his dressing gown as he went. He unlatched the door and opened it a crack. A young bellboy stood there with a note on a tray. Sherlock Holmes took the note, dropped a coin on the tray, and closed the door.

It was from Sassanof. A snowstorm between New York and Chicago had shut down the railroads. Their departure would be delayed. Holmes went back to bed. There was one thing he needed to do before he left New York, but there was no urgency about it if they were not leaving that day. The greater urgency was how to fill his time. So he went back to sleep. He woke about noon, dressed, and joined the rest of the company in the dining room. Afterwards he returned to his room and bundled up the "American clothes."

He walked to the theatre, entered through the stage door, and made his way to the costume rooms. He left the bundle there with a note apologizing for their state. As he was making his way out of the theatre, he heard voices around a corner that made him stop in his tracks. One was Mr Palmer, the manager of the theatre. The other was Captain Bernard.

"'Will Taylor?' No, officer, there hasn't been any playwright hanging about the theatre by that name," Palmer was saying.

"Tall, thin fellow with black hair."

"No writers like that have been around here."

"Let me know if you see him."

"What is he wanted for?" Palmer asked.

"Oh, nothing like that," Captain Bernard, said laughing and

trying to lighten the tone. We found his notebook last night and want to return it to him."

Bernard's attempt at making light of his search was not convincing even if one did not know what Holmes did. If they had merely found the notebook, then how could he describe this Will Taylor? Holmes waited until Bernard had gone and Palmer had moved to another part of the building before making his way to the stage door and back to the hotel. He collected more newspapers and returned to his room. He lit his pipe and read the newspapers.

Sherlock Holmes had seen news stories about the storm for several days. On March 17th, the papers reported that several trains of the Mountain Division of the Union Pacific were blockaded by snow in the Sierra Nevada. By the 18th, the storm was raging in the Rocky Mountains. On the 21st, it was wreaking havoc over Michigan, Wisconsin, Iowa, and Missouri, but especially Illinois. It reached New York on the 22nd.

Yet it was not the storm that concerned Holmes nor the policeman (or men) who may be hunting for him. It was the empty hours. He had gone from doing secret surveillance between eight theatrical performances a week to no obligations at all other than that he be ready when the train was. He did not think it was wise to walk the streets. He was rid of the clothes he had worn and he had his makeup kit with him, but he was not keen to play tag with these people unnecessarily. One important thing he had learned from his investigations was that it was difficult to know whom to trust, especially among the police.

The day passed and then the next. The winds howled and snow fell. He read the papers, played his violin, and paced the floor of his room like a caged tiger. On Wednesday there was a knock on his door as he was playing a piece by Paganini. He set aside his violin hoping it was word that they were soon to depart. Sassanof was at the door. Sherlock Holmes invited him in.

"Ah, I had heard that you played the violin. It has its own way of speaking, doesn't it?"

"Indeed."

"We missed you at dinner. In fact, we've missed you at a

number of meals recently. However, what you do on your own time is your business. While you seemed a bit distracted during the last few performances, I don't believe the audience noticed. You will be glad to hear that we have received word that they are clearing the tracks and we shall be departing for Chicago in the morning."

Chapter 18

Westward

"I travelled in my youth, took to the stage...."
Neville St. Clair, "The Man with the Twisted Lip"

Holmes was glad to be leaving New York. He had known from the beginning that his work for Hargreave was not a puzzle he could resolve to his usual satisfaction. Yet the proceedings had been instructive, and had reminded him that acting was merely a path to his career as a detective. On the other hand, the last few days of inaction waiting for the snowstorm to pass had been extremely annoying. He was looking forward to being on stage again.

The air was cold and the snow was deep when they boarded the train in New York. They pulled their overcoats and scarves close, and hurried to find a seat hoping the car would warm up once they were under way. Soon the engine began chugging north along the Hudson River pushing the snow aside as it moved. The trees and fields were draped with snow. Ice clung to the shore of the river and stretched its fingers across the water. The view out the windows only made the passengers feel colder. The conductor lit a stove at one end of each car, but its warmth did not spread far. Some passengers stood huddled next to it for a while vainly hoping to take some of the heat back to their seats with them. Near Albany, the train crossed a bridge over the Hudson and headed west. They passed through more forests, farms, and villages. More than half a day later they rattled past the famed stockyards and arrived at Chicago's Great Central Station.

The snow was even deeper in Chicago when they arrived there. Attempts had been made to sweep off walks and streets, but the effect was to create narrow passages between piles and drifts of snow, which stood several feet high in some places. The women struggled to lift their skirts over the accumulated ice and snow, and shake it out of the folds as they entered the carriage. The cold and snow distracted them from the views of the city. Yet now and then, as they rode through the streets they saw blackened brick and stone that stood out in stark contrast to the snow, a reminder of the great fire that nearly destroyed this city only a few years before. They were on their way to McVicker's Theatre which had been built in August of 1872, a year after the fire destroyed its predecessor. The theatre was owned and managed by James H. McVicker, a man who began his career in the theatre as a comedic actor before changing to management. Mr McVicker greeted them and gave them a tour of the theatre, then begged that they excuse him.

"I have an appointment with the architect who designed this building. Some questions came up after the recent snowstorm that I wish to discuss with him. Nothing that should concern you."

Mr McVicker left the English actors upon the stage and headed towards the front of the building. A carriage pulled up as Mr McVicker looked out front. He stepped out and offered his hand to the man who descended to the curb. A young woman peeked out the window of the carriage and another scolded her and pulled her back.

"I hope you do not mind," the man said with an accent that spoke of a past east of the Black Sea, worn smooth by decades in the States. "My cousin and her daughter are visiting from New Jersey. When her daughter heard that my work was taking me to a theatre I had designed, she said she wanted to see it. She insisted on coming along. These children born in America, they are headstrong."

"Not at all, Mr Adler," James McVicker said. "Please invite her in to see your lovely theatre."

The two women descended from the carriage. Mr McVicker led them through the vestibule and opened a door at the back of the auditorium for a peek.

"It is so beautiful," the younger woman said. "It makes me want to sing."

"Sshh. Please, you will disturb the actors. They are rehearsing."

"Oh, may I watch?" she said with excitement. "I have never seen a play."

"Come, Irene, we must go and let these men do their work," her mother said.

Irene sat down.

"Please, just for a few minutes," she said.

Her mother threw up her hands.

"*Shtiferish meydl!*" (Naughty girl!) her mother whispered.

"I will be quiet!" she whispered back.

Mr Adler looked helplessly at Mr McVicker. He had no idea how to handle young women.

"Well, I don't see that there could be any harm," Mr McVicker said. "This should only take a few minutes."

Her mother sat down next to her looking annoyed, but resigned.

"You act like *shikseh*," she whispered to her daughter.

"Sssh!" her daughter responded.

"I will only be a moment," the architect said and left them alone in the auditorium.

The actors on the stage were busy running through lines and planning the stage business of their first performance. They took no note of the two ladies who sat for a few minutes in the back of the auditorium. Soon Mr Adler came for them and they returned to the carriage and departed. Mr McVicker joined the actors on the stage and asked if there was anything more he could do for them.

"We do not usually host touring acting troupes. So I am less familiar with what your needs might be."

Sassanof wanted to confer with him on staging and schedules and the two managers retired to discuss those business details.

Sassanof wanted his actors to continue the tetralogy that had been so successful in New York and Boston. However, rather than run those four plays during the matinees as well as the evening performances, he wanted them to test the plays of another of Shakespeare's tetralogies: *Henry IV 1 & 2*, *Henry V* and *Richard II* in the matinees. They would offer each individually at first then promote the sequence if they were well received. Mr McVicker agreed. They hoped the variety would draw patrons to return frequently.

They also hoped the weather would be more accommodating.

It was an ambitious plan which kept the cast very busy throughout their short run in Chicago. When they were not on stage, they were studying their lines for the new plays. In fact the actors were somewhat relieved when another snowstorm struck on the 28th and performances were cancelled that day and the next. They used those days for reading lines together at the hotel. The new plays did not come off as polished as those the cast were more familiar with. At the end of their four weeks in Chicago, Sassanof concluded that he had been pushing the company too hard and they should rely on the plays already in the repertoire. The receipts had been good but not as good as in Boston or New York. The short, crowded schedule in Chicago meant that Holmes had no opportunity to make the acquaintance of the police in Chicago. However, he did find his way to the Western Union offices a few days after they arrived in Chicago and again before they left town to send his wages to his brother.

The original plan had been that they would take the train to Philadelphia on May 1st. Instead they were taking a night express from Chicago to Omaha. That trip would take about eighteen hours. From Omaha they would take the Union Pacific railroad west to California. As they boarded the train at the Chicago Great Central Station, Holmes noticed that Sassanof was looking more anxious than he had on any previous part of their tour. The black valise with chrome hinges and corners that he was clutching probably contained the receipts from their runs in Boston, New York, and Chicago. Sassanof had paid cast and crew before leaving Chicago to distribute some of it amongst them, but he was most likely carrying substantially more. Holmes suspected their manager intended to deposit it in a bank in San Francisco for the duration of their visit there but felt keeping the surplus with them on the trip across country was necessary to cover any expenses they might encounter. Undoubtedly, he was nervous because he had heard of the train robberies in the western parts of this country.

As the train pulled past the stockyards on that spring evening the smell of manure and hay washed over them. Soon it was replaced by the scent of sweet prairie grasses. They passed by some farm fields, but increasingly they were entirely surrounded by undulating grasslands. Early in the evening, a young boy called a "butch" came through the railway car carrying a tray of goods in his hands with bags containing more hanging from his shoulders.

"Newspapers! Magazines! Peanuts! Candy! Some fruit for you, ma'am? *Guide to the Rocky Mountains*! *Adventures of Kit Carson*! *Red Knife, the Chief*, latest from Beadles & Adams, finest publisher of western adventure! Post Cards! Peanuts!"

The sun sank slowly behind the horizon and the train rushed on through the night. Most of the passengers settled in to get some kind of sleep. In the coach car they arranged coats and bags to establish some crude comfort. It was fitful sleep due to the rattling and bumping of the car, and the occasional whistle as the engineer warned any late travellers on lonely roads they crossed. The passengers who woke as the rays of dawn peeked in the windows of the railroad car saw the scenery outside the windows had changed. Rolling prairie had giving place to a succession of low brown bluffs. They passed a lake covered with ducks then more greening hills dotted with herds of grazing cattle, followed by more bluffs.

The remaining passengers were finally jarred from their slumbers by the reappearance of the butch offering packaged rolls and more reading material. When the boy had cleared the aisle, Holmes stood and stretched. He walked the length of the car and back again. He lit his pipe. A herd of shaggy ponies ran by outside the windows. Then the train passed more low hills and mires surrounded by budding willows. The whistle was sounding with increasing frequency which must mean they were nearing a town. The train rolled past a series of low buildings. He heard a passenger say it was Council Bluffs. A few minutes later the train turned westward and rattled over a long bridge. The brown Missouri River flowed sluggishly between its iron piers.

On the other side of the bridge was the city of Omaha in the state of Nebraska. One of the drawbacks of the night express from Chicago was the necessity of staying overnight in Omaha to catch the next train west, but after the long night on the train a hotel bed sounded inviting. The members of the Corycian Company left their trunks in the custody of the Union Pacific Railroad and proceeded into town to find lodging for the night. The streets of Omaha were dirty and ill-paved. The owners of shops lounged about in the doorways as if they had little commerce to keep them busy, despite the daily influx of train passengers. In any case, their demeanour was not inviting. The members of the theatrical company found a hotel and secured rooms. Then they sat down together for breakfast. Some of their company announced plans to nap after breakfast to make up for the fitful sleep the night before and others their intention of spending the rest of the day in their rooms merely to avoid the glum, dusty streets.

Holmes was among those who chose to nap in the morning, but later in the day he set out to stretch his legs. Omaha was not a very large town. He soon found he could tour the entirety of in a short period. As he strode down one dusty street, he heard gun shots coming from behind a building. He walked around it to look and found a tall, sandy-haired young man of fourteen or fifteen shooting tins off a fence. Holmes watched from a distance for a while then walked up when the shooter stopped to reload. The boy looked up at him as he approached.

"Hello, my name is William Escott. You shoot quite well," Holmes said.

"Nate Smith. Thanks. You don't sound like you are from around here."

"I'm not. I am from England."

"That's a long ways off, isn't it?"

"Yes. Beyond the Atlantic Ocean."

"Ever fired a gun?" the boy asked as he snapped the gun back together.

"Yes, shotguns mostly. Never a handgun," Holmes replied

"Want to give it a try?" the boy asked, offering his pistol.

Sherlock took the gun and examined it. It felt warm against his palm as he turned it over.

"A Colt .45?"

"Yes, called a Peacemaker," the boy said. "It was my father's."

"It has a good weight to it. I assume it has quite a kick. Shooting a handgun is different—"

"Are you gonna talk or shoot?"

Sherlock Holmes smiled, aimed the gun, and squeezed the trigger. Wood splinters flew up as the bullet nicked the top edge of the fence under the tin. The vibrations alone caused it to fall off the fence.

"My aim was a little off," Sherlock said.

Nate stared at him.

"You're kidding me. You want me to believe that was the first time you shot a pistol?"

"It was," Holmes assured him.

"Damn. I'd hate to see what you could do with practice."

"Considerably better, I would hope," Holmes said. "I underestimated the necessary angle."

"But how'd you get that close your first time? It took me weeks of practice to get that close."

"I have some knowledge of the mechanics, the force of the gunpowder, the ballistic trajectory, and I observed you handling the pistol," Holmes said returning the gun to the boy.

"Damn. Ever been in a gunfight?"

"No."

"I'm ready for one. Been practicing the 'quick draw.' Set the cans back up and I'll show you."

"Cans, tins, yes," Holmes mumbled.

"What?"

"Nothing important, just vocabulary," Sherlock Holmes said.

"You English fellers talk funny."

"That is precisely what I meant," Holmes responded as he reached the fence.

He picked the cans up from the ground, balanced them on the fence, then moved back and watched the boy draw and shoot from the hip. One can after the other flew off the fence.

"You aim entirely by the feel of the gun in your hand?" Holmes asked.

"I guess so. From practice I just got a feel for where it is aimed."

"What do you intend to do with such talents?"

"I'm going to shoot me some gunslingers."

Just then a woman came around the building.

"There you are, Nate. Come along. It is time for supper."

"All right, ma. This is Will. He was watching me shoot."

"Good day, ma'am," Sherlock Holmes said.

"Good day to you, sir," Mrs Smith said herding her son towards his supper.

Holmes walked back to the hotel where he and his fellow actors were spending the night. The company dined together that evening then separated again until the following morning. When Holmes arrived at the platform, he found it crowded with immigrants heading to California. There were men with wild, unkempt hair and beards, wearing ragged overcoats and clutching parcels, and tired women trying to control restless children. Sassanof encouraged members of the Corycian Company to stay together as if he was fearful of losing one of them on their way west. As they were boarding the train, Nate ran up to Sherlock Holmes.

"You did not tell me you were taking the train," the boy said.

"Well, I am."

"Don't be rude, Nate," his mother said catching up to him.

"Quite all right, ma'am. You are also taking the train?"

"Yes, but just as far as Laramie," she said, attempting to straighten Nate's unruly hair with her fingers. "We are going to live with my sister and her husband. Since Nate's father died, I just don't know how to handle him."

"Ma!"

"He seems a fine boy."

"He doesn't always mind and he reads too many silly dime novels."

Sherlock Holmes smiled.

"I was reproached for the same faults."

She looked at him.

"You're not wearing a holster and a gun."

"No, ma'am."

Holmes did not know what to say to Mrs Smith to make her less anxious, if anything. Soon the whistle blew and the last of the passengers scrambled aboard. The train pulled away from the station. Nate had convinced his mother to sit behind Holmes. As the train gathered speed, Nate leaned over the seat and quizzed Sherlock Holmes about where he was going and why over his shoulder.

"We are actors," Holmes told him.

"Actors? You tell stories on a stage?"

"Somewhat like that."

Langdale Pike piped up.

"Oh, come now, Escott, you can do better than that."

"What do you propose?" he replied.

"That we give these ladies and gentlemen a sample of our talents. Act 1 Scene 1 of *Romeo and Juliet*?"

Claude Dewarr looked at Joseph Reece.

"I'll be the Montagues to your Capulets."

"Done!"

The two young men jump into the aisle and began the fight between the servants that begins the play, each reciting the words of two characters. They made it a fist fight rather than a sword fight and Pike leapt in as Benvolio on cue to part them, followed by Dewitt, Escott, and Devigne in their usual roles. It slid almost seamlessly from the fight in Act 1 to the fight in Act 3 without any planning. It was a brawl in the aisle of the railway coach accompanied by Elizabethan dialogue that resulted in two dead, though the dead rose and dusted themselves after the others scattered back to their seats. Their fellow passengers applauded.

"Ordinarily we are up on a stage with costumes," Holmes explained to Nate.

"And swords," Anthony Dewitt added with a twinkle in his eye.

"Swords? Do you sword fight?" Nate asked.

"Yes," Holmes said.

"In fact, he taught the rest of us how to do it," Dewitt said.

"Any guns?"

"No guns," Holmes said.

The butch came through and Nate's mother bought one of dime novels he was offering for Nate to read. She didn't approve of them but she felt he was bothering the actors. Soon the boy settled down to reading about Kit Carson.

For a few miles the train travelled along the bluffs then headed out on the prairie. The land was flat and dotted with wild flowers that bobbed above the windswept grass like gulls at sea. The train stopped for a short break at the dining station at Grand Island where the passengers consumed tea, antelope chops, and steaming sweet potatoes before hurrying back to the train.

They were a few dozen miles west of Grand Island when a voice called out from above, "There are some riders following the train."

It was the brakeman who spent most of his time atop the cars. After his announcement, they heard his footsteps along the roof heading towards the engine. Less than a minute passed before they heard someone leap upon the steps of the car followed by another. Then the back door flung open and two men pushed inside and slammed the door shut behind them.

While most of the passengers saw only the guns in their hands, Sherlock Holmes scanned then from hats to boots. Their hats were common American felt hats, battered, dusty, and stained with sweat. They had tattered kerchiefs tied about the lower half of their faces. Their shirts were old and worn, in need of mending and cleaning. One of them wore a ragged grey jacket and both wore grey trousers, the remains perhaps of a military uniform. Their boots were scuffed and scraped. They were long past any sign of polish and the leather was cracked. Both men were perspiring freely. Perhaps it was just the result of their exertions catching the train, but he did not think so. These were nervous and desperate men.

Holmes eyed the other passengers. The male passengers had frozen. The women clung to each other. Sassanof was clutching the valise tighter. No one in the car was armed, except one. Even as the thought crossed Holmes' mind, Nate stood up from the seat behind Holmes, turning back towards the robbers and drawing his gun. Holmes jumped from his seat to push Nate down, but it was too late. At the sight of the gun, one of the nervous robbers fired. Nate fell. His mother cried out. The other robber cursed.

"There wasn't supposed to be killin'," he cried.

Holmes grabbed Nate's gun as it fell. Crouched now between Nate and the robbers with the Colt 45 in his hand, he fired and struck the shoulder of the robber who had fired at Nate. The other robber yelled again, but did not fire. He grabbed his wounded companion, flung the door open, pushed him out, and jumped from the train himself.

The passengers were stunned. The entire episode had lasted only a few minutes. Holmes turned to the boy. Nate had been struck squarely in the chest and the wound was bleeding profusely despite his mother's attempts to staunch it with her handkerchief. Nate looked Sherlock Holmes in the eyes. He reached up and placed his bloody hands over the smoking gun still in Holmes's hands.

"Keep it," he said and closed his eyes for the last time.

Holmes looked up at Nate's mother.

"I never want to see that thing again," she said.

Before he could respond, Ida pushed past Holmes to comfort the grieving mother. He stood and backed off, took out his handkerchief, and used it to wipe the boy's blood from his hands and the pistol. Then he stuck the gun in his pocket. He walked to the back of the car and closed the door left open by the would-be robbers through which dust and coal smoke was entering the car. He leaned against the wall, loaded his pipe, and lit it.

The conductor had been alerted by the brakeman and entered with a drawn gun. He soon realized the excitement was over. He notified the engineer and the brakeman, but there were no towns in this part of the state. There was no point in stopping the train. They would report the murder and attempted robbery at the next stop. Nate's body was wrapped in a blanket and moved to the luggage car. The train continued westward.

The next stop was the dining station at Sidney, Nebraska. It was a crude structure of boards and canvas. The passengers scrambled out with wary looks down the line behind them and sought the meagre shelter of the station. The telegraph boy lagged behind setting his box near one of the telegraph poles that ran along the railroad tracks.

"What are you going to do?" Sherlock Holmes asked.

"There is no telegraph at this station," he said. "I am going to tap in and wire ahead."

The boy climbed the pole and connected a wire to the telegraph line. He scrambled down and connected his telegraph key to the wire and began manipulating it. Sherlock Holmes watched him. They were the only ones out on the plain next to the train. The revolver still bulged in his coat pocket. Holmes did not imagine himself as guarding the telegraph boy. He did not expect the robbers had followed the train. They had been scared off by the deadly exchange and mostly likely headed the opposite direction. Holmes did not want to talk about what had happened and he wasn't hungry either.

He was, however, curious. He had sent and received telegrams before but never seen a telegraph in operation. The boy had released the key and it soon began producing sounds. The boy seemed to understand the sounds it made as if it was a spoken language. He wrote down the response. When the boy was done and was detaching the wire, Holmes asked about it.

"That's Morse code?"

"Yup," the boy said.

As he was placing the wire back in the box, he pulled a yellowed paper from it, unfolded it, and handed it to Sherlock Holmes. Holmes saw it was the key to the code.

"May I study this?" Holmes asked.

"Uh huh. Just give it back to me before you leave the train. I know the code, but I keep it in the box in case someone else needs to use it who does not."

Just then Langdale Pike wandered out from the station.

"Escott, you had the correct idea. They served the most wretched stew with some mysterious meat."

"Prairie dog," the telegraph boy said.

"I am almost afraid to ask what a 'prairie dog' is," Pike said.

"See those little things on that hill yipping at us?" the boy said.

"Good heavens. Looks like a giant rat standing on its hind legs. I think I am going to be sick."

It was the first conversation Holmes had had with any of the Corycian Company since the encounter with the robbers. He was glad it had been on a different topic. The passengers in the rail coach had been eerily quiet since the incident, except for the occasional sob from Nate's mother. Holmes had feared that once in the station, comment would burst forth. Whether it had or not, the other passengers came trailing behind Pike, but said nothing to either of them.

The message the telegraph boy had received was that the Laramie County sheriff would meet the train in Cheyenne and nothing could be done before then. He passed this information to the conductor from whom it spread among the passengers, and the car returned to an awkward silence.

In Cheyenne, they were met by both the sheriff and another problem. When they reached the town, the conductor told them that the train would be delayed.

"There is a herd of buffalo on the tracks west of town," he said.

"Well, make them move," Sassanof said.

The conductor smiled.

"You don't make a herd of buffalo move by just blowing the train whistle. We aren't going anywhere for a while. Neither is any other train heading west. The railroad has wired for some buffalo hunters but it might be several days before they arrive."

The delay was somewhat fortuitous because otherwise the train would not have waited for the inquest and the passengers in the last passenger coach car would have been forced to take another train. Sheriff Nick O'Brien boarded the car to speak to the passengers. His brogue identified him as a native born Irishman transplanted to the American West, a revelation that surprised the English ladies and gentlemen among the passengers. His accent was a bit worn from decades in the States, but unmistakable to them.

"From ah've been told, the uh, incident, occurred in Nebraska and thus out of our jurisdiction. But oit would be impractical to send ya back to Nebraska, and the trains from Nebraska are being held up until we cahn clear the tracks west of here, oi've been deputized t' hold an inquest here on behalf of the state of Nebraska. A jury hahs been rounded up and is ahwaitin' us in the courthouse. So if ya would follow me, whe'll try to conclude this mahtter ahs soon ahs possible."

Sheriff O'Brien descended from the train. No one moved for an instant. Then Ida led Mrs Smith from the train car and the rest followed. Sherlock Holmes trailed the other passengers and noticed that two deputies followed him. The line of passengers proceeded through the dusty streets with the demeanour of a funeral procession and filed up the courthouse steps. The brakeman was already in the courtroom before them and he was called to testify first. He described how he had seen the two men ride their horses up alongside the train and was afraid they were going to try to mount it. He had warned the rear passenger car and then gone forward to warn the others. He could not describe the men because he had seen them at a distance, riding fast, and wearing masks. The conductor then testified that he had approached the car cautiously, but discovered the robbers had already come and gone.

Then they called Sherlock Holmes to the stand as William Escott. He had decided to remain in that identity, for only one man in the room knew him as anything else. He told how he had heard the men climb aboard the train and turned around in his seat towards them. When he realized that the boy was going to challenge them, he had tried to pull him down below the seats but reacted too late. He then used the boy's gun to shoot one of them.

"Whaht did they do then?" the sheriff asked.

"They panicked and jumped off the train," Holmes said. "I don't believe they had ever robbed a train before."

"Why do you think that?"

"They were very nervous. I think that even the shooting was

nervous reaction to the sight of the gun."

"Cahn ya describe them?"

"Their faces were covered. So I doubt I can provide much that is useful," Holmes said but then proceeded to provide their heights and a detailed description of their clothes."

"Worn grey pahnts and jahcket?"

"Possibly part of a uniform," Holmes said.

"Loikely confederates," the sheriff said.

Nate's mother and the other passengers confirmed his testimony and had nothing to add. The coroner's jury quickly returned a verdict of manslaughter and the witnesses were dismissed.

Sassanof went to send a telegram to the theatre in San Francisco to tell them they might be a few days late and then to find rooms for the company. Several of the men from the train wanted to ride out to see the herd of buffalo. Holmes joined them as they found a stable and hired some horses. When they said what they were about the stableman told them that the herd was northwest of town.

"You can just follow along the railroad tracks right to them. A number of people from town have gone out to shoot at them but it was not been enough to disturb them. They are feeding off the fresh spring grass and don't seemed to be planning to move until they've eaten their fill. Don't get too close. They can be mean, and deadly."

They followed the stableman's directions. It felt good to lope along after being cooped up in the train. They followed the tracks past a rocky ridge. A quarter mile ahead they saw a dark heaving sea of bison that covered the tracks and stretched northward between the ridge and the mountain front. The large shaggy animals were snorting, milling about, and eating whatever they saw. They had arched backs, horns that curved up from the sides of their head, and bushy tails to swat at flies.

"That's bloody amazing," Langdale Pike said.

"There must be thousands of them," Dewitt said.

The actors kept their distance from the herd and watched from horseback. But some of the other young men rode towards the herd firing guns. A few of the larger beasts turned and charged towards them, forcing all the young men to retreat.

The ride out to the herd seemed to have broken the dark mood, or perhaps it was the ride combined with the inquest. There was some amount of relief to having the story out. In any case, the young men were more talkative as they rode back to town. After they returned the horses to the stables, the actors heard that their manager had reserved rooms for them at the hotel. The ride had given them an appetite so they repaired to the dining room of the hotel for dinner.

In the dining room the heads of large game animals stared down on the diners from the ceiling. It was somewhat disturbing and occasionally the actors and actresses would glance over their shoulders at the glass-eyed beasts. After dinner they toured the town. Cheyenne was more substantial than Omaha, but still much smaller and rougher than the American cities they had visited in the East. In addition to the courthouse and the hotel, it had five churches, two theatres, a jail, a city hall, and a schoolhouse, plus a number of concert halls, saloons, gambling establishments, houses, and stores. The people in the town were a mix of railroad workers, ranchers, farmers, miners, and the shopkeepers who served them.

While the rest of the company were at supper that evening, Sherlock Holmes stepped out into the dark and paused to light his pipe. He strolled away from the buildings and the voices into night, leaving a trail of smoke behind him. The night was calm and a million stars twinkled overhead. Some of the stars to the south were different stars than those he knew in England. The moon was the same, though higher in the sky. He sensed someone else was there, yet no one had come from the buildings behind him.

"I have no money on me," he said to the night.

"I have little use for white man's money," came a response from the darkness. "But you do not sound like most white men."

The words came from behind him and to the west. He turned towards the voice, but he could see nothing. The voice was that of a young man.

"I am not an American," Holmes said, "I am from England.

England is across the ocean to the east."

"Where the white men first came from?"

"Some of them."

One shadow separated from the rest and formed a silhouette against the stars.

"My father was a white man, a trader. Life was good when I was small. The white traders and the Indians lived in peace. Even when he sent me to school in St. Louis, life was better than now. Now white men herd us like cattle and kill our women and children."

"I mean you no harm."

"You are not afraid of me."

"Should I be?"

"Most white men fear the Indian like they fear a wild animal."

"Do you intend to hurt me?"

"I could."

"You have no weapon other than that rock in your hand."

"I could have another."

"You would not be brandishing that rock if you had a better weapon. I do not fear the rock."

"You have tobacco."

"I do. Would you like some?"

"I have nothing to trade."

"Then it will be a gift."

The shadow came towards him. Holmes heard the rock fall. He held out his tobacco pouch. The young man produced a small pipe from a satchel he carried. He filled the pipe and returned the pouch. Holmes lit a match and the Indian took it and lit his pipe. Then he sat down upon the ground with his ankles crossed and his knees akimbo. Holmes joined him and the two of them smoked in silence for some time. In the moonlight Holmes could see that young man wore his hair long tied behind his back. He wore no shirt, only breeches of some type of leather. At last Holmes broke the silence.

"In my country is it a tradition for people to introduce themselves when they meet. My name is Sherlock Holmes."

"I am called *Haycott Payay*. My father also gave me the name James, James McBeal."

"Your father was a Scot?" Holmes asked with surprise.

"Yes."

"I was born not far from Scotland."

"He said it was across the ocean. We are nearer kin than these Americans."

"Perhaps we are. Who are your mother's people?"

"We call ourselves *Tsitsistas*. White men call us Cheyenne."

"Like the name of this town."

"Yes."

"Why are you here?"

"This is my home. My people have roamed these lands since long before the white men came. Two generations ago some of our people went south with the *Hetanevo'eo'o* Arapahos, but the white men have killed the buffalo and the deer, and cut the trees, and eaten the forage our horses need. Then they say that we mean them harm and shoot our people and burn our camps. We became angry and went to war with them. Then we made peace, but they herd us to a reservation. There is little game and not enough to eat. Even when my people try to do as they say, they beat us, make us prisoners, and shoot at us. Some of us escaped and ran. We hoped to join our brothers in the north. It was a slow journey looking for food and hiding from the soldiers. I travelled with some elders. I tried to help them, but they did not complete the journey. They joined the ancestors. I had to go on alone. At last I am here."

"Why are you here now?"

"I am here because the buffalo are here and our northern brothers will come hunting them. I will join them."

"If the soldiers catch you, they will take you back?"

"Or kill me."

"Then why are you near these buildings risking capture?"

"Looking for food. I have not eaten in many days. I smelled your tobacco. It had been many days as well. Thank you."

"Wait here. I will bring food."

The young native melted into the shadows. Holmes walked to the hotel dining room. When he returned to where he had left the Cheyenne there was no sign of him. As Holmes looked around *Haycott Payay* reappeared and took the plate he was offered. They sat down upon the ground again. The young Cheyenne ate the meat and fried potatoes hungrily. When he was done, Holmes spoke again.

"Would you give me a gift in return?"

"I have nothing."

"Could you teach me to disappear into the shadows as you do?"

"Now? Too much to learn in one night."

"We will be here as long as the buffalo block the railway tracks. We will leave when they are gone and so will you."

"If I find my brothers before they are gone, I will not come back here."

"I understand. We will each leave when we must."

Haycott Payay showed Sherlock Holmes how to become part of a shadow rather than trying to hide behind it. After a few hours of study they parted and Holmes returned to the hotel.

In the morning the actors heard from the hotel manager that a message had been sent to Mrs Smith's sister and she had come down to Cheyenne and taken Mrs Smith and her son's body back to the ranch. The news brought the tragedy fresh to their minds and lowered their mood. Then Sassanof announced that he had booked them for a performance that night at McDaniel's Theatre. They were going to do *Romeo and Juliet* in their usual attire since their costumes were packed in their trunks in the custody of the railroad. After lunch they went to survey this theatre. They passed through a bar covered with frescoes of Mount Vesuvius and the Bay of Naples, and into the "theatre" which was a large room full of chairs and tables. The stage was narrow. The drop-curtain was covered with Greek nudes. Statues of the Venus de Medici and another undressed lady of colossal proportions posed at the wings. At each side of the hall are tiers of boxes reached by long narrow flights of stairs. Next door was the gambling salon, a large room with a bar at the end and long tables at each side arranged for *rouge et noir*, roulette, keno, and poker.

"How low we have sunk," Sebastian Devigne whispered to Claude Dewarr, out of Sassanof's hearing.

Yet Devigne played Romeo with all his usual passion to the hooting and shouting of the audience. This audience was different from those they had played to in the East. They were noisier, less sophisticated and obviously intoxicated. After the performance Holmes took some food to the area where he had met *Haycott Payay* the night before. The Cheyenne appeared and accepted the plate. As they smoked their pipes afterwards, Holmes explained why he came later that evening.

"I have seen how white men tell their stories on a stage. This is what you do?" *Haycott Payay* responded.

"This is what I do now, but I am training to discover bad men and stop them."

"This is why you want to learn these things?"

"Yes."

Haycott Payay nodded.

Sherlock Holmes handed the young Cheyenne his tobacco pouch.

"Take this. I can get more."

Haycott Payay took it and tucked it in his bag.

"Now, I teach you more."

He showed Holmes how to follow prey without being seen or heard, even in daylight. Holmes practiced the techniques as he learned them. It was an odd game played in the dark between the young English detective and the young Cheyenne warrior, but it was one that would serve Sherlock Holmes well for many years.

The next morning the Corycian Company learned they were to be spared from repeating their performance at McDaniel's Theatre. Word spread over breakfast that before dawn a group of mounted Cheyenne had swooped down on the buffalo herd. They had killed several dozen in rapid succession and driven the remainder northward. As they were hauling away the spoils of their hunt, soldiers from Fort Laramie had advanced on them. The Cheyenne being pursued by the soldiers had pushed the buffalo even further north before fading off into the mountains. Railroad men were currently inspecting the tracks. If they were sound and clear the trains would move that day.

A couple of hours later they were told that they should be prepared to board that morning. The passengers surged to the platform and piled back in the railroad cars as soon as they could. The engine throbbed and hissed steam. The whistle blew. The doors slammed and the drive wheels began turning, pulling the cars west of town. It wasn't long before they reached the area that had been occupied by the herd. All around them was turmoil. The grass was pounded down and the soil churned up by thousands of hooves. Manure dotted the landscape and as they pull through the area the buzz of flies was so loud that they could hear it over the sound of the train.

"My God, it looks like there was a battle here," Pike said.

"I wonder how long it takes to recover," Holmes asked.

"A few good thunderstorms will do it," said the conductor. "The hail pounds down the soil, breaks up the chips, and the rain washes them away."

"Chips?"

"Buffalo Chips. Dung."

"Ah."

Soon after they passed a station appropriately named Hazard. The train steamed westward and upward as if to mount to the sky. The terrain was different from the prairie they had crossed in the Nebraska. The grass fell away as they mounted between piles of granite. They passed other small stations. The engine laboured pulling them higher and higher, finally reaching a treeless windblown summit where it stopped. There was a roundhouse, a turntable, and a windmill next to a water tank. The small town of Sherman could be seen a short distance away. The engine took on coal and water and the entire train was inspected. Then they headed down from the summit through a grove cut through solid granite. They came out of this artificial cavern on to a spindly steel bridge that swayed under the weight of the train and threatened to plunge them to the chasm below. As the train crawled slowly across the long vibrating span some passengers held their breath then let it out with a sigh when the tracks rested on solid earth again. The train passed through long roofed galleries of planks and beams nailed together in the crudest manner. Then they lurched down the mountains toward Laramie City where the train stopped and the passengers were shepherded into the Thornburg House for the midday meal. Some of the ladies seemed a bit weak in the knees entering the dining hall after the ride through the mountains and were hesitant to board again after their meal. Yet they soon were all back in their seats, and the train plunged downward through grey mountains, rumbling through more snow sheds, winding over narrow gorges, and shooting past many small stations. By the time the train stopped at Rawlins, the passengers gratefully descended from the train, many with nerves on edge from the wild ride. They were ushered to the Maxwell House and had no idea what they ate. All they knew was that the ground was solid and unmoving below their feet. After supper, the conductor hurried them back on the train with a knowing smile.

The train began climbing again after Rawlins, but it was a slower ascent than that out of Cheyenne. The sun was low in the sky and soon set behind the mountain they were ascending. It was dark by the time they reached the other side and began a long, slow descent. Most passengers settled down to sleep as the train crossed the deserts of western Wyoming. Dawn was breaking as the train was pulling into Green River City, whistle going full blast. Stretching stiff joints and feeling falsely reassured that they had passed the worst of the journey, the passengers filed into the Desert House for breakfast.

Holmes knew better. He had purchased a guide from the butch that described the route. He knew the journey ahead was much more dramatic than that behind them, but he had also ridden trains through the Alps years ago. He was not surprised by the plunges and climbs they had met so far. At the Desert House they were served fried eggs and hoe cakes with syrup and thick slabs of butter, with tea and fresh milk.

The air was thinner and crisper here. Much revived the passengers climbed aboard the coaches again. From Green River the train began another slow ascent, gently passing several stations, travelling through a tunnel cut through a mountain, and then descending again towards Evanston. Here they entered a verdant river valley where the train stopped for dinner. The dining hall at Evanston was called the Mountain Trout House. It lived up to its name by serving them fresh mountain trout, warm bread, and baked beans.

Not far out of Evanston they left Wyoming and entered the territory called Utah. They also began to descend in a rush between the great cliffs of Echo Canyon before turning at nearly a right angle and sweeping across another valley then past a station labelled "Devil's Gate." They swung around a mountain and through a narrow pass and over a trestle bridge and out to a green valley again. The train roared on through the valley as if anxious to meet the mountains on the other side and plunged into Weber Canyon. Suddenly the Great Salt Lake spread out before them as they exited the canyon. Then down and northward around the lake at nearly a level grade, roaring past Promontory Point station where the golden stake had connected east and west, and on around the lake then west as if to chase the sun before it set. But the train stopped before the sunset at some nondescript and nameless dining station somewhere in the alkali desert where they were served some unknown hash that they ate without thinking with eyes wide with the sights seen.

The sky was still aglow when they wandered out to the coach and claimed their seats again. The sun was behind the great mountains ahead which they had failed to notice before. They travelled on a couple more hours. Then they stopped in the dark, not just to take on coal and water, but to add another engine. Those who noticed trembled at what must lie ahead if two engines were needed when one had been enough for all they had encountered so far. A hint of something new was mixing with the smell of coal smoke in the night air. Then the two engines began to turn their powerful wheels and they slowly ascended the winding canyon of the Truckee River rising eighty feet to the mile. Pine and fir forests replaced sagebrush. Snorting and puffing they rose until Donner Lake glimmered below them in the moonlight encircled by forested mountains.

Sherlock Holmes did not sleep that night. He still saw the image of Nate lying dead in his mother's arms. Yet it was a thought that had passed through his mind at that moment that haunted him more: Nate Smith had been about the same age as Jonathan Beckwith. He had not thought of Jonathan since they had rescued Arthur and Edward the previous summer. He had no idea whether he was in Yorkshire, or London, or somewhere else. He had felt responsible for the boy when they were together, but realized at that moment he did not even know if he was alive. He had not known Nate more than a day yet had felt culpable for his death. He had been too slow to realize what the boy would do. Yet with the thought of Jonathan it struck him that he could not save everyone. That thought was in direct opposition of the oath he had sworn when he had decided to become a detective a few years before. It was not a notion that set easy with him.

With these thoughts churning about in his head, Sherlock Holmes watched the train crest the Sierras in the moonlight, and noticed how quiet the train became as it descended without the aid of steam, sometimes nearly nose down. He smelled the hot metal of smoking brakes and saw sparks shooting from the train wheels in the dark.

The train did not stop at Dutch Flat, but roared past, whistle blowing. Those miners still abed heard the train's scream and rolled out to light the fire and boil the coffee. Holmes saw the blasted and water-worn slopes surrounding the gold mining camp flash past and minutes later he felt the train careen around a sharp turn and drop at Cape Horn as it clung to the face of a cliff over the gorge of the American River two thousand feet below.

The train rushed on as the sun rose behind it, finally slowing to a stop at Colfax in the state of California on the western face of the Sierra Nevada Mountains. The morning air was fragrant and children swarmed the platform selling strawberries. Mysterious smells emanated from Chinese shops lining the railroad. The passengers were led to a dining hall contracted by the railroad where they were offered fried ham, potatoes, fruit, and eggs.

The train left the extra engine behind at Colfax and headed west at a more sedate pace through forests and past farm fields. There were more frequent stops to off-load and on-load passengers. By the time they reached Sacramento the pine and fir trees had given way to cedars, palm trees, and prickly pear cactus. They had lunch at Sacramento and boarded for the last time with a mixed of excitement and exhaustion.

When the train at last reached Oakland, members of the Corycian Company rose stiffly from the passenger car and descended to the platform. Weary but excited, they were immediately entangled in the bustle of transferring themselves and their luggage to the ferry. They stretched their legs on the long wharf, trying to avoid being separated in the throng of humanity heading to the ferryboat. They embarked and huddled together against the railing. As the ferry pushed off, they inhaled the salt air, and cleared their lungs of the coal smoke. They had thirty minutes to take stock of their surroundings. The sun lay low in the west, tinging the ocean gold -- the Pacific Ocean! They had crossed both an ocean and a continent in the last six months and found themselves at another ocean. That alone was remarkable to contemplate. Behind them were the mountains they had crossed. Before them was San Francisco.

250

Chapter 19

San Francisco

> *"It must have been a young man, and an active one, too,*
> *besides being an incomparable actor."*
> Sherlock Holmes, *A Study in Scarlet*

From across the bay, San Francisco seemed to squat uncomfortably on a cluster of hills. Even as they drew closer to the city, the sun sank below the horizon and details faded. In the twilight, San Francisco became a silhouette of low buildings against the blue sky. At last, the ferry found the pier with a thump.

"All ashore!"

As they disembarked, the ferry passengers were assaulted by an army of hack drivers, express-men, and hotel runners clamouring for attention. Randy Foster made arrangements for transportation of the Corycian Company and their luggage. They piled into cabs. Their destination was a boarding house called Normandie House on Stockton Street, east of Chinatown. The crates of the theatrical costumes and properties would be transported to the theatre in the morning. The English travellers looked out the windows as they were driven through the streets. Some streets were lined with shops with brightly lit front windows full of merchandise and lamps outside their doorways inviting shoppers in. The windows of hotels and saloons glowed,and light spilt out of their doors as they swung open to admit or discharge patrons. Yet other streets were dark or dimly lit like mysterious voids.

The carriages stopped before a simple wooden structure with "Normandie House" written over the door. It was two stories with bow windows on both floors. It was not a glamorous structure, but their needs were simple.

"All I want is a hot bath and a soft bed," Ida Newton said.

The actresses, and Sally, the dresser, echoed her sentiments. But some of the young men had other ideas when they realized that the famed Barbary Coast was a few blocks away.

"I'm ready for a little adventure after being cooped up for so long," Anthony Dewitt said.

"I am curious," Joseph Reece said. "Men in the pub in Cheyenne were talking about the Barbary Coast."

Claude Dewarr and Sebastian Devigne fell in with their plans to explore the Barbary Coast. Sassanof knew he could not stop them. If he attempted to forbid it, they would slip out anyway. He knew what an adventure this tour was to these young men, and they had been well-behaved thus far.

"Don't be out too late. We will rehearse tomorrow morning. We are two days behind in our schedule already."

The young men agreed.

"And stay out of trouble!" he reminded them.

Langdale Pike turned to William Escott.

"I am famished and have a notion for some Chinese. I have been told Tong Ling's in Jackson Street is quite good. Care to join me?"

Curious himself, Holmes agreed.

In 1876, San Francisco's Chinatown was seven blocks long and three blocks wide, but it housed over fifteen thousand Chinese. It was a maze of narrow roads and alleyways crowded with a mix of dingy brick buildings and flimsy shacks. That evening the streets were teeming with Chinese men wearing close fitting silk caps or flattened conical straw hats. Their hair was shaved in front and worn in long queues down their backs. They wore long jackets with wide sleeves over loose trousers with wide legs. The two young actors saw few women out on the streets of Chinatown. People from other countries passed Pike and Escott as they walked by shops with sign-boards over doors or window-frames with Chinese characters painted in gold, black, and red, lit by flickering candles.

Tong Ling's restaurant lay on the outskirts of Chinatown only a few blocks from Normandie House. Two large Chinese lanterns hung from a small balcony above the entrance. As they approached the door, a Chinese man with a straw hat passed in front of them with baskets laden with vegetables suspended from either end of a bamboo pole. Suddenly a group of outlandishly-dressed young men shot from behind the two actors. One of them upset the man's baskets with a blow from a short, stout stick. His companions pushed the Chinese man to the ground. Before the young man holding the bludgeon could hit the fallen man, Sherlock Holmes stepped forward and yanked the weapon from his hand from behind. The young man spun around and the others followed suit. As the gang turned upon Holmes, he saw that they were a mix of boys and girls. Their leader looked to be about Holmes' own age. He wore a ruffled white shirt, black string tie, velvet waistcoat, olive frock coat, knee-high boots, and tight fawn-coloured trousers. His younger companions were dressed similarly, even the young girls. Their leader extracted brass knuckles from his pocket and slid them on his right hand as he squinted at Holmes.

"You will pay for that," he said.

But his composure was disturbed by a cabbage that smacked him in the back of his head. As the young men had faced each other, people had swarmed from the surrounding buildings. They had picked up the fallen vegetables and began pelting them at the gang members. Pike, who was in the line of fire for some of the vegetables that missed their targets, began sending them back at the gang. The vegetables were followed by sticks and pieces of brick until the interlopers were convinced to withdraw. Holmes extended a hand to the Chinese man who had been knocked down, and others gather up his baskets and the bruised vegetables. He bowed to Holmes and hurried off.

"I keep forgetting how dangerous your company is, Escott," Pike said from behind him.

A man was waving to them from the doorsill of the restaurant.

"Come in! Come in! I give you a good meal," called Tong Ling.

They entered. The interior of the Chinese restaurant consisted of a single large room filled with numerous small tables. The furniture was made of black, polished wood. Red and gold paper lanterns hung from the ceiling. A savoury odour pervaded the room. Their host led them to a table. Chinese diners at the tables they passed smiled and nodded before returning to their meals.

"Thank you. Thank you for saving my friend. Those hoodrums attack us for no reason. Beat us and try to cut hair."

"Hoodrums?" Pike asked.

"Forgive my English. 'Hoodlums' those are called around here. You are not from here."

"We are from England."

Tong Ling looked sharply at them.

"I have met Engrish men before. Not like you. Here we feed you a good supper. You not pay."

Another man appeared with a tray and served them tea in little cups. Tea was followed by a stream of blue china plates containing dishes savoury and sweet.

"Your intrepid nature does have its benefits," Pike said.

"Such as?" Holmes asked.

"A free meal."

"That was not my plan," Escott retorted.

"You had a plan? My plan involved consuming vegetables, not throwing them or ducking them. That is still my plan."

After they had eaten, their host reappeared and asked if they were pleased.

"Yes, quite pleased. A friend in London had recommended your restaurant and he did not exaggerate."

"Pardon me for asking, but you said the 'hoodlums' as you called them, try to cut hair. Why would they do that?" Holmes asked.

"They try to cut this," he said, displaying his own queue. "My countrymen come to your country and work hard for many years, but they hope to return one day. The Emperor requires that we wear our hair this way. If it is cut then we would be accused of treason and hanged. So we cannot go home if it is cut."

"Do these hoodlums know this?"

"I do not know. I do not think they care."

After they left the restaurant, Escott and Pike wandered through the dimly lit streets of Chinatown. For the most part they were ignored, but a man at the entrance of one building gestured to them with a long stem pipe and invited them in. They looked in the doorway and saw a room filled with a double tier of bunks. Nearly all of them were filled with men with little trays holding a lamp and a horn box filled with the black opium paste. Most of the men were Chinese, but there were a few from other countries there, lost in the dreamy smoke of the opium. Pike and Escott shook their heads and continued on. Eventually they found themselves in Broadway where the gaslights glowed brightly. There they met Claude Dewarr and Joseph Reece.

"Have you seen Devigne or Dewitt?" Reece asked.

"No. Why?" Escott asked.

"We were separated."

"Perhaps they returned to the lodging-house?"

"Perhaps."

The four actors walked the two blocks back to the Normandie House. Reece and Dewarr regaled them with their adventures in the Barbary Coast.

"It is a mass of dance halls, concert halls, saloons, one right after another: the Thunderbolt, Cock of the Walk, the Billy Goat, the Big Dive and many more."

"All very flashy."

"Bright lights, music, and the girls!"

"We looked in at a few and they wanted to give one on Pacific Street a try."

"It is called Bull Run," Reece said.

"We went in and had a drink and talked to some girls."

"We stayed for a few minutes, but we wanted to look around more so we left. When we peeped in later they were gone."

"Devigne and Dewitt were nowhere to be found."

"We asked a few people but no one seemed to know when they left or where they had gone."

"We started back towards the lodging house, then we met you."

There was no sign of the others at the boarding house.

"We should look for them."

The four young actors headed west again.

"Show us where you last saw them," Escott said.

Reece and Dewarr led them to Bull Run. It was a three story building on Pacific Street. Laughter and music spilled out on to the street.

"It was in here. A couple of the girls had latched on to them and persuaded them to buy them drinks."

Before the entrance was a large screen covered with paper painted in bold colours. Beyond the screen men and women were drinking and dancing. The women were dressed in brightly coloured dresses that exposed their legs and bosoms. One of them approached Claude Dewarr.

"You are back and you brought some more friends," she said fawning over him.

"We are looking for our friends. Have you seen them?" he responded.

"I have a very bad memory. Buy me a drink and I might remember," she responded.

"Sorry. We just want to find our friends and leave."

A man at a nearby table stood up.

"Don't be rude to the lady. Buy her a drink."

"Please, I did not mean to be rude. Here," Dewarr said, tossing a coin to the girl.

Some other men approached looking menacing. The four actors were now backed against each other surrounded by a drunk and nasty looking crowd. Escott spoke softly to his companions.

"Let's work our way to the door. Stay together!"

Then he loudly addressed the crowd.

"No insult was intended. We are visitors to your country. We shall be on our way."

Langdale Pike led the way for the sole reason that he was facing the way they had come. He was drawing on his acting skills to try to look both large and threatening and congenial at the same time. In truth, he was terrified. A public school education had not prepared the young lord for this. An isolated bit of fisticuffs was one thing and this was entirely another. He politely said 'excuse me' and 'good evening' to each of the rogues and girls he passed.

Reece and Dewarr had gotten their education on the streets of London and were more familiar with this type of situation. They stepped sideways on either side of Pike silently staying alert. Escott brought up the rear watching for any sign of attack. As Pike reached the door, a man blocked his way. A man facing Escott drew a knife and another broke a bottle and advanced. The actors braced themselves.

"Excuse me," Pike said to the man in front of him, "I have enjoyed your hospitality immensely, but I do believe the time has come for us to leave your jolly company."

The man grinned and stepped aside. The actors rushed out the door. The crowd behind them roared with laughter.

"I am uncertain whether they intended to harm us or merely to make fools of us," Pike said.

"It could have been either," Escott said.

"I for one do not wish to stay around until they change their minds," Dewarr said.

"My curiosity has been amply sated," Reece said.

"We need to find Dewitt and Devigne and leave," Escott said.

"Let's look in these alleyways," Escott proposed.

They explored in pairs, but never far from the other two. They were actors, not fighters, and they clung to what little safety they had in numbers. The alleys were dark and little was to be seen. In one Escott saw a dim candlelight mounted next to a door. Beneath it, some men were loading a bundle of some sort into a horse cart. Escott signalled to his fellow actors to follow him. He patted the horse as he walked past it.

"What are you about there?" he asked.

"None of your business," one of them responded.

Two men dressed as sailors blocked his way, but Escott pushed past them. He reached into the cart and pulled back a tarpaulin. He saw four young men, including the missing actors. They seemed asleep or worse. It was too dark to tell.

One of the sailors grabbed his arm and Escott hit him with a right jab to the face then ducked the swing of the second sailor and delivered a solid body blow.

"Come on," he called to the other actors as he jumped on the cart. He reached for the reins and kicked away the sailor who tried to stop him. His three companions managed to fight their way past the sailors and tumble into the cart. Escott slapped the reigns as another man came out the door and yelled at them.

"Hey!"

But the actors were off down the alley and along the roads of the Barbary Coast until they reached Broadway and turned the horse east towards their boarding house. As Escott drove, the other actors examined the cargo. The four young men under the tarpaulin were alive, but unconscious. No amount of slapping or jostling woke them.

"I believe they have been drugged," Pike told Escott.

At the boarding house they transferred the cargo to the actors' rooms. Escott turned the cart around, descended to the cobblestones, and slapped the horse on the hindquarters. He walked back up the steps of Normandie House as the cart rattled westward. Dewitt, Devigne and the two other young men were still unconscious, but otherwise seemed unharmed. They decided to let them sleep it off. The actors were dumped on their beds and their fellows in chairs. Then the remaining actors retired to their own beds, having seen enough of San Francisco for the night.

With the sunrise the well-rested women were bustling about and getting laced and booted, excited to see the new town. The actors were slower to rise. When they did, they, like their sisters the night before, first called for hot water. Regardless of how dusty their train journey had left them, their adventures in the Barbary Coast had put them in contact with filth of another sort. While the water was heating, Escott, Pike, Reece, and Dewarr converged on the room assigned to Dewitt and Devigne. A moan was the only response to their knock. So they entered anyway and drew back the curtains. Reece and Dewarr had brought pitchers of cold water, which they proceeded to dump on the two drowsy actors and the two strangers.

Devigne shot up in bed.

"Bloody hell!"

One of the strangers jumped up.

"Who the hell are you?"

"We are the actors of the Corycian Company. I am Langdale Pike," he said with a small bow. "This is William Escott, Joseph Reece, and Claude Dewarr."

Each gave a bow in turn, as they were introduced.

"The miserable pair in the beds are known as Sebastian Devigne and Tony Dewitt," Pike continued.

"We rescued you last night," Dewarr said.

"Someone drugged the four of you and dumped you in a cart," Reece added.

"We prevented you from being 'shanghaied,'" Escott said, "pressed into service on a merchant marine ship."

"My god! I'm Matt Johnson and this is Tom Walsh."

"Oh, my, head," Devigne moaned. "Last I remember was drinking with those girls. Everything is fuzzy after that."

"The girls probably put something in your drink."

"How did you find us?" Dewitt asked.

"That's a tale in itself. But water is heating. If you will clean yourselves up, there is some form of breakfast in preparation below. You are welcome to join us."

"No, we should be getting back. Our parents will be worried sick."

Johnson and Walsh hurried off as quickly as their throbbing heads would allow, and the actors saw to their ablutions. As they descended for their breakfasts, Sassanof, Foster, and the secretary were heading over to the theatre. The carpenter, Walter Blanchard, was going with them.

The ladies of the company were in the sitting room talking with fellow lodgers and peering out the bay windows at the fog that blanketed the city.

"Almost makes you feel at home!" Rose Morris exclaimed.

"I never thought I'd be homesick for a good pea-souper," Louise Harris sighed.

The actors consumed copious amounts of coffee, burnt

bacon, cold eggs, and something the cook called "biscuits," that were not at all like English biscuits, and which had been drowned in some form of gravy. They did not care what it was. They were starved. Pike regaled the actors, actresses, and fellow lodgers within earshot with the tales of the exploits of the night before, only slightly embellished.

The sun was beginning to burn through the fog and the young men were feeling alive again — though Devigne continued to complain of a headache — when Randy Foster came back to retrieve them. Devigne accepted the landlady's offer of some willow root powder that she claimed worked wonders. The ladies took up their bonnets and bags, and the gentlemen their hats and makeup kits. Then they set off in a couple of hired carriages for the theatre. The drive was not long, just a few blocks down Stockton Street, then into Bush Street. They passed a portion of Chinatown on the way and saw Chinese men and women going about their business. Most especially notable were the men coming from the hotel district pushing carts of laundry to Chinatown.

The California Theatre was a brick building that presented a simple face to the world. The only ornamentation was a series of arches above the windows on the upper stories. But inside the theatre there were elaborate murals of San Francisco, and a panoramic view of the bay had been painted on the drop curtain on the stage. The theatre had been built seven years before by William Ralston, at that time the treasurer of the Bank of California. Ralston built the theatre to showcase the talents of actors John McCullough and Lawrence Barrett. It was quite successful its first few years, but the Bank of California, which owned the theatre, failed in 1875, and soon thereafter, Ralston died, leaving it with an uncertain future. The current manager, actor Charles Barton Hill, was embracing opportunities to bring in talent from the East Coast and Europe.

The Corycian Company actors were greeted inside the theatre by their manager who spoke to them briefly before introducing them to Mr Barton Hill and a representative of a local newspaper. Sassanof told them there had been some miscommunication in the telegrams. In San Francisco, it was the custom to have performances seven days a week and matinees on both Wednesday and Saturday. Sassanof agreed to the Wednesday matinee, as they had also done in New York, but insisted his actors needed their Sundays. The theatre managers had agreed to arrange for other performances those days.

The more immediate question was that evening. The delay in Wyoming meant they were two days behind. Those had been their rehearsal days. Would they be prepared to perform that evening? Sassanof believed so, but he wished to sound his performers on the matter before committing them. He noticed especially that Devigne and Dewitt looked under the weather, though he had not yet heard the cause. He assumed it was merely the aftermath of too much drink the night before.

"My head is improving, but I would be most appreciative if you could find me some coffee less wretched than that at the lodging house," Sebastian Devigne said.

The other young men shared a look. The coffee had been tolerable, but they feared nothing would taste good to Devigne in his current condition. In any case, he agreed he could perform that evening.

"We have entertained fellow passengers on heaving decks, aboard trains roaring across the prairie, and in the back room of a saloon in some dusty town. Surely we can rise to perform in this lovely theatre," he said. "I think it will be a welcome change."

Dewitt was in accord.

"Suffering will merely sharpen my wit. The show must go on!"

Sassanof introduced them to the theatre managers and informed them that they would stage a play this evening.

"But can you provide us with an audience?" Sassanof asked.

"That is where I come in," said the newspaper man. "We will have the news of your arrival and performance this evening on the streets before noon."

"We have the broadsides printed," Barton Hill said. "We were just waiting for you to arrive to put them up. I'll set the boys to it right away."

THE CONSULTING DETECTIVE PART II: ON STAGE

The actors were shown to their dressing rooms. Walter Blanchard was already unpacking their costumes and Ida and Sally were hanging them up and making them presentable.

They would do a rehearsal of *Henry VI Part I* that morning and a full dress rehearsal in the afternoon followed by the performance that evening. Devigne was correct. After the long journey across mountains and plains, it was refreshing to be performing in a real theatre again. During the first rehearsal they adapted their stage business to the California Theatre stage and they worked with the house gasman and stage crew on the timing of lighting and curtain changes. The theatre had a few appropriate back-cloths but for the most part it was up to the actors to set the mood.

After the first newspaper hit the streets, other papers sent men to write on the English troupe visiting San Francisco. The journalists were permitted to sit in on the dress rehearsal and talk to the actors afterwards. This American style of journalism featuring interviews with the actors was still new to them, but members of the Corycian Company understood that the purpose was to promote the play and they did their part. By the evening they were in all the papers and curious patrons began appearing at the box office. When the curtain rose the auditorium was more than half full. This was quite pleasing in the circumstances. They certainly had performed for fewer in London before. Their hope was that good notices and word of mouth would fill the theatre the following nights. It was not the Corycian Company's best performance, but it was sufficient to impress the San Francisco papers. That's what they discovered the following morning. That evening they had dined together at a restaurant and then retired to their beds in Normandie House. The following morning when Langdale Pike rose he found a pencilled note tacked to the door of the room he and Escott were sharing.

Gone for a walk will meet at theatre at 10 am.

WE

He was not surprised. He knew Holmes had a greater need for solitude than the past week had allowed. After the boy was killed on the train Holmes had tried to be off on his own, especially in Cheyenne, but too often the company was thrown together out of necessity. Pike passed the message on to their manager.

Sherlock Holmes had dressed quietly and crept from the room and out the front door before dawn. The fog was not as thick as it had been the previous morning, but it did lie about the streets in wisps and knots. He stopped in front of the boarding house to light his pipe. He headed west down Broadway. In the grey predawn light the Barbary Coast looked both less glamorous and less intimidating. The northern limits were marked by a row of Mexican fandango houses, ironically directly opposite the county jail. They, like the other buildings of the Barbary Coast, seemed to have subsided from exhaustion. No doubt their patrons had as well.

The fog increased as he neared the waterfront. Here, like the docks of London, the workday had already begun. Fishermen were heading out to sea. Express wagons pulled up full of parcels. Ferry boats were being loaded and unloaded. Steamships were preparing to leave. The sun was creeping over the mountains to the east. He leaned against the pier and stared out at the Pacific Ocean. Oystermen passed with their morning haul. Gulls cried overhead. He walked down to pier where their ferry had come in the night before. Another was steaming in from Oakland. He watched it disgorge its passengers. Automatically he analysed the occupation and visible history of each one. It was a good mental exercise. After a while, he pulled his watch from his pocket and looked at the time. Then he turned eastward and walked along Pacific Street. There were some stone buildings, but more were made of wood. Few exceeded two stories in height due to the risk of "shakes." He wondered if they would experience any earthquakes during their stay. The shops were open now, offering the usual assortment of hard and soft goods. There were quite a number of restaurants including one oddly named The Poodle Dog.

As he arrived at the theatre, he heard the clop clop of horses on cobblestone behind him. He turned to see two hacks drive up and his fellow actors and company spilled out.

"Good morning, Mr Escott. I trust you had a pleasant walk?" Sassanof asked.

"I did indeed."

"Good, then let us get to work."

Their second day in San Francisco was more productive and their second performance was marked with more of the flare the company was known for. The seats were filled that night. The following day was a Wednesday and Sassanof had decided that they should perform their old standard, *Romeo and Juliet*, for the matinee. For the balcony scene they used a rig the theatre had from a previous production. It was not as beautiful, nor as high as the one they had used in London. Rose still insisted that Walter Blanchard examine it before she mounted the steps.

As usual, *Romeo and Juliet* was well received and the Saturday matinee was sold out as soon as it was scheduled. On the fourth day they performed *Richard III* and Escott's impersonation of the title character received very positive notices. By the second week, the company had settled into their new routine, filling the theatre each night, and twice on Wednesday and Saturday. The actors had learned their lesson and stayed clear of the Barbary Coast, seeking more reputable taverns or saloons when they felt the need to imbibe. Escott continued his early morning walks and began reading the San Francisco papers regularly. The local news was not particularly interesting. There was the occasional assault and petty thievery. Local and national politics consumed copious column space, but held no interest for him. Occasionally the papers reported crimes from other states, such as the successful train robbery in Texas on May 12th which the papers reported several days later. The newspaper attributed it to the James-Younger gang which was responsible for a number of bank robberies across the country.

In his walks, Holmes visited all parts of the city, but most often he went to the waterfront which was the liveliest area early in the morning. He observed the normal arrival and departure of ships and the movement of people and cargo. Occasionally he saw something unusual. What he saw on the morning of June 14 turned out to have much greater significance than he realized at the time.

That morning he was watching a steamer named the *Sacramento* arrive. He observed the sailors and the stevedores go about their work. A foreman was examining some freight on the wharf. Another man approached him and asked him to examine some boxes in the hold of the Sacramento that seemed to be damaged. Not long after, a crate was hauled up from the ship and placed at the end of the wharf. It was a pine box, strapped with hickory or oak-split straps. It was about three feet long, two feet wide, and two feet tall. It was stained and leaking some oily substance that began to stain the wharf. A second, larger case was brought up and placed next to it. It was also badly stained with oil. Several men gathered about the boxes. Some were from the ship or the Pacific Mail Steamship Company that owned the ship and some from the express company to which both boxes were consigned to be transported to their final destination. The employees of the express company were hesitant to take possession of damaged goods and those from the ship denied having done anything to the boxes to cause any damage. They determined from their examination that the first box had leaked upon the second but they were uncertain exactly what it was leaking. One man touched the oil with his finger and smelt it and invite others to smell it. Then he tasted it. That did not seem to resolve the issue. Finally they turned the case over on one end which seemed to cause the leaking to stop. They were discussing sending it elsewhere to be examined further.

Holmes checked his watch. It was time to head to the theatre. He left the waterfront behind and walked east past the shops to the California Theatre. He greeted the other actors who were also arriving and changing into their costumes for the matinee. Soon he had transformed into Tybalt and was waiting in the wings for his entrance in the first scene. *Romeo and Juliet* proceeded as usual before a nearly full theatre. The company completed Act 3 and Escott retired from the stage after the death of his character. He removed his costume and makeup. He was in the wings considering returning to the lodging house rather than waiting for the final curtain call.

On stage, the actors were continuing with Act 4 when it struck. At the first movement, the performers on the stage looked down at their feet, fearing a repetition of the stage collapse they had experienced in London. However, the audience, being more familiar with San Francisco's earthquakes, stampeded to the exits. The loud noise that followed meant that the players were not far behind them. However, Holmes had noticed something else. The movement of the ground and the noise had been accompanied by a wind that had coursed through the theatre, first blowing the heavy stage curtains downstage and then pulling them upstage. Yet not quite. There was a cant to their sway. He, too, ran out to the street and then west on Bush Street. The streets were full of confused people. About a block down he began to see broken glass in the streets and people with minor cuts. By the time he reached Montgomery Street the damage was severe, especially to the south of Bush Street. South of Pine Street all the glass was shattered in all the surrounding buildings, fragments of window frames and doors littered the streets, and pieces of clothing and personal effects lay among them. Nearly everything had been demolished within fifty feet of the intersection of Montgomery Street and California Street. Based on remains of signs, the ruins included an assay office, an express office, and a social club. The men digging through the debris were being directed by a man Holmes recognized as one he had seen on the wharf.

"Can I be of assistance?" Holmes asked.

"Yes, thank you. I've sent for some more of my men from the waterfront, but we can use every hand to find the wounded and bring them to safety."

He discovered later that this man was Captain Cox of the Pacific Mail Steamship Company. But for now, Holmes took his instruction moving debris and searching the ruins, knowing only that he seemed a man of authority who was familiar with the building. Soon they were joined by Captain Lees of the San Francisco police and fifteen of his men. Captain Lees took command when he arrived. Twenty-five of Captain Cox's men arrived from the docks shortly after. Dozens of others joined them throughout the day.

Sherlock Holmes helped move debris in the express building. The air was choked with dust and debris that kept raining down from the ruins. He tied his handkerchief about his face and others followed suit. They moved roof beams and parts of walls that were blocking the front of the building. They found wounded and carried them out. As they worked, it became obvious that the origin of the explosion had been in the yard behind the express office. Clearing the path to the yard was grisly work. Among the wreckage they found fragments of human remains and personal effects scattered amidst wood and brick. When they reached the yard, they found two dead bodies. Their clothing was torn, and their flesh shredded. Then Holmes saw something twitch beneath them. It was a man's hand. He called others to help move the corpses. The man below was badly injured, but he still breathed. They carried him out of the remains of the building, but he soon expired. They found other bodies in the yard, including two horses still harnessed to a cart. Behind the horses, possibly shielded from the blast by them, Holmes found another man alive and not far from him a man who had been beheaded. That was characteristic of many explosives. While the blast moved out in all directions, the pattern of damage could be altered by the shape of the explosive itself or by objects in the path of the blast, for better or worse. He turned and looked back across the yard. There at the centre of the destruction was a hole about three feet in circumference. The cobblestones had been depressed to a depth of nearly sixteen inches. Holmes walked to the hole and looked in. Some broken pine boards were embedded in it. They had been three feet long and looked like they had been bound together to make the bottom of a box two feet wide. The sides were torn off with only splinters remaining. He believed he had seen that crate that very morning on the waterfront.

One of the searchers called that he had found another man alive. Holmes joined him and helped carry the man out and place him in an ambulance that was taking wounded to the County Hospital. Out on the street, he looked around at those he had been working with. Their hair was covered with dust and dirt and their clothing was so caked as to be unidentifiable. New volunteers were arriving and Captain Lees was urging those who had come first to go home and get some rest. Holmes removed the handkerchief from his face and pulled out his pocket watch. It was nearly time for the evening performance. He could clean up at the theatre. He walked back the route he had come attempting to wipe the debris from his clothes as he went. When he arrived, he found a placard announcing that the evening performance had been cancelled. He turned and walked up Stockton Street past Chinatown. Some people stared as he walked by. As he mounted the steps of Normandie House, Louise Harris ran out.

"Good heavens. Are you hurt?" the actress asked, confirming that he must look a fright.

"No, just rather filthy," he responded

"Where have you been?" their manager asked.

"Helping find injured people at the site of the explosion," he responded.

"You saw it?" another person asked.

"Yes. More than anyone would want to. It is not a pretty sight."

Holmes bathed and changed and took up his violin. He didn't need to ask why the evening performance had been cancelled. The city was in shock. He spent the evening alone with his music. He couldn't really say why he had gone. Perhaps he had just developed an instinct to run towards danger. There was little real mystery other than the mystery of life and death. He did not go back again but followed developments in the newspaper.

In the subsequent days, the debris was cleared, the dead buried, and the wounded treated. Performances resumed on Friday. The following Monday the inquest began. By then the *San Francisco Dispatch* was reporting that all the dead and wounded had been identified, though in the case of those found in the yard behind the express office, it was more by location and the evidence of those who had seen the men there than anything intrinsic to the bodies themselves. As he had seen, the physical damage was so great that they were unrecognizable. Holmes attended parts of the inquest when he could between performances. He heard testimony by some of the men he had seen examine the boxes on the wharf. They testified that the explosion had been caused by the leaking box he had seen arrived on the wharf. It had come from New York by way of Panama and had been destined to be delivered to a man in Los Angeles, a city further south along the coast of California. The second case seemed to be an innocuous case of silverware. The witnesses described sending them both with the drayman to be examined at the express office.

He also heard the testimony of several chemists who had determined that the leaking substance had been nitro-glycerine. One of the chemists demonstrated nitro-glycerine's power by hitting a drop of it with a hammer in the courtroom. It made a loud report.

Captain Cox testified to taking splinters from the stained part of the wharf and performing a similar test on them with a similar result. He also delivered splinters from the stained part of the wharf to the chemists for chemical tests.

The coroner's jury came to the inevitable conclusion that the ten people were killed by the explosion of nitro-glycerine when a mallet and chisel were used to open a box containing it. They further found that whoever had shipped the unmarked box of nitro-glycerine was guilty of a "heinous crime."

Buried beneath the stories about the explosion, news had begun to trickle in of more Indian battles in the Black Hills northeast of Cheyenne. Then came the American Independence Day, which San Franciscans celebrated with fireworks, picnics, and games. The holiday spirit did not last long. On July 6th, the newspapers reported that General Custer and his troops had been killed on June 25 by Sioux and Cheyenne warriors at a place called Little Big Horn. The news was delayed due to the time required for word to be brought down from the mountains by the survivors. Holmes could not help wondering if *Haycott Payay* had participated in these battles. It was not a time to mention that he had befriended a Cheyenne in Wyoming. While earlier in the year he had read articles sympathetic to the Indians, now the temper turned decidedly against them and the many outrages against them seemed to be forgotten. Lost in the midst of the many articles about the battle of Little Big Horn in the following days was the news that the James-Younger gang had robbed another train in Missouri.

Weeks later Sherlock Holmes folded up the last of a stack of newspapers. A maid was accused of robbing a former employer. Some jewellery thieves had been caught. Two boys had broken into a candy shop. A coroner's inquest returned a verdict of death by hydrophobia in the case of a man who was bitten by a dog and died twenty-five days later. Holmes shivered. He had escaped that grisly fate himself.

There was crime in San Francisco, but there wasn't much mystery about it, at least not since the explosion in June and that had not remained a mystery long. The explosion had been the chief topic of conversation until the news of the fate of General Custer and his men. Even that had faded from the public consciousness as the summer had progressed. Then reports from Minnesota claimed that on September 7th a bank robbery by the James-Younger gang had failed, and Cole, Bob, and Jim Younger had been arrested. This was hailed as welcome news by bankers and railroad operators and passengers. The general hope was that the rest of the gang would be captured soon.

The months in San Francisco had been pleasant enough. Most days were sunny once the morning fog burned off. The summer had not been too hot and the approaching autumn did not seem to be too cool. While the proceeds from their performances had been lower than they had been in New York, Boston, or Chicago, the California Theatre was desperate to retain good acts and had encouraged them to stay longer.

However, there was nothing to engage the interest of an English detective and the actors were homesick. Nonetheless, it was a report of snowfall in the mountains that finally convinced Sassanof it was time to go home. He feared that of they did not leave soon they would be stranded on this continent for the winter. He had other reasons for returning to London as well. Repairs to their theatre should be complete, though the Baron had not been effuse about the matter in his few letters, and their tour had been quite profitable. Sassanof was ready for the triumphant return that he and his partner had planned.

Chapter 20

Return to England

*This strange, wild story seemed to have come
to us from amid the mad elements*
Dr Watson, "The Five Orange Pips"

The final week of performances by the Corycian Company was announced and train tickets were purchased. This time the plan was to take trains directly across the continent to Baltimore, another port on the East Coast, and board a ship there. Sassanof had learned, however, from their delays travelling westward, that it was not advisable to reserve their place too early and risk missing their boat. Instead he exchanged telegrams with a shipping agent in Baltimore and arranged for him to purchase tickets for their passage back to England when Sassanof instructed him to do so by telegram. Funds had been wired ahead to cover the cost.

Their crates of costumes and properties were packed and farewells said before they boarded the eastbound train. Sassanof once again was clutching the valise as they chose their seats. To him the U. S. bank-notes contained within represented not only their expenses for returning to England, but the funds to save the Corycian Company. It was capital that he had raised through proper management of their performances without the efforts of Baron Von Marienburg. In fact, he had given his partner in England no indication of how much he was bringing back with him in the wire he sent informing him of their imminent return. It was enough to fund their gala return to London and pay their patient investors a dividend.

The members of the theatrical company thought of themselves as jaded and experienced travellers until the climb over the Sierra Nevada in broad daylight. They saw now the peaks and gorges they had missed in the dark on the way west. They were horrified at the depth of the American River gorge and the careless way the train seemed to swing around Cape Horn clinging to the cliff over it.

The weather remained clear through the canyons of Utah, but as they reached Green River snow began to fall. It danced and whirled about the train as it sped forward. It began to stick to the rocks and bushes. Three inches of snow were on the ground when they reached Laramie, but there was none at Cheyenne. As they approached that town, they saw the valley where the herd of buffalo had delayed them in the spring. Tall dried grass surrounded the tracks. There was no sign of the animals' passage. They did not stop in Cheyenne this time. When the train reached the prairie once more, they met a new phenomenon. Outside of Pine Bluffs it began as a rattle on the roof of the railroad car that increased to a dim. It seemed as if their car was being pelted with rocks, but what they saw out the window was hail as large as green peas, but as white as snow bouncing and piling up along the tracks. As it was slacking off, a crack and flash made them jump, followed by a deep rumble. Heavy rain followed. The thunderstorm continued far into the evening. The din of the rain and the thunder made it impossible for anyone to sleep for hours. Yet the train rushed on through the night.

The clouds were gone by morning. A light wind was blowing from the east as the rising sun crested over golden waves of tall grass. They stopped at Elm Creek for breakfast. By late morning dark clouds were gathering on the eastern horizon. They were higher in the sky by the time they stopped for the noon day meal. Holmes stood for a while staring east before boarding the train. There was something wrong about those clouds and there was an odd haziness in the sky. As the train roared eastward the haze increased and a whiff of something strange was in the air. Those were not ordinary clouds.

Sherlock Holmes was not certain who first said the word, but soon it was on every lip and as the dark billows reached over the train they could see flames stretching along the eastern horizon and smell the sickly sweet scent of burning grass. The conductor tried to assure the passengers. Such prairie fires were common this time of year, he said. The engineer had received reports of the blaze during their stops. The right of way was clear and the rails ahead were undamaged. As the fire was moving west, the most prudent thing was to run through it. He told them how to wet their handkerchiefs and hold them over their mouths and noses to make breathing easier.

They were not convinced. As the smoke about them grew thicker, their doubts increased. Still the train sped toward the inferno. It even increased in speed. Suddenly the fire was all around them, the ground black and red, and flames hissing and snapping on every side. They could feel the heat, and the smoke was choking them. Yet before panic overwhelmed them, they were through, and passing a charred prairie with occasional wisps of smoke rising. Someone started applauding and in their relief everyone in the car joined in. It was dark by the time they reached Omaha and staggered to the hotel. The following day they would catch another train to Chicago and from there to Baltimore. For now all they wanted was to sleep in a real bed. Yet their dreams were haunted by tongues of fire rising up out of mountain gorges.

In the morning, they dined together in the hotel. No one mentioned the young man they had met when they left Omaha on the westward journey who never reached Wyoming. When they arrived in Chicago and had their tickets in hand for the train to Baltimore, Sassanof wired ahead to the agent to book them passage sometime on October 24th or later. That should give them enough time to transfer their luggage from the train yard to the ship. They learned when they arrived in Baltimore that eastbound ships often had fewer passengers than westbound and such was the case for this passage of the *Devonshire*, leaving on October 24th. The agent had booked them two in a cabin and the ship's master was glad to have them.

Anthony Dewitt and William Escott shared a cabin. No performances were expected of the weary actors this trip. Most of the Corycian Company spent their days up on deck staring out to sea and their evenings in the salon or in their cabins. Anthony Dewitt did indeed have a chance to hear his cabin mate play his violin on more than one occasion. He learned the secret was to enter quietly and remain quiet. If undisturbed, Escott would keep playing.

Looking forward to a raucous swarm of siblings at home in London, Dewitt considered it a treat to lie back on his berth and listen to the music.

The sun had been bright and seas calm when they had steamed away from Fell's Point, through Baltimore Harbour to the Chesapeake Bay, and thus to the Atlantic Ocean. On the third day, tattered clouds gathered in the sky and the winds increased. The waves tossed the ship about turbulently. Then the sky broke with a rush of wind and drenching rains that chased all but the sailors down below.

As the members of the theatrical company retired from the deck, they were startled by the cry from the sailors of a man over board. They looked at each other to determine whether they were all accounted for and soon realized that they were missing their manager. The ship's crew pressed them down below. This was the sailors' bailiwick. They gathered in the second-class salon and waited. Soon they were joined by a shocked and soaked Michael Sassanof whom the sailors had fetched up from the sea. After a change of clothes, and with a hot cup of coffee in his hand he told them of his misadventure.

"I don't really know how it happened. You know how the rain began quite suddenly and it was hard to see on deck. One moment I was making my way along and the next I was in the water. The wind was so fierce that it almost felt like I was pushed by a human hand. I had never been so frightened in my life. The waves kept crashing over me. I was certain the ship would go on without me. Miraculously they spotted me and pulled me up."

The winds blew from every quarter and the sea broke over the deck. The storm roared like a monster set on devouring them. The ship tossed so violently that cases of sea sickness increased and even walking below decks was hazardous. As they left the dining room after supper on the evening of the second day of the storm, Escott and Dewitt found Sebastian Devigne lying unconscious at the bottom of a staircase with blood pouring from a head wound. They took him to the infirmary. Besides a nasty lump and a sore head, the ship's doctor said he would be fine. Devigne himself remembered nothing. Most assumed he had fallen due to some heave of the ship. Holmes was sceptical. He did not remember the seas being especially turbulent at the time. He began asking members of the Corycian Company where they were when Devigne fell.

"Do you think someone pushed him?" Pike asked.

"I do not know," Holmes admitted. "You are sharing a cabin with him, correct?"

"Yes, but Dewarr, Reece, Foster and I had gone to the salon for a game of whist. So you can eliminate all of us."

"That narrows the field considerably."

"You think it was one of the company?"

"I don't know why anyone outside the company would have any reason to harm him."

"Unless he was participating in some secret liaison with another man's wife."

"Do you know of such a thing?"

"No. It was just a suggestion."

"It's late. Most passengers have retired for the night. I will continue my inquiries in the morning."

That night the wind blew itself out and by morning the storm was only a memory. The smoking-room, the saloon, and the deck became lively and people found their appetites again. Sherlock Holmes continued questioning anyone he met on board throughout the day. With the passengers now scattered throughout the ship he had not yet been able to question all other members of the theatrical company though he had managed to talk to a number of the crew and other passengers.

After supper he retired to his cabin, thinking perhaps he was chasing a will o' wisp. He played his violin for a while and then grew drowsy and set it aside. He closed his eyes and slept. He had no idea how long he slept, but he opened his eyes to find the face of Walter Blanchard, a carpenter and handy-man of the Corycian Company, staring down at him. Blanchard was leaning with his full weight on his hands which were grasped about Holmes' throat, not only choking his breath, but constricting the blood flow to his brain. Sherlock Holmes knew he had mere seconds before he would lose consciousness, and that would be a sleep from which there was no waking. The carpenter had strong hands and Holmes could not pull the man's grip away from his throat. The berth was wedged against the wall and Blanchard was on the other side. There was no room to roll and throw the man off. Holmes flailed his hands about for some weapon and one fell upon the neck of his violin. He hesitated for a fraction of a second as spots were forming before his eyes. Then he gripped the neck of the instrument and slammed it as hard as he could against Blanchard's head. The blow was sufficient to startle his assailant into loosening his grip long enough for Sherlock Holmes to gasp a single breath. He aimed the second and third blows at the man's face.

Even as Holmes was physically fighting for his life, another part of his brain was cataloguing the damage to the violin based on the sounds it made. The instrument sang a low pitched protest ending in a sickening crack as the back concussed against his attacker's head with the first blow. With the second blow the back gave way in a chorus of splintering sounds accompanied by a 'sproiing' as the strings were released from their tension. On the third strike, the neck snapped and the strings whipped like metal tendrils towards the man's face. By instinct, Blanchard's hands had flown to his face, releasing Holmes' throat. While drawing rapid painful breaths, Sherlock Holmes jabbed at the man's eyes with the broken neck of the instrument and threw himself upward as the man backed off. Soon the two of them tumbled to the deck and were struggling on the floor attacking each other with the fragments of the violin.

Then there were footsteps outside the cabin and Anthony Dewitt entered and pulled Blanchard away. Blanchard immediately wrenched himself free from Dewitt's grasp and bolted out the door. Dewitt ran after him. Holmes inhaled slowly as passengers drawn by the fracas gathered outside the cabin. Several members of the Corycian Company entered as he sat up amidst the strings and scraps of wood that had been his violin.

"Are you all right?" Michael Sassanof asked.

Escott nodded and swallowed, his throat was too sore yet

for speech.

"Liar. He nearly made mincemeat of your throat. Up on the berth. Get the ship's doctor in here."

Anthony Dewitt returned to the cabin out of breath.

"Gone," he gasped.

"Gone where?" Langdale Pike asked.

"Overboard."

"He jumped overboard?"

"No," Dewitt said finally catching his breath. "He ran up on deck. I followed but he was running like a mad man. He slipped in the dark and fell over the rail. I looked but could see no sign of him. The crew is searching."

"Why did he attack you?" Sassanof asked.

Sherlock Holmes shook his head.

Why had Blanchard attacked him? Was it because he was investigating Devigne's fall? Was he responsible for Devigne's fall? If so, why? Dewitt's words stuck in his mind: "a mad man." Was it just a coincidence that two men who had tried to kill him in the last two years were described as mad men?

In any case he could not continue his questioning now. Sassanof was correct. Despite the attentions of the ship's doctor, Sherlock Holmes was unable to speak for several days. Otherwise the results of the battle were scratches on his face and hands and bruises around his throat that all healed in a few days and left no scars. But the destruction of the violin inflamed old wounds buried deep beneath the surface.

The following night Holmes stood against the rail looking out at the luminous waves in the dark. Somewhere beyond the horizon was England. In his hands, he held a box with the remains of the violin. His mother had insisted that he learn how to play while they were living in France. This violin had been purchased there. How long ago? Nine years? His teachers had been excellent. His mother had urged him to practice frequently after they had returned to England and often asked him to play at family gatherings. She had encouraged him to take it with him to Cambridge. Little did she know that within three years after they returned to

England he would play it at her funeral, or that three years after that the violin would save his life.

He recalled the incident on the way to her grave. His father had turned him away due the rain. He was right, but somehow her death had seemed less real as a result. He had never gone to the burial plot afterwards, never seen her tombstone. He had said at the time that he felt nothing about her death and that was true. Yet even a vacuum where little had been noticed before is a change. He lifted the box and dumped the contents overboard, a burial at sea.

For three days afterwards, he stayed in his cabin. He sent out notes that excused his absence by his lack of voice, but there was more to it than that. After he regained his voice the first mate came to the cabin to take his statement about the incident. Blanchard was never found and they discovered nothing of interest among his effects. No one knew why Blanchard had attacked him and possibly Devigne. They might never know. However, they had to file a report.

"You are travelling under the name of William Escott. Is that your real name?"

"My name is Sherlock Holmes, and I am a private consulting detective."

He explained in a few more words what had happened and signed the statement the first mate wrote up, but his own words were ringing in his ears. Sherlock Holmes, consulting detective....

He knew what he must do. He had learned many useful things the past two years but now it was time to move on.

He approached Sassanof.

"I would like a word, in private, if I may," Holmes said.

"Then come along, Mr Escott."

"I'm going to be leaving the company when we arrive in England," he said once they were alone.

"I hope this attack—"

"It is not that."

"Have you received another offer?" Sassanof asked.

"No, sir. I am leaving the theatre altogether. There are other worlds calling me," Sherlock Holmes said.

"It is hard to argue when you put it like that," Sassanof said.

"You can tell the company when you please, but I would prefer it be after I left. I don't want to make a big show of it," Holmes insisted.

"I'll respect your wishes, Mr Escott. I can't deny that you have made me a pretty penny and I'd like to make some more. But I sense your determination and I don't think your heart would be in it even if I talked you out of going. A man should throw his whole heart and soul into whatever he wants to do."

"Thank you," Sherlock Holmes said and shook his hand

Chapter 21

A Wake for William Escott

The stage lost a fine actor, even as science lost an acute reasoner,
when he became a specialist in crime.
Dr Watson, "A Scandal in Bohemia"

The night they reached London William Escott died. Sherlock Holmes had intended that Escott die that night, but it happened in a different manner than he expected.

The ship had entered the Thames Estuary late at night. It arrived at the London docks in the wee hours of the morning before even a promise of dawn. The rest of the passengers were asleep, but Holmes had been pacing the deck for hours, impatient to be off. While the gangplank would not be put into place for hours, Holmes was willing to sling his bag on his back and descend to the dock via a rope ladder. He left instructions for his trunk to be sent to Montague Street.

He made his way across the slumbering city and let himself into the rooms with the latchkey. He crept through the sitting room in the dark to his room, threw himself upon the bed and fell asleep. Many hours later someone was shaking him awake. He rolled over to blink at his brother Mycroft.

"Good morning, Mycroft," he said shutting his eyes again.

"It's evening," Mycroft said. "I noted your presence this morning but decided not to wake you then."

Sherlock Holmes opened his eyes again.

"And why now?" he asked.

"I thought you might want to read this," Mycroft said holding out a newspaper.

There was something about his brother's manner that made Sherlock sit up and take the paper. It was folded back to an interior page and a small paragraph was circled. The headline read: "Actor Drowned." Sherlock frowned and read on: "Police have reported that a body was pulled from the water near the London docks this morning. It seemed to have been in the water a number of hours which made identification difficult. However, sources believe that it may be the body of a young actor by the name of William Escott. He is reported to have left a recently docked ship before dawn and has not been heard of since. The body is of a young man of similar type. The police reported no signs of foul play. 'He had talked of ending his career when we returned to London,' said the manager of the acting company which had just returned from a tour of the States, 'but I had no idea that's what he had in mind.' Police are continuing to investigate."

"You do seem to have a talent for making dramatic exits," Mycroft said.

"Even when I don't intend to, it seems," Sherlock said. "I knew nothing of this. I have no idea whether this poor fellow was in the water anywhere near where I passed or whether it was at all close in time. What time is it now?"

"Half past six," Mycroft said.

"Thank you for bringing this to my attention. If I write up a note could you see that it is sent while I clean up? I need to set things straight."

"Certainly."

Holmes wrote a note addressed to Lord Cecil at his club.

Heard about Escott. Must speak to you. Meet at the Criterion Bar at half past seven. Bring Sassanof. No one else.

He left it unsigned certain that the young lord's insatiable curiosity would bring him around and left it to his devices to round up the manager. Having handed the note over to his brother who dispatched a servant with it, Sherlock Holmes shaved off his beard and began trimming his hair.

"So Escott dies anyway," Mycroft observed.

"Well, yes, that was my intent, but not quite like this. I'm not going to revive him merely to kill him again. However, I think I owe it to Sassanof to tell him that it wasn't me. There. I think that will do for now. I will have a barber touch it up later."

"You are looking well," Mycroft said.

"Thank you. It has been quite an adventure."

"As your letters seemed to indicate," Mycroft said.

"Now I've saved enough to pay my debt to the college and embark on my real career."

"Sherlock, you might want to read this," Mycroft said handing him a letter.

It was on Sidney Sussex College letterhead and was signed by the Master.

Dear Mr Holmes:

I am writing to acknowledge receipt of the final payment due upon your debt to the college. I wish you success in your endeavours.

The letter was dated the previous January.

"You paid my debt to the college," Sherlock said to Mycroft.

"Yes, I did," Mycroft admitted. "I knew that you would make good on it, but I was concerned that if it were drawn out too long that they would contact Father about it. So I paid it and have been applying the money you have been wiring to me to repay that loan. It has not been any hardship for me. I am well-paid and my needs are few."

Sherlock shook his head.

"Thank you. I will pay the remainder to you tomorrow when I unpack my bags," Sherlock said. "Right now I need to attend my own wake."

Sherlock Holmes pulled the brim of his top hat down over his face as he approached the Criterion. He noted Sassanof and Lord Cecil sitting at the bar as he entered. He sidled into a booth in the corner, ordered a pint, and asked the bar maid take them a note. He looked down at his drink as they approached.

They sat down.

"So what's this you need talk about—," Sassanof began.

Holmes looked up.

"I'll be danged," Sassanof finished, sitting down, and staring at Holmes.

Lord Cecil did not miss a beat. He held out his hand.

"Sherlock, it is very good to see you again!" he cried. "It's been a long time, hasn't it?"

"Yes, indeed," Holmes replied with a twinkle in his eye.

"Have you met Sassanof, here?" Langdale said.

"We've met, but I don't think we were properly introduced," Holmes said.

"Ah, well, I can fix that. This is Michael Sassanof, the manager of the Corycian Company. Sassanof, this is my old college chum, Sherlock Holmes."

"Pleased to meet you," said Sassanof still somewhat in shock. "So that wasn't you?" Sassanof asked in a whisper.

"No. I didn't even hear about it until this evening. I slept all day. My brother woke me to show me the paper. I thought I should set things straight."

"We're mighty glad to know it wasn't you. But then who was it?" Sassanof asked.

"I have no idea. I didn't see anyone like that when I left the docks," Holmes said.

"What if the poor bloke has family looking for him — with the corpse misidentified — the face was all bloated and well, nibbled on," Sassanof shuddered.

"I thought about that. I have an idea. You can go back to the police and tell them that you thought of something else that would make it certain. I have a large scar on my ankle from a nasty dog bite during college. See?" Sherlock said exposing the scar where Victor Trevor's dog had bitten him.

"I remember that," Pike said.

"Or Pike can do it. Tell them that you just remembered it and wanted to look to be sure. When they say no, then you can say then it can't be Escott."

"I can do that," Pike said.

"Just don't raise a hue and cry over what became of Escott. He's gone, and I'd rather he stay that way."

"I appreciate you setting us straight," Sassanof said.

"Well, I thought I owed that much to you, and I knew that Pike would recognize me if we ran into each other on the street, and you might, too, since this is how I looked when we first met."

"So now you are going to concentrate on the detective business?" Pike asked.

"Yes," Holmes said.

"Ha. See there's the solution," Pike said with triumph. "If anyone is too nosey about Escott, we'll tell them that we hired a private detective named Sherlock Holmes who traced him and found out that he just had taken up a new career out of the limelight."

Holmes laughed.

"You do that," Holmes said.

They had a couple more pints and talked for a while longer.

"I should be going. Pike, we should keep in touch. Here's my card," Holmes said giving one to each of them. "I shall keep an eye on your company and be a patron when I can afford it, Sassanof. If you ever know of anyone who needs to consult a detective, I would be pleased with the referral."

With that, Sherlock Holmes tipped his hat and left them and his career in the theatre behind.

There were mysteries to solve.

THE CONSULTING DETECTIVE PART II: ON STAGE

Epilogue

In unpacking his trunk, Sherlock Holmes came upon his copy of his version of *Richard III*. He placed it in the post with this cover letter:

> *Dear Mr Irving,*
>
> *I enclose my playbook to the production of Shakespeare's Richard III as I drafted it in 1875. I have retired from the stage and have no further use of it. If you should find it worthy of production, I would appreciate a box to view it. I do not wish to have my name connected to it. I added no lines to the Bard's own words.*
>
> *Sincerely,*
> *Sherlock Holmes*
> *fka William Escott*

Weeks later he received a response:

> *Dear Mr Holmes,*
>
> *I have a box reserved in your name at the Lyceum for our first night of Richard III on January 29, 1877. Will you not come and see if I do him justice?*
>
> *Yours Truly,*
> *Henry Irving*

Acknowledgments

I am grateful to Sir Arthur Conan Doyle for introducing the world to the greatest detective of fact or fancy. I also thank Sherlockians everywhere for keeping green the memory of Sherlock Holmes, and providing countless resources for understanding Holmes and the world he lived in. I am especially grateful to Derrick Belanger, Leah Cummins Guinn, Ron Lies, Frank Mentzel, Sara Salazar, Kate Workman, and Diane Zike for reading and commenting on the manuscript.

"William Escott" was suggested as Holmes' stage name by William S. Baring-Gould and derives from an alias Holmes used in the case of "The Adventure of Charles Augustus Milverton" compiled in *The Adventures of Sherlock Holmes*. The stage name "Langdale Pike" was also suggested by William S. Baring-Gould and is the name of a character who appears very briefly in another context in "The Adventure of the Three Gables" compiled in *The Casebook of Sherlock Holmes*. I expanded and transformed the character of Langdale Pike when I created the character of Lord Cecil Hamley in Part I of *The Consulting Detective Trilogy* with the expectation that his stage name would be Langdale Pike. William S. Baring-Gould also suggested the character of Michael Sassanof. Baron Von Marienburg's character was suggested by a comment in "The Adventure of the Mazarin Stone."

As readers of *Part I* of this trilogy know, Dr George Mackenzie was loosely based on Dr George Mackenzie Bacon who was the medical superintendent of the Fulbourn Asylum (aka Cambridgeshire Pauper Asylum) at that time. There is no record of Dr Bacon treating a patient with cocaine, though papers from that time period record that many doctors tried using it to treat many different things.

Jonathan Beckwith was first seen in *The Crack in the Lens*, had a prominent role in *Part I*, and appears in a separate Young Adult book, *The Adventures of Jonathan Beckwith*, which overlaps with this book. Two of the adventures which appear in Chapters

4, 7, and 8 of this book also appear in that book from a different perspective. Jonathan will appear briefly in *Part III* as well.

Sherrinford Holmes was also suggested by William S. Baring-Gould as the eldest Holmes brother. I greatly developed his character in *Part I* of this trilogy, in *The Crack in the Len*s, and in *The Adventures of Jonathan Beckwith.*

Chapter 6 is based on Sir Arthur Conan Doyle's short story, "The Actor's Duel," (aka "The Tragedians") which was first published anonymously in *Cassell's Journal.* Large portions of the dialogue and action in that chapter are from that short story. That story is in the public domain. I also found references to a real knife fight on stage between two Chinese actors in California fighting over a woman. That might be where Conan Doyle found the inspiration for his story. The attack on Escott in Chapter 11 echoes the murder of actor William Terriss by another actor outside the Adelphi Theatre in London on December 26, 1897.

The explosion in San Francisco in 1876 in Chapter 19 was based on a real explosion there a decade earlier. Information related to that blast came from: Robert West Howard, *The Great Iron Trail*, New York: G. P. Putnam's Sons 1962; *Placer Herald*, Auburn, California, April 21, 1866; *Parrot v. Wells, Fargo & Co.* 82 U.S. 524 (15 Wall. 524, 21 L. Ed. 206) Legal Information Institute, https://www.law.cornell.edu/supremecourt/text/82/524 ; "The Use of Black Powder and Nitroglycerine on the Transcontinental Railroad," The TransContinental Railroad, Linda Hall Library http://railroad.lindahall.org/essays/black-powder.html ; http://www.pbs.org/wgbh/americanexperience/films/tcrr/ ; Nilda Rego, "Days Gone By: Wells Fargo Blows Up," Mercury News, July 14 2015; "The Nitro-glycerin Explosion, Inquest Testimony," *Daily Alta California*, April 21, 1866 p. 1, col. 1; *Stockton Daily Independent*, April 16-21, 1866, Stockton: San Joaquin Co., CA, http://www.newspaperabstracts.com/link.php?id=56159. Thanks to Steven Jaume, Associate Professor, College of Charleston, South Carolina for confirming one clue concerning the explosion.

Leah Cummins Guinn helped me find London want ads. For information about the lease at 24 Montague Street, see Mi-

ACKNOWLEDGMENTS

chael Harrison's "Why Didn't I Check Montague Street (Especially No. 24)" in *Baker Street Journal*, Vol. 20 No. 4 December 1970 p. 196-200. Some of the descriptions of Victorians and their occupations which are recited by Sherlock Holmes are based on *London Characters and The Humorous Side of London Life,* a collection of public domain works by London sketch artists collected at http://www.angelfire.com/ks/landzastanza/london.html. An invaluable source while writing all of my books has been Lee Jackson's *Victorian Dictionary* which can be found at http://www.victorianlondon.org. The website's name is deceptive because it is far more than a dictionary.

I read numerous Victorian novels, biographies, autobiographies, reference books and websites to recreate London, New York, Boston, Chicago, and San Francisco from January 1875 to December 1876, The following books and websites provided background and details which enriched this story: Herbert Fry, *London in 1885*; Captain Walter W. Jaffee, *The Sherlock Holmes Illustrated Cyclopedia of Nautical Knowledge*; Bruce Wexler, *The Mysterious World of Sherlock Holmes*; H. R. F. Keating, *Sherlock Holmes: The Man and His World*; Charles Viney, *Sherlock Holmes in London*; Gustave Dore and Blanchard Jerrold, *Victorian London - Publications - Social Investigation/Journalism - London: A Pilgrimage,1872* can be found on Lee Jackson's website; "Josiah Pierce on Passage to England," *Maine Memory Network* MMN #31740; Details on specific ships: http://www.norwayheritage.com/. Information about sweaters: Charles Kingsley, *Cheap Clothes and Nasty*, 1859, *Alton Locke*; Henry Mayhew, *The Morning Chronicle: Labour and the Poor, 1849-50*; Henry Mayhew, *Letter XVI, Tuesday, December 11, 1849*.

Sources for information on the theatre in England and America: George Rowell, *Theatre in the Age of Irving*, Totowa, NJ: Rowman & Littlefield, 1981; John Russell Brown, ed. *Oxford Illustrated History of the Theatre,* Oxford University Press, 1995; Daniel Blum, *A Pictorial History of the American Theatre 1860-1879*, Crown Publishers, 1969; Lionel Brough, "Benefits," *The Stage Door,* (date unknown); "Art on the Stage," *The Building News*, June 29, 1881, p. 150; Maxwell Ryder, *Elocution and Stage Training*, London: The

Era Offices, 1901, 2nd ed.; *Cosmetics and the Skin*, http://cosmeticsandskin.com/bcb/greasepaint.php; 1*9th Century The Gaslight Era*, Stage Lighting Museum, http://www.compulite.com/stagelight/html/history-4/history-4-text.html; George C.D. Odell, *Annals of the New York Stage: Volume VIII (1865-1870)*, New York: Columbia University Press, 1936. Information on the Fifth Avenue Hotel can be found at http://daytoninmanhattan.blogspot.com/2014/03/the-lost-5th-avenue-hotel-5th-avenue.html.

Much information for the journey west to California came from Dee Brown, *Hear the Lonesome Whistle Blow*, London: Vintage Press (1977); M. Florence Leslie, *California: a Pleasure trip from Gotham to the Golden Gate, April, May, June, 1877*, New York: G.W. Carleton & Co. (1877); Barbara Berglund, *Making San Francisco American: Cultural Frontiers in the Urban West, 1846-1906*, Lawrence: University Press of Kansas (2007); Herbert Asbury, *The Barbary Coast: An Informal History of the San Francisco Underworld*, New York: Alfred A. Knopf 1933; Charles Nordhoff, *C.P.R.R., The Central Pacific Railroad*, 1882, reprinted Silverthorne, CO: Vista Books (1996) http://cprr.org/Museum/index.html. Information for the return trip to London and some insights into America were found in Joseph Hatton, *Today in America: Studies for the Old World and the New*, Harper's Franklin Square Library, New York: Harper & Brothers, July 15, 1881.

About the Author

Darlene A. Cypser is an attorney and historian living in Colorado. Darlene became an avid follower of Sherlock Holmes when she was in high school. Since then she has corresponded with a number of Sherlockians around the world. She a member and former Chief Surgeon of *Dr. Watson's Neglected Patients*, a scion of the *Baker Street Irregulars* located in Denver, Colorado. She is also a member of the *Hounds of the Internet* and the *Hudson Valley Scion-tists*. She has had four articles published in the *Baker Street Journal*.